'A profound and ... marriage from which the woman rescues herself... in an age when the odds against her doing so were immense. Catherine's heroic determination to make her own future is what drives the narrative forward. The writing is visually rich and packed with detail, and the story is beautifully told. I couldn't stop reading it.'

JAMES ROBERTSON

'Ajay Close is a terrific writer, her prose is tight and lucid and sometimes quite beautiful. This story of the doomed relationship between the Scottish writer Catherine Carswell and her first husband, talented but severely mentally ill painter Herbert Jackson, takes us from the headiness of whirlwind romance to the first inklings of unease and... into full-blown nightmare. Close displays real skill and insight in making something both moving and compelling out of such challenging material. Highly recommended.'

CAROL BIRCH

'A passionate, brutal tale – full of tender moments and barbaric acts. The emotional landscape is vivid and refreshingly candid, with some brilliant portraits of selfishness, and the vignettes - so sharp-eyed and merciless - are a real treat.'

SUE PEEBLES

'A brilliant and compelling new book from Ajay Close. A story of passionate love turning into a damaging marriage as Catherine Carswell fights first to understand what is happening to her and then to free herself and her child and make a new life for them both. Ajay Close has written a story about the life of a woman in the early 20th century which speaks across time to all women everywhere.'

SUE WILKINSON

The Daughter of Lady Macbeth

'Sensual, wise and raw, *The Daughter of Lady Macbeth* gets to the heart of what it means to be a mother, or wish you were.'
ROSEMARY GORING

'Through her engaging writing, Close manages to get under the skin of her characters and the reader becomes caught up in their story. Their pain springs off the page, as each woman confronts the demons from her youth. A gripping read about redemption, love, and self-discovery.'
The Lady

'As befitting something which references one of Shakespeare's darkest female characters, *The Daughter of Lady Macbeth* has a shocking, violent and mysterious opening. Both time-lines will keep you guessing.'
Stylist Magazine

'*The Daughter of Lady Macbeth* is an honest and often relent-less exploration of relationships, identities and the friction between them.'
Scottish Review

'Close is exploring important matters; nature and artifice, mothers and daughters, husbands and wives, loyalty and betrayal. Her prose, as usual, is beautifully polished but this is her most emotional novel to date and is partly inspired by her own experiences. As a picture of a marriage crumbling under pressure it is melancholy and all too genuine.'
Book Oxygen

'...has a raw, desperate quality which strikes at the very heart of human frailty.'
Undiscovered Scotland

A Petrol Scented Spring

'A fascinating insight into one of the most compelling stories in the history of the women's suffrage movement.'

The Times

'I was riveted and gripped by it.'

MURRAY LACHLAN YOUNG on *A Good Read*, Radio 4

'Close writes with breathless wit, dizzying passion, a quick sympathy for her two heroines, and an unflinching eye.'

Kirkus Reviews

'A captivating and nuanced read... Close writes witty and humorous dialogue that has the duck, dive and jab of a boxing match between characters.'

Scottish Review of Books

'Uncompromising in its honesty and compelling in its narration... Ajay Close has hit on a real-life story that may prove to be one of the gems of the year.'

The Herald

'A thought-provoking and revealing read... Close's sophisticated writing is never less than engrossing.'

The Scotsman

'Close's dialogue is superb, as is her insight into the complex mix of human imagination and emotion. A truly gripping novel.'

Scottish Review

Born in Sheffield, **Ajay Close** worked as a newspaper journalist, winning several awards, before becoming a full-time author and playwright. Her first novel, *Official and Doubtful*, was longlisted for the Orange Prize. Her fourth, *A Petrol Scented Spring*, was longlisted for the Walter Scott Prize for Historical Fiction. Her play, *The Keekin Gless*, was staged at Perth Theatre. *The Sma Room Séance* toured east Scotland and was performed at the Edinburgh Fringe.

Also by Ajay Close

What We Did In The Dark

Ajay Close

SANDSTONE PRESS

First published in Great Britain by
Sandstone Press Ltd
Willow House
Stoneyfield Business Park
Inverness
IV2 7PA
Scotland

www.sandstonepress.com

Editor: Moira Forsyth

The moral right of Ajay Close to be recognised as the
author of this work has been asserted in accordance with the
Copyright, Designs and Patents Act 1988.

The author gratefully acknowledges support from
Creative Scotland towards the writing of this book.

The publisher acknowledges subsidy from Creative Scotland
towards publication of this volume.

ISBN: 978-1-912240-89-0
ISBNe: 978-1-912240-90-6

Cover design by Stuart Brill
Typeset by Iolaire, Newtonmore
Printed and bound by CPI Group (UK) Ltd, Croydon, CR0 4YY

For Jim

I made what may be called a rash and foolish marriage to a man I scarcely knew. In reality – the reality that is oneself in so far as this at any moment can be termed real – it was a desperately rational act.

Lying Awake, CATHERINE CARSWELL

1939

I had the dream again last night. Not Italy this time, but London. I was a stranger, barged by the sightless crowd, with the greasy pavement under my shoes and my nostrils red-raw in a young woman's face blanched with cold.

I turned from my reflection in the tinselled windows, along a narrow mews where the warm smell of horse vied with the stink of petrol, to emerge in a square. Brass plaques reflected a bruised yellow dusk. To my left, gated greenery, a blackbird on a railing, trees turned to velvet shadows against the dimming sky.

The office was comfortable, in an old-fashioned sort of way, with creamy gaslight and treacle panelling. A girl with a scar on her upper lip wetted a cloth with methylated spirits and dabbed at the hammers of her typewriter. She glanced at me, and quickly away. I knew then I had done something shameful, but the old man was kind, exclaiming at my icy handshake, seating me by the glowing coals. When I brought the teacup to my lips, it smelled faintly of meths.

There was a tap at the door.

My heart lurched in terror and, more terribly, with a sort of gladness.

I knew you at once, although your hair was white and your boxer's body stooped and frail. You had shaved off your moustache, but your eyes were the same.

At last I found my voice to say, 'But you're dead.'

And you said, 'Am I?'

PART I

Youth again, though so delightful to the unthinking eye, is the season of green sickness, of ill-assurance, of desperate melancholies, of the agonies of misprised love and irremediable mistakes.

Lying Awake, CATHERINE CARSWELL

1904

It was early September, but the Berkshire afternoon was as warm as Glasgow in June. From the train I saw crows picking over yellow stubble, orchards of reddening apples, barns of russet brick, a pulsing of white scuts as rabbits fled up the grassy embankment. A farmhand set down his scythe and drank from a jug and, just as if the curtains had drawn back from a stage, I knew the long years of dreaming were behind me. Life, my real life, was about to begin.

I had had this thought before, more than once.

'Miss Macfarlane?'

The boy swung my carpet bag into the trap, placing a hand either side of my waist to lift me up after it.

'Do you do that for all the ladies?'

'No, Miss.'

I laughed, and spent the rest of the journey avoiding his glance.

The summer 'cottage' was a substantial house, the crooked squares between its ancient timbers sealed by buttercream, a thatched roof like an ill-fitting wig. (I made a note to remember that simile at dinner.) A thrush sang from the yew hedge, nasturtium trumpets flamed, lavender spikes trembled under the ministrations of bees.

'Cathie!'

'Professor Raleigh.' Too late, I remembered I had to call him Walter now.

He seemed to have grown even taller in the months since we had last met: taller, and more confoundingly debonair. He advanced, trousers flapping around his long legs, arms opening in welcome. That faint tremor in his hands, a congenital weakness turned to witty effect. Seeing the glint in his green eyes, that drooping moustache, I thought, *If I ever met your twin, I would marry him like a shot.*

'We're just sitting down to tea, if you don't mind being kept in suspense about where you'll be sleeping. Don't worry about washing off the smuts – they're very becoming.'

For a moment I was stuck for words, then I recalled the trick of it.

'There was a man in my compartment eating pickled sardines. I spent a good deal of the journey with my head outside the window.'

'Ah yes, the sardine-eater. Have you met his continental cousin, the breather of garlic sausage?'

We smiled at one another, and I said it, although I had promised myself I would not.

'Why are you leaving Glasgow?'

'You might as well ask a fowl why it would leave the lidded pot. Eight lectures a week, a hundred-and-fifty a year. At present I'm merely parboiled. Another two terms and I should have been soup.' His voice dropped to a more intimate register. 'And you will visit us in Oxford. Unless you disgrace yourself this week.'

He motioned me down the path, advancing a long arm as if to curve it around my waist, one of those phantom gestures of his. How I loved his ungainly grace. (Unconfessable thought. Like our bodies, our remarks must never quite touch.)

The cottage was cool and dark after the vivid garden, with a smell of beeswax on old wood, the floor listing slightly under my feet, the echoing tick of a longcase clock. He stooped to pass through the doorway at the end of the hall. In the greenish light filtered through the leaded glass, I saw a small party was in progress. Two men got to their feet. The women turned towards me.

Transfixed by Lucie Raleigh, I did not listen to the introductions.

I had pictured her as Guinevere to the professor's Lancelot: a languid, willowy queen. In reality she was compact and energetic with a pleasing, squarish face. Slightly inturned upper teeth grazed a plump lower lip. She seemed surprisingly youthful for a woman in her late thirties.

'Miss Macfarlane was Walter's most brilliant student in Glasgow,' she announced to the company. Then, to me, 'The children will be back very soon. They're all frightfully excited about learning the piano.'

I sat down.

Professor Raleigh hung back from the circle of chairs, folding himself into the window seat.

'We were just planning tomorrow's outing.' Lucie's charming inflection rendered me peculiarly helpless, as if the words she wound around us were very soft, very strong wool. 'Mary wants to see some hideous exhibition in Swindon, but perhaps you'd prefer an interesting ruin.'

'That's rather hard on your husband.' A droll, drawn-out, provocative voice, its owner looking almost exactly as I had imagined Lucie. 'Walter's more of a column – or possibly an obelisk.'

'A jolly obelisk,' said my whiskery neighbour, who was German.

'Covered in terribly amusing hieroglyphics.' This from a Fauntleroyish young man with a flop of brown hair.

'Quite indecipherable to the rest of us.' The queenly woman again.

'To you,' Lucie purred. 'But not, I'm sure, to his most brilliant student.'

I had to speak or be written off as a dullard.

'After you've been bamboozled by Professor Bradley's lectures, Professor Raleigh is clarity itself.'

'Really?' Lucie said. 'He doesn't rattle off a few random facts, then spend the best part of the hour reading out his favourite speeches from the Bard?'

In truth, this was exactly what he did. I glanced towards the window, but the professor's face was obscured against the light. 'He reads better than any actor.'

'He does, doesn't he?' his wife agreed. 'We were wondering if we should do some Shakespeare while you're here. That is, if you'd find it amusing. We're all such show-offs, one forgets it's not to everyone's taste.'

I said I would love to read a play.

'Not *read*,' said Fauntleroy, '*perform*. Costumes, scenery, props – sword fights, too, saints preserve us.'

'But not one of the tragedies,' Lucie intervened. 'By our age you've had enough of those, and the history plays have so few decent parts for women. Besides, it's only the comedies Walter takes seriously.'

Picturing myself as Viola, in doublet and hose, I suggested *Twelfth Night*.

'We thought *Much Ado*,' Lucie said smoothly. 'It's so refreshing to watch a pair of lovers of a certain vintage. Not so ancient as Anthony and Cleopatra – that's just sordid – but old enough to have learned there's more to love than ecstasy and death.'

'Stair rods?' her husband offered. 'Marmalade? Life insurance? Bridge?'

Ignoring him, Lucie continued, 'Though I wonder if Beatrice wouldn't have been better off marrying Don Pedro.'

'Oh *no!*'

My fellow guests smiled and I saw that I had been cast in the role of *ingénue*. I did not like this any more than I had liked Lucie making it clear I was there to mind the children. I had no wish to spend this week being patronised as the help.

8

I stood up.

> 'What fire is in mine ears? Can this be true?
> Stand I condemned for pride and scorn so much?
> Contempt, farewell! And maiden pride, adieu!
> No glory lives behind the back of such.
> And Benedick, love on – I will requite thee,
> Taming my wild heart to thy loving hand:
> If thou does love, my kindness shall incite thee
> To bind our loves up in a holy band.
> For others say thou dost deserve, and I
> Believe it, better than reportingly.'

There was a small astonished silence. My face grew warm. 'Well,' said Whiskers, 'I can see why you're top of the class.' The professor patted his pockets in a syncopated rhythm. 'They're in your raincoat,' Lucie murmured. Turning back to me, she said, 'We're having steak and kidney for dinner. I do hope you're not a vegetarian? You don't have that look – you know what I mean: as if they're bald even though they've got hair. But if you are one, you must say. I'm sure Cook can rustle up a coddled egg.'

I assured her I was quite omnivorous.

'How extremely accommodating of you.'

At midnight in the sewing room on the three-quarter-length divan (knees tucked up to keep my feet under the covers), I reviewed my new acquaintances. Before coming to Glasgow, Professor Raleigh – *Walter* – had held the literature chair at Liverpool University. Whiskers (Professor Kuno Meyer) taught Teutonic languages there. The foppish boy, Lytton, had been another brilliant student of Walter's and held the extra claim of being his sister's nephew by marriage. I would have been deadly jealous, but I had no jealousy to spare: it was all directed at the honourable Mary Chaloner Dowdall. According to Whiskers (who sat beside me at dinner), she was a famous Bohemian who had once ridden through Liverpool in a Romany wagon, bare-legged, wearing a short, striped petticoat and spangled headkerchief. She was not so very much older than me, four years at most, but the gulf between us was plain for all to see. The queenly Mary had *finish*. Along with her lovely, intelligent face; her long, slender, gypsyish limbs; that air of being aloof one minute and, the next, intent as a hunting cat. I would have been horribly in love with her, had I been a man. Luckily she had a husband, a barrister detained in the north by a very important case.

The next day, Walter sat beside me at lunch.

He was no more attentive to me than to any other guest, but I was near enough to breathe in his faint smell of Morgan's pomade mixed with shirt starch and cigarettes. The nape of my neck prickled at his proximity. Our feet touched. I murmured an apology. He smiled at his plate.

'I hope the boys aren't being too much of a nuisance,' Lucie said.

'Not at all,' I replied, knowing everyone had heard Valentine slamming his fists on the piano keys, roaring, '*I hate it, hate it, hate it!*' while Hilary tried to hide his pious smirk. Little Adrian was my favourite, in his velvet smock and knicker-bockers, slipping his soft hand in mine. Thankfully, there was a nurse to see to the baby.

After lunch, Walter returned to his study. One more day and his book on Hakluyt would be ready for the printers. Kuno and Lucie claimed a corner of the parlour for a game of chess. Mary retired for a nap. We had been up so late last night, and Cook's suet sat rather heavy on the stomach. Lytton borrowed an umbrella and set off for the village post office, taking the children, who were to spend the afternoon with their grandmother. Unexpectedly, I was free to do as I pleased. Lucie said she admired my pluck, going out for a walk in this filthy weather. I was to be sure to gird myself in a waterproof and sou'wester.

'Cathie!'

As if by magic, Walter appeared behind me in the lane, out of sight of the house and doubly concealed by his voluminous oilskins. He was carrying a pudding basin.

'For the plums. I'm going to pillage the vicar's trees. You shall be my accomplice.'

But he took the road leading away from the church.

'I like a woman who matches my stride. Lucie has me creeping like an undertaker while she trots alongside me on her little terrier's legs.' He stopped on a bridge over a railway cutting. 'Perfect timing: here comes a ripper!'

A plume of smoke hurtled along the cutting towards us. The express was moving so fast that the engine rocked from side to side. The whistle shrieked and we were wreathed in the delicious smell of washday ironing, a metallic drag in the thundering rhythm, a bass note I felt in my bones. We turned and watched it speeding away towards London. Walter's smile made me wonder if I had cried out in excitement.

The vicar's orchard sat across the road from the church, behind high walls of ancient brick. Fruit lay rotting in the grass, worm-holed or swollen and burst. The tree we chose wept like a willow under its burden. So many plums, with a blueish bloom that wiped away to reveal the same shade of pink as the old brick walls. A twist, the merest touch, and they fell into the palm. Only one resisted. When I tugged it free, a drop of syrup seeped from the umbilical dimple, like serum from a wound.

Stretching to reach one of the higher clusters, I nudged a pocket of leaves and a teaspoon's worth of rainwater ran down the inside of my sleeve. I gasped. Walter turned at the sound. The tips of his long fingers circled a fruit, gently squeezing. He plucked it and bit, spitting out the stone, bringing the residue

11

to my mouth. My lips grazed his fingers as I took it. His eyes held mine. Woodsmoke drifted from the vicarage chimney. Our oilcloths creaked as I pressed myself against him, lifting my rain-wet face, my juice-sweetened mouth, to his. Was that surprise, or alarm, in his eyes? He glanced over my shoulder before planting a quick, fatherly kiss on my nose.

'We'd better chivvy along and fill Cook's basin,' he said.

I picked plums as if my life depended on it, as if they were all that stood between my family and starvation. As if I were stripping the tree of my shame.

We retraced our steps over grass that was turning to bog. Rain bounced on the paved road, forming a brown river in the gutter. Walter slithered on a fallen leaf. Our glances met and veered away. We parted company inside the cottage garden. I took the kitchen path, he made for the front door. For the past ten minutes neither of us had spoken.

The boot room was warm and dry, the brass hooks concealed by layers of tweed and wool, the floor cluttered with hazel sticks and perished gumboots. I pressed my face into the comforting mound of dusty-smelling coats. I was twenty-five. Father had been dead three years. My sister Fanny was in London and engaged to be married. How long before Grant found a farm, and Gordon passed his architect's exams and was snapped up as a husband, leaving Mother on my hands? As was only fair. I had had my years of freedom. What had I gained at the Frankfurt Conservatory and Glasgow University? The knowledge that I was a mediocre pianist, and Professor Raleigh's regard, a treasure lost with that clumsy lurch into his arms.

'That's right. You'll feel better after a good cry.'

Walter had shed his oilskins.

'I'm not crying.' Though I could feel my blotchy face and reddened eyes.

He came in, closing the door behind him. The lock made

the lightest of clicks. His hands framed my brow, pushing back the strands of hair that had come unpinned under the sou'wester. He kissed my eyelids, nose, cheeks, chin, lips. The surprise of his tongue in my mouth. 'Ssshh,' he said, when I tried to speak. A woman's voice echoed down the corridor, and he was gone.

The rain persisted. We drank tea and ate buttered muffins. At five o'clock Lytton returned and we played charades, swains against damsels. The swains mimed the Wreck of the Hesperus, Lytton clinging to Walter, who swayed like a metronome as the ship's mast, while Kuno puffed out his cheeks to blow a hurricane. We damsels were weak with laughter by the time our turn came. The honourable Mary spurned the murder of Julius Caesar (my suggestion) and Orpheus in the Underworld (Lucie's), insisting on the beheading of Mary Queen of Scots. To no one's surprise, she took her namesake's role. Lucie was executioner. Whom was I to play? In a flash of inspiration, I remembered the little Skye terrier that emerged from his mistress's skirts after the second, fatal chop.

And so it happened that the caller shown in by the maid found Mary fallen elegantly on the floor, near a cushion trussed into the shape of a head with a diadem improvised from a pearl necklace, while I romped on all fours, barking soundlessly.

'I'm afraid you've missed tea,' said Lucie, who had entered into the spirit of the game less wholeheartedly.

I look up.

You are standing in the doorway. Black hair showing the first flecks of grey, a black moustache. The sort of conventionally handsome face sketched above a three-guinea overcoat in the back of the *Strand Magazine*, I think, until I notice your eyes. The upper and lower lids are unusually heavy, yet not sleepy – oh, quite the opposite of sleepy. Your pupils drill directly into mine.

'Catherine, this is my baby brother, Herbert.' A warmth in Lucie's voice, almost as if she liked me.

You are known to the others, your arrival casting a fine net of constraint over their hilarity. Kuno mutters, 'Jackson.' Lytton nods. Mary looks down, smoothing her skirts.

'What have you done with the children?' Lucie asks.

'They're in the kitchen, cadging jam tarts from Cook.'

'Well at least you haven't left them by the side of the road somewhere.' She turns to me. 'He can be fearfully absent-minded when he's making sketches for a new painting.'

The charades are abandoned. A fire has been lit against the rain, but the day holds no chill. We are all pink-cheeked and slightly overheated. The swains are in their shirtsleeves. Only you are cool. A smell of outdoors clings to you. Already I can see you are one of those men who smile rarely, making gayer souls look like fools.

Over dinner the conversation has an extra sparkle, as if everyone is striving to impress – or is it to exclude? – the newly arrived guest. Walter declares the Irish are all like people in bad plays. The Scots? A passionately officious race. 'The whole country is like a company floated to exploit something.' As for the Welsh with their reeking root vegetable, they were a joke in Shakespeare's time, and remain so to this day. Kuno wonders how he would summarise the English.

'No race has a more highly developed sense of the ludicrous.'

'That's a bit of a backhander,' Lytton says.

Walter denies it. 'If forced to choose between virtue and a sense of humour, only a barbarian would opt for the former.'

'He's said that before,' Mary drawls, 'written it in a letter, I shouldn't be surprised.'

'How can you tell?'

15

'Your syntax had a touch of the fountain pen about it.'

'As is so often the case,' Kuno adds.

And now we must all have a stab at defining the English.

Lucie offers, 'They discipline their children and indulge their dogs.'

Lytton: 'They speak the language of Shakespeare, and read the yellow press.'

Kuno: 'They overboil their vegetables.'

Lucie again: 'Forgive their ungrateful guests.'

Kuno claps his hand to his heart and bows.

Mary: 'They write poems about the smack of willow on leather, but not about their wives.'

The candles drip honeyed light across the table. Our fingers ply the heavy silverware, lift the ruby wine in the crystal glass. Glancing up, to Kuno's abundant red beard and the sparse grey hairs across his pate, the exaggerated cut of Lytton's velvet jacket, the rather homely bump at the end of Mary's nose (hidden from me until now by her blazing belief in her own beauty), I wonder: is this what an artist sees?

Lucie nominates William Morris as the quintessential Englishman. Yes indeed, Mary says: all those brick terraces glimpsed from the train, papered in Honeysuckle and curtained with Pomegranate. Walter remarks that, despite his skipper's beard, there was a streak of the schoolgirl in Morris's soul.

It is my turn.

'The English regard God as their butler.'

Kuno snorts with mirth.

I remember this look of Walter's from tutorials, when I said something that exceeded his idea of me.

'Very good,' Mary says, 'but what does it mean?'

Lytton answers for me, 'They count on Him to keep the foreign riff-raff out of Heaven.'

'Doesn't every nation hate foreigners?' You have been quiet for so long, it is mildly shocking to hear you speak. 'Surely it's natural enough.'

16

'Not to a Scot,' I say. 'When my father was alive, our house was filled with Indian rajahs, freed negro slaves, South Sea Island princes, Jewish evangelists. By the age of twelve, I was giving English lessons to Polish refugees.'

'How extraordinary,' Lucie murmurs.

In the parlour afterwards, Mary sings Gray's *Elegy* to the tune of 'Tom, Tom, the Piper's Son'. Lytton shoehorns Keats's *Endymion* into 'Oranges and Lemons'. My splicing of 'The Lady of Shalott' and 'Three Blind Mice' wins a round of applause. Walter proposes Word and Question. We draw slips of paper from two hats and retreat to write our poems.

My verse scans perfectly, rhyming 'bunion' with 'onion' to answer 'why did the late Queen dislike Spaniards?' After Mary's wittily risqué stanza, it seems no more than the work of a diligent schoolgirl. Kuno produces a limerick that is all the funnier for being delivered in a Hamburg accent. Lytton recites his doggerel in Cockney, pairing 'sorrow' with 'horror' and 'ho-hum' with 'bluetongue' ('how did Bo Peep lose her sheep?'). Inevitably, it is Walter who carries the day, with his answer to 'Is art the highest vocation?'

> 'The Artist and his luckless wife
> They lead a horrid haunted life,
> Surrounded by the things he's made
> That are not wanted by the trade.
>
> The world is very fair to see;
> The Artist will not let it be;
> He fiddles with the works of God,
> And makes them look uncommon odd.
>
> The Artist is an awful man,
> He does not do the things he can;
> He does the things he cannot do,
> And we attend the private view.

The Artist uses honest paint
To represent things as they ain't,
He then asks money for the time
It took to perpetrate the crime.'

'Fix!' cries Lytton. 'You drew your own question.'

'Quite inadvertently.'

'And you just happened to have been working up a poem along the same lines?' Mary drawls.

Walter's lips twitch. 'That would be the act of an absolute bounder.'

The front door bangs.

'Herbert's wound troubles him at night,' Lucie says. 'It makes him rather abrupt.'

Mary is persuaded to play the piano. She is not as expressive as I should have been, but looks very handsome at the keyboard.

Lucie draws me aside and asks if I would mind bringing you in. You may have gone back to your lodgings in the village, but she rather suspects I will find you lurking in the garden.

As soon as I leave the house I taste the smoke from your cigarette. You are standing by the gate. The moon has turned the path chalk white. Seen from behind, you could be anyone, a stranger. I could creep up on you and silently undress. Touch you on the shoulder. Let those rakish eyes look their fill. Six months hence, visitors to the Royal Academy would view me naked from head to toe, silvery with moonlight.

I blame Walter for stirring up these indecent thoughts.

Your head lifts. A lurch in my stomach as if I had stepped through a rotten floorboard. You turn towards me. Fear: what else is youth? Terror of uncharted waters. The compulsion to press on.

'Will you come in?'

'Why, are they missing me?'

'Not as far as I can tell.'

Your mouth does something hidden by your moustache. The next moment the humorous spark, if that is what it was, is gone. 'These infernal games. While your friends in there were *being amusing*, I was watching their countrymen die on the South African plain.'

'Were you badly wounded?'

You stare rudely.

'Lucie mentioned it,' I say.

Again that unreadable movement of your mouth. 'She must have meant my injured feelings.'

'She sent me to fetch you.'

'She is my guardian angel.' I hear this as sardonic, but perhaps it is not. 'And Raleigh's.'

I guess what you are thinking, but I do not expect you to say it.

'Are you his mistress?'

'No!'

'You turned him down?'

'Walter has never been anything but entirely proper with me.'

'Because you're promised to another?'

What makes me say it? 'Because I'm not *amusing*.'

This time the smile shows under your moustache.

'Then we're two of a kind,' you say.

Next morning the halcyon weather has returned. The boy who brought me from the station drives us to the Downs. Since there are ten of us, plus an enormous picnic basket, he makes three trips, departing after the third with instructions to collect us mid-afternoon from White Horse Hill.

It is glorious to be out of doors with the bees sucking the last honey from the vetch and the butterflies stravaiging and a kestrel hovering above us in the hazy blue. You bring a sketchbook, setting up your folding stool and squinting at the landscape so intently that no one tries to talk to you. While the others walk on ahead, the children and I borrow a dish from the picnic basket and gather the fat black brambles that grow so abundantly here. We eat at least as many as we consign to the bowl. The boys' mouths are stained purple. Mine too. How sweet the squashy berries are, though not as sweet as this rest from witty talk. To think I used to pity the Benedictines their vow of silence. I have not been in Berkshire three days, and already I feel like weeping with relief whenever I lock the lavatory door. *Peace, at last*. The bairns and I are perfectly happy talking nonsense until Lytton arrives, sent back by Lucie to chivvy us along.

What a gossip he is. Apparently Kuno is brilliant, much more original than Walter, although conversationally rather pedantic in the German manner. I am not to be fooled by Mary's aristocratic airs: her late pa was a stockbroker.

Fought her grandpapa tooth and nail to get his hands on the baronetcy. The widowed mother is a recluse. A pity the same cannot be said of Gabrielle, Mary's oldest sister. A sapphic. Addicted to ether, and a second-degree sorceress in the Golden Dawn.

'And Herbert?' I ask.

Yes, you are an artist, of sorts, but no more talented than your sister, and rather less prolific. It takes you such an age to finish anything. You could hardly be more different from your late father. Here I have to confess my ignorance. 'Mason Jackson, of course.' Lytton is surprised I have never heard of him, but sure I would recognise his illustrated editions of Dickens and Shakespeare. Pen and ink sketches, rather heavy on the cross-hatching.

'He was no Dürer, but they have a certain vulgar brio. The illustrated papers couldn't print enough of 'em. Jackson *fils* has turned his back on journalism, though not before journalism turned its back on him. Mostly he does portraits. Mary sat for him a few years ago.' Lytton pulls the sceptical face he wore when I recited Beatrice's speech from *Much Ado*. 'Made her look rather shrewish. Without Walter and Lucie, he'd be up a gum tree. Walter swung him a teaching job in Liverpool and got him into the University Club, then he chucked it all to go off to the Transvaal with the Royal Engineers. The art school was very decent, brought in a chap to keep his seat warm: not a pretty painter, but the real thing. Charmed the socks off Mary and her husband. Of course, when the war was over, Jackson was rather surplus to requirements.'

After lunch I find myself walking with Lucie. We breast a hill to discover a herd of deer grazing below us.

'Oh look!' I exclaim.

'They always remind me of cheap furniture,' she says. 'Square-cornered and cumbersome and a rather unlikely colour.'

I stare at the deer, trying to turn them into chests of drawers, but they remain obstinately themselves.

'They're hopelessly short-sighted. A stag will lock antlers with a bicycle's handlebars in the rutting season.'

'Love is blind,' I remark. Rather wittily, it seems to me.

'Lust more than love, I'd say. But perhaps you think they're the same thing?'

My eyes stray towards Walter, twenty yards ahead with Mary and Lytton, each long stride taking him further away. What made him choose Lucie, out of all the young women he must have besotted? She is not as beautiful as Mary, and plainly not half as smitten as me. Once in a while her eyes will seek his with a coded glance, but he pays her no particular homage that I can see.

As if the advance party has breached some invisible boundary, the deer turn and flee, springing on their carved haunches.

'Do you wish to marry, Catherine?'

What an extraordinary question.

'If I meet the right man.'

'Oh, I'm sure you will. In my experience these things happen when you least expect them.' Lucie shows me her pretty teeth. 'Some fellow you don't know from Adam crosses your path, and nothing is ever the same again.'

Not long after this she trips. One minute she is walking alongside me, the next, she is on the ground. I call Walter, but his efforts to get her back on her feet are met with moans of pain. The party gathers in a circle. Mary reports that her ankle is hot to the touch. We will never reach our destination by four o'clock. Lucie decides you and I must go on ahead and bring the trap back with us. We are on the point of setting out when Walter speaks up. He is hopeless as a sick nurse. Having walked with me before, he knows I am as strong as a carthorse and will set a fearsome pace. He alone has the long legs to keep up with me. All in all, it would be better if you stayed behind with your sister.

Lucie tries to catch his eye, but he is busy telling the boys to behave themselves while we are gone. He hands over his cigarettes to see Kuno and Lytton through the wait, entrusting his hip flask to Mary in case a nip of something medicinal is required. Toodle-oo. We should only be a couple of hours.

My heart is beating fast but I say nothing.

And maybe his motives are purely pragmatic. We stride out like athletes, with no spare breath for talk. Of course I long to be taken in his arms. But if it has to be one or the other, I would rather discuss poetry.

I was one of four non-graduating students allowed to attend Professor Raleigh's honours class. Every morning that first term I ran downhill to his nine o'clock lecture, never thinking for a moment that he had noticed me. It was *Hamlet* we discussed, that lunchtime in the library. (Wednesday was stringy mutton, the one dish I could not abide.) I spoke, and Walter listened. Not a courtesy I could count on later. Sometimes my weekly tutorial was more like a lecture to an audience of one, and how bad tempered I would be afterwards, but I never showed him my impatience, because it was a privilege to be singled out, and there were other days when our minds truly met, and we read to each other to illustrate our arguments, or read together, Isabella to his Angelo, Katharina to his Petruchio, and I thought, *I was born for this*.

When we have walked half a mile or so, Walter turns away from the path, along a winding track that descends, gently at first, then more steeply. He claims it is a shortcut. My sense of direction leads me to doubt it, but surely he would not make Lucie wait unnecessarily. Another half-mile and we are in a sort of chasm, between high hedgerows dense with hips and haws and berries, scarlet and carmine and blood-blister black. It is so lovely here, with the hedge sparrows' scribble-song all around us and a light blizzard of thistledown in the air.

Walter breaks our silence. 'Two men making love to you. What a busy week this is turning out to be.'

Astonishment stops me in my tracks. 'You can't be referring to Lytton or Kuno, so I take it you mean Herbert?'

'You hadn't noticed?'

I am not convinced by his amused tone. *Could Walter be jealous?*

'He seems very personable,' I say.

'Does he?' The amusement sounds genuine now. 'I suppose he's young, not bad-looking, a former soldier: all the qualities to turn a woman's head.'

'You think?' It is like being back in his rooms at Glasgow University. I would say anything to impress him, if only I knew what he wanted from the conversation.

'And free to marry.'

'I'm not looking for a husband at present.'

'But if a suitable candidate should appear, you won't forget your old admirer?'

It seems to me there are three people in this country lane: Walter, my own self, and a doppelgänger visible only to him. My lips try out the teasing, voluptuous smile such a woman might wear.

This is nothing like our kiss among the coats. Then he was tender, now he is forceful, pushing me against the bank, an animal smell breaking through the clove-like scent of pomade, my mouth so full of his tongue I cannot ask him to slow down.

A rose hip hits him on the leg and bounces to the ground. Mary is standing a few feet away.

'Good shot,' he says, straightening up.

I brush seed heads off the back of my dress.

'The driver passed us on the road so we flagged him down.' Mary's drawl acknowledges nothing, and everything. 'Kuno has taken Lucie back to the cottage.'

'Good of you to run and fetch us,' Walter says. 'You must have put on a spurt.'

'Yes, I'm sorry about that.' She raises her eyebrows at me. 'I'll make sure I dawdle next time.'

Every step of the walk back is an agony of shame. Mary and Walter talk of friends in Liverpool. A notorious Bohemian with several illegitimate offspring, 'Sampson', 'Ehrenborg', someone Walter calls 'the Mighty Atom'. I think, *Perhaps they are excluding me out of charity, giving me time to regain my composure*, but now the conversation takes a turn that cannot be for my benefit.

'I take it Lucie sent you.'

'We agreed it might be prudent.'

'Ah yes, prudence: your signal virtue. Especially in gypsy caravans.'

'What's a poor maid to do when she's seduced, sire?'

They share a few moments' throaty laughter.

'So you found us up on the road, marching along.'

'If you say so.'

'Discussing Jane Austen.'

'"It is a truth universally acknowledged..."'

A glance between them.

'Lord knows why we call you the gentler sex,' he says.

The trap is waiting on the roadside. The children have been dropped off in the village with Lucie's mother. Lytton, Walter and Mary make the next trip, leaving you with me.

We watch them dwindling into the distance until they disappear over a hump in the road.

'Will we walk to the top of the ridge?' you say.

I shrug. But it is better to be moving, changing the scenery, even if the same trapped thoughts are circling in my head. Their throaty laughter. *Especially in gypsy caravans.*

'Packing already?'

I carry on folding my clothes. It is almost midnight. Walter comes into the sewing room, closing the door. I do not look up.

'It was my understanding you weren't leaving until Saturday?'

I say nothing.

'Are you not enjoying your stay here?'

I continue packing.

'Lucie will be heartbroken, not to mention the children.'

I have stowed every garment within reach in the bag. My stockings are still in the drawer, but I cannot retrieve them without turning to face him. I take the shawl out and refold it.

'Please, Cathie, stop fussing with that.'

I hear him step towards me.

A few hours ago, I would have found this suspense delicious. What a ninny I am. It is Mary he wants. I cannot blame him. Any man asked to choose between us would feel the same. But it was cruel of him to toy with me. I would rather die than admit any of this.

'Mary is an enchanting woman,' he says. 'No mere mortal could resist her. Highly intelligent, too. As is Lucie. I could not love a stupid woman. But what I find most alluring in them both is their generosity. So many women see love as barter: a night of pleasure for a house, servants, *position*. They make me shudder. Mary understands that love is not a hat that fits one head only. Men and women are more alike than is commonly supposed. Lucie has my heart, and Mary, and still it beats for you.'

I turn around. He is in his nightshirt.

The look on my face makes him smile. 'Surely you knew?'

It seems to me I did know, and yet I did not.

'You're so different here,' I say.

'Am I really?' His eyes look into mine. 'Perhaps it was too much to ask, but you have been such a charming guest. The children adore you. And it will be much easier now Lucie knows you.'

I do not ask what will be easier. It is the fourth year of the twentieth century. Am I less generous than Mary? If I feel myself touched, head, heart and soul, as Walter touches me, do I not owe it to myself – to Life – to respond?

He draws me towards him.

When I glance at the door, he whispers, 'Everyone's asleep.'

We are up and out early next morning into a day without a breath of wind. The air smells as if God has just bitten into a Cox's Pippin. Mist lines the river valley like pocket lint.

We have borrowed five dogs and five guns from the local estate. Lucie, whose ankle is *quite better thank you*, announces that you and I will share. Neither of us shows much enthusiasm for this arrangement. Walter says he will take turns with his wife. 'There's nothing like a gun for fostering an interest in nature.'

Kuno raises a finger to his lips, partridge being famously sensitive to noise. We spread out across the field, you and I at the eastern end of the line. All at once the children charge, arms flailing, yelling at the top of their lungs. The first bird breaks cover. Mary fells it. Her grey-muzzled retriever bounds towards the trees. The second bird is mine. I am a good shot, having had years of practice on summer holidays in Perthshire. I hand the gun over, but you set it down to deal with our cocker spaniel, Queenie, who is only half-trained. I pet her silky ears while you prise the fowl from her jaws.

There is a burst of laughter from the other side of the field. Walter has missed. He mugs an annoyance that, beneath the pantomime, seems real enough. When I turn back, you are watching me.

'Will you take a shot?' I ask.

'I'd better keep an eye on our bitch.'

'I can do that.'

'No need.'

You hung back from last night's parlour games too.

'Why should I have all the sport?'

'I've seen enough of guns.'

'In the Transvaal?' The volley of shots ceases. I lower my voice in the sudden hush. 'Surely the fighting was done by infantrymen. Weren't you a Royal Engineer, tasked with maintaining railways and bridges and telegraph lines?'

'It's a pity you weren't a general, to make things so orderly.'

The others are laughing again.

'How alien daily life must be to a returning soldier,' I say. 'How petty it must seem – all of it, not just the parlour games.'

'It's like standing outside a window in a snowstorm looking in on a warm room...'

Hearing a crack in your voice, I nod. *Go on.*

'I should like to smash through the glass, but the flying shards might cut the people inside. At the very least, I would let in the freezing air, destroying my dream of sanctuary. And so I stay out in the cold.'

Lucie calls my name. I turn round. She points at the partridge now flying out of range: my bird.

Mary takes aim and it drops out of the sky. Queenie's head jerks at the shot. She takes off at the same moment as Mary's retriever, ignoring your efforts to call her back. The two dogs race, their paths converging. The still air carries the sound of snarling. The retriever emerges with the dead bird, Queenie chasing her across the field, snapping at her throat. Mary breaks off a long switch. There is a terrible squeal.

'*Ho!*' I shout. Such a rage in me as I sprint towards them. I grab the switch from Mary's hand. Smartly Lucie steps between us. Lytton and Kuno have separated the dogs. Mary insists Queenie had been about to turn on her: she should be shot. 'She's a pup!' I shout. Walter observes that in such cases it is best not to take chances. 'Hogwash,' you say. No one mentions that the honourable Mary has narrowly escaped a thrashing. Although it is not yet noon, Lucie decides to return to the home farm where lunch has been arranged. To keep the dogs apart, you and I wait a few minutes before setting off.

'Why did Mary look at you?' I ask, when we are alone.

You sit on the ground with the spaniel in your arms, stroking her back. A pink weal marks her gingery muzzle.

'Just before she struck Queenie,' I say. 'She looked straight at you.'

You carry on stroking, one muddy paw cradled in your hand.

'Were you in love with her when you painted her portrait?'

'Is that what she says?'

Queenie whines at the harsh note in your voice.

'I can see for myself how beautiful she is.'

What must it be like to possess such a woman and then lose her? Are all others insipid, like water after strong wine?

'You have no idea of the evil there is in the world,' you say.

'In Mary?'

'In almost everyone.'

After lunch, you sit alone with your sketchbook while I join the others in a walk, but we are paired on the ride back to the cottage. The sun is sinking, its light pouring across the Downs like camomile tea. The alliance between us this morning feels very distant. Racking my brains for something to say, I ask you to show me your drawings. You refuse.

At first I think you want me to coax you. I say I understand that a sketch is by its nature unfinished, but your studio is in London and we are in Berkshire and I am eager to see some of your work.

'Do you think I've been sketching you?'

I deny it.

You smile behind your moustache.

The trap rolls on towards Fernham. The horse seems tired. The boy flicks at its hind quarters with the whip, whistling an aimless tune between his teeth. You sit opposite me, watching the fields go by, swaying with the bumping of the trap. How strange that you and Lucie should be brother and sister. She is such an English rose. You could almost be Spanish. Your tawny skin seems thicker than an Englishman's hide, but so supple. Your hair, only half-tamed by macassar oil, still shows its wave. A complicated face, with your broad, handsome, surely broken nose, those dissolute-seeming eyes, and yet some fierceness pulling against the sensuality. Something not quite right about your clothes, although chosen with a dandy's care. The sailor's peacoat and starched white shirt, that military wristwatch.

'I should like to have met you in uniform,' I say.

'Am I not enough of a gentleman like this?'

I can hardly admit I was thinking of your narrow, muscular frame. The sense I have of force only just held in check.

'You have a military bearing.' The trap takes us a few yards closer to the cottage. 'I meant no offence.'

The boy is still whistling his tuneless melody.

I lower my voice. 'Does it not seem odd that we're either completely silent with each other or talking as bluntly as family?'

You think about this. 'Not so very odd.'

'Do you speak to all women like this?'

'To my landlady, no. To my sister, probably.'

'And everyone else?'

'I prefer the company of my easel. Some weeks I don't speak to a soul from one Sunday to the next.'

'I should be bored out of my wits.'

'I'm often bored by talk, but never by my eyes. I've learned more about you from looking than I could glean from a month of conversation.'

Our glances meet. We listen to the wheels on the road, the jingling harness.

'So tell me about myself.'

'You're finding all this fun more wearing than you expected. You're wishing you'd stayed at home...'

I squint at you, against the light.

'...instead of accepting another woman's hospitality to spoon with her husband.'

'*I beg your pardon?*'

'And now you're putting on a show of being affronted by me—'

'I have no feelings whatsoever about you.'

'—when really you're angry with yourself.'

The boy's patched coat gives nothing away, but I am sure he is listening.

'Did your sister tell you to say this?'

'No, although my sister understands the situation. Probably better than you do.'

The trap lurches over a pothole. You are waiting for me to ask what you mean.

'Would you rather I didn't go on?'

I give you an unfriendly look, but if you clam up now I will die of curiosity.

'Walter pays the same attention to every lady who crosses his path. Mostly they laugh it off, but every once in a while the inexperienced ones open their hearts to him.'

I understand now that I have never known humiliation. Girlish embarrassment, yes, but nothing as corrosive, as all-consuming, as this. I am on fire: my face, my vitals, the blood in my veins. Moments from last night flash before me, no longer tender, or passionate, just sordid.

I pull the sketchbook from your satchel. Little Adrian asleep; Walter in an armchair, stroking a slit-eyed cat; Lucie in melancholy profile. You grab the book from my lap. For a second we hold it taut between us. The spine rips.

You say, 'If you were a man, I'd box your ears for that.'

The old lady on the platform opens the door and peers into the packed compartment. Beside me, you tense in readiness to give up your seat. I would think less of you if you did not, but I am loath to lose the pressure of your thigh, the warmth of your arm against mine. The intruder retreats, closing the door. To my left, a lawyer's morning coat and grey-striped trousers. On your right, a portly gentleman in tweeds (the reason we are so squashed together). Opposite, a lady-schoolteacher type, two clerics and a salesman whose enormous suitcase extends perilously beyond the overhead luggage rack. What do our fellow passengers make of us: brother and sister, cousins, sweethearts? Or do they sense the truth: that we are virtual strangers thrust by chance into such immodest proximity?

Outside the fogged windows, Berkshire becomes Oxfordshire, every moment taking us further from Walter. In a few hours I will be back in Glasgow, trying to look interested as Mother extols the virtues of the latest patent liniment. Perhaps we will share our dinner with some moth-eaten prophet she has discovered in the Gallowgate. Or she will have changed churches again, and I will find the parlour filled with a new circle of censorious widows eager to pass on the Lord's disapproval. *Not just travelling unchaperoned, but with a bachelor, and foreign looking, and devilishly handsome.* A panther, it strikes me now: your sleek, supple hide cloaking muscle and sinew.

You insist on accompanying me across London. Under the glass canopy of Euston station, the air is chill as on the banks of a great river. The shriek of locomotives vies with the station master's whistle, the slamming of compartment doors, the hubbub of a hundred heartfelt meetings and partings.

'I'd rather not take this train.'

I have reasons. The pity of wasting such a glorious morning in travel. How seldom I am in London. How I detest eating lunch on a train. Is that a smirk behind your moustache? You have an appointment at your club at half past ten. If I am happy to wait, you will be free by noon. There is a little restaurant around the corner, a respectable establishment popular with maiden aunts. I will be back in good time for the three o'clock express.

A school of arms!

You are amused by my surprise. Did I think you would belong to the sort of club that charges its members to sit in button-backed armchairs and read the newspapers? You had your fill of that in Liverpool. A nest of bullies and gossips, just like school. After a day at the easel, a physical contest, man to man, is just the thing for your aching muscles. They are all vigorous, good-natured fellows here. Anyone with a nasty streak would soon be drummed out.

The ladies' sitting room overlooks the fencing hall. A smell of powdered rosin and sweat rises from the men below. Some are stretching, awaiting their turn with the foils. Others watch from benches. The wooden floor is marked with broad red stripes, allowing four separate contests to proceed simultaneously. The swordsmen dance up and down their allotted ground, left arms raised in a courtly flourish. Then, all at once, an interval of effortful grunting, the deft flurry of foils, and the hit, after which they separate. I would like

33

to select a favourite and silently cheer him on, but how to choose when all look so alike in their white suits and padded breastplates, faceless behind their masks. It is a little like dreaming, watching so many ghostly antagonists fighting without motive or passion or the possibility of blood.

And yet my eye finds one of these grunting phantoms more sympathetic than the rest. I make him my champion. My ear picks out his stertorous breath, the thump of his soft-soled boots on the wooden floor. He and his opponent seem evenly matched, moving forward and back, neither gaining much ground. Attack, feint, lunge, parry, counter-attack, circle parry, disengage. No hits. For a long time it could go either way, but eventually my man's movements grow sluggish, his foil less exact. Under the arms, his white jacket is wet. I watch the ebbing of his stamina, the effort to draw breath. The other's eye is a fraction sharper, his hand a split-second faster. My champion knows it, and the prospect of defeat lends his swordplay a new fury. The thrilling pace is almost too quick for my unpractised eye to follow. It cannot last. My man begins to flail and stumble, lunging too violently, exposing himself to the counter-thrust.

A hit.

The men step back, lowering their foils. My champion rests a hand on his heaving chest and pulls off his mask to reveal a violent flush. The victor, too, unmasks. You! In my astonishment I laugh out loud. You look up, catching my eye.

In Glasgow there is an unbridgeable gulf between the burly coalmen shouldering their hundredweight sacks, the draymen hefting casks of ale, and virile intellects like Walter, pale from long hours indoors, eyes red-rimmed from straining to read fine print by lamplight. I never dreamed of meeting a man with an artist's soul and the ruthless physicality of a soldier.

The restaurant is hardly bigger than a shop. The dim interior with its densely patterned wallpaper encourages conversation in lowered tones. To me the place feels delectably illicit. We take a table in the corner furthest from the window. Three prosperous-looking men sit over snifters of brandy. A pair of elderly widows despatch plates of breaded plaice. In the other shadowy corner, an exquisitely pretty woman is whispering with an older man too ugly to be her father. When you turn to see what I am looking at, your face shows such disapproval that I am moved to defend her. We can't *know* she is a paid companion. Yes, he is old and fat and balding, but then so is the king and, if rumour is to be believed, he has broken his share of hearts.

'Because he was Prince of Wales.'

'Partly,' I concede. 'But don't you think grossness can be attractive – at least, when it's in tension with other, finer qualities?'

'No, I don't.'

'Perhaps women are more susceptible to it.'

'And perhaps you're in a contrary mood, and you'd argue with me whatever I said.'

'I would not!'

Your heavy-lidded eyes fix on mine. 'Then those maidenly blushes hide a streak of depravity.'

There is a delicious edge to this teasing. I think your foil is safely blunted, but how can I be sure?

'Never lie to me, Catherine. I shall always know.'

'Is there no end to your talents – portraiture, swordsman-ship and mind-reading too?'

You smile. 'You have an unusually candid face. It shows every thought, like a pool rippled by the wind, never quite at rest.'

I am too pleased to know what to say.

'Has no one ever told you?'

I shake my head.

'Your eyes darken, or lighten. Your colour changes, flushing or paling—' your hand stops just short of my cheek '—here. And here.'

You find me beautiful. It is as if I have been teetering across a rickety bridge, refusing to look down, my whole life. And now that you have handed me across to firm ground, I know I was never in danger of falling.

'When a woman looks in the glass,' I say, 'that is, when *I* look, I refuse the face I find in that first instant, composing my features, almost without thinking, to achieve a more alluring reflection. I've had so many years of practice, it's the work of a moment.'

'So you've no idea how you appear to others?'

'How can I know?'

'I could paint you.'

And of course this is what I hoped you would say.

You ask what I did before studying at Glasgow University. I tell you about the Frankfurt Conservatory, how I went there in love with my own talents and, within a fortnight, knew myself quite ordinary. Even as I persevered, making the most of the opportunity I had been given, a spark in me had been snuffed out. Walter blew it into life again. He gave me an ear for the music of words. Not just Shakespeare and Donne, but the cadences of everyday conversation, the scope for playfulness and virtuosity over the breakfast table. His praise, quite unlooked for, resurrected my old brilliant self. Two blissful years as his student. If I had forgone Frankfurt, I might have had four and taken my degree, but the end would have come just the same. Brilliance might be charming in a girl, but it is no use to a grown woman, unless I marry well, like Mary, and can afford to host a salon. All my education has only rendered me less suited to living with a widowed mother who is good-hearted, but exasperatingly slow: a muddle-brained, trusting innocent. How can I leave her defenceless in the world? But how can I bear it, if I do not?

You listen without judging me, having your own forbidden thoughts about the futility of teaching. You have given up your position in Liverpool and plan to earn your living as a civilian engineer.

'But you'll still paint?'

You look down at the tablecloth. 'It's no great loss to the world.'

'Even if that were true, it'd be a loss to you.'

It is so long before you reply, I wonder if you have taken offence.

'I'm not sure it's healthy to define oneself by a talent no one else believes in.'

'*I* believe in it.'

The feeling in your eyes makes me think of a dog on a chain. Leaping up, to be yanked back down again.

'Jackson! I thought it was you.'

A ruddy-faced man looms over our table. One of the brandy drinkers. There is a smear of custard in his half-handlebar moustache.

Your glance flickers, as if calling on all your reserves of patience. 'Scotty,' you say flatly.

'What a turn-up, bumping into you down here.'

Scotty turns to me. You do not introduce us.

'Just the other day, Gordon Duff was saying "I wonder what's become of Jackson." The club's all at sixes and sevens, what with moving down the hill and all. No end of new blood about the place. That chap Muirhead they got in to fill your shoes seems very popular. Amusing fellow but solid, y'know. Not like whatsisname. Had to count the spoons every time he got up from the table. Dowdall says he's a genius, but everything he painted looked sloppy to me. He'd do better swearing off the gin and getting fewer parlour maids in the family way. Still, rather them than Mrs D, if you catch my drift. What *was* his name... Julius, was it? Something of that sort. We miss those boxing classes of yours, y'know. Are you still fighting? In the ring, I mean.' He prods your arm. '*In the ring*, eh, what? Never mind, old chap, just a joke. So, how are you making a living these days? I suppose studio work don't put much jam on the table.'

He reminds me of a clockwork mouse I had as a child. It kept going, even when it met the skirting board, until the mechanism ran down.

One of his companions pays the bill. Scotty glances over his shoulder.

'Well, I should really get back to, ah... Things to do, y'know. I'll give the chaps your best.'

'I'd rather you didn't,' you reply in the same flattened voice as before.

'Oh, ah, as you wish.' He sneaks another look at me. I make sure not to meet his eye. 'Good luck, old chap.' With a nod in my direction, he moves off to re-join his friends, who rise from the table and follow him out to the street.

'I'm sorry about that,' you say.

'Who is he?'

Raising a hand, you get up to peer through the window. Satisfied, you sit down again. 'He had the room across from mine at the University Club in Liverpool. For years I counted him as a friend.'

'But not now, I gather.'

'Many false friends have shown their true faces over the past two years.'

'He seemed harmless enough.'

How cool you are suddenly. I curse this habit of commenting on things I do not understand.

The waiter passes our table bearing plates of empress pudding for the widows.

'What's the matter, Catherine?'

'I hope you never despise me.'

You search my face. A blush rises up my throat and across my cheeks. I feel as if my skin were glass, as if you read my thoughts almost before I think them. Your gaze locks on mine, transmitting a beam of smoky light.

'I hope so too,' you say.

After Berkshire, the Glasgow air tasted unwholesome. The pinch-faced, bow-legged children in the street disturbed me as they had not before. 'Never mind, Cathie,' Mother said, 'you'll soon forget you were ever away.' I snapped at her: was that supposed to be a consolation, the years stretching ahead of me, day after dreary day with nothing to look forward to, my one taste of Life receding ever deeper into the past?

(And this was not the worst. There was something much more dreadful. Every day it grew more certain, though I tried to push it from my thoughts.)

For once, Mother did not urge me to remember the Everlasting Arms. With that innocent genius she had for hitting the nail on the head, she suggested we join another church and make an effort to befriend the mothers of marriageable sons. With the Lord's help, I would find a husband. He and I could take over her bedroom. She would move into Fanny's room.

I told her I had to go; Phyllis was expecting me.

But Phyl was hardly more comforting.

'Why are you so in awe of them? I should think you'd be glad to get away. They sound revoltingly smug.'

We were in the studio at the top of her parents' house. To maximise the light, she had whitewashed the walls, ceiling and floorboards. Gray spatters marked her linen smock and the improvised turban covering her hair. Her eyes, fringed by near-invisible lashes, were like the sea in winter. The only splashes of colour were the yellow stains on her smoking fingers.

I told her I was not *in awe* of anyone, least of all Walter and his friends. Nonetheless they had done me a service, revealing the paltriness of my existence. It was high time I found my true path. I was not like the girls we had gone to school with, and not like Phyl either, more's the pity. I would have given my right arm to walk about smelling of hot wax and plaster of Paris, or turps and linseed oil, to take a lump of clay and mould it into beauty. But the hard fact was I had no vocation, and longing for one would not bring it about. If I had a gift, it was for appreciation. Not just of works of art, but of the artistic moment in life, the *magic*. Phyl had the talent to make that magic with her own two hands. I could only put myself in the way of it. Without it, my soul would wither and die.

Phyl raised a spectral eyebrow.

'You think I'm talking grandiose nonsense.'

She did not deny it.

'I should accept I'm just ordinary and find a nice ordinary husband so I can bear his ordinary children—'

'*What?*'

'But I'm not ordinary. I wish I were – oh all right, I don't. It doesn't matter what I wish for. We Macfarlanes are peculiar. Who else has rice and milk soup for Sunday lunch to save the servants a little trouble? Who else's mother has been passing off her wedding gown as an evening dress for thirty years? Father wasn't much better, sending off his ships full of cloth with no idea whether they'd be paid for. Oh, we give ourselves airs, we tell ourselves we're less worldly, more sensitive. Perhaps we are. Or perhaps we're ridiculous. Either way, we're not going to change. You think magic belongs to artists, and those of us in second class must make do with bandstand concerts and toasted marshmallows, but you can't put us all in the same pot.'

She was looking at me as if I had taken leave of my senses. 'Has something happened, Cath?'

I nearly told her, but I could not face listening to her practical suggestions. Or else it would defeat her, and then I would truly despair. I took two cigarettes from the packet on the table. She fished the matches out of her smock pocket without comment, although I almost never smoked.

When we had both exhaled, she extended her right hand palm up, slowly turning it over, showing me the swollen knuckle, the nicks and burns and silvery scars. 'Does this look so very magical?'

'It does to me.'

She laughed. 'You can't put all artists in the same pot either. I've met one or two who lay claim to the creative ecstasy you imagine, but I don't think much of their daubs. All right, let's say this magic of yours exists: where is it? In your brain, your heart – or out there, like Mr Marconi's aetheric waves?'

'It's both.'

'Why would you build your happiness on something that appears out of nowhere—' she reached up and plucked a yellow birch leaf out of my hair '—and then, *pouf*, it's gone?'

'You're wrong. We don't always see it, but it's always there.'

Her smile turned sad. 'You're so like your mother. This aesthetic rapture you're chasing, isn't it just God by another name?'

'Not God but his creation. Here, now, in this room, or picking plums in an orchard, or playing charades in a parlour, or... or watching men fight in a fencing hall. It's being alive in every way, body and soul.'

I stubbed out the cigarette I had barely smoked and opened the window. The wind drove a faint smell of autumn from the Botanic Gardens. Dahlias and beech mast.

'It seems to me this holiday of yours has done you no good at all.'

How badly I wanted her to know, and how reluctant I was to admit it.

'I thought, if nothing else, you might enjoy a little masculine attention.'

I opened my mouth to speak.

'And I don't mean from that old professor.'

My face must have fallen.

'*Cath, what is it?*'

I wanted her to tell me that every woman had the odd late bleed, and a life without risks was no life at all, but the minute I said the man was Walter, she would know I had been used.

'There might have been a *little* masculine attention.'

'Oh yes?'

'Professor Raleigh's brother-in-law was staying in the village, an artist. He...'

'Out with it.'

'He said I reminded him of the Madonnina.'

'On top of Milan Cathedral? You weren't wearing a crown of stars at the time, by any chance?'

'Absurd, isn't it?'

'Completely absurd. But you were flattered anyway.'

And so I told her about your eyes; your broad, broken, sensual nose; the richness of your skin against the white fencing suit; the uncanny way I had chosen your opponent, as if I wanted to be the one down there trading rapier thrusts with you.

'You haven't fallen in love?'

'He lives in London.'

She squinted at me. 'That's all right then.'

'He gave me this, just before I got on the train.'

She put down her cigarette and took the sketch of me picking brambles the day of the picnic. I watched her eyes move across the paper, and back to something worth a second look.

'He's had work shown all over. Liverpool, here, the Royal Academies in Edinburgh and London.'

'Has he?' she said. 'Well, perhaps love makes him fumble-fingered, as well as blind.'

Walking back to Kersland Street, I saw a figure waiting across the road from the house, too far away for me to make him out. But somehow I knew.

Hoping to impress you, I take you to the Willow Tea Rooms. We inspect the top-floor billiard room and keek around the pretty leaded-glass door of the *salon de luxe*. Mr Mackintosh's brother-in-law was a colleague of yours at the Liverpool art school. MacNair's home, too, was decorated in this modern style, you say. Spending an evening there was like dining inside a coal scuttle. 'This pink-and-silver is much more pleasing. A pity it attracts so many stout Glasgow matrons. It can't be good business to make your customers feel like hobgoblins in fairyland.'

Our giggling draws a waitress who shows us to a table in the gallery. You give the oddly proportioned chairs a sceptical look. Your taste is traditional, although by temperament you are a radical. You insisted that men and women were taught together in Liverpool, even when drawing from life. The chatter with the naked models could be quite bawdy, but all in fun. Your students were great jokers. One girl, returning after a short holiday, found her painstakingly worked clay sculpture sown with cress, its contours hidden by a mass of little green leaves. The sort of trick men find more amusing than women, I say, but no, most of your day students were female. Lively girls. Always putting on plays, or dressing up as Titania and her fairies in *tableaux vivant* in the art sheds. I smile at the idea of art in a shed, but you say the studios were precisely that: ramshackle wooden huts, stifling in summer and freezing in winter. When the rain hammered on the tin roof, you couldn't hear yourself think. The railway line passed close by and, even with the windows shut, the soot found its way in. You were forever having to wipe smuts off the plaster cast of Michelangelo's *David*.

I laugh at your stories, but I am burning to ask, *Have you come all this way to see me?*

I tell you about Phyl, and how I am torn between envy and concern for her. Such arduous, lonely days in the studio but, at the end of them, a bas-relief on a public building seen by thousands, tens of thousands, ever after. I chose music, for the joy of Bach and the camaraderie of an orchestra (and the flattery of applause) yet I was always better at painting. Had I gone with Phyl to Glasgow School of Art, and thence to Paris, like you, how different my life would have been. Or maybe not so different, I admit, maybe just a dilettante painter instead of a dilettante pianist.

You give me your smoky look. 'And you and I wouldn't have met.'

That evening you are waiting on the same corner. Closing the front door, I think how easily it could be August, not September, and the man across the road a handsome stranger. Would I be struck by your supple skin, your hair turned to indigo by the setting sun? Would I wonder about the woman you were waiting for?

I should warn you we are sure to be seen by someone who will take the first opportunity to inform my mother, but I am loath to seem more conventional than your students. And what harm is there in showing a visitor around? I learned to play peever on this pavement. In that shop, I spent half my weekly pocket money on a ha'penny box of sherbet with a dainty wooden spoon. One-legged Alf has been standing on that corner for as long as I remember, yet there is always some chump convinced he knows which cup hides the sixpence.

I am gabbling, but no matter. You are charmed by my chatter, as by my silence. By my intelligence, and my nonsense, my mystery and my artlessness. I almost wish Phyl were with us so I could tell her, *This is what I mean by magic.* In the dusk, Trinity College tower seems carved from pink sugar. The air is drugged with the scent of late roses. The grand houses of Park Circus could be the painted backdrop to a stage.

The view from the top of the park makes your breath catch, just as I hoped. The Palace of Arts seems borrowed from a Russian picture book. Below us, tall chimneys, buttery points of light in the slate-blue fug, the winding river a rumour in the dark. We set off down a shadowy path that is wide enough for two, and still our shoulders and hips manage to bump. You offer me your arm. The season is more advanced here than in England, but we both find the chill stimulating. You have heard autumn is the time to be in Italy, when the sun has lost its fierceness but the days are still warm. I tell you I visited relatives in Rome and Florence when my father was alive, and learned Italian at the Conservatory... You hold up a hand, peering into the shadows. I hear the distant rattle of trams, or perhaps the river, before the creature lifts its head and the rising moon is reflected in its eyes.

'Dog?' I breathe in your ear.

'Fox.'

And now it is gone, but the spell it cast over us lingers. We tread more stealthily, more alive to what might be just out of sight. Dare I say it aloud?

'This park is famous for lovers after dark.'

'Is that why you brought me here?'

'Of course,' I say. 'You can't visit Glasgow without seeing the famous lovers of the West End Park.'

Next morning I wake to find the golden sky awhirl with leaves. All I can recall of my dreams is a tender, delicious feeling, like eating coconut ice in a warm bath. I accompany Mother to church, but my thoughts are not all of Heavenly things. Then hours in front of the glass deciding how to dress my hair, swithering between the grey and the emerald silk.

Three o'clock comes and goes. And four. And five. Did I imagine last night? Are you some tawdry cad stepped from the pages of a penny dreadful? At six, the doorbell rings. A boy in livery hands over an envelope.

Philp's Cockburn Hotel,
141 Bath St,
Glasgow

Dear Miss Macfarlane,
    Ever since I left you I have been angry with myself for not having come to see your mother. I have no excuse except my headaches, which is a poor one.

Yours always,
Herbert Jackson

I plead a monthly pain to get out of evening church. Although I often walk past the Cockburn Hotel, I have never ventured inside. In other circumstances, I might be impressed by the extravagant design of the Minton tiled floor. I march up to the reception desk and demand you be fetched from your room. The clerk informs me Mr Jackson is in the Turkish baths, receiving a massage shampooing from the medical rubber. If I am happy to wait, he will send the boy with a note.

Fifteen minutes later you stand before me, your hair damp, your cheeks so pale that any doubt is dispelled. I resent this sickliness in my virile lover, but enjoy taking charge of a lieutenant who once commanded a section of soldiers. These headaches are the very devil, you mutter. You never had a day's indisposition until a couple of years ago.

I tell the waiter to bring beef tea and arrowroot biscuits.

'I wondered if you were regretting last night.'

I wait for you to deny it, to look shocked, or shifty, or *something*. Will you force me to say it?

'The offer of marriage, I mean, not the kiss.'

Your proposal took me aback. The next moment I wondered if I had not willed you into making it. It was such a perfect solution.

You frown. 'You got my letter?'

That note addressed and signed so formally, as if we had barely shaken hands, never mind crushed lip to lip. 'It was rather stiff.'

The waiter is back to ask if we have any objection to Oxo, as the kitchen has no Bovril. I tell him Oxo will do very well.

You wait for him to walk away. 'I've thought of nothing but our wedding night since the day we met.'

And now I begin to enjoy myself. The scent of lump sugar dissolved in tea. The *trring!* of the brass bell on the reception desk. The numbered keys in their cherrywood slots. How fortunate men are, to roam wherever they please.

'And you will roam with me,' you say.

'Which is not the same thing.'

'You can't think I would ever desert you?'

'A moment ago I didn't, but now you've planted the possibility in my head.'

I am a clumsy flirt. You lean torwards me, a catch of anxiety in your voice. 'Catherine, promise you'll never doubt me.'

How thrillingly earnest you look.

'There are people who may try to turn you against me. Promise me you won't listen to them.'

'What people?'

'Liars. Scoundrels. My own family.'

I recall your remark about false friends. 'But why?'

Your eyes fasten on mine.

Two feelings in perfect balance: excitement, and apprehension. Who are you, this stranger I have decided to marry?

'I want to be completely honest with you, Catherine. I've not been able to work for two years. God knows what your mother will think. I am accused of the vilest deeds by men who don't even have the decency to repeat their slanders to my face. I have no right to ask any woman to share these difficulties, least of all a woman like you, but I think, with your help, I can see my way out of them.'

Your brown hand rests on the table between us. I lay my own white hand on top. 'Tell me everything.'

'As soon as we're man and wife.'

When the bell rings, Mother calls out, 'Cath, he's here!' so piercingly you must hear her in the street. The mantelpiece clock chimes the hour, although it is seven minutes past. I fly to the door ahead of Lizzie our maid, prompting a snappish, 'Am I opening it or are you?'

Still, at least Gordon and Grant are not here to embarrass me with the chamber pot story.

Ours is not a fashionable home. I have decided to laugh off Father's Chinese sword and helmet; the crimson drawing-room carpet that clashes so horribly with the salmon, watered-silk walls; the half-finished canvas of an Italian shepherd on an easel in the corner, with a drapery over one side of the frame as if Uncle Frank had just this minute put down his brush and popped out to lunch. No man in love could hold these against me. But what will you make of Mother?

She is not exactly fat, but shapeless as a bolster, and in no way flattered by her black dress, cut down from a crinoline that is one of my earliest memories. Its swishing hem gathering little clouds of fluff from the parquet. Her flat cheeks are babyishly unlined, her hair thin, her teeth a glimpse of calamity in the sweetest of smiles. Her fingers must always be busy, rubbing at a spot on her dress or testing her chin for the rogue hairs her eyes are too weak to see in the glass, eyes that remind me of nothing so much as the pacified gaze of a brown cow. It is easy to miss the fleeting pucker of her lips. Even I cannot always tell when she is in on the joke.

Once you are sitting in Father's old chair, I am just as anxious that she should form a good opinion of you. She is sorry to learn your late father's paper carried no devotional articles, but glad to hear you are staying in a temperance hotel. There is an awkward silence when she realises you have no position, and another when you say you are a member of the Church of England. She supposes my example will lead you to the evangelical path. My father had his share of misfortune in business, and always kept a roof over our heads. God willing, you will do no less, but she cannot risk me being left destitute if you should die first. A life insurance policy will set her mind at rest.

I have never seen Mother so business-like.

'Don't gape, Cath dear.'

You give her a charming smile, which she fails to return. 'So you have no objection to the match?'

'It is rather sudden.'

'The first moment I saw Catherine, I knew.'

Still she does not thaw: my mother, who dimples at tradesmen to put them at ease. At last she says, 'It's up to Cath. She goes her own way, always has.'

You kneel at my feet on the faded Turkish rug. 'Miss Macfarlane, will you do me the honour of becoming my wife?'

I have felt like this on clifftop walks when the path wound too close to the edge. This same mad urge to do the fatal thing, this same bubbling hilarity. How can it be funny? You would be humiliated, rightly furious. I would never see you again. Mother would ask me over and over, what was I thinking? Walter would break with me. No invitations to Oxford, no amusing letters recommending this or that book.

No father for my child.

I come to my senses. 'I'd be delighted, Mr Jackson.'

Lizzie finds some elderflower cordial to toast our engagement. There is no end of matters to discuss. What I will need by way of a trousseau; whether the widow in Gibson Street who refashioned Mother's crinoline is equal to a wedding dress; how sad it is Father did not live to see this day. Apart from anything else, he would have known what to do about the kirk. Mother has doubts about our minister's position on the second coming, but it might seem peculiar to find a new congregation and raise the subject of a wedding within the first few months.

You and I exchange glances.

'We thought we'd marry at Herbert's church in London.'

Disappointment vies with relief in her face. She runs a frugal household. But it is such a long way for our Scotch relatives to travel. As far as it would be for Herbert's English ones, I point out. I like the idea of a London wedding. If it were possible, I would preserve my spinster self intact in Scotland, while becoming this wholly new English person, Mrs Herbert Jackson. I keep this curious thought to myself. Mother observes that London can be lovely in the summer.

'I'm afraid we can't wait till next summer,' you tell her. 'We're rather hoping to get the business over and done with in a fortnight.'

'Heady stuff, that elderflower cordial,' you say as we leave the house.

You're right: I feel quite drunk. 'It's been in the pantry for years.'

'She must know.'

'How? She won't even take a medicinal brandy.'

All at once it is irresistibly funny. We shush each other, trying not to make a show of ourselves in the street, but the thought of public opprobrium only adds to our mirth.

Arm in arm, we climb the hill between the tenements, some golden sandstone, some red. The close mouths with their painted glass fanlights and green china tiles; the bay windows stacked one on top of another, each with its yashmak of patterned net.

'I saw Gemmell, Raleigh's doctor, this morning.'

'About your headaches?'

'He sees no reason why I shouldn't marry.'

This brings me up short. 'You were afraid there might be?'

'I wanted to be absolutely sure, for your sake.'

It is the sort of balmy afternoon when pupils gaze out of classroom windows, impatient for the bell. I feel as if I am strolling through my childhood for the very last time. The churches we joined, and left. My old school. The square where Fanny, Gordon, Grant and I played hide-and-seek. The street corner where I sang, dressed as a boy, Fanny accompanying me on the violin. Mother was mortified, although happy to spend the coins tossed into my hat. On wet afternoons Fanny and I would play at married ladies, paying calls, remarking on the weather. When it came to having babies, we threw our dolls at the ceiling so they dropped down as gifts from God.

'What are you smiling at?'

You laugh when I tell you.

I look you in the eye. 'Shall we have children?'

The dog leaps in your glance. 'If God is generous.'

I show you around the Botanic Gardens. You pick up a horse chestnut, splitting the green case with your thumbs to extract the glowing conker. A man walks a few yards ahead, his Border terrier sniffing at every tree. When he turns to call the dog to heel, I catch sight of his face.

'Don!'

He looks as pleased to see me as I am to see him.

'Don, this is Professor Raleigh's brother-in-law, Herbert Jackson.'

You have let go of my arm. I link us again. 'Herbert, this is Donald Carswell. We saw many a late night putting together the *Glasgow University Magazine*.'

Nods are exchanged, but no handshake.

You toss the conker up and catch it. The terrier sniffs at your shoe.

'Herbert and I are to be married.'

I thought he had guessed, but the look on his face suggests otherwise.

'Next month,' you say.

'Congratulations…'

I feel as if I should apologise to him. You smile under your moustache.

'…she'll make a bonny bride.'

'Won't she, though?' you say.

I have never thought of Don as a *man*. You bring out a side to him I have not seen before. A stranger might use the same words to describe you both – tallish, saturnine, well-spoken – yet I can hardly conceive of two more different types: you muscular, pachydermous, swarthy; Don hollow-chested, with a Scotch pallor between his blue chin and black brows. Why is it so impossible to say, *Herbert, this is Don, who got the fellows in tweeds to shuffle along so there was room for me at the table*? When they made a fuss about not lighting their pipes in front of a lady, it was Don who told them not to talk such rot, Don who taught me to mark up the galleys, who told me I wrote as well as any chap, then tactfully underlined the hanging preposition in my first paragraph. Such a good friend, and yet I cannot say to him, *This is the man I am going to spend my life with. Like him, for my sake.*

Perhaps he hears without it needing to be said. 'I wonder we've not met before. Glasgow's such a village.'

'I've been living in London, though a regular visitor up here.' You look about yourself appreciatively. 'A handsome city.'

'There are worse places for newly-weds to set up home.'

You turn to me. 'What do you think, sweetheart, shall we live here?'

Don shoots me a questioning look. I suppose it is odd, with the wedding so soon and no plan for what happens after.

'I'd prefer London,' I confess.

'Or Italy. When you think about it, there's nothing to keep us here.'

'A new start,' Don says in such a despondent voice that I

almost reach across and touch his sleeve. As you are with us, I can only ask him to pass on my good wishes to his mother (who detests me).

'How long has he been in love with you?' you ask, once we are out of earshot.

'I never knew till now.' There is a shameful pleasure in this admission, the betrayal of one man binding me more tightly to the other. I suppose marriage will be full of these forks in the road.

No. 2 the Studio
Redcliffe Square
Kensington
22nd September

Dear Heart,

Do you know that your coming down to the station to see me off stirred me more than a band of military music? I have been looking into my affairs and hope to be settled soon. I was just writing a telegram to you when your letter came this morning and set my blood tingling. If you write to me often I shall leave what I have to do here half-finished and come and carry you off. To think of you keeping awake till two o'clock in the morning. You must not do it! I must find you well and bonny when you come. I have had a letter from Lucie in Glasgow. Perhaps you will see her. Don't be influenced by her. Be brave, sweetheart, and trust me. If you love me as I love you, I shall have no fears at all. I shall write no more now and as soon as I know you are wearing my ring – I'm already wearing yours – I shall make no further secret of our engagement. Now, sweetheart, arrivederci until I can see you and kiss you.

Yours always,
Herbert

I enjoyed my brief engagement, visiting the dressmaker, shopping for gloves and stockings. I cleared out my wardrobe, discarding anything too girlish. I meant to be the worldly sort of wife. Everything about me, the way I dressed my hair, the cut of my coat, the tilt of my hat, would be poised, amused, knowing. One day my path would cross with Mary Dowdall's and she would hardly recognise me. Mother was still sulking over your haste, but at least she did not guess why I was eager to comply. My friends were more enthusiastic. When I showed them your photograph, they smiled and admitted they, too, might have galloped up the aisle. Only Phyl refused to share in my happiness.

'Since nothing I say will make any difference, better to say nothing.'

'So you disapprove.'

'Cath, it's as if you've locked your brain in a cupboard. When you talk about him, it's like listening to a story from the *Lady's Pictorial*. So darkly handsome. The unruly way his hair grows. Next you'll be telling me he has a *panther's grace*. I can't picture an ordinary man in a drawing room: I see him racing towards you on horseback, the light of battle in his *smouldering eyes*. Do you know, you haven't reported a single interesting remark of his? Have you ever had an actual conversation, an exchange of views?'

'He's in love with me.'

'Then be his lover. Why do you have to marry him?'

'You don't understand.' And I didn't explain.

'I've known you for twenty years. How long have you known him: three weeks?'

I was about to tell her to mind her own business, but the worry in her sea-coloured eyes gave me pause. 'Is that it, then, you're washing your hands of me?'

'Don't be an idiot. When it's all gone wrong and you're back in Glasgow, I'll be the only one you can face.'

On the Wednesday before the wedding I took the train to London to stay with Fanny. She could not understand why I had to drag her to an art gallery when we had so much of my trousseau still to buy.

'Cathie, that painting: it could be you!' She read the title. 'Oh. *Portrait of a Young Man*.'

'Herbert said there was a resemblance.'

His long hair was dark but, yes, his flattish, rather feminine face reflected the light like mine, and his features, although not identical, combined to similar effect. I had looked up Bernardino Licinio in the library. A pupil of Bellini's. I had hoped for dancing eyes, a mischievous smile, at the very least a certain soulfulness, but the young man's expression was earthily resigned. His not-quite-clean left hand rested on a skull.

'How depressing,' I said.

'Well, it is a memento mori.' Fanny had an infuriating habit of stating the obvious. Or perhaps she was being tactful, by not remarking on the fact that I reminded you of a man.

Mother, Grant and Gordon travelled down on Friday. That evening we took a stroll along the Thames. Gordon reported that catching the express had been predictably nerve-wracking. Hustling Mother out of the house while she protested that she had forgotten to pack the sal volatile, her embroidered hankie, her hairbrush; the headlong dash down the platform to climb aboard before the station master blew his whistle. This set us reminiscing about childhood holidays. The trains we missed, the luggage we left behind. Even Mother joined in the laughter.

A flock of geese haunted the muddy riverbank. Charmed by their pink feet, Grant tried to stroke one and got pecked for his trouble.

'Let's come back here tomorrow night,' I said.

Gordon laughed.

'What's so funny?'

Fanny slipped her arm through mine. 'This time tomorrow you'll be on your honeymoon.'

The day dawns as crisp and blue as a bride could hope, but proceeds in a muddle. Mother is still in her nightclothes when the carriage turns up to take us to the church. I have to dress her, trying to keep my sleeves out of the way as I pin her hair. I am so anxious about being late I forget to look in the glass.

You have arranged to meet us outside the church so Mother can witness your will and insurance policy, but when we arrive at St Luke's there is no sign of you. A portly stranger introduces himself as Cousin William and takes us across the road to your studio. We climb three flights of stairs to find you gone. 'He had been waiting some considerable time,' William says tartly. On our way down again, we pass a man in a paint-spattered smock. He stares at my wedding lace. I ask if he has seen you. 'No, I'm glad to say.' Down in the lobby, a woman is sorting through the post. When I catch her eye over the banister she bolts like a rabbit down its hole. The instant we set foot in the church, the organist strikes up the opening bars of Wagner's 'Bridal Chorus'. There is no time to check my appearance before Gordon steps forward to escort me up the aisle.

'Smile,' he says in my ear, 'you look like a hedgehog with toothache.'

You should have warned me you had so many relatives. The Macfarlane and Lewis side of the church is pitifully sparse. Turning my gaze to the numerous Jacksons and Tippets, I spot Walter straight away, six inches taller than everyone else. Lucie sits between the boys in a lilac dress twice as lovely as my wedding gown. The bony matron beside Hilary must be your mother. I tell myself her expression is solemnly joyful. Gordon's arm drags at mine, reminding me to slow down. Small, stately steps, taking care not to trip on my hem. The arcades are picked out in red, white and black like a bookmaker's waistcoat. There are statues of saints above the pillars. A muscular marble Sebastian pierced with metal arrows. Mother won't like that. Bad enough that there is an altar; did they really have to cover it with a golden cloth? I have an ink stain on my sleeve after signing the insurance papers. Did I smear it on my cheek while tidying my hair? Mother is so short-sighted she would never notice, and Gordon is quite capable of finding it funny.

How handsome you are in morning dress, even if your smile is rather tense.

Just after the vicar asks if any man can show just cause why we may not lawfully be joined together, the door opens at the back of the church. Two soldiers in scarlet tunics walk in. I take them for late guests, until I see your face. They advance into the nave. The congregation turns to look. My heart starts to pound. I have the mad thought that they have come to arrest you and I will never see you again. The taller one wears an insolently mocking expression. The other – stout and red-faced with sparse blonde hair – doffs his cap to me. His wet lips shine, catching the light from the high windows. The vicar continues with the ceremony.

'*Do you, Herbert Parry Malpas Jackson...*'

Your breath is faintly eggy as you make your vow. No sooner have the words left your lips than the stout soldier says in broad Scotch, 'Sorry – wrong church.' His slack grin and the clumsy way they turn and retrace their steps betray them. They are drunk.

The door closes with a bang. For a moment I cannot think why the vicar is giving me that fishy look. I stammer out my promise to love and obey, forgetting the cherishing. Afterwards in the vestry, while the others are signing the register, you whisper that you knew they would turn up. You are surprised they did not try to stop the ceremony. I ask who they were. You mouth, '*Later.*'

The wedding breakfast is held in your family home, where every surface is smothered in white roses and maidenhair ferns. I always thought I'd have sweet peas at my wedding. The guests mill about, ignoring the place settings, talking at the top of their voices. Fanny asks if I am all right. *Of course*, I say. She gives me a doubtful look. While you are being congratulated by several artistic young ladies who would plainly like to be standing in my shoes, I am introduced to Aunt Sarah, and her friend Miss Turnbull, and Uncles James, Edward and Alfred, and cousin Edith, and cousin William's wife Mary, and second cousins Percy, Sydney and Cecil, and the Richardson wing of your family, which is so numerous I don't even try to remember their names. On the other side of the room, Gordon and Grant have detached themselves from Mother and cousin Gussie and accepted glasses of champagne. I am about to go and join them when my new mother-in-law turns her toothy smile on me, praising the elegant simplicity of my dress (chosen so it could be dyed and worn to parties in the years ahead). 'Such a pity you couldn't come to dinner on Thursday. I'm glad to see your sister has recovered.' I try to look as if I know what she is talking about. Lucie comes over to kiss my cheek and call me 'sister'. Your brother Arthur has sent congratulations by telegraph. He is sorry he cannot be here, but it takes so long to travel from India. Cousin William pats my hand and assures me, mystifyingly, that 'all will be well'. Second cousin Maud says we must come down to Southwold. You arrive at my side. For one blissful minute we are alone in the crowd. 'You're doing very well,' you say. I bring my brow to your lips, murmuring, 'When will it be over?' You give me a warning squeeze. Again I ask about the redcoats. 'They'll have been at Crathie's wedding.' A brother lieutenant who tied the knot yesterday, just down the road. You were not invited. Before I can ask why, a newspaper colleague of your late father's arrives to shake your hand, and now your old fencing master, and a boisterous pair of fellows you boxed with at Westminster School, and still I have the sense that you, too, are almost peripheral to the occasion. Gordon walks past with another two glasses of champagne. 'Are you all right?' The tinkling of spoon on glass prays silence for the speeches. Your best man, a Scotch doctor, describes apple scrumping, flour bombing and other boyish mischief. Walter's witty address includes an anecdote about the many hospitable professors whose floors have been ruined by turpentine. To my relief (and pique), he barely mentions me, but later, when I duck into an empty bedroom to look in the mirror, his face appears behind mine.

'Do you have a kiss for your brother-in-law?'

'Our kissing days are over,' I say into the glass.

'Don't be hard, Cathie, it doesn't suit your Tess Durbeyfield bloom.'

'Is that how you see me: one of Hardy's tragic heroines?'

He looks sombre. 'I hope not.'

I was always susceptible to the complex timbre of his voice. Hearing it now, I seem to see him with my old eyes. The soulful droop of his moustache, the glinting gaze whose humour is a sort of rapacity.

'I have a present for you,' he says.

And now I notice the package in his hand, small enough to be hidden from Lucie. I turn and reach for it. He snatches it back, forcing me to advance. I take hold of it, but he does not let go. Our mouths are inches apart. It would be the easiest thing in the world to kiss him.

I tear open the brown paper.

'Carefully,' he admonishes.

'*Oh, Walter.*'

It is a Venetian glass perfume bottle with a patterned brass collar and lid: a translucent swirl of green and amethyst, flecked with gilt. So exquisite, my mouth waters. So delicate that when I close my fingers around it, it disappears.

'Just between us,' he says.

The kiss is meant to be a peck on the lips but somehow it lingers, entering my bloodstream like strong drink, passing through my breasts to the fork between my legs. Our glances meet and he pulls away, frightened by what he reads in my eyes, or by what I might read in his.

'Ah, Cathie,' he says hoarsely.

For one terrible moment I think he knows. Will he reproach me for not telling him? Be grateful to me? But now I see it has not crossed his mind.

Out on the landing, Lucie's voice calls, 'Walter?'

He murmurs in my ear, 'Be careful.'

Within the hour, you and I are boarding the boat train at Charing Cross.

PART II

Since I remember I have more than anything else wanted to be deeply loved.

Lying Awake, CATHERINE CARSWELL

PART III

1939

I write, therefore I am. Nothing can stop me. Not the lawyers' letters about my memoir of D. H. Lawrence, not the bullet in the post after my life of Rabbie Burns. Critic, biographer, novelist, journalist. In an idle moment the other day I totted it all up: two million five hundred thousand words, give or take the odd radio talk. Not bad for a late starter. I wonder if you knew. I picture you in that place leafing through a much-fingered copy of the *Observer* and seeing my name. Perhaps you decided it was some other woman, but for a moment the possibility must have occurred to you. Were you impressed, even proud of me?

No, I suppose not.

Once I got going, it became second nature. There is copy in everything. I wake in the morning. We have run out of tea and there is none to be had at the grocer's. I grind my teeth with irritation, then think of the lives lost as the torpedoed cargo ship went down. On my way back, I call on Fanny. She is turning the flat upside down, which she calls a *good clear-out*. All those years collecting pretty things for her home, and now all she wants is to be rid of them.

There is nothing that happened to me before I turned twenty-five and after the age of thirty that I have not set down on paper, but I never published a word about our marriage. It was a point of honour. Seven days ago I began writing this. Perhaps it is my way of having a clear-out.

If these pages found their way to you – but why limit the absurdity, why not say, if we met – would you call me a liar?

Or would you understand at last?

In my twenties, I believed in forever. *As long as you both shall live* meant something quite different to me then. An hour – a minute, in your company – seemed an eternity. How fleeting time feels, now I am better acquainted with death. Father has been gone forty years, Mother twenty-nine, Walter seventeen. Lawrence, the most fiercely alive of all, died the month I turned fifty-one, a year after Lucie's letter informing me that you were gone. And still I ask myself, did it have to be like that? Could we not have managed it differently?

1904

When will I be alone with you?

The boat train is busy. Anything more than polite conversation is impossible. Strange, to sit so close to you and still to be locked inside my own head, to sense the straying of your thoughts who knows where. I seem to hear Phyl's mocking voice: *I suppose you thought marrying would turn the two of you into one.* Outside the window, children strip the hop gardens of Kent into enormous wicker baskets. I point out an oast house with a roof like a witch's hat after the witch has walked into a lintel. Starlings perch on telegraph wires. A black stallion rolls in a meadow. A storm is coming, battleship clouds driving in from the north, but we are snug inside our carriage speeding into the future.

We are booked on the packet steamer. The purser finds us chairs on the port side, and hands us a travelling rug smelling faintly of fish. I hang over the rail and watch the sea. The wind waters my eyes, tugging my hair from its pins, whipping it across my face. The ship's engine vibrates in my bones. Your warm hand closes over mine. The sinking sun paints our faces rosy gold, lays a glittering path across the waves.

'What are you smiling at?'

It is one of our games. My secretive smile, your question.

'Oh, I don't know. I'm bound for Italy with my husband. We were married this morning. What are *you* smiling at?'

'The most beautiful creature on this boat.'

We return to our deck chairs and hold hands under the blanket, watched by an older, elegantly dressed woman whom I think much more beautiful. She was on the train too, in our carriage, travelling alone. She must envy us our youth, our being in love. Discreetly I point her out. You beckon the purser and ask to be moved to the starboard side. Going below deck to wash, I spot Mr Joseph Chamberlain, until recently a member of the government. There is a queue for the lavatory. It is almost dark when I get back with my news.

'So they're following me.'

Is this a joke? I remind you of your promise to tell me about your troubles. You glance at the young man loitering by the ship's rail. Your mouth covers my ear, your hot breath: 'When we're alone.'

I turn and press my lips to yours. A taste of tobacco in your warm wet mouth, the smell of your skin under your clothes, the way our bodies fit together, the narcotic slowing of blood flow and breath until the tide turns and we are swept away.

This is real. Nothing else.

Modesty forces us apart. Your panting voice rasps in my ear, 'You'll drive me mad like this.'

'And you me.'

Night falls. We take a turn around the deck, pausing at the stern. Standing here, we might be the only two people on board. A phosphorescence in the churning wake. Further out, sea and sky interchangeably black.

'Will you tell me now?'

Your letters have been intercepted. By your mother, for one, out of a misguided protective urge. Your old Liverpool colleagues are less well-disposed to you, in league with other members of the University Club. At least you know who they are, unlike the second, shadowy faction plotting against you.

'When I came back from Africa my old friends were queer. Offhand with me one minute; the next, making insinuating remarks. At first I put it down to my roughened nerves. I'd seen it happen before: men who fought alongside me – good men. One day you'd trust them with your life. The next, they'd be jumping at shadows.'

'You actually fought?'

'That's the general idea, with war.'

I blink. You have not been sarcastic with me before.

'By then the enemy had gone on commando. They attacked in small bands, every last man a crack shot. It was impossible to keep track of them...'

You give me a sudden, searching look. Have you guessed how little heed I paid at the time, how I never read a newspaper in all the months you were risking your life?

'No man truly knows himself until he's been in a war. Beforehand, I dreaded having to fight. In fact, an exchange of fire clears the head marvellously. One does the needful, almost without thinking. It was the weeks that passed with no sniff of the enemy that wore the men down. Forever alert for the jangle of a rein, a puff of dust, the sixth sense that something was wrong. Day after day, nothing happens, and yet you could be shot – *bang!* – at any moment.'

That *bang!* makes me start.

'And that wasn't the worst of it. Anyway, it wasn't my nerves, in Liverpool. They were spying on me, talking about me behind my back. Oh, they were slippery about it, but every so often they betrayed themselves, knowing something they couldn't have come by honestly. I was the only one in our little circle who'd acted on the fighting talk they'd come out with night after night. For a while, I thought that might explain it, but they're beyond shame. I see now I was naïve to hope I could leave my troubles behind by leaving Liverpool. England is a small place. Wherever you go, there are fellows who know someone, or whose cousin is married to someone. Impossible to tell who's spreading this tittle-tattle out of malice, and who's simply gullible enough to believe what he's been told.'

'What tittle-tattle?'

You vent your frustration in a noisy sigh. 'I wish I knew. It's all so damnably vague, the sort of viciousness men whisper in corners, then deny to one's face.'

'But there must be *someone* who could tell you.' I realise how provoking that sounds. 'I'm sorry: if there were an obvious answer, you would have thought of it by now. It's just that I hate injustice. I find it physically unbearable – any sort of injustice, never mind when the victim is my husband.' I shiver. 'So you'll never find out?'

'Oh, I wouldn't say that. They'll be on their guard against me, but they don't know you.'

We plough through the waves towards France, breathing in the tang of salt and tar and engine oil, the growl and throb of the ship under our feet like some great beast. I am grieved by your troubles, but glad of them too. Life: thrilling, extraordinary, unforeseen – what else have I longed for? Let your enemies come, the more dangerous the better. We will face them together.

The boat docks at eight. A deckhand uncoils a rope thick as my arm and flings it across to a man in oilskins with a Port Authority cap. A second rope flies out from the stern. A porter takes our luggage away to be chalked by the customs men.

We have supper in an *estaminet*. You would have gone to a hotel, but wanted to avoid the woman from the train. And anyway, it is more fun to sit among men in overalls grimy from a hard day's work. You have a tin ear for languages, so I translate.

'His sister's husband vomited over the padré in chapel... the sister has locked him out... she says he's a drunkard, but he'd eaten a bad mussel.'

'You're making this up.'

I flex my eyebrows. 'Maybe,' I say, 'and maybe not.'

'I hope you're not going to disappoint me, Catherine...'

Phyl may mock, but you *are* like a panther.

'...or I shall have to punish you.'

Within the hour we are on the train heading south. The journey takes all night and most of the next day. For long stretches we have the carriage almost – but never quite – to ourselves.

You tell me about your father who died last Christmas. Eighty-four, and still a force of nature. An artist, but first and foremost a newspaperman. A legend in the trade, a tyrant in his own home. If a volcano erupted in Krakatoa, or a mudslide drowned a township in America, there was a *News* man on the spot within days. Not that things always went according to plan. Every few weeks he would burst through the front door shouting '*Lucie! Arthur! Bertie!*' It was your job to search the encyclopedia. The other two went through the library shelves. Your father stood over the table, roughing out a street scene, while you called out 'turbans' or 'rickshaws' or 'camels', and he added them to the falling masonry and figures fleeing in panic. Once, the three of you went to the office to see him draw on the engraving block. He took you down to the print room where the giant rolls of paper sped through the machinery until you grew dizzy with watching and half-deafened by the racket. He gave you the very first copy, inky and warm off the press.

You liked him best in a crisis. It was the weeks when deadline day passed without a hitch that made you anxious. Then the merciless eye so dreaded by his staff would turn inward. Sixty years of age, and what did he have to show for it? A peddler of lurid sensationalism to the masses. Oh yes, he illustrated Dickens, Shakespeare: cheap volumes that sat unread in front parlours in Pontefract and Huddersfield. This was when your mother would send you children upstairs to wait until the slamming front door announced his departure. Off to the Cheshire Cheese public house, where he would quarrel with the first friend unwise enough to flatter him.

I think about Lucie peering through the banisters, satisfying herself the coast was clear. I am your protectress now.

'You must have feared him less as you grew older?'

It is not quite a laugh, more a rueful breath. 'You'd think so, wouldn't you? Maybe if I'd stayed at home. I left school with Arthur. He'd won prizes enough for both of us. I went to Paris. It was agreed I'd be better out of my father's sight. He was proud of Arthur for his Oxford scholarship, and proud of Lucie for finding such a clever husband. Me, he despised.'

'Because you reminded him of himself.'

You look up. 'Why do you say that?'

'You inherited his talent, maybe a talent that surpassed his. At any rate, you had the courage to aspire to art.'

'I taught drawing to young ladies passing the time between school and marriage.'

'To get the wherewithal to paint.'

The air between us thickens. The lamps on the ceiling make the rushing darkness beyond the windows a black mirror. Were it not for the elderly Frenchwomen sitting behind us, you would take me in your arms. I hardly know which is more delicious: the embrace we long for, or its deferral.

The conductor enters our carriage.

'You were saying about your father,' I prompt in a demure voice, but my eyes are bold.

A grin flashes behind your moustache.

'He went on working into his seventies. My mother wanted us to be reconciled. She persuaded him to sit for me. A portrait in oils. For years I'd lived off an allowance she made me. I couldn't refuse her, any more than he could. Neither of us wanted to sit in that room day after day. I'd hardly seen him for years. He had the same silver hair and white beard, the same big head, but his mouth had sunk into itself. His skin – you know how silk crêpe will rot? The blazing eyes I'd dreaded as a child were like holes in a mask. Empty.'

We are silent while the conductor checks our tickets.

'Did you paint the war?' I ask, to change the subject.

'My sketches were not suitable for publication.'

I hear the irony, but cannot tell whether it is directed against others or yourself.

'It must be hard to draw such unspeakable things, much less do them justice.'

A banal remark, yet you seem to hear some acuity in it. 'People would believe anything – *anything*, no matter how grotesque – rather than the truth.'

'"There is nothing covered that shall not be revealed",' I say, quoting St Luke.

Your eyes drill into mine. 'Bless you for that, my Madonnina.'

We wake stiff from sleeping upright. Surreptitiously I pinch my cheeks to put the colour back into my face. In the dining carriage, the waiter brings us warm crusty bread and coffee so darkly potent that the morning swims around me. After many hours of watching the passing countryside in the company of a coughing Frenchman, we arrive in Como.

Our room is under the creosoted rafters supporting the *pensione*'s pitched roof. Two single beds have been pushed together and made up with one wide cover. The landlady says we must be tired after our long journey. When she has gone, you open the window, scanning the narrow street from end to end.

'Do you know what I'd like more than anything?' you say.

'What?'

'A hotel dinner.'

The marble lobby of the Grand Hotel Plinius is filled with expensively dressed couples on their way to the dining room. Large gilded mirrors hang on the walls. Turning full circle, I see four Catherine Jacksons, all with violet semicircles under their eyes and slivers of darker cloth where Mother's seamstress let out the darts to bring their dresses into fashion.

'Should we find somewhere a little less grand?'

You lift my chin. 'You're more beautiful than all the duchesses and contessas in here, and I am the man with you on my arm.'

Under the weight of a starched napkin, I feel less shabby. We order oysters and *fegato alla Veneziana* and I take a little watered wine and feel drunk with transformation. I am a married woman with my husband's hungry eyes upon me. Under the table, your thumb circles my palm, probes the valleys between my fingers. I tell you about the holidays of my childhood. The house that smelled of chimney soot, stewed tea, pork dripping and mice. The bathwater drawn from a pond that arrived with small frogs, tadpoles, newts and leeches. When you pull a disgusted face, I say we children couldn't have been more delighted. I loved those summers. Fanny and I ran wild in trousers and jerseys. Week after blissful week of climbing, boating, swimming without costumes. Then the dreaded return to Glasgow, and woollen combinations, long chemise, wadded stay belt, white long-cloth knickers, flannel petticoat, thick black stockings. Mother would be scandalised to hear me itemising my underwear, even with my husband, but I mean the very opposite of flirtation. *This is me, stripped of mysterious feminine paraphernalia. A person, like yourself.*

You recall Lucie bawling in protest at a particularly hated undergarment. It is almost your first memory.

How much we have in common. Favourite poets, composers, even fictional characters. The games we played as children. The detested nightly spoonful of cod liver oil. I could weep for that little boy plucked from the nursery, dressed in scratchy collar and tailcoat and delivered to the well-bred barbarians of Westminster School. You laugh: better the odd honest thump than the sophisticated cruelty of little girls. Out of nowhere, I remember Marion Torres and the nights I cried myself to sleep. I thought my chest would break open with unhappiness, and yet now, seeing your eyes soften, I am almost glad it happened.

With Walter my brilliance was always conditional. He retained the teacher's prerogative of disappointment, and I was careful to show him only my best side. I want you to know everything about me.

The opulent dining room shimmers, the chandeliers' dazzle given back by fork and spoon and earring and necklace, and by my own bright eyes. My cheeks are warm with wine and admiration. Not only from you. At first I think you will be pleased to know yourself envied by richer men. Did you not say as much in that gallant speech in the lobby? But you pay less and less attention to my conversation.

'What's the matter?' I murmur.

'That greasy Italian over there. He's hardly eaten a bite. He can't drag his eyes away from you.'

'Which one?'

'By the fireplace. *Don't look*. I've half a mind to go over there and demand we settle this like gentlemen, at first light.'

A duel! I find the idea rather thrilling. You rise from your chair.

'Herbert, *no*, please.'

You sit down again. The waiter approaches, thinking something is wrong, veering away when I give a fractional shake of the head.

'It's a question of respect. A man who looks at another man's wife like that might as well walk over here and help himself to the food off my plate.'

'So I'm a glorified calf's liver?'

After a suspenseful moment, you laugh.

On the way back to the *pensione* we stray into the ornamental gardens beside the lake. The night is touched with frost. Our breath wisps like smoke. You ask me to waltz. 'Without music?' I say. You take me in your arms, murmuring, '*One* two three, *one* two three.' I hum 'The Blue Danube'. Held like this, I sense things about you I can hardly translate into words. A lightness on your feet, in your touch, and at the same time a sureness that says, *Give yourself up to me, let go.* How magical it is, gliding over the grass, the glimmer of stars above us.

I whisper, 'I'm so glad I married you!'

Not half an hour later, you rap on the door of my dressing room.

'Yes?'

'Is anyone with you?' Your voice is sharp.

'No.' I laugh, saying this.

'Then why is the door locked?'

'I don't know.' I open it. You look angry. 'Old habit, I suppose.'

You push past me, into the tiny room. 'I heard you speak.'

'Did I?' I have a habit of talking to myself. I don't always know I'm doing it.

You look out of the window, almost as if you expect to see someone hiding on the ledge. Finding nothing out of the ordinary, you return to the bedroom. I carry on unpinning my hair. When I emerge, you are slipping something under your pillow.

'How furtive you look,' I say teasingly. 'What have you got there?'

You put out the lamp.

Next morning when I wake, the sun through the louvred shutters makes twin ladders of light across the ceiling. An unfamiliar odour under the covers, not unpleasant: the smell of our two sleeping bodies combined. I slide out of bed and pull back the shutters. Four floors below us, the narrow street is split by shadow. On the brilliant side, old women water the pavement to keep down the dust. A mule draws a cart. A pigeon flies arrow-straight the length of the chasm, north to south.

How soundly you slept, all through our wedding night.

Behind me, the mattress creaks. I turn to find you sitting up and smiling.

'Good morning, wife.'

While you are in the water closet, I find the pistol under your pillow.

Como is ringed by peaks. Cloud strings snag in the crevices of the mountain above us. Further off, the Alpine foothills gleam pale oyster. The lake is endless as the sea, yet flat calm and smelling of river, and greenish-purple, as if used to rinse a watercolourist's brush. A swan descends, wings beating the air, webbed feet splattering; the next moment, gliding elegantly away from us.

We explore the narrow streets behind the lakefront hotels. The small shop windows are crammed with merchandise. This one candy-striped parasols; that one, ironmongery; a third, ladies' hats; a fourth, the lace-trimmed shelves of a *pasticceria*. Little dogs with foxy faces follow their owners into the butcher's without anyone turning a hair. The men serving behind the counters have the high-coloured, hook-nosed, theatrical handsomeness of Mr Punch.

The engineer in you is eager to see the *funicolare*. It seems to me half fairground ride, half clockwork toy. I am enchanted by the driverless carriage, the doors that would be crazily angled on the flat but seem perpendicular against the steep platform. We sit at the front, so you can observe the steel cable. The doors slam, a bell rings, our rumbling ascent begins, balanced by the descent of a second carriage on a parallel track. I clutch your arm as the carriages pass, inches from collision.

So this is married life. Your hand in mine as we climb the mule track past gingerbread cottages and terraced gardens. The smell of woodsmoke so heady it could be incense. A wayside chapel. Birdsong. The fragrance of the pines. The levelled area amid the treetops with its view of mountains mussel-shell blue in the haze.

My heart takes a while to steady after the effort of the climb. So high, we might be floating on a cloud. A dog's bark echoes somewhere below us. How beautiful the nape of your neck is. The tousled hair above your brow. Your broad, handsome, brutish nose. Your lips. Our mouths meet in a chaste kiss that turns to passion, as running water will fill a cup to overflowing. I push away the anxious thought. All will be well. It is as you said: you were so tired last night.

When at last we pull apart, you say, 'You're the love of my life.'

We take the ferry to Bellagio, with its belle-époque villas, its narrow, stepped streets. There are tables on the lakefront where French and German and American tourists sit in the shade of a pergola strung with vines. Mallards waddle between the chair legs begging for tidbits. Coots paddle around the quay making their strange piping cries.

Our landlady, Signora Ferri, is delicately formed, her wrinkled skin framing the curious gaze of a child. She apologises for the cold but she did not expect frost at night so early in the year. If we want logs to burn, we will have to pay extra. Last year they would have been included in the price, but what is she to do? Everything in Lombardy is so expensive. Noticing there is only one blanket on the bed, I ask for another. She seems not to understand, then points to my wedding ring and brings her hands together in a gesture that needs no translation. Sitting down to eat, we find the meat in the cold supper she has left us is mostly gristle. The towels have been worn to threads by her own household before being offered to her paying guests. At dusk we discover there is no oil in the lamp. A search of the cupboards yields a single candle stub.

I am glad to be staying with Signora Ferri. The one thing she has not thought to charge us for is laughter, and we have such fun at her expense. In bed that night, between the icy sheets, we joke that she will be wanting another two lire for a sunny day, for fresh air when we open the windows. For that spider in the corner, keeping down the flies. We laugh until tears run down our faces, the knowledge that she lives upstairs and must surely hear only increasing our hilarity. You crush my cold foot in the furry crook of your leg, but it's no good, my teeth still chatter. Giggling, we pull on our clothes, trousers, a fisherman's jersey you brought for walking in the Alps, my flannel dress and stockings, to fall asleep like children, hand in hand.

Next morning the signora brings down a tray with yesterday's rolls and a jug of gritty coffee. As soon as she has gone we escape to the lakeside. The sky is a dull white, the air chill. We bathe our faces in the steam of bowls of hot milk. The waiter brings us two sugar pastries so delicious that I order another. Afterwards, you smile at my disappointment. Have I not learned that the secret of all pleasure is knowing when to stop? 'Is it?' I say, looking into your eyes. 'Surely not *all* pleasure?' I have embarrassed you. You clear your throat and signal to the waiter for the bill.

In time the cloud hanging over the lake thins to a layer like a crocheted christening blanket, the sun keeking through its fine holes. They are burning leaves in the olive groves. When I remark that the smoke smells of caramelised sugar, you say I am such a greedy girl that everything smells of sweetmeats to me. You will have to watch me or I shall grow fat. By noon the haze has cleared. The walls around the orchards are warm to the touch. Clumps of tiny purple flowers have rooted in the mortar. Lizards the length of my forefinger creep out to bask. They lie so still, you do not see them until I point them out, their blinkless eyes, their pulsing throats. Touched by the sun, their brown, speckled skins glint gold.

On the esplanade above the boathouses, a group of sweating seminarians hold an interminable pose for a photographer half-hidden by the black skirts of his camera. You wish you had your sketchbook. A half-mile further on, a dozen shirt-less men are erecting a wooden amphitheatre in the grounds of the Grand Hotel. A small crowd has gathered to watch. I study the faces, and am studied in my turn, the men gazing into my eyes in that direct, unabashed, questioning way I remember from visiting Florence with my father. You ask if I have some understanding with them. Yes, I say, if you mean the understanding that exists between men and women everywhere, but in Italy is nearer the surface. I am pleased with this answer. It seems to me to strike exactly the note of sophisticated frankness a married woman should maintain with her husband.

A boy is selling ice cream in lick glasses. My water ice is like perfumed snow. Wiping my sticky mouth after finishing it, I notice you have only eaten half yours. 'How much do you love me?' I ask. Licking the path your tongue has smoothed over the cold sweetness feels as indecent as anything we will do in the dark tonight, or perhaps tomorrow. *Please, God, let it be soon.*

We talk about staying till spring to see the cherries and camellias in bloom, quitting our miserly landlady and taking rooms with a lake view. After breakfast in the sunlit court-yard, I will go out, leaving you to your easel. Halfway down some narrow *salita* I will find a dressmaker who can follow my sketches using the local silk. You protest: is this to be a regular occurrence? An investment, I say. I will need a certain level of finery to make the acquaintance of all the rich women at the Villa Serbelloni needing a handsome young artist to paint their portraits. My introductions and your talent will provide us with a living. I will befriend another artist's wife – or perhaps a poet's, so she will not be jealous of all the commissions I secure. She will complain of her husband's other women, and I will pity her, knowing myself loved so devotedly. Around five, you will clean your brushes and wander down the hill. We will sit at the water's edge watching the Menaggio ferry come and go, as the sky turns the colour of poached salmon and the sun sets behind the mountains quick as a dropped coin.

You bring my fingers to your lips. 'When I think how easily we might never have met, and now you're my whole life.'

Such wonderful things you say to me.

'I wish I could hold you in the palm of my hand.'

'I would carry you in my pocket all day long.'

'I would put you in my mouth and suck you like a sweet.'

In a shop built into the hillside selling majolica bowls and gilded papier mâché trays, we buy a peacock-green silk eiderdown.

'One day,' you say, 'when we're very old, we will die in bed under this quilt.'

At lunch we overhear a party of tourists discussing a ball to raise funds towards the building of a laying-in hospital. You loathe formal dances. How cruel to deprive me, I say, when we waltz so beautifully together. You laugh. I look into your eyes. '*No.*' I bite my lower lip. At last you sigh, shaking your head. '*Thank you,*' I whisper.

Dusk finds us strolling through the Melzi gardens. Light above us, darkness below. Not a breath of wind, and still the coloured lanterns strung along the path seem to shiver. From inside the villa, the faint notes of a polka. You draw me off the path, under a palm.

'There'll be a queue of young men wanting to dance with you.'

'I'm sure there won't.'

You put a fingertip to my chin, lifting my gaze to yours. 'There will.'

'But I shall dance only with you.'

You kiss me, and we go in.

I had no idea there were so many elegant people in Bellagio. I argued night and day until Mother agreed to my oyster satin with its modest stitching of pearls: I might as well be wearing sackcloth. The dance floor is awhirl with spangled chiffon and embroidered tulle, like dewy cobwebs glittering at sunrise. How many of these filmy marvels will survive the exertions of the night, a heel through the hem, the sweat of tarantellas and Schottisches and mazurkas?

You were not exaggerating when you spoke of loathing these occasions. Your handsome features seem carved in stone. The orchestra is playing the opening bars of a tune I don't know. I draw you onto the floor. When the extraordinarily tall man on my right seizes my hand, I am as taken aback as you are to be captured by the woman on your left. We are linked in a large circle, evidently some sort of reel. Four steps forward to tighten the ring, then four back. Dropping hands, the women step forward and retreat. Just as I am getting the knack of it, the giant takes me in his arms. My eyes meet yours. For a moment I think you will break his hold and drag me off the floor, but that would throw the whole dance into confusion, and besides, the woman on your left is waiting to be claimed. My new partner spins me around and we cross hands to promenade for the count of eight before the circle reforms and the sequence begins again.

I never knew until now why Father disapproved of Fanny and me shuffling around the floor in Mr Webster's dance class. The abandon I discovered, waltzing with you on the Como lakefront, turns out to exist in others' arms. The voluptuous pleasure of yielding to a man, feeling myself taken, not as clever Catherine, or funny Cathie, but as the woman I am underneath. As soon as each of these strangers lays hands on me, I have him: the proportions of chivalry and mastery in his nature. I know how it would be to mate with him. Not just to lie with him (but yes, that too): to live as his wife. All this in the first moment of being held. Turning in the latest new embrace, I glimpse your face rudely averted from the woman you are leading, to keep me in sight. Your eyes proclaim your agony so nakedly, it is easier to look away, to fix my gaze on my partner's shoulder and surrender to our fleeting, intimate exchange.

The music accelerates. Pink cheeks grow crimson. The whirling bodies radiate heat. My partner, having ascertained that I am Scotch, gives a piercing shriek, his attempt at the cry of a Highland chief. Now everyone is doing it. A new wildness enters our movements. There is less courtesy, more rough familiarity, in the way each man takes possession of me. We turn and trip and turn again, spinning across the floor. I am dizzy, as if drunk, intoxicated by the pull between my body and these others, by an exhilaration like sprinting full-pelt, lungs bursting, yet wanting to leap higher, spin faster, to lose myself in the delirium of the dance.

We have come full circle. You are about to reclaim me when the music stops. The look in your eyes frightens me.

'Let's get your coat,' you say.

My body is deliciously loose and glowing, my damp skin just starting to cool.

'*Catherine.*'

'We've only had one dance.'

'I told you I hate these affairs.'

'Just one more...'

But you are adamant. You cannot stand the heat, or the racket. The stink of bay rum and tuberose on sweating bodies is getting on your nerves. You have plans for the morning. You do not want to be shut in a darkened room with one of your headaches.

I swallow my disappointment and collect my coat, thinking we will go straight back to our lodgings. But in the chill, dark gardens, where the strains of a waltz can just be heard, you take me in your arms and we glide *one*-two-three *one*-two-three between the palms.

Everyone is going to the circus.

Children race past us, their parents ambling along behind.

Here and there, a hunchbacked *nonna* still wearing the fashions of twenty years ago. I recognise a waiter from the lakefront café, the woman who sold us our bedcover, the pretty girl from the *pasticceria*.

We were taken to the circus every Christmas in Glasgow, but there was always a stiffness in Mother's smile that judged the treat too vulgar or ungodly (or perhaps Roman Catholic). So much nicer to go with a husband who shares my excitement. It could almost be summer, with the outdoor chatter, the scents of myrtle and night-blooming jasmine, the bats flickering over the lake. A sudden blare from the direction of the Serbelloni gardens shocks us into silence. Just as I identify the sound, I hear the word on other lips. *Elefante, elefante.*

We pay our fifty centesimi and go in. Sawdust underfoot. The stink of coal oil lamps in the back of my throat. The seats are wooden planks arranged in tiers. No sooner are we settled than everyone shuffles along to accommodate another family. A few seconds later, someone else. We are quite squashed by the time the ringmaster appears in his top hat, tailcoat and white gloves to promise us *meraviglie e terrore, risate e lacrime.* Wonder and terror, laughter and tears.

First come the tumblers in long-sleeved vests and short, puffed breeches, walking on their hands, followed by a French poodle on its forepaws. The band has a refrain for every performer. A drumroll and cymbal clash for the tumblers, a mincing penny whistle for the dog, a wailing pungi when the contortionist fits herself inside a bottle. How entrancing it is. The chalky ring of light, white plumes on the dancing horses, the jugglers' spinning diabolos and rings. A baggy-skinned lion opens his jaws to accommodate the tamer's head. The elephant turns on the spot, and receives his applause with a charming clumsy bow.

The audience is a show in itself, calling out when the monkey steals the ringmaster's hat, screaming when the tumblers dive through flaming hoops, clapping and cheering

84

so loudly I can hardly hear the band. When the trapeze artist high above us lets go and flies through the air to be caught on the upswing by his partner, every one of us takes the same sharp indrawn breath. He somersaults in mid-air to land on his feet, arms raised in triumph. We are still applauding when the white-faced clowns shamble into the ring: a tiny Pierrot with baggy pantaloons and pokey hat, Harlequin in flashing red and black. The vulgar rasps of his trombone, alternating with the midget's squeaking trumpet, are exactly like a conversation. I turn to share the joke, but your face is grim. 'Are you unwell?' I whisper. Before you can reply, I am distracted by the entrance of a red-nosed Auguste whose hair stands vertically off his balding head. I do not know why he should remind me of my father, but the thought lends a poignant touch to his antics. He crosses the ring playing a tuba – *oom-pah, oom-pah* – big shoes flapping, his trousers dropping and rising in time to the music.

He sets up a blackboard. Pierrot and Harlequin sit on a low bench alongside a little white dog in a ruffled collar. The children around us squeal in delighted recognition. Auguste has a teacher's long stick. Each time he tries to point to the board, it wilts. The dog barks. Pierrot produces a soprano giggle, Harlequin a bass guffaw.

You ask, 'What are they saying?'

As the jokes are all visual, I whisper that it doesn't matter.

'I would rather judge that for myself.'

Auguste makes Pierrot bend over. The little man grimaces against the expected beating, then opens his eyes in surprise. The stick droops. The audience howls with laughter. Me too.

'*Tell me*,' you hiss.

I shake my head, not wanting to miss a moment of this joyful silliness.

Auguste tests the stick, bringing it down hard on his open palm. This time it remains rigid. He bends double, rocking with pain. Behind his back, Harlequin mimics him.

'*Catherine.*'

A man sitting in the row in front glances over his shoulder and whispers something to his sweetheart. She turns to look at us, catching the eye of the woman sitting to my right. In their shoes, I too might smirk.

'*What is he saying?*'

I put my finger to my lips.

Incensed, you pull my hand away. 'It's about me, isn't it?'

We walk back to our lodgings in silence, blind to the beauty of the night. You are angrier than when the man admired me at dinner in Como. Every time our neighbours laughed at the clowns your eyes darted left and right. I was afraid you were going to start a fight. We walked out halfway through, there was nothing else for it. You stood up and I followed, blocking others' views, stepping on their toes, *scusi, scusi*, to the end of the row, down the rackety steps and around a good third of the ringside to reach the exit.

'I suspect we've been followed here.'

I have turned to look behind me before I understand that you mean *followed to Italy*. Every moment of our stay, while I amused myself with ice cream and circuses, your troubles have been preying on your mind.

'Would they really come all this way?'

'Distance is nothing to them.'

We have reached the formal gardens lining the esplanade. Five swans are sleeping on the grass, folded into themselves like ladies' hats.

'Herbert, why do you keep a pistol under your pillow?'

'I have to be able to protect you from them.'

And here it is again: the delicious ache I feel twenty, thirty times a day. I long to do what other wives do in the dark, giving myself utterly, nothing held back. I am beginning to think you don't feel the same.

'My love, you have to tell me what this is all about.'

86

'You must know. Everyone knows. It's been in the newspapers.'

'Which newspapers?'

'All of them. Not spelled out, of course. They do it in their hateful roundabout way.'

I frown.

'We talked about this on the boat.'

'You didn't tell me everything.'

Although there is no one to hear us, you lower your voice. 'I am spied on. To what end, I don't know. That's what I need *you* to find out for me.'

I think, *If you are really of such interest, you must have committed a crime.*

'It seems an awful trouble to go to, unless you've given them some cause.'

'You don't know what people are like.'

How can I deny it? The congregations we worshipped with in Glasgow were such blameless souls, I never understood why the minister's sermons were so preoccupied with evil. My fellow students were guilty of nothing worse than vanity. The foreign visitors who crossed our threshold seemed proof of graciousness in every land. And yet wars break out, and men are murdered.

'There were things I was kept in the dark about.'

Things? It dawns on me you are talking about the Transvaal. 'Discreditable things?'

You seem to hold your breath.

'Done by our forces?'

Your mouth makes a sort of shrug.

'And they suspect you of knowing?'

You meet my eye. 'You think?'

'It's possible.'

I like the sound of this new, worldy, judicious self, but it makes me nervous. Sooner or later you will find me out. I don't even know why we went to war.

'On the boat, you said, however terrible it was waiting to be ambushed, that wasn't the worst thing...'

Your eyes narrow.

'...What was the worst?'

You take a long breath. 'With the Boer, one knew they were the enemy. One could trust them to behave accordingly. With our side, I could never be sure.'

All at once you are decisive. You cannot have me caught up in this. It is too dangerous. You should never have married me. I must leave you and return to my former life in Glasgow.

'No!' Under my indignation, I think, *Already you are tired of me*. 'Do you really believe I would turn my back on you for the sake of a quiet life? Your enemies are my enemies. I have taken a vow to stand by you for better or worse.'

How thrilling it is to be taken in your arms.

'My own bonny, brave sweetheart. Do you really have the courage for this?'

'I was always a daredevil,' I say, smiling.

Your lips drag against my cheek, your voice deep in my ear. 'Strong as a little leopard, and twice as fearless.' You hold me at arm's length, exultant. 'My Madonnina, we'll get the better of them yet!'

Dear Arthur

We arrived at HQ an hour ago and were shown straight to our tents, but, being too excited to sleep, I may as well bring you up to date with the past three weeks. Look up Germiston in your atlas: we're on the outskirts, in the shadow of Rhodes' gold mines. As you can imagine, our position is pretty well guarded!

I have been given command of a couple of dozen Aberdeenshire engineers. They breed them big up there. Most have a head's height on me, and all speak with the queerest sort of accent. For the first week I could make neither head nor tail of most of what they said, and Corporal Robb thought he'd have some sport with me by laying it on even thicker. He is an untrustworthy lout, as is my second corporal, but Sergeant Greig is a decent chap.

We were at sea seventeen days. When we docked in Table Bay, Cape Town was crawling with plague, so we marched the men straight to the train. There was an idiotic mix-up at the station, the sort of thing I am on my guard against now. None of these fellows has the sense he was born with. They were told to collect a blanket and seven days' bully beef for the journey up country. You should have seen them: carrying full kit, trying to squeeze through the entrance to the rations store with their comrades coming the other way. I gave the order to leave their kit bags on the platform and, once they had collected blankets and rations, to board the open trucks of the train. Then I was summoned to the officers' carriage for a briefing. By the time we set off, it was pitch black. When we stopped at a wayside station for supper, Sergeant Greig approached me to ask when the men would be reunited with their bags. I said surely they had their kit with them in the trucks? 'No, sir': nothing but a blanket and the clothes they stood up in. Of course, I blew my top. Why in God's name would they be separated from their bags, did that make any sense? 'No, sir.' Well then, why had they left them behind? Do you know what he said? 'It was your orders, sir.'

It took us a week to travel here from Cape Town, so I got a good look at the country. At every cutting, two sentries with lanterns were posted on watch, and yet it was hard to believe in the war until, leaving De Aar, I caught my first glimpse of the wreckage from an ambush. It gave my blood a jolt to see the engine, wheels to the sky, and the mangled cars a few feet from the newly repaired track. Then I noticed the row of graves. A couple of days later, south of Kroonstad, the captain got word that the Boer had boobytrapped the line, cutting off a party of ours. We officers went to sit with the men in the trucks. You can imagine how our ears strained and our eyes raked the landscape. I could hear Lieutenant McLean addressing his section in the next truck. I dare say there is a comfort for the men in listening to an officer stating the obvious, but I was damned if I could think of anything beyond telling them to charge magazines and keep their wits about them. I saw Corporal Robb exchange a smirk with Second Corporal Sillars but, not wanting to get off on the wrong foot, I overlooked it. I would not make the same mistake now.

We waited there all day, staring at nothing in the blinding light. Nightfall was a blessed relief. By chance, a fellow called Paton turned up, an Aberdonian railwayman known to my NCOs. He'd found a couple of bottles of whisky from somewhere and the men made a fire and had a concert, singing 'Rolling Home to Bonnie Scotland' and 'Auld Lang Syne' amid much toasting and laughter. I was afraid the racket might alert the Boer, but Captain Walsh said the men could do with some release after the tension of the day. He urged me to join them. I rather wish I hadn't, but I suppose forewarned is forearmed.

They were sitting with their backs to the officers' carriage and I arrived without them knowing I was there. The NCOs and their old acquaintance were in a huddle apart from the rest. From their talk, I gathered Paton had served his time as a sergeant in the Engineers and, having nothing to sail home for, had found work with the Imperial Military Railway. He seemed amazed that Greig and Robb had not stayed in Scotland with their wives. 'Don't come crying to me when they blatter you,' he said (or something along those lines). Sergeant Greig said there were ten of us to every Boer, and Robb laughed: 'Ten times as many mammy's boys to burn their peeliewallie skin red raw.' I should have alerted them to my presence, but this was the first chance I'd had to observe them when their guard was down, and I admit there was a pleasure in it, like sighting a chap with your rifle when he doesn't know you exist. Stout fellow that he is, Greig said the sappers would do very well, to which Robb replied, 'It's Jack the laddie ah fret aboot,' and of course I knew who he meant.

'Ye reckon he's aye been Jackson?' Second Corporal Sillars said. Greig asked what else? 'Mowgli. Umbopa.' They laughed. Robb swore I was Indian, then changed his mind: 'Eyetie. Or Jewboy, mebbe.' 'Big neb, richt enough,' Sillars said, 'looks smashed to me.' Robb sniggered, 'A fighter who cannae duck a punch. That's a' we need.'

I thought how Lieutenant McLean would have handled this, drawling, 'I'd drop you in the first round, Corporal,' then reaching for the whisky bottle, offering it next to Robb, who'd have taken it with a sheepish grin while the others laughed. Only they would never have said Indian or Eyetie or Jewboy about Lieutenant McLean, so I barked at them to stand to attention and report to the officers' carriage at first light.

There is more to tell, but I must turn in now. Might I beg a favour before signing off? After all the promises I gave Mater about drinking boiled water and taking holy communion and making sure the captain knows I'm a Westminster man, I can't seem to write her so much as a postcard. Be a good chap and keep her happy with a few harmless facts.

Your affectionate brother,
Herbert

1904

You start bringing your sketchbook on the walks we take after breakfast. I suspect you are planning a portrait of me. If I come too close, you cover the paper with both arms. While you draw, I write letters, reading them aloud to you before I seal the envelope. The rest of the time, I stare at a book. Back in Glasgow I could finish a novel in two days. Here, I am too distracted. When you ask what I am thinking about, I reply 'a hat I saw yesterday' or 'what we'll have for dinner'. I am ashamed of these evasions, but I can hardly say, *I'm trying to understand why you don't desire me.*

Again and again I have kissed you, nuzzled you, pressed myself against you, trying everything short of taking you in my hand. How can you resist me? We must consummate our marriage. It is more than four weeks since Walter walked into the sewing room. How long before my condition starts to show? My heart beats so anxiously, the skin flutters on my breast. How can you not notice? It is a terrible thing I am doing, but what choice do I have? If I confess, you will never forgive me or the bairn. You might even tell Lucie. And taking the long view, it is not as if I were smuggling a stranger's blood into the Jackson clan, merely altering cousins to half-brothers.

The postman delivers the first replies to my letters. No word from Mother, but Gordon and Grant are both well. Fanny is full of plans for her own wedding next year. She writes of Hop in that tone of loving disparagement I have often wondered at in wives, as if men were little boys to be managed past their thoughtless impulses. Am I expected to reply in similar vein? I imagine reading such a letter aloud to you.

I have not quite forgiven Phyl her gloomy predictions, but I am glad to see her italic hand and hear her sardonic voice speaking through the lines. She has a new commission, a bas-relief of Industry and Science for McGeoch's warehouse in West Campbell Street. As I am not available to model for Science, she will have to make do with the servants. If only Ethel the parlourmaid did not look quite so much like a hamster. In postscript, she sends her best wishes to my husband and hopes he and I are now thoroughly acquainted.

I glance at your face bent over the sketchbook. How fierce you look, frowning against the midday light. On the slope above us, a cypress looms black against blue sky. A bee drunk with lavender staggers on the breeze. The sun warms the sly jokes folded in my hand. I take out my pen. *Dear Phyl.*

I tell her your teeth are whiter than most Englishmen's, or seem so: after a few days in the Italian sun, your skin has darkened, as if soaked in brandy. You are blind to a new trimming on a hat, but charmed by the mole on the side of my neck. Though you are not one to talk of souls, I fancy yours is like the cypress: solitary, upstanding, thrawn.

There are other details I keep to myself. What happened at the circus. The nightmares you wake from soaked in sweat, but can never remember. Daily we watch the tourists at the lakefront tables, couples attaching themselves to couples, families to families. Unlike Walter and Don, you do not enjoy conversation for its own sake. It is a question of self-respect, as if words were coins and only a fool pays out more than strictly necessary.

Taking up my pen again, I explain how you volunteered to serve in the Transvaal. Night after night at your club, you listened to the Boer-lovers' treasonous pi-jaw being shouted down by professors of botany lusting to give the blighters a bloody nose. Walter was the only one who talked sense: we had to fight because it was impossible for Dutch and British ambitions to flourish side by side, and because the empire that let South Africa slip through her fingers would make a poor guardian of Canada, Australia and New Zealand. We were British: we owed the civilisation we counted as our birthright to a thriving mercantile community. War was an ugly necessity. We could not parley with an enemy that was armed to the teeth and determined to eject us.

Drawing was not a parlour skill to the Royal Engineers. They needed men who could sketch the banks of a river and design the right bridge to cross it. Teaching for a living had frayed your self-respect. Belonging to a regiment, you felt more fully a man than you had in years. But the soldierly ideals instilled in Birkenhead turned out to be a poor preparation for Africa. All you will say is that reports of the war in the British press were little better than bedtime stories, and they were right to censor the facts – no one who knew the truth could call himself a patriot.

I love you the more for setting you down on paper like this, seeing you neat and whole. The letter needs one last paragraph, congratulations on Phyl's commission, enquiries after her family, but you are tired of sketching, so I fold the sheets of paper inside *Middlemarch*, to finish later.

How happy we are, despite my guilty secret, every day a raft of new pleasures: lake trips, scenic walks, a bookshop with an English shelf, a charming osteria. But not today. Even before opening the shutters, I recognise the sort of ashen morning I dreaded in my spinster years. Flavourless, colourless, interminable.

By nine we are on Via Roma, thoroughly bored. Having only just had breakfast, we cannot take coffee in a hotel.

A church, I suggest, but one gilded altarpiece looks much like another to your eyes. We cross the street to the covered arcade. There are leather goods and bolts of silk in the shop windows. When these are thoroughly examined, we stare at the bills pasted to the walls. A Swiss soprano sang Schubert's Lieder here last week. Two weeks ago, it was a selection from *Pelléas et Mélisande*. A theatre company is to perform *Twelfth Night* at the Villa Carlotta in November.

You look away from the posters, to my face.

'What?' I say.

You nod at a line drawing of a gypsy girl standing between a soldier and a lanky toreador. A production of Bizet's *Carmen* in the Serbelloni ballroom.

'We're too late, it was last month.'

Your voice drops. '*Look* at it.'

I squint at the poster, not sure what I am meant to see.

'Well?' you ask.

Can you mean the bosomy Carmen? 'Me?'

'*Us*.' A testy note in your whisper. '*Our marriage*.'

I stare at you.

'Don't try to spare my feelings by pretending.'

'I wasn't.'

'Then why are you smiling like that?'

'Like what?'

You tilt your head and simper. I refuse to believe it is an accurate impersonation.

'I'm not the fool you take me for,' you say.

'What?'

'Oh for God's sake.'

I remember this bruised feeling under my eyes. When I was a child, it presaged tears.

'Apparently *I* am the fool,' I say, 'since I haven't the first idea what you're talking about.'

You jab your finger at the wall. 'I'm talking about *that*!'

'A poster: is that all that's bothering you? I'm more

concerned that we've not been married seven days and already you seem to hate me.'

'I don't *hate* you, I just expect an honest answer to a straightforward question.'

'It's an advertisement for a production of *Carmen*.'

'I can see that, even with my rudimentary grasp of Italian.'

I don't know what to say.

You give an exasperated hiss. 'It's there in black and white.'

I point to the lines of type. 'The name of the opera? The composer? The company?'

'*Why* do you deny it?'

I come to the crucial detail. 'The performance, on the first of September. It was printed before we'd even met.'

'Precisely!'

At last, a glimmer of light. I have never seen *Carmen*, but I know the story features passion and jealousy. Does the toreador in the illustration not have something of Walter about him? Now I am afraid.

'Oh.'

'*Oh*,' you mimic, but you seem pacified.

Do you know? Is that why you will not consummate our marriage?

I whisper, 'Forgive me.'

You take my hand. Our first real quarrel. I am still not sure what it was about, but it is over now.

Later you find my letter to Phyl.

It is partly my fault. You saw me writing it. I did not read it aloud to you. Naturally you are curious. You take the copy of *Middlemarch* from my bedside. I am in the other room, reattaching one of your shirt buttons. An alteration in the air causes me to turn my head.

'What's this?' you say in your quietest voice.

'It's not finished.'

'Really? You don't think it says more than enough as it is?'

'Phyl is one of my dearest friends. We tell each other everything.'

'Including my business, it seems.'

'Your business is my business now.'

'And that makes it Phyl's business too?'

'Yes.'

'And who will Phyl choose to tell, and who will that person tell in his turn?'

'I'm proud of you. I want her to know. One day you two will meet and be friends.'

'If I live.'

'Now you're being ridiculous. There's not the faintest chance that letter will be seen by anyone else. And even if it were, it wouldn't *threaten your life*. I know why you're annoyed: because I made a joke about husbandly inattentiveness.'

That does it. You say you were prepared to forgive an honest error of judgement, but what I did was quite deliberate. I do not seem to realise that in binding myself to you in marriage I have bound our fates. By putting you in danger, I endanger myself. You cannot allow that. You tear the letter in half, and half again, throwing the pieces into the grate. You will have to keep a careful watch on me. It saddens you, this loss of a trust that was so dear to you.

I tell you not to be so melodramatic. Your face darkens. I can see you are about to respond with something truly hurtful. The quarrel will burst into flames and burn all night; everything will be fuel to it.

'Herbert, I'm sorry. Don't let's argue. It breaks my heart. I was thoughtless to write what I did. I'll be more careful in future.'

It costs me dearly to say this, but you do not seem to recognise it as an apology. You say it is not just *what* I wrote, but the deceit. Why would I hide the letter in a book if it was really so thoughtlessly written? I knew what I was doing and sought to hide it from you, and now I am lying about it.

I retract my apology. The quarrel flares up just as I feared. Soon we are arguing about which of us will sleep in the chair, since we are equally determined not to share a bed. The shouting – all mine – is only brought to an end by Signora Ferri rapping her broom handle on the floor that forms our ceiling.

Dear Arthur,

I received your letter this morning and am still chuckling over your *contretemps* with the Memsahib-to-be. It's the first good laugh I have had since leaving home. Who would have guessed little Pensa had a dragonish side? I trust harmony is now restored.

Just after I last wrote I had rather an unwelcome surprise. You will recall I had been given command of an Aberdeenshire section lacking a lieutenant, with orders to replace a section from the same company whose tour of duty was at an end. Those men are halfway to Blighty by now but, at the last minute, their lieutenant, Bill Crathie, decided to stay on. He is rather like Rutledge, captain of rugby in my year, if you remember him: a ruddy complexion and a mop of flaxen hair. To hear the whoops of joy when my NCOs clapped eyes on him, you would have thought they'd been given a week's leave in the fleshpots of Paris. I gather the captain back in Aberdeen is his cousin. Not that this was mentioned when Captain Hunter had me in to explain that, as Crathie knew the men, he would be taking over. So there you have it: they promoted me to lieutenant, only to strip me of my command within a month. Had I deserted, I would have been court-martialled, but as this is the regiment's doing, I must look cheerful about it.

After three weeks of kicking my heels here, I had a stroke of luck. Sergeant Greig took a detachment to a little piece of nowhere in the Orange River Colony needing a well and windmill pump, and the whole lot of them went down with dysentery. I led the replacement detachment: six sappers and twelve native labourers, with Second Corporal Sillars as my NCO.

One day, Arthur, you and I must sit down and compare

your experience of the brown man and my impressions of the black. There are two hundred of them attached to the 47th. They like to wear military uniform, but after their own fashion. One dresses in an Engineer's tunic with a pair of tattered trousers and a shapeless, broad-brimmed hat. Another wears military breeches with a vest and dirty neckerchief. All go barefoot, the soles of their feet being tough as boot leather. The one I have most to do with wears a stovepipe hat, flannel vest and trousers cut off just below the knee. Though it is devilish hard to guess their ages, I'd say he has a good twenty years on the others, who look to him for guidance. He goes by the name of Solomon, although the Kaffirs address him by some other, quite unpronounceable moniker. I first noticed him arguing with the ox-cart driver over the best route to avoid an enemy ambush. He would not say how he knew their whereabouts, but assured me that, if I trusted him, he would be my eyes and ears. When I replied I should be glad to be warned of the Boer, he said the damndest thing: 'I see all your enemies, *sah*, far away and near.' Then he turned to look straight at Sillars. You will be wondering why I tolerated the fellow's liberties. Well, for one thing, he was right about my second corporal, and for another, he speaks two or three tribal languages and knows the veldt like the back of his hand. I rather took to him, and found the hours passed more quickly in his company.

It took us a week to complete the drilling and rig up the pump. We were packing up when a messenger arrived with orders to build a blockhouse to defend the well. It was a pity Captain Hunter had not thought to send the fellow with a wagonload of corrugated iron. There was little chance of requisitioning any down there: General Kitchener has ordered that every farm is to be blown up or burned. Nevertheless, I set out on a recce, taking four sappers and half a dozen natives.

The first two farms we came across were roofless shells,

the third intact, leading me to assume the inhabitants were friendly. The old apple-cheeked Dutchman spoke excellent English, introducing his daughter and her three children, and assuring us there had been no commando in the area for over a month. It was a surprisingly civilised home to find out in the wilds, the dresser shelves filled with blue-and-white china and a very decent watercolour on the wall. Moir and Baird were greatly taken with the daughter, a handsome woman with copper-coloured hair. She led them out to the pump for a drink of water, leaving me with her father. We had been jawing away for a good ten minutes when Solomon appeared outside the window and signalled that I should join him. He led me to the stables, where we found three hot and sweaty mounts. I sent him back to the wagon to alert Lennox and Dyce.

My first sniff of the enemy. You will be wondering if I was afraid. I can honestly say I was not. Looking back on it now, it's almost as if I acted in my sleep.

For all our stealth, they knew we were there. Lennox and Dyce had just entered the yard when the first shots rang out from the hayloft above the barn. I took cover behind a water butt and felt the bullets whizz over my head. Lennox joined me, Dyce ducking back behind the farmhouse. Baird heard the exchange of fire and walked the old Dutchman's daughter into the yard with his pistol to her head. She is a tall woman and he was pressed so hard against her back that the enemy had nothing to fix their sights on. When they reached us, Lennox slipped in as close behind Baird, while I kept up a volley of fire at the opening above the barn door. Hearing shots to either side of me, I saw Moir had joined Dyce. Solomon was peering around the corner of the dairy. Somehow he'd got his hands on a Mauser.

It is taking so long to get this down on paper, yet it all seemed to happen at once. Lennox, Baird and their hostage entered the barn. I saw smoke coming out of the loft. The Dutchman's daughter began to yell. My men emerged, shutting the barn doors behind them. The smoke grew thicker, the screaming hysterical. Queer how a woman's voice can get inside a fellow's head and make coherent thought impossible. The trapped men shouted to us in their double-Dutch. Their rifles were thrown from the loft. I gave the order to hold fire. 'It is a trick, *sah*,' Solomon said. I turned to find him crouched at my side, his shoulder bleeding. The horses began to whinny in panic at the heat and smoke on the other side of the stable wall. The barn door opened and the Dutchwoman emerged, screaming at us not to shoot. Looking up, I made out the shape of a man amid the smoke pouring out of the loft. I shot him in the arm, aiming for his heart. The sappers looked at me in confusion and I remembered my order to hold fire. The woman yelled at the Boer I'd shot, telling him to jump. His legs jarred horribly on the ground before he crumpled. The sight stalled the fellow who took his place. His comrade pushed him out, then jumped himself. We all heard the bone snap. The woman howled as if the pain were her own. I told my men to secure the prisoners, and ran into the house. The 'friendly' Dutchman was in the kitchen with his terrified grandchildren, a pistol in his hand, an old thing as likely to blow up in his face as to hit its target. When he saw my rifle, he dropped it on the floor. I killed him with a single shot.

Of course, there could be no blockhouse building after that. We had to get the men to a military prison, and the woman and children to the refugee camp. I promised her the old man would have a decent burial, but I suspect the natives saved themselves the trouble and left his body to the flames. Certainly they re-joined us soon enough. The Boer horses were exhausted and would have held us back. Moir shot them, which set the children wailing again.

We put the prisoners in the Dutchman's cart. The woman and her children rode with us. She wanted to bring their clothes and blankets and cooking utensils, and even the piano. I said I should make myself a laughing stock returning to HQ with a piano. She tried to bargain with me: what if she and the children wore their spare clothes? Impossible: it was almost eighty degrees, with no shade in the cart. Besides, General Kitchener's orders are quite clear: scorched earth. The natives drove the sheep and cattle into a pen and slit their throats. I thought she would press the faces of the two younger children to her breast, but they all watched as Moir and Baird tore off the tin roof and set fire to the farmhouse. She was white with strain, but shed no tear, and did not speak to me again.

When we got back to camp, we put her and her children under canvas. The Boer fighters slept in the open, tied up, watched by Knowles. I retired to my tent, to be woken by the children's screams. The woman had stolen across to the prisoners and had been about to take possession of Knowles's rifle when, luckily, he awoke. By the time I arrived she was tied up and Lennox was holding the children at gunpoint. I told him to lower his weapon, and they ran to her. Seeing this, Sillars begged a word with me in private. Lennox had been right, he said: the Boer were quite capable of using children to escape. Was I aware of General Kitchener's order that enemy prisoners wearing items of British uniform were to be shot? I did not take his meaning at first: the prisoners were not in any uniform, British or Boer. He unravelled one of his puttees and handed it to me, and then I understood. I told him I didn't know what sort of slipshod training he had had, but under my command everything was going to be done by the book. Instead of taking this reprimand with a brisk 'yes, sir', he stared at me. I knew then there had been plenty of insubordinate talk with Robb. Or was it Lieutenant Crathie he put his trust in? A second corporal would never show a lieutenant that sort of insolence without support. Anyway, a couple of days later we arrived back at HQ, all present and correct.

And there I had better leave this letter.

Affectionately,

Herbert

1904

A knock at the door.

'Catherine, are you all right?'

'I'll be out very soon.'

'Are you constipated? Should we ask the pharmacist for some syrup of figs?'

I never dreamed married life would be so confining. I am never out of your sight. I tell you, much as I love you, I need half an hour a day alone as others need food or sleep. Without it, I no longer know who I am. What nonsense, you say: I am your bonny, blue-eyed wife.

By now the urge to solitude has become a compulsion, but if I say, 'I'm going out for a walk', I know you will want to come with me. If I try to dissuade you, you will be hurt. We will argue. Even if I get my own way, the walk will be ruined. One morning I slip out of bed before dawn, avoiding the creaking floorboard, closing the door very gently. I tell myself this stealth is consideration for your rest, but my blood pounds as it did when I committed some calculated transgression as a child.

I walk for miles, until a pallor shows above the mountains to the east and the hooded crows rise from their roosts to fill the air with hoarse calling. When I return to Bellagio, the sky above the lake is a watercolour in pale grey and lemon. Oarsmen stand, smoking and yawning, awaiting the first passengers of the day. Ducks stalk the esplanade, ever hopeful, pecking at nothing. The proprietor of the lakefront café hails me with a beaming '*Buongiorno, Signora*.' I am surprised to be recognised, and then struck by my surprise, by how invisible I feel lately.

I sit at a table, looking out across the lake, my mind spilling over with thoughts I banish in your presence. The pattern of our days: cooing one minute, squabbling the next. To the best of my knowledge, Mother and Father never exchanged an angry word, although Fanny and I had fierce spats, and the boys were always bawling 'I hate you!' at each other. Sometimes I feel more like your sister than your wife, as if our life together were a contest only one of us could win. And yet you call me *Tswekere*, a word you learned in Africa. It means 'sweetness'. You tell me I have saved you. Without me, you would not have had the heart to carry on. Last night, in bed, I took my courage in both hands and asked why our marriage is still unconsummated.

You sighed as if you had been waiting for this. 'Haven't you guessed?'

I have done nothing but guess, coming up with a dozen reasons, each more wounding than the last. 'Is it that you don't like me... like that, now you've seen more of me?'

You touched my face so tenderly. 'You are everything I could wish for. I'm the one who's deficient. I thought marrying might cure me, but it's no use.' You turned, to lie on your back. 'You needn't worry, I shan't trouble you in that way.'

'It would be no trouble to me.'

'Nevertheless, it's out of the question.'

'But why?'

'It's not something I can discuss with my *wife*.'

'With whom else?'

'I thought a doctor. That man Gemmell. Not that he was any use.'

'But couldn't we just try, to see what happens?'

106

How mature and reasonable I sounded, even as the thwarted child in me thought, *I married that ruthless fighter in the fencing hall, so how is it I have ended up with you?*

'If we were to take off our nightclothes, if you took me in your arms and kissed me...'

You shook your head.

'I'm sure many men have been agreeably surprised.'

Your eyes turned to slits. 'And how would you know that?'

'The world is full of children.'

'And none of them will be fathered by me.'

I imagined marriage as an Eden of perfect frankness, but our interests are not identical, and not every truth is kind. I could have pressed you to explain, but at whose expense? Yours. And for whose benefit? Mine.

'Your coffee will be growing cold.'

I look up, startled, thinking you have tracked me down, although the voice is golden, with a slide in it where English accents are crisp.

I take a sip. 'You're right: stone cold.'

He is an American, but of Italian descent. Courteous, dapper, his bushy hair bright as blue smoke against his olive skin.

'Should I leave you to your thoughts?'

Even if you were to arrive, how could you reasonably object? He is old enough to be my father.

He is taking the grand tour with his mother. She sleeps late, is bored by art but will not admit it. She insists on accompanying him to churches and galleries, then marches him past Giottos, Michelangelos, da Vincis in a frenzy of impatience, to idle away three hours over lunch. He does not really mind, having proposed the trip for her benefit. She is such a sociable old soul, and she spends far too much time at home with only her dogs for company. He can return alone next year and feast his eyes on everything that has passed in such a blur.

His coffee arrives. His look says I have his full attention.

I confess I hardly know what to tell him. The account of myself I would have given ten days ago is out of date, but I am so new to wifehood I have nothing sensible to say about it.

'Your husband is...?'

'A painter.'

'And you?'

'I played the piano. Not well enough to make a career of it.'

'You'll find your vocation.'

He says this quite matter-of-factly, and all at once the world around me is magical. Sparrows at the empty tables, shopkeepers unbolting their shutters, a light breeze coming off the lake, the reek of the ferryman's pipe. How acutely I feel the surface of my skin, the border between what is and is not myself.

'May I ask your vocation?'

'Idling.' He smiles. 'Falling into conversation with interesting women...'

A flirt, I think disappointedly, my own smile fading.

'Inadvertently offending them.'

I look up. 'It happens often?'

'Generally we get past the misunderstanding.'

'And when you don't?'

He shrugs. '"This above all: to thine own self be true".'

'And you apply this credo quite indiscriminately?'

He laughs. 'More with some people than others, I suppose. Does that make me a hypocrite? Perhaps. But it allows my mother to sleep at night.'

When I get back, you are pacing the floor. You throw yourself upon me. '*Thank God!* I thought they'd taken you, lured you away under false pretences, or—' that tender break in your voice I love so '—God knows what.'

You won't work today. We will do something together, a drive or boat trip: my choice.

I would like to see the castle above Varenna. You frown.

We would be better postponing that until we leave for Milan. I wonder if you are confusing Varenna with some more distant place. It is a short lake crossing, barely an hour. You make an impatient noise: you know perfectly well where Varenna is. Why must I contradict you all the time? Can I not trust your judgement for once? Not when that judgement is wrong, I say, and the next thing I know, you have decided we will quit Lake Como altogether. There is a ferry sailing at one o'clock. You write a note to the agent who arranged your life insurance and hurry out to the post. While you are gone, I slip upstairs to break the news to Signora Ferri. An acquaintance has told you how beautiful Milan is at this time of year, and now you must see it at once. I am afraid she will claim to have turned away other lodgers and insist we pay her the next month's board but, to my relief, she laughs.

'*Gli uomini sono tutti pazzi*,' she says. *All men are mad.*

You return from the post office out of sorts. 'I went up to tell our landlady we're leaving.'

'I already told her.'

'So I discovered.'

'I thought it'd be easier, as I speak Italian.'

'If I can communicate with the Basuto I think I can manage with an Italian housewife.'

'Yes, of course.'

'A housewife who now thinks I have to hide behind my wife's skirts.'

'I'm sure she doesn't.'

'Tied to your apron strings.'

I have never seen you so angry, I think. But I have. More than once.

Dear Arthur,

How does it feel to be a respectable married man? I hope Gilbert did a good job with the ring and the speech and dancing with the prettiest bridesmaid, though not as good a job as I should have! I suppose you will be off to India soon. You must send me your address by return, if you hope to hear from me before Christmas.

We are roughing it rather at present, making a new line of blockhouses along the border with the Orange River Colony (which the enemy call the 'Boer Free State'). Crathie and I have four working parties under our command. We ride along the line in opposite directions, recce-ing the sites and re-allocating men if any party falls behind. I take Solomon with me as my scout. He rides well enough, and is no use as a labourer with his shoulder not healed from the bullet he took at the Dutchman's farm.

It has turned extremely cold lately. I am told it is usual to make the natives sleep in the open, but I would not shut a dog out in such filthy weather. At night my parties sleep in the blockhouses, soldiers and Kaffirs alike. The air in there gets pretty ripe. I have heard Sillars and Robb grumbling about it, but neither has questioned the situation to my face. I have been adjusting my style of command. You may smile at the thought of your little brother acting the martinet, but bear in mind how I dealt with the old Dutchman. Moir and Baird told the others of our little adventure, which has done my reputation no harm.

I felt a certain responsibility for the Dutchwoman and her three children, and continued to take an interest once they were settled in the refugee camp. Her name is Johanna. I hoped to send you a sketch of her, drawn from memory, but I cannot seem to do her justice. Her pallor has a steely gleam, the line of her jaw sharp as a blade, but I have seen her coppery hair loosed from its pins, when she seems another woman entirely. I see now I disadvantaged her unduly by leaving her possessions behind. Most of her neighbours in the camp have changes of clothing, a medicine box and a few valuables they can sell *in extremis*. In the weeks I spent at HQ, I fell into the habit of bringing her odd items to amuse the children, a green beetle in a matchbox, a cast-off snakeskin I found up on the Rand. She permitted this, I suspect, less for the things themselves than for what she might need of me in future. The refugee camp is a harsh place. The women feign friendship with each other, but each would see the others starve if it meant an extra plate of porridge for her offspring. Before I was ordered down here, I visited Johanna daily and I fancy she looked out for me, although she met all my attempts at conversation with scornful or satiric looks. Once or twice she wanted some special thing of me, a bar of soap, a narrow-toothed comb to pull the lice from her children's hair. It was they who asked, stammering out the few words of English she had made them learn by heart.

At first I was insulted by her silence but, as the days passed, I found it rather a relief. Has it ever occurred to you, Arthur, how little there is that cannot be said with the lift of a brow or curl of a lip? We have become acquainted, she and I, as surely as if we had met in a Kensington drawing room. I have learned her habitual gestures, the softening in her face when the children address her, the look she sends to stop their quarrels, the laugh she swallows in my presence when one of them says something that tickles her.

I have also learned the ways she shows her enmity. How could it be otherwise? I executed her father. By lying to us, he left me no choice. Doubtless she would say, by knocking at his door I left him no choice but to lie. This is what it means to be at war. Had she spoken to me, I should have justified myself thus, and pride would have compelled her to hurl abuse if I came near her. As it is, her children are better fed, their scalps no longer itch, the beetle's sprint when released from its matchbox makes them laugh. Most importantly, they have a protector – or had, before I was sent down here. One afternoon, while her mother's back was turned, the girl Mariam smiled at me. At the man she had watched shoot her grandfather! I could have knelt at her feet and wept.

She is a funny little thing. Indeed, all three of them are. I cannot remember seeing such queer-looking children, ugly as little monkeys. It is surprising, with such a comely mother. The father must be unusually hideous. I have seen the camp register, and know that the elder boy, Christiaan, is nine years old, Pieter is seven and Mariam two. On my last day at HQ I tried to sketch them, but their mother snatched the sheet of paper from my book and tore it to shreds.

I think of them at night, in my blockhouse, as I think of you, Arthur, hoping you remember your little brother no less fondly.

Herbert

1904

When we get off the train in Milan, the air tastes of warm dust. The wind is blowing from the south. I squeeze your hand. The cab driver takes us to his sister's *pensione* near Porta Ticinese: 'Very clean, very nice.' We leave our luggage and go straight out again. In Glasgow the shops will be closing. Here, the city is just coming alive. Our little single-decker tram hurtles through the streets, clanking against the rails. I see it first: a great cliff of pink marble luminous against the dimming sky. The tramcar stops, we disembark.

'Can you see her?'

I look up, straining my eyes. 'Can you?'

'*Damn it.*'

'Never mind. She'll still be here tomorrow.'

'There she is.'

The Madonnina stands on her pinnacle, bright gold against the pearly sky, her head in its circle of stars, the gilded column of her throat. Is that really how you see me: the calm blank stare, those open arms?

'What do you suppose she's thinking?' you say.

'"Can I get down now?"'

You tut.

'Or perhaps she's boasting. "Look! No hands!"'

We are in a garden in the sky. A pink marble garden, dense with marble topiary, the roof a gentle slope under our feet.

How quiet it is, apart from the squabs crying in their nests. Keeking through the tracery, I see another roof like a ship's quarterdeck and, beyond, tiny figures on the street. An invisible hand pushes against my breast, strong as a voice saying *No*.

'I thought you could climb like a monkey.'

'I never found a tree two hundred feet high.' I like it when I make you laugh. 'You could have warned me she'd be wearing a bedspread.'

'It's cold up there!'

I turn away.

'You're disappointed?' How easily you read me.

'I thought she'd be more beautiful. She's just there to support the lightning conductor.'

'She's keeping us safe,' you say.

In the afternoon it rains. I write some letters. Sighing and fidgeting, you leaf through your sketchbook. Eventually you leave the room, returning with a pile of clothes.

'Didn't you tell me you used to wear trousers on holiday?'

'As a child.'

'Here you are, then.'

I put down my pen.

When I emerge from the dressing room, your look takes me back to that first night, on the moonlit path at Walter's summer cottage.

You put out your hand as if to introduce yourself. 'Herbert.'

I cannot think of a name.

'Fabio,' you suggest.

We shake hands like men.

The streets are mostly empty, and the few people about too intent on getting out of the wet to notice us. How different I feel in your clothes. I would like to race you along the pavement, only your shoes are much too big for me, even with the heels padded with newspaper. A little boy on the tram tugs

114

at his mother's sleeve. She hisses at him to be quiet. We are poker-faced, but laughing inside. A white dog wags its tail as if in on the joke. By now the West End Park will be a blaze of gold, but the trees in the Giardini Pubblici are still green.

'Here will do,' you say.

In the shelter of an enormous cedar. So dry and dim, we might almost be indoors. You shed your jacket. I do the same.

'And your shoes.'

You roll your shoulders, rise up on the balls of your stockinged feet. Your right hand lashes out to tap my cheek. I give a startled cry. Your left hand taps my other cheek.

'Don't!'

'Stop me, if you don't like it.'

Your white shirt glimmers in the shadows.

'Raise your hands like this. No hitting below the belt.'

I adopt the pose. You lunge, landing the flat of your hand on my shoulder.

'And again!' you say.

I flail at you. You duck away.

'You'll have to be quicker than that.'

You feint towards me, pull back, take half a dozen dancing steps.

Another tap, this one more of a smack. *'Come on!* If we were in earnest I'd have knocked you out by now. Look at you: your chest is wide open.' You jab at me in demonstration. 'And your head.' Another jab. 'Try to block me.'

I dither my hands in a way that makes you smile. I smile too. You smack me in the ribs. 'I make that five hits!'

I try to hit you back, but it's no use. Your blood is up. The faster you move, the more decisively you make contact with your swift, hard pats. They do not hurt exactly, but the humiliation stings. The suddenness of each blow, your panting grin, the triumph in your voice as you keep score: all this is intensely aggravating.

'*Six!... Seven!... Eight!* Wake up!'

I do my best, but you are too quick for me. My patch of ground is uneven underfoot. I wonder if you manoeuvred me towards it deliberately. Each time you parry my attempt at a blow, you laugh.

'*Nine! Ten!*'

My face is hot.

'*Eleven!... Twelve!* Watch me: try to anticipate what I'm going to do.'

With a shriek, I lash out. You block me.

'Better,' you say. '*Thirteen!... Fourteen!*'

I am almost weeping with frustration.

'*Fifteen!* Don't drop your guard!'

And at last, you cut through the years to find the savagery that caused Mother to curtail her children's wilder games. I do not care how ungainly I look, how undignified my gasps and grunts. We have been married nine days and you have done no more than kiss me.

I make contact: a ringing slap on the jaw, less controlled than your pats. My hand smarts, my blood sings.

'Enough,' you say, stepping back. 'I think you were getting the hang of it by the end.'

You take me to lunch at a restaurant in the Piazza Belgioioso. We are the only patrons under the age of sixty. You hope the menu is not tailored to ageing teeth: all consommé, creamed spinach and blancmange. We giggle over our waiter, the very image of Mr Balfour, with his basset-hound eyes and those wings of silvery hair. Today we are conspirators, making fun of everything. The extravagant chandeliers – Signora Ferri would be horrified! The diameter of that woman's hat! The noisy table over there. Professors? I shake my head: second violins from La Scala. You order *caviale, frittelle di pesciolini, ossobuco* and a bottle of Prosecco. I say we will have to go back and sleep all afternoon.

'And why not?' you murmur, with your old smoky look.

116

My pulse quickens, though I am wary, after so many false alarms.

Around us, married couples chew placidly.

I ask, 'Do you think they're still in love?'

'Why shouldn't they be?'

'Don't men marry women for their beauty?'

'Their beauty, the candour in their skin and eyes, their hearts at once so fierce and soft.' Your voice cracks. 'What I'll never understand is why women marry men.'

'Men too can be beautiful.

You laugh.

'What about the young man in the portrait by Licinio – isn't he beautiful?'

'Very, but I have a theory about that. There's no record of Licinio ever marrying. He had a brother, Arrigo, also a painter, and supposedly another, Fabio, who drew maps.'

'Fabio?' I say.

'I believe Licinio married in secret, but his bride was so lovely he feared she'd be taken from him, so he passed her off as this boy, Fabio, and they walked the streets of Venice side by side in doublet and hose. To the world, she was his "brother", his comrade in arms. But in the privacy of their rooms, she was his wife.'

I lean across the table towards you.

People are staring. You sit back, out of reach.

'Anyway,' I say, 'men have a different kind of beauty. Less exquisite, but more durable. I think you will be even more handsome when your hair is grey, your face a little heavier, and all your experience is written in lines around your eyes. You'll go out to lunch with your handsome, noisy friends and the young girl who clears the tables will try to flirt with you.'

'My friends will be handsome too? I must make sure you never meet them.'

'They won't be as good-looking as you.'

The caviar arrives.

117

'Salty,' I say.

'You don't care for it?'

'Knowing it's a delicacy, I like it – but if you told me the poor ate nothing else, I would pity them.'

'What a barbarian you are! Without me to watch you, you'd live on marrons glacés.'

'And Prosecco.' I look into your eyes. 'And love.'

'Which tastes like what?'

'Like I thought caviar would: strange and new and delicious.'

Your eyes lose their shine. 'New,' you echo.

'Well – mysterious. I should like to know you as thoroughly as I know myself, but always to marvel at you as I did the day we left Walter's.'

'Was I so marvellous?'

I take a swig of Prosecco. Too much. It makes me cough. 'At the fencing school, you were so ruthless with your opponent. Then you took off your mask and I realised who this... this *fiend* was. Your hair was damp and curly, and I could taste the faint tang of your sweat in the air.'

I look down at your hand caught in a diagonal of sunlight spilling across the tablecloth. Tiny bubbles float to the surface of my Prosecco. I think, *I will remember this moment for ever*: the elderly clientele, the chandeliers, the two of us a little drunk, talking about love.

I tell you this.

'Am I not enough for you: you need Venetian glass and a roomful of spectators?'

'Of course you're enough, but we live in the world, and so does our love.' I lean forward again, not too far, just enough to be gilded by that slice of sunlight. 'What is it like for you, loving me?'

'Like it was for Licinio, owning a treasure every man in the world wants to steal.' You glare at me, almost as if I were your enemy. 'That table of talkative old men: if I left now, any one of them would come over here. Oh, they'd be

118

gentlemanly about it, offering you their protection, finding a cab to take you home, but in their hearts they'd think only of ravishing you.'

I glance across the restaurant, not altogether displeased by the thought of their secret lust. 'You don't make love sound very enjoyable.'

'With good reason.'

I kick your foot under the table.

'But it's Nature's way. Look at the blackbirds: up at dawn, whistling themselves hoarse to keep their rivals at bay.' You lower your voice, holding my gaze. 'It's very precious to me, knowing no other man has touched you...'

My mouth seems to have forgotten how to smile.

'...knowing you love me with every fibre of your being.'

After the *ossobuco*, the waiter brings us *crema al pistacchio* and brandy and coffee. It is past three o'clock when we emerge into the bright, cold afternoon. We have agreed to take a walk in the Parco Sempione, but first I need to collect my shawl. At the *pensione*, I raise a finger to my lips. You close the heavy street door behind us. There is no sign of the cab driver's sister. Our bedroom is shuttered. The plain deal wardrobe gives off a scent of pine woods, half fragrant, half fusty. I slip off my shoes and feel the chill of the stone floor. Such a strange look in your eyes. It could be longing, or terror. I whisper in your ear, 'Shall we take a siesta?'

Every night since our wedding, you have put on a striped flannel nightshirt. I have worn a nightgown of Swiss cotton. Sometimes I have lain in your arms. Sometimes our bare ankles have touched. You have planted a kiss on my brow before rolling onto your back to sleep. You have never seen me naked.

You pull my hand away from your shirt buttons. I kiss your mouth. The Prosecco helps.

'Catherine...'

'*Ssshhh*,' I whisper. 'Call me Fabio.'

At first I feel less like your lover than your nurse, easing your arms out of the sleeves, unlacing your shoes, laying you down, tugging at your trousers. You permit this, without going so far as to cooperate. I stroke you with my fingertips, learning you by touch, your warmth, the places where your smooth skin cedes to fur. You are not that virile swordsman I thrilled to, any more than I am the Madonnina. We must each find a new self in the other. Your body tenses under my hands. I murmur lovingly until you relax. It is like entering a castle in a fairy tale, opening door after door into chamber after chamber, finding in each room another door with a different lock. Just as I lay my hand on the key, you moan and turn onto your front. So I must start again, stroking the soles of your feet, your hairy calves, the nape of your neck, kissing your spine all the way down to the furry cleft, caressing you until your buttocks no longer clench and I dare to slide a finger between them, making you shudder. And at last I rouse you to passion.

I have thought so often of our kiss in the West End Park, your ragged breath, how you pressed yourself against me, then pulled away, ashamed, hoping I had not understood. I have forced myself to ration this memory lest repetition wear out its delicious potency, fearing it might prove as close as you and I would ever come to bliss. And now I think, *What a mouse I was, eking out my crumbs from the feast.*

Next morning I wake to my monthly bleed, six weeks late.

Dear Arthur,

I presume you have heard the Despot is ill. Lucie writes that Mater is worn out with worry. She has asked me to request compassionate leave, but I can't see what good it would do. The voyage takes three weeks, by which time he will either have rallied or breathed his last.

You will understand if I write little of how the war is going. Regulations aside, I suspect your daily newspaper knows more than any of us. What I can tell you is how ravaged this land is. I find myself thinking of the plagues of Egypt, only instead of frogs and locusts, we have the pom-pom and Lee Enfield. Otherwise it is fairly similar. Fire; hailstorms; livestock carcases littering the veldt, bellies swollen with putrefaction and swarming with flies. Our lads try to despatch them efficiently, but I have seen ewes twitching in agony while their lambs huddle into the steaming entrails for warmth. We have started poisoning the wells, which is quicker than having to round up the herds, and the lack of clean water makes life harder for the enemy.

Six weeks ago Crathie was recalled to HQ, leaving me with command of the section. No sooner had he left than things turned pretty lively. That is just his luck. His weeks in charge here went swimmingly, and the minute he left, a supply train was blown up within sight of us, killing one man and wounding another twenty. The saboteurs got through the wire, despite our sentries. The blame was laid at my door, on account of an order I gave that would have been commended in any other circumstances. Not infrequently, a rat on the wire will trip off our alarms. The sentries react with bursts of gunfire, which are observed by the nearest blockhouses. They too open fire, which spurs on their neighbours, and their neighbours' neighbours, until several miles of the line are blasting away at nothing. It is quite a sight, the veldt all lit up with these fireworks, but it is a deplorable waste of ammunition. On the night in question, the wind got up and our watchman reported the tinkling of tin cans on the wire. I told him to assume they were disturbed by the weather, but to keep his eyes open. Unfortunately, there was no moon.

I had spent that night with Robb's work party and the corporal himself witnessed my end of the telephone call from Captain Hunter. As the day wore on I was aware of the sort of gleeful scandal I remember from school. The men's loyalty is all for Crathie. They are such asses, it did not occur to them that, being under my command, they shared in my disgrace.

I took Solomon on a scouting expedition beyond the furthest extent of the wire, crossing into the Orange River Colony. The wind stirred the reddish grass under a sky that made me think of Mater's painted biscuit tin. I had never felt so aware of the immensity of this land and its utter indifference to mortal concerns. I fell into a sort of trance, thinking of nothing, seeing only the neck of my mount and the pale clouds she snorted into the air. Solomon was shivering, so I gave him my greatcoat. I have written 'thinking of nothing' and yet a part of my mind was musing on how queerly unobtrusive he can be, and how little escapes his notice, and how this must be why Robb and Sillars dislike him so, believing he reports everything to me. When I asked him what my NCOs said behind my back, he did not answer at first, showing me those yellow tusks of his and a wide stripe of his grape-coloured gums. I could see he was calculating how much it was wise to reveal. I ordered him to spit it all out, omitting nothing, and eventually he did.

They said I was a boxer, and Robb would not put money on me in a fight, but Greig said a many a mongrel's bite was as fierce as a bulldog's. And Sillars? I asked. Sillars said mongrels were not born to lead, but everyone knew where they stood with a toff like Lieutenant Crathie. Here Solomon grew cagey. I knew there was more, and had to browbeat him rather until at last he told me, 'They say your mother was a niggah, *sah*.'

When we got back to the line, I told Sergeant Greig the men were grown flabby, both in body and in their mental habits. In future, rum rations would only be issued once a week, and to earn them, every man was to do a half hour's daily sparring practice. The most proficient would compete for a ribbon. This scheme has produced very satisfactory results. On Sunday evenings I put the men through their paces and demonstrate the correct delivery of hook, jab and uppercut. Initially, both corporals proved rather slow at dodging and blocking. I fear I have made Robb's ears ring more than once. The men are now fitter, and their reactions quicker, which can only make them better soldiers. Sillars has shown considerably more mettle since I bloodied his nose and blacked his eye.

Give my best regards to Pensa.

Affectionately,

Herbert

1904

I hoped we might stay a month or two in Milan, but you are anxious to move on. There are so many cities to see: why would we deny ourselves by remaining in one place? I say it is dispiriting to know that the minute we arrive anywhere, you begin planning our departure. You do not reply and, as I am determined to learn wifely tact, I let the matter drop.

We take the train to Perugia.

You want to stay in a rooming house recommended by a swordsman at your club, only your friend did not remember its name, or the name of the square, just that there is a pretty church around the corner. We could take a *carrozza* from the station, but one of us would have to explain this to the driver and, as you find it unmanly to have me do the talking, you prefer to leave our luggage on the platform and walk.

The afternoon is close, the path steep. We have no idea where we are going. At every fork in the road you falter. When we pass a row of shops, I offer to ask for directions. 'No.' *Why not?* 'There's no need.'

Two weeks ago I could speak to any baker or grocer, and now I am a wife who sees the rational course of action but must follow my husband in patent folly. Nor am I permitted to express my reservations, though I know they will be held against me when the error is proved.

We are both sweating in our coats by the time we find the square. The *pensione* is full. The landlady suggests we try her friend in Via Baglioni. Saying this stretches her command of English to the limit. Nothing would be easier than for me to continue the conversation in Italian. I raise my eyebrows at you, and receive a stony look. We resume our wandering through the mazy streets, passing a priest, a peasant leading a donkey, a washerwoman, each of whom would gladly direct us. You insist we are on the right road. As you are so sure, I say, why not indulge me by letting me ask? You will have the satisfaction of being proved right, and I will be spared another half-hour's suspense. Barely controlling your exasperation, you say if I will just show a little patience, by the time we reach that church on the hill we will have our bearings. I think perhaps we will laugh about this later, when you are not so very angry. But the truth is, I am angry too.

'Will it always be like this,' I say, 'you wanting to go one way and me another, and you hating me for it?'

'I don't *hate* you, I just don't see why you have to make such a *fuss* about everything.'

In every *piazza* there are ragamuffin boys eager to conduct a pair of well-dressed strangers through the streets. Any of them would lead us to Via Baglioni, but you wave them away. Perugia brings out a side to you I have only glimpsed before: acutely sensitive to embarrassment, hating the thought of losing face by admitting you are a stranger. You pay a high price for this masculine pride. Over the next few days, I will see strain etched around your mouth when you are doing nothing more taxing than speaking to porters and waiters. They will see it too. Sometimes they will look at me, gauging my reaction, wondering what I am doing with such a man. Loyally, I will bury this knowledge, saying nothing as you labour through the simplest transactions, your supposedly explanatory gestures jagged with frustration.

Next morning, we return to the railway station to find that most of our luggage has gone missing. Only the carpet bags remain, the porter having stowed them in an office, leaving the trunks on the platform. I say this is preposterous, no one could make off with two heavy trunks without attracting attention. The station master shrugs. If we did not want to risk losing our possessions, we should not have left them behind. When I mention the police, he becomes more civil and promises to make enquiries. Even as I thank him, I know this is the last we will hear. All my pretty things gone. The trousseau Mother and I worked so hard to assemble, my beaded oyster satin, our peacock-green quilt. At least I still have Walter's perfume bottle. I notice how pale you have become. Your darting eyes scan the other platforms as if the thieves might be lurking nearby. Of course, the loss of your sketchbooks is a grave blow, and all your clothes, but you seem positively unnerved. You don't even object to me handling the matter in Italian.

Perugia is a working town that goes about its business blind to the antiquities on every side: Etruscan, Roman, mediaeval, Renaissance, rococo, all hugger-mugger on the same small hilltop. Via Baglioni is the next street down from Corso Vanucci, yet our lodgings are plain and clean and inexpensive. Our landlady, Emilia, is quick to show her snaggle-toothed smile and as generous as Signora Ferri was mean. She has a three-year-old grandson, Gianni, a black-eyed imp who would follow me not just around the house, but through every street in town, were his *nonna* not there to restrain him.

Every morning we walk up the hill to see the masterpieces collected in the Palazzo. You unfold your stool. Students with the tight curls of Roman statuary loiter in front of the paintings. When they stray too near, you cover your new sketchbook. Once or twice, I see them smile at this. You are so anxious since our luggage was taken, forever braced against some threat. It makes me ache to watch you. To pass the time, I compose a letter to Phyl, describing the bone-white pallor of travertine walls against the night sky; the local boar stew flavoured with herbs; the pear *crostatini* in

Sandro's *pasticceria*, where the boy wraps our treats in scarlet paper tied with gold ribbon. I wish she were here to see the fourteenth-century nativity painting with the bagpipe-playing shepherd and dog dancing on its hind legs. Or that infant Christ pulling at the Madonna's hair. My favourite shows the baby Jesus sitting on Joseph's shoulders exactly as Gianni is carried by his father. When I draw it to your attention, you say the artist did not care about *people*, only composition, colour and light.

One afternoon we visit San Lorenzo's cathedral. It has the usual mercantile atmosphere: its high ceiling amplifying the hubbub of conversation and the chink of coins in the offertory box. The locals light candles and pray to a statue of the Virgin that reminds me of the mannequins in Cochrane's shop window (albeit with less lifelike fingers). Above the main altar, an exsanguinated Christ is lifted down from the cross amid so much storm and wind he looks seasick rather than crucified. A chapel by the entrance houses the city's most famous relic: a circle of cloudy agate that is claimed to be the Virgin's wedding ring.

We stand behind the red silk rope, a few feet from the gilded reliquary. An elderly Perugian asks if we are English. You nod, so now it is impossible to say I am Scotch. He explains that the reliquary has fifteen locks, each key being kept by a different priest. Once a year the fifteen meet and the treasure is brought out. Newly-weds come to watch, each wife hoping for the honour of trying on the ring, but the privilege is not without risk, for the agate changes colour according to the fidelity of its wearer.

The next day we visit Sant'Angelo, which seems more like a Roman temple than a place of Christian worship. After so many vaulted ceilings teeming with fat *putti*, the sparse interior is balm to my dazzled eyeballs. Just a few fading frescos, a Christ with rolled hair and forked beard, a Madonna whose doughy features are younger than the face of the infant in her lap. So cool and light in here; such colour as there is, muted as a reverential murmur.

'Isn't this more holy than the gilded opulence of San Lorenzo's?' I say. 'God feels closer here, somehow. Maybe the Mohammedans are right, and the divine is cheapened by depiction.'

You walk away to examine a fresco.

'Don't you think?' I wonder if you heard me. 'Herbert?'

'Thank God I lived for thirty-six years without the priggish renunciation of the Scotch Protestant aesthetic.'

Startled, I say an impartial observer would hardly call me ascetic. Do I not commend the loveliness of our surroundings, the ingenuity of Etruscan arch and Roman aqueduct, the genius of dossal and triptych, a hundred times a day?

'No. You don't commend: you *devour*. Everything is gobbled up and chewed to a paste until it no longer bears the slightest resemblance to itself. Then you vomit it up as words.'

'And is that so very different from you turning the world into pictures?'

'It is my living.'

'I see very little evidence of it.'

A low blow. I should not have said it.

We walk back to our lodgings. Another woman would salvage a little restorative solitude from your sulk, but I am never so distractingly aware of you as when we are at odds. In my head I continue the quarrel. The more I delight in a thing, the less capable you seem of taking pleasure in it. Is this my fault? Would you rather I were miserable, and incurious, and hard to please?

Emilia has cooked us a fricassee of minced rabbit. The tension between us makes it hard to swallow.

I am desperate to end the silence, but unable to think of anything to say. At last, I try, 'Why do you hide your drawings in the Palazzo? After all, you're only copying.'

'*Copying?*' you echo.

'Are you not?'

'I'm working up sketches for a painting. I cover the book to stop others stealing my ideas.'

'Oh, Herbert, I'm so glad! I thought you'd... How exciting! You must tell me all about it.'

'I'd rather not. You would have to apply your *intelligence* to it, and that would see off my inspiration.'

Is this really what I am to you: an opinionated flatfoot trampling the delicate flower of your sensibility? 'I sometimes think everything that made you fall in love with me threatens you now we're married.'

You look up from your plate, amazed. 'Why would you say something like that? We've only just got over one quarrel.'

'No we haven't. You've spent the past half-hour sulking. You're angrier with me than ever.'

Emilia arrives to clear away.

You lower your voice. 'I'm sorry to see you're so unhappy with me but, if you recall, you were the one who encouraged me so assiduously in Berkshire. You can hardly blame me for responding...'

Emilia turns and goes back downstairs.

'...I wasn't to know your affections would prove so short-lived. If they were ever real, if you weren't in love with Walter all along, and only dallied with me to ginger up his interest.'

Such a hard look in your eyes. What have I done to make you so resentful? Is it because of what happens in the night?

We do not quarrel continuously; there are peaceable hours. A lunchtime brass band concert in front of the Prefettura, where the sun, filtered through the trees, casts lacework shadows on the biscuit-coloured ground. A windy day when leaf litter whirls in miniature cyclones and laughing students run past us chasing a fugitive hat. A late-evening walk heady with anticipation of the night to come, the sky above us a bowl of blue plums with a creamy pinch of moon. No longer taking these happy moments for granted, I cherish them all the more.

One warm day we make an excursion to a hilltop *castello*. The driver of the *carrozza* asks if we wish him to wait. By now you have picked up enough Italian to get by, if only you would make a joke of your limited vocabulary, but self-mockery is not in your nature. The driver asks again, is he to wait? Not understanding the question, you ignore it. He hands me down from the step and asks for three lire. It is too much, but the price of not speaking Italian is being made to pay *alla Inglese*. 'Two o'clock,' you say, holding up two fingers. Taking this as an attempt to haggle, he empties his face of expression and thrusts out his hand. Again you show him two fingers. 'I think...' I start to say. Your look silences me. You sort through a handful of coins. The driver takes what is offered and spits on the ground at your feet, driving away in a cloud of dust.

You flush with aggravation. 'I suppose he'll come back?'

'I very much doubt it.'

To make matters worse, the castle is shuttered and locked. We make a circuit of the walls and agree it looked more impressive from the hill foot, where it seemed cut from a medieval tapestry. There is a small chapel nearby, little more than a stucco hut with a bell suspended above the pantile roof. A priest emerges, a vigorous man of about your age with thick black hair and an inky beard. I have never seen a holy father smoking a cigarette. He drops it on the ground and looks at me. Were he not sworn to celibacy, I would call his gaze lascivious. He sets off down the road, cassock skirts swishing with each long stride. You give his back a baleful stare. I assume we will follow him down.

'Where do you think you're going?'

To avoid him, you take a zigzagging beaten-earth path that soon peters out. Our descent becomes a scramble, here rock rose, hawthorn, a treacherous tangle of ivy and gnarled roots, there parched earth and stones shifting underfoot.

'Take it slowly,' you say.

But it is your slowness that makes you slither. I am a hare not a tortoise. Better to trust to momentum, taking the slope at a clip, grabbing the odd steadying branch but never quite stopping. When I look over my shoulder, you are fifty yards behind.

There is a pine wood halfway down the hill, dark and cool. Anchoring myself to a tree, I look back. You are still on open ground, your knees locked, your whole body braced with the effort of keeping your footing. Even at this distance, I can see you are annoyed. Sharply you call my name. I am invisible amid the pines. Your head swivels, scanning the hillside. I know why: you think the handsome priest has cut back through the wood to meet me. A double pleasure in this thought: imagining myself and the priest, skirt to skirt, mouth to mouth, and imagining you watching. On a reckless impulse, I start to run. It is like being a girl again, the daredevil girl I used to be, hurtling too fast over ground too steep. There is a patch of sunlit earth where the trees have been felled. You catch sight of me, shouting at me to wait. I sprint towards the next clump of pines, taking cover behind the thickest trunk, catching my breath. You have reached the outskirts of the wood, close enough now for me to see the twist of fright in your rage. My heart goes out to you, but I am frightened too. Why are you so angry? It is only a game, like the game we played in the park in Milan. Only now I have the advantage. I break cover, running headlong. You see me, but can only inch down the hill in old-ladyish pursuit. A giggle escapes me. I reach another stand of trees, stop, then run, stop, run. I cannot remember when I last laughed like this, helpless against the waves of hilarity. And at last, provoked to recklessness, you give chase, running, slithering, breathless, cursing, blind with fury, bellowing at me to wait, until you trip on a root, to break your fall, face first, against a pine.

Now it is not funny at all.

By the time I arrive, you are on your feet again. Your left eye is closing. Blood trickles down your cheek.

'Are you all right?'

You turn towards me. I notice the quiet of the wood, the lack of birdsong or insect buzz.

Back at Via Baglioni you call me thoughtless and selfish. I am not a child, and should stop behaving like one. I could have fallen and been badly hurt. A nice honeymoon we would have had with me on crutches. When you call me, you do so for a reason: you expect me to obey. I stare at the floor, remembering what happened amid the pines, the force you put into that push, jarring the back of my head against a tree, bouncing my brain in my skull.

Dear Arthur,

I received your letter this morning. You are ahead of me with news from Lucie. I am glad to hear the Despot is on the mend, but he is well over his Biblical three score years and ten. We must expect more of these attacks.

Things have been rather dull here for a couple of months – and latterly, anything but. Ten days ago I was roused from sleep to find the Boer had set fire to the veldt and the wind was driving the flames towards us. I told the men to pick up their shovels and dig a firebreak. Attempting to pass this order down the line, I found our telegraph wires had been cut.

The trench did its job and the fire burned itself out, but we had the stink of it in our nostrils for days. I told Solomon to reassure his fellows that lightning never strikes in the same place twice, but three of them ran off. A couple of days later I was informed of a problem back at the blockhouse where I was quartered. Sillars had ordered a native to be stripped and bound to the wheel of a wagon, ready to be flogged at first light. I returned at dusk to discover the man was Solomon. When I asked his offence, Sillars said it was theft from my own possessions. I tell you, Arthur, I felt sick to my stomach. One hears talk about the dishonesty of the natives, but I had thought Solomon of another ilk. I could not stand the thought that he had taken advantage of my good nature to make me his dupe. I asked him if what the second corporal said was true, and he denied it. He had the inward look he wears when baited by my men, like a suffering Jesus. I told him to speak up and tell me his side of it, but he said nothing more. His lips were cracked and swollen, and crusted with a dark matter I realised was blood. There was a revolting stench and, looking down, I saw that he had soiled himself. I asked how long he had been tethered like this. Since he was caught red-handed, I was told: nine hours.

I asked what he had stolen, and Sillars smiled in a repulsively sly manner. Drawings, he said. What drawings? 'Of ladies, sir.' He meant my studies of Johanna, and some sketches I had done to keep my hand in: recollections of the models in my life-drawing class. Well, then I knew it was I myself who was Sillars's target, and my scout merely the unfortunate proxy. I gave orders that he was to be untied and taken inside the blockhouse. I excused him from duty next day, leaving him to sleep until the afternoon, when I brought him a tot of rum. His account was rather more plausible than the version I had been given: it was Sillars who had been rifling through my belongings and Solomon who had caught him at it. When I told him I believed him, he said, 'But yesterday you believed Corporal Sillars, *sah*.' I had an impulse to beg his forgiveness, although of course I did not. It galled me that I could not punish Sillars, but I had the morale of the section to consider. I did not think the men would wear me taking the word of a black fellow against their second corporal.

Today, quite out of the blue, Crathie turned up with papers calling me back to HQ. He is taking over command here. I am to get myself to Vereeniging Station. A supply train will carry me the rest of the way. No reason was given. I will take Solomon with me and write again as soon as I know more.

Yours, as ever,
Herbert

1904

Gianni sits on my knee. As you do not like us speaking Italian, I am teaching him English. *Cup. Plate. Fork. Butter.* You say we must leave Via Baglioni.

'Butter.'

'*But-ter.*'

'You don't want to know why?'

'I already know,' I say. 'You're jealous of your three-year-old rival.'

Your voice drops to a hiss. 'Do you notice nothing? They were watching us from the roof when we came in last night.'

You have not mentioned your enemies for several days.

'They signalled a warning to their accomplice, who was inside searching our closets.'

Gianni listens intently, not understanding a word. He lifts his solemn eyes to mine. I pull a comical face. He giggles. You slam your hand down on the table.

'Does it strike you as funny?'

Gianni starts to cry. I take him down to his *nonna*.

When I return, you tell me they are everywhere, a network of informants monitoring our every move, signalling to each other with winks and smiles, or waving handkerchiefs when we pass. Yesterday, a youth with a bugle. Oh, they are resourceful, recruiting children, and waiters, and engine drivers. Do I not remember the whistle when we boarded the train in Milan? They coordinate their efforts via coded articles in the newspapers.

Is it now, my first doubt? Or have I known for weeks, keeping the knowledge like a locked room? All at once the door is ajar, but I am not ready to go in, not yet. I say you are quite worn out by your troubles. I will be more vigilant in future, but you must promise to be more relaxed. Try to enjoy this beautiful place. After all, there may be an innocent explanation.

'I see,' you say. 'You're with them too.'

Most days we wake to a faerie world painted in shades of white, a lilac brightness behind the mist. By eleven, the veil is gone, leaving a high blue sky with floury smears. Snails have left their glinting silver scribble on the paths overnight. The sun is so low that, as we walk east, the street flickers through my squinting lashes. The trees in the Giardino del Frontone glow the greeny-gold of old brass.

How lucky we are with this never-ending autumn. I can hardly remember my spinster self, and yet the sun shines as warmly as the day we met.

Early morning. I am in Emilia's kitchen playing with Gianni. She shouts for me. I rush upstairs to find you in a tangle of sweaty sheets. When I touch my hand to your brow, you cry out.

These nightmares afflict you two or three times a week. You speak, not coherently, but saying enough for me to gather that you are in Africa, there are others around you, something terrible is about to happen. Today you are not merely distressed, but in pain. When I sponge your brow, you flinch. I bring a glass of water to your lips. You gag. All this time your eyes are closed. I ask, is there anything I can do? You shake your head, then groan at the motion. Suddenly you get out of bed, pushing past me, stumbling to the basin where you retch violently, although there is nothing in your stomach but bile.

Emilia and I make the bed with clean sheets. I smooth the covers over you, hoping you will wake restored. You thank me for my *kind wishes*, but by now you are familiar with these attacks: you will be sick again, and afterwards will feel just enough relief to fall into another sleep, from which the pain will wake you, and on and on it will go until the evening, when, God willing, the bout will have run its course. I am to sit in the other room, silently, having closed all the shutters. Any disturbance, even a sliver of light under the door, will aggravate the pain.

Downstairs, Emilia gives me directions to Dottore Bianchini's office.

The doctor is the first bald man I have seen in this hirsute city. His apartment, with its framed copy of Botticelli's *Primavera*, reminds me of my home in Glasgow – my former home. I have no home now, other than you. The doctor invites me to sit down. A little information now will save time later. I describe your sensitivity to light, your inability to hold down food or drink. He asks what brings this on: cheese, port, cigars, game, thundery weather? I consider and reject them all. He tips his head on one side. Real or fancied worries? I meet his eye. He wants to know how I would describe you: sanguine, choleric, phlegmatic, melancholic?

The cockatiel in the corner gives a piercing screech. I jump. The doctor drapes a chenille over the cage.

'A vigorous man,' I say, 'yet not altogether strong. His speech is quiet but...'

The doctor nods encouragingly. '*Sì?*'

'But he's not always as calm as he seems. Once he has an idea in his head, it's hard to dissuade him. At times he...'

'*Diventa tiranno?*'

'*Sì.*'

I have dismissed this thought so many times, yet in the

mouth of a stranger, your tyranny takes on the colour of objective fact.

I am ashamed to let the doctor into our rooms. The stink of vomit, the china basin by the bed with its spoonful of yellow bile. When you see I am not alone, you grow still as a cornered animal. Dottore Bianchini brings a chair to the bedside. As he speaks no English, I must translate. How long have you had these headaches? Do certain thoughts bring them on? You refuse to reply, or even to look at me. The doctor tells you the cycle of nausea and sleeping must be broken. He takes out a powder, stirring a spoonful into a glass of water. You are to take a small sip every few minutes. If you feel bilious, you are to wait for the feeling to pass. On no account must you give in to it. I take some lire from your dressing room and show him out.

'Pour it away,' you say when I get back.

'It'll make you feel better.'

'It will weaken me, if it doesn't kill me.'

I touch your fiery brow. You move your head away. You are sorry to deprive me of the chance to play ministering angel, but if I really wanted to help you, I would not have invited Death into our bedchamber. You cannot believe how easily I have been duped. '*Oh bella Signora. Your husband ees a lucky man: such a beeyootiful wooman and so eentelligent...*'

I tell you this childishness insults us both.

'You're so greedy for flattery you can't see what's staring you in the face. *He is in league with our enemies.*'

I bring the glass to my lips. 'If it's deadly, I'll die first.'

Your arm shoots out from under the covers. Shocked, I misunderstand, but it was the glass you struck, not me. There it is at my feet, miraculously unbroken, its contents a puddle on the floor.

Mid-afternoon. You have been sick again, and are sleeping. The minute I step into the street it begins to rain. At least it is dry in San Lorenzo's, with a comfortable buzz of talk, the smell of incense and wet coats. The Virgin's jewelled crown winks under the electric lights. I have a sudden whim to light a candle.

The tiered rows of flames give off a surprising heat. I feel so Protestant my hand shakes. Should I make my wish at the instant the wick catches? I cannot quite put it into words, and now it is too late. The flame wavers in the draught, thickening and narrowing around its colourless heart. My eyes blur with tears. How silly. What is there to cry about? Just these people so at home here, and the little golden flame flickering so bravely.

'Mrs Jackson?'

I jump, ready to explain that I will come back tomorrow with money for my candle. The American I met on the Bellagio lakefront is standing beside me. That plume of hair like bright blue smoke.

'Richard Moretti,' he says.

'Of course.' I offer him my hand, then have second thoughts. 'Perhaps it's not done to shake hands in here?'

'We'll have to see if they throw us out.'

We walk away from the kneeling supplicants. His frivolous remark has put me so at ease, I almost take his arm.

'You're a Roman Catholic?'

'Oh no,' I say, as if the idea were too absurd, then realise he saw me lighting the candle. 'When in Rome...'

'And did it help?'

Tears spill down my cheeks.

'I'm sorry.' My voice high and quavery, my hand rising to my face, adding to the spectacle.

He touches a tactful finger to my elbow and steers me across to the chapel containing the Virgin's ring. We stand at the silken rope, with our backs to the cathedral. To my relief, he does not ask what is wrong. I sneak a sidelong glance at him. Time has loosened the flesh under his jaw and thatched his eyebrows untidily, but the eyes themselves are clear and steady, and his clothes are beautiful.

'Impressive,' he says, meaning the gilded reliquary.

'I'm not sure Joseph of Arimathea would recognise the ring.'

'A doubting Thomas? Next you'll be telling me you don't believe it changes colour.'

'If it doesn't, it should.'

His mouth prepares to laugh, expecting a sally.

'Love changes from hour to hour.' *Too candid*, I think, especially after tears, but now I remember: he claims to prize truth above all. 'Before my wedding, I thought marrying would make me perfect.'

'And now?'

'Women are the powerless sex. We learn to please our masters from the cradle. Fathers, professors, husbands. It doesn't make us false, or not necessarily, but nor are we as *fixed* as men are.'

'Unless secured with fifteen locks.'

We both look at the reliquary.

I say, 'I hated it on sight without understanding why.'

You are waiting in the darkened sitting room when I get back.

'Are you feeling better?'

'Yes,' you drawl, 'I'm sorry about that.'

'I don't understand.'

'There'll be no more sneaking out to meet your lover.'

I go to hang my coat in the dressing room. All the drawers are open. My new dresses have been pulled from the rail. I rehang them.

'If you must ransack my clothes, can you please put them back afterwards?'

You smile as if this were some footling attempt to change the subject. 'I heard him in there.'

'Who?'

'Who do you think? Your lover.'

You have not accused me of adultery before.

'And did you find this lover of mine when you searched the cupboard?'

'He heard me stirring and made a run for it.'

'You saw him?'

'He was too quick.'

'Shall we ask Emilia if she saw him?' This is sheer bluff. I do my utmost to keep Emilia in ignorance of our difficulties.

'What's the point? She'll say whatever you tell her to.'

I go into the bedroom and open the window, pull back the covers to air the sheets, pick your nightshirt off the floor, and return to the sitting room.

'You know there is no lover.'

Which is just what you hoped I would say.

'No lover?'

I have the strangest feeling under my arms.

'*No lover?*' you repeat more distinctly. Your right hand is clenched in a fist. 'Then who gave you this?'

In your palm sits Walter's perfume bottle. You must have searched thoroughly. I had wrapped it in a handkerchief and tucked it at the back of one of the drawers.

You raise your eyebrows. I say nothing.

You get up and cross to the open window, holding it between forefinger and thumb. Just above the horizon, a crack has opened in the clouds. Touched by the pinchbeck rays of the setting sun, the swirls of purple and green glass seem even lovelier than they did in Kensington. You move your hand beyond the sill, watching my face.

'Give it back.'

'If you tell me who gave it to you.'

'It wasn't a lover. I have no lover.'

'Then it can't matter if you tell me.'

Richard Moretti's face appears before my mind's eye. A

slight furrow forms between his untidy brows, but his eyes have perfect confidence in me.

'It was a wedding present from Walter.'

'Thank you,' you say mildly, bringing your hand back inside. My breathing eases. You walk over to the fireplace and hurl the bottle at the hearth, where it smashes. I hear the tinkling fragments bouncing on the stone, a faint creak as the brass collar rolls from side to side.

You look at me like a chess player inviting my next move.

I nearly say it: *I could kill you.*

'Catherine! Come back here!'

I run down six flights of stairs and out to the street.

Some of the men you believe are in love with me: Gianni's father; the vice-consul who lent me his hymnal during English matins at the Hotel Grande Bretagne; the consumptive-looking youth we buy stamps from at the post office; the red-haired student playing his violin outside the Conservatorio; any number of diners at the Ristorante Progresso.

This being Italy, how can I swear they have not noticed me? But if they did, it was only to forget me as soon as the next pretty girl crossed their path. I am the one who remembers, hoarding their glances like treasure.

The garden terrace overlooking the north of the city is deserted. I thank the rain for that, even if I am soaked through. There is a circle of dry ground under the tallest laurel, whose trunk is almost warm through my wet dress. For a moment I am three years old again, wrapping myself around Father's leg, taking an odd kind of comfort in the pattering sound of the rain above me. Scratch of bark. Smell of wet leaves and thirsty earth.

I wish I had never set eyes on you.

I mean this with all my heart, yet it means nothing. We are husband and wife. Already you know me better than

142

any man alive. Of course the accusation that I have taken a lover is nonsense, but why did you choose today to make it? I was so glad to see Richard Moretti, so stimulated by our brief conversation, so restored to myself. Somehow you sensed this. You have a preternatural instinct for anything that draws my attention away from you: Phyl's letters; the handsome priest; a splay-pawed puppy straining on the leash. You would like to smash them all as you smashed Walter's pretty bottle. When you are sketching and I loiter aimlessly, waiting for you to finish, you pull on my jesses at the exact moment my thoughts take wing. Did you not decide to leave Bellagio the very day Richard introduced himself?

I wish Phyl were here to tell me I am imagining this.

Dear Arthur,

I hope you and Pensa managed a proper Christmas out there. Mine was decidedly queer: biltong for lunch and a carol service in the sweltering dusk with the men all slapping at mosquitoes.

Things got very bad here in the months I was down in the ORC. I hardly recognised the place on my return. The Boer ambush so many supply trains, we have scarcely enough food for the troops, let alone anyone else. My days are spent supervising the digging of mass graves near the refugee camp, where a dysentery epidemic rages unchecked. I called there the day I got back. After so long away, I expected to find Mariam grown, but she was smaller, slighter, lost within her clothes, with the shrivelled face of a tiny crone. Johanna too was changed, her eyes dull in shadowy sockets, her face little better than a skull. When I said her name she shooed the children into their tent, pulling the flap shut behind her. Retracing my steps through the camp, I took a good look around. It was like walking through Hell. Many of the children have fared worse than Johanna's. Their shoulders, knees and ankles seem monstrously swollen, the flesh having fallen from their bones. Some are toothless from scurvy. The worst cases have lost their palates too.

A day or so later I was in town with Solomon, supplementing our rations from the shops. I saw Johanna across the street, that filthy dress she has worn for months drawing stares from the civilian ladies. Solomon was less surprised to see her. He told me the refugees with money obtain passes into town, buying a little more than they need to trade when they get back to camp. When I said we both knew Johanna had no money, he returned that infuriatingly secretive look of his. I said he had better explain, it would go worse for him if I found out later, so then he told me: 'Men pay her, *sah*.' She is not the only one. Every half-presentable woman under the age of thirty has done it. There is an old Dutch farmer who gives her the odd shilling, and the camp superintendent is rumoured to put extra salt and coffee in her weekly ration. By the time Solomon had finished his grim report, she had disappeared.

That afternoon I went to the refugee camp. She wasn't about, although the day was very warm and most people were outside. For the first time I entered her tent. It was sweltering in there and the stink was appalling. Johanna was sitting on the ground, mending a shirt, with the children crouched behind her, using sticks to draw in the dirt. I told her I would have given her money, had she asked. Her knowing smile made my blood boil. When I said I would not have expected anything in return, she replied, 'You mean you want what I have to sell, but you do not want to pay for it.'

I tell you, Arthur, I could have struck her. Struck her, or pressed her down on that bare earth floor and taken some recompense for all the kindness I have shown her family. I said she must have laughed long and heartily to have chanced upon such a fool as myself. She answered sarcastically. What good luck I had brought her! Her father killed, her home burned, her children starved, her honour sold for a few cups of meal. And now we had found a new trick to play on her. She opened a twist of brown paper: her sugar ration. I noticed a few blueish specks amid the dark brown. She said it was bluestone vitriol. The previous week, ground glass. When I looked at her as if she were mad, she shouted, 'You are poisoning us! You burned our pasture and slaughtered our herds and took us off the veldt "for our own protection", and now we are too heavy a burden. You cannot feed and clothe us and tend our sick and hungry children, but nor can you send us back to our roofless farms: the world would see you for the brutes you are. So you let the children sicken or starve, and the rest of us you give a little push, because it would suit you very well if every last one of us died out.'

I was not about to dignify such arrant nonsense by denying it, so I asked why she slept on the ground. She laughed in my face, leading me out of her tent into that of her neighbour, and then her neighbour's neighbour, and she would have continued to the end of the row, had I not resisted. Each was the same. I asked what they did when it rained. 'We sleep in the mud.' I said I would find her two camp beds, which was all the tent would accommodate. She and Mariam could share one, and the boys lie top and tail in the other. She asked if I was going to get beds for Hannah and her children, and Trude and her children, and Sophie, and Anna? Of course not: it would be the devil's own job to get my hands on two. In that case, she said, she would have to guard her tent or someone would steal them, and most likely burn them for fuel, and even if she managed to keep hold of them her friends would call her the Englishman's whore, her children would be shunned at the morning school they ran among themselves, and her days would be even more miserable than they were presently.

What could I say? She was cutting off her nose to spite her face, to spite *me*. I left the camp and have not been back, but I am haunted by the wizened faces of her children and the desperation I saw in her eyes. Tell me, Arthur, what would you have done in my shoes?

Herbert

1904

In late November we leave Perugia for Florence.

By now your grasp of Italian is good enough to order in restaurants and buy writing paper and stamps. With anything more complicated, you stiffen in what I recognise as self-consciousness; to others, you seem coldly aloof. All Florentines are proud. I watch as the face of the waiter or shopkeeper freezes into a mask. I miss Emilia and our old thoughtless chatter. Here I speak only English, and only to you.

Some days we get through three courses at lunch without exchanging a word, surrounded by a dozen voluble conversations. I would eavesdrop, but your will is like a high wall, sealing me off from our neighbours. On the street you hold my hand so tightly that we draw curious glances. I bump into an old lady. You call me clumsy. Can I not look where I am going? But to steer an unimpeded course down the street I would have to wrench my hand from yours and free my thoughts from their anxious awareness of you, and that you would never allow. If I say this, you will call me absurd. We will quarrel. I will pay for my candour with hours of misery. So I say nothing. Unchallenged, your view of me infects my own. I *am* clumsy, and absurd. Italian men no longer look at me. I catch my reflection in the mirrored glass behind a chemist's counter: a pinched, plain, dull-eyed woman. Her expression reminds me of you.

One morning we climb the four hundred and sixty steps to the balcony above Santa Maria del Fiore. In the piazza below us, tiny people trail long, off-centre shadows. I envy their lives, so small and complete and perfect. Faint sounds reach us. The voices of children, chanting priests on their way to Mass. How steeply the curve of the dome falls away. How easy it would be to climb over the metal balustrade and pitch myself forward.

We emerge from the darkened stairwell into the brilliance of the square. Waiters plump as bullocks loiter in café doorways. Blinkered horses stand patient while the *tassisti* flirt with pretty girls. They belong here, the blood runs red in their veins, while you and I are pale ghosts haunting the past.

Our lodgings overlook the Ponte Vecchio. You roll back the rugs, seeking the trapdoor you are sure our landlord Tommaso uses to gain entry when we go out. There are two walk-in closets with hooks on the walls. Every night you search mine for the lover hiding behind my clothes. You retire early and will not hear of me staying up. I cannot afford to turn this into a battle – what if you guess? (*How can you not guess?*) So I come to bed. The mattress pitches as you climb in beside me. You put out the lamp. The blackness is absolute.

I cough and turn over.

You sigh.

'Sorry,' I say, and cough again.

'*Catherine.*'

We lie with a modest few inches of mattress between us. It may not happen for an hour or more, but I have learned to stay awake. Being dragged out of sleep is worse. Those first moments of not knowing who or what or where I am.

I cannot recall when my skin last tingled at the thought of the night ahead. The reasons I give for wanting to stay up, the hundred-and-one little tasks that *cannot wait*, are not entirely pretexts, but dread swims beneath them. It can only be a matter of time before you notice my loss of feeling.

How we lie to ourselves.

I *feel*. Ah, God, if only I did not.

You touch me and, like Alice, I shrink to a smallness in infinite space. Such loneliness, estranged from you and from myself. I am not my corpse, this bundle of organs wrapped in skin, but still my flesh crawls. Your fingers are razorblades flaying me in fine strips. My hands clench against the urge to push you off. You are everywhere, above, below, inside and out, your heat, your smell, your breath... but where am I? Can the self vanish, leaving nothing but this twitching husk? *What is the matter with me?* You buck and groan. And sleep, thank God.

You are teaching me to draw. I want to capture the view from our window but you tell me that would be running before I can walk. I have a clumsy hand and no idea how to look. The first exercise you set me is a cut loaf. I sketch it along with the board it sits on, the knife beside it, the table and a stretch of wall. You take your pencil and strike jagged lines through everything but the bread.

'Try again.'

And I do try, studying the crust and the greyish crumb, the little pockets of air, the way its just-cut yielding stales so quickly. Perhaps I need a new way of looking to adjust to being a wife. I make the mistake of saying this, rousing you to a contempt tinged with fury.

'Can you not let one thing in God's creation just be itself? Do you have to torture everything into meaning?'

You want me to be just like you, I think. To see the world like you. To draw it like you. Only not so proficiently.

My education continues in the Uffizi Galleries, where the custodians hang grey net at the windows to protect the masterpieces from sunlight. I thought I had seen every last canvas, but I have not been in this room before. A master is trying to instruct an unruly class of schoolboys. I turn away, to find myself standing in front of Piero della Francesca's twin portraits of the Duke and Duchess of Urbino.

They are painted in profile on separate panels joined by a single frame so that they seem to be facing each other, trapped in their terrible intimacy for all eternity. Adjacency makes opposites of them, his skin darkly weathered, hers the deathly pallor of a goose egg. He is ugly, powerful, dressed in red like his bloody appetites, rapacity in the hatchet of his nose, the girth of his neck, the fleshy moles on his cheek. Somehow the woman before him deforms his nature to make him coldly exacting. Disapproval is etched in the set of his mouth, sarcasm in the lift of his brows. Instinctively, I would take her side, but she is so hard to pity. Such composure in her subjection, such withholding. Under those demurely hooded eyelids, her stare is quite level. Her eyes, pale as ice, seem to say, *Yes, I submit, but you will get no joy of it.*

'You've been standing here for ten minutes.'

You are tense. I knew it before you spoke. Intuition threads between us like the webs of barbed wire you strung across the African veldt.

'There are better portraits,' you say, 'works of genius.'

But I cannot take my eyes off the duke and his duchess. 'Have you ever seen two people who hate each other more?'

'You read too much into it. It's just a dynastic portrait.'

'Of a couple who should never have married.'

You look away from the paintings, to me. 'Is that what you see?'

'She steals the light from his face, drains it of vitality. Yet if you look at him first, he bleeds her white.' A tremor in my voice. 'They're destroying each other.'

'Why are you saying this?'

'Don't you see it?'

'Who would you rather have married?' you hiss. 'Some old brute who'd leave you to your own devices all day, and then ravish you at night? Is that what you want? Or would you have taken Walter, only he wasn't available? How much more fun you'd be having with him, spouting your pretentious rubbish at each other.'

Always this scintilla of truth in your grotesque accusations.

I say, 'When did you stop loving me?'

'Oh no, it is you who stopped, if you ever loved me in the first place.'

How will we get through the rest of our lives?

'Here it comes,' you say in disgust, 'the waterworks.'

'Please, Herbert.'

'Don't make this into my doing. How did you think I was going to respond?'

'I was talking about the painting.'

'Why don't you tell the truth, for once?'

'Because you prefer lies.'

Your face empties of expression. You walk away, into the next room. I stay rooted to the spot, waiting for the spectators to move on.

When at last I stir, you are nowhere to be found. You have never left without me before. I am frightened, but also excited. I have spent so long trying to forestall the worst. Let it come.

You are waiting at our lodgings. You stalk into the bedroom, slamming the door. I take off my coat and open the copy of *Middlemarch* I have been trying to read ever since we left England. The print dances before my eyes. You emerge from the bedroom and stand over me, arms folded.

'Do you have anything to say to me?'

I look up.

'Do you think it's right to talk to me like that in front of all those people?'

'I didn't set out to—'

You cut me off. 'You don't think it's right? Then what have you got to say?'

You are talking to me as if I were an errant child.

'You refuse to apologise?'

I pretend to read my book, waiting for you to tear it out of my hands.

Quietly, you say, 'If I died tomorrow you would be free of me.'

I look up, astonished.

'Don't tell me it hasn't occurred to you.'

'Why would you *die*?'

'There are people it would suit very well; it may be you are one of them.'

My heart clangs.

'If I met with an *accident*, you'd be a free woman again, but with a widow's respectability, able to go where you please unchaperoned – *do* as you please. And with five hundred pounds' insurance money.'

I remember how I thought of falling from the Duomo. Is it normal for newly-weds to be preoccupied with death?

'I thought you would at least pretend to be appalled,' you say.

I imagine your flesh cold beneath its fur, the smoky light of your gaze forever extinguished. Never again to hear that crack in your voice. Tears stand in my eyes. 'Of course I don't want you to die.'

But behind my distress, an inner voice says, *He doesn't mean a word of it. It is just his latest weapon in the war between us.*

We get past this quarrel, and the following evening, at supper, I ask you if we will settle in Florence? Much as I enjoy the roaming life, it may soon be necessary to make a permanent home. Somewhere comfortable, and affordable, where you can find paid work.

'Why?'

'Can't you guess?'

You look up from your plate.

'We may have a child.'

'Impossible.'

Such an unexpected reply, I hardly know what to say.

'I thought you wanted children.'

'My wishes don't come into it.'

I laugh softly, remembering too late how you hate this.

'It's women who arrange these things, while their damn-fool husbands accept who knows whose bastard...'

I sigh.

'You don't deny it, then?'

'I am not about to present you with someone else's child.'

'You'd be well advised not to.'

'I haven't looked at another man since the day we married.'

'If that is true, we have no need to settle anywhere.'

'And if I conceive a child?'

'Then I shall know.'

'Know what?'

'That you have a lover.'

'I don't need a lover – I have you.'

'And I am not a fool.'

I am so tired of this wrangling, I could sleep for a thousand years. 'I am never out of your sight.'

'And how you long to escape me.'

'Sometimes I do. I can't really think about anything when I'm with you...' A new possibility occurs to me. 'Are you telling me there is something medically wrong with you?'

'I'm starting to find this conversation distinctly unsavoury.'

'Have you been told by a doctor—'

'Enough!'

I flinch as from a blow, though it is only your jabbing finger.

'*I will not accept another man's child.*'

We carry on eating our supper.

All at once you spring up from the table and cross to the

window. You have heard someone on the roof. The next thing I know, you are out on the veranda, balancing on the wooden balustrade.

'We're five floors up. You'll break your neck!'

'I shall if you don't leave me alone.'

You reach up to grip the overhanging eaves. For all your strength, the angle defeats you. You can only lift yourself so far. Your feet dangle above the balustrade, your whole body quivering with strain.

'Herbert—'

You scream, *'Shut up!'*

You must know you cannot do it, but the more I urge you to see reason, the more determined you become. I cannot bear to watch. You will kill yourself out of rage. Rage, and grandiosity. This obsessive belief that you are beset by enemies. You refuse to give it up – you would rather give up your peace of mind, our love, even your life. We both liked the romance of a conspiracy against you. The pistol under your pillow; the muttering in darkened railway carriages that was almost as delicious as kissing. But the truth is, no one cares what you do.

I return to the sitting room. A few minutes later, you join me.

'They got away,' you say.

Dear Arthur,

Much thanks for your letters. I got the second ahead of the first, and so received your reassurance before knowing Pensa was unwell, a very satisfactory way of hearing bad news. I am sorry this silence of mine has worried you. What I have to tell you would never have got past the censor. I will be entrusting this letter to a fortunate fellow certified unfit for duty. He is sailing tomorrow and will post it from Southampton.

For months they have been assuring us the war is nearly over, but I see no evidence of it. It could go on like this for years, the mounted columns sweeping up a few Boers here and there, the rest escaping through the wire, which is accounted our fault as Engineers and nothing to do with General Kitchener's crack-brained scheme to turn half the continent into a sieve. At any moment of night or day, three-quarters of our men are roaring drunk. There is the odd skirmish. Our officers surrender, knowing the Boer has no way of keeping them prisoner, and thinking nothing of the disgrace so long as they are spared a Mauser's bullet. They slink back to their regiments naked as the day they were born, stripped of boots and uniforms by an enemy so short of clothes they cover themselves with dresses and poke bonnets. Our commander-in-chief is rumoured to be in the throes of a nervous breakdown. They say he keeps a caged starling he found up a chimney, and cares more for that bird than for all the quarter of a million men at his disposal.

Are you shocked, Arthur? Believe me, this is not the half of it, but I must get on with my own tale.

There was nothing happened under my command that was not reported back to Crathie. The gossip circulated among his brother officers, and somewhere along the chain all sorts of unsavoury rumours were added. I had no inkling of this until

Captain Hunter summoned me to ask why I was consorting with an enemy spy. I questioned Solomon, who admitted he had worked for the Boers in the Free State, but swore he owed them no loyalty. They treated him brutally and, furthermore, were farming land stolen from his forefathers. I made it known that if I heard any man speaking ill of him, the fellow would regret it. Far from quelling the scandal, this only encouraged new and beastlier lies about the supposed 'liberties' I permitted my black servant.

I now believe I was recalled to HQ on the Despot's account. The army is terrified of anyone with the influence to turn the tide of support at home. There is usually a copy of the *Illustrated London News* in the officers' mess. Every so often Captain Hunter will ask what I thought of this or that article, his casual tone belied by a piercing look. When I say (truly) that I have not seen it, he thinks me devious as well as disloyal.

My section returned here in late January. I should say, Crathie's section. Sillars has been his man and boy, having worked as a fitter at his family's shipyard. He and Robb bore me a grudge from the start, simply because I was not Bill Crathie. Greig I think more honourable, and it has cost him a mention in despatches. I wish you were here, Arthur. We would spend a day with them, keeping our own counsel, and when we retired I would ask you, are they so much worse than other men? It may be we are all fiends when the wind blows from the wrong direction. All except Crathie, who is irreproachable in every way. That is his genius.

I have mentioned the sickness in the refugee camp – ha! See how the habits of censorship are ingrained in me. I mean, of course, the concentration camp. At first, disease carried off the weak and, while cruel, this has always been nature's way, but the weak have been gone for months now, and still they die. I have been in the habit of going there every morning, and cannot remember a day when I did not have to vary my route through the rows of tents to avoid one or more makeshift

156

funerals. The chief culprits are dysentery and enteric, but measles has attacked a fair few, and hunger finishes them off.

You will guess what drew me there. Johanna's ability to buy extra rations was short-lived. No one wants to take his pleasure with a whore three-quarters starved. For weeks I saw nothing of her. She had made it very plain how unwelcome my kindnesses were. But at last, she had to throw herself on my mercy. She was a sorry sight, her face tallowy, her hair lank, her dress so grimy it was hard to remember what colour it had been the day I first saw her. Had she come to me in such a state a year ago, I would have vowed to horsewhip those responsible, but who is to blame? The Boers for hiding behind their women's skirts? Or did the women bring it on themselves by taking the role of quartermaster? She would say we British are the guilty party, yet she had to beg me to spare her children's lives. I watched her swallow the remnants of that pride of hers, purging the hate from her eyes. To be honest, I loathed her no less: for what the war had done to her, and for what she in her desperation did to herself.

I gave her a couple of mealie cobs from Solomon's sack. She wept with relief, bringing my hand to her lips to kiss. I pulled away and she saw the revulsion in my face. After that, she understood the terms of my assistance. We were to return to our earlier relations. No smiles or words of gratitude. Daily I went across to the camp with what little I could scavenge from the stores, always handing it to the children. I had to steel myself not to flinch at the once-soft skin drawn so tight across Mariam's bones.

It had been a long time since I had sketched anything. There is an accuracy of looking when one draws. Mostly I walk around with my eyes half-shut. Who would choose to see these once plump and rosy children brittle as matchwood, their ears enormous on the sides of their shrunken heads, their eyes dark pits of incomprehension and reproach? If it is hard to see their misery, it is worse when they smile, their gums protruding out of their grey little faces. Formerly they scampered, now they sit, listless, on the damp ground. They must have told their mother what I was doing, but she did not come out of her tent to snatch the sketchbook from my hands. It may be she knew that drawing them, *seeing* them, would bind me with an obligation stronger than my old affection.

Matters came to a head three weeks ago. The officers' quarters are some distance from the internment camp, but the shots that night were rare enough to wake me. Next morning I learned that Johanna was locked up. Her children had never tasted the extra rations I secured. She had passed every last biscuit to their father, who had been making weekly forays on to the Rand, meeting her after curfew. She – or rather, *I* – had been all that stood between his unit and starvation, until that night, when they were surprised by a sentry who shot the husband dead. Two others got away.

I admit I admired her loyalty and half-envied that dead Boer, while cursing her for making me her stooge. I did not speak to her. It would only have raised her hopes and, as I was implicated in her treachery, I could do nothing for her. Captain Hunter hauled me over the coals, calling me a bloody fool, and worse. As he spoke, the American financier Pierpont Morgan was arranging to lend the empire a further £32 million, on top of the £240 million he had already brokered for this war. Did I imagine he was doing this out of the goodness of his heart? He saw profit in backing the winning side. This foul-up was just the sort of affair to shake his confidence. Henceforth I was not to set foot in the refugee camp. He did not want to hear my name coupled with *that Boer bitch* again. Of course, my infamy spread like wildfire. Who could resist the tale of a lieutenant gulled by his Boer doxy into procuring supplies for the enemy?

After that I met insolence and insubordination at every

turn, with the exception of Sergeant Greig, who took all my commands with a brisk 'yes, sir', relaying the order as Crathie's to make sure the sappers jumped to. Not that I had much occasion to command them. They spent their days digging graves. Solomon was reassigned to the burial party. One night he appeared in my tent, sweating and short of breath, urging me to go with him. I asked where and why, but all he would say was 'Please, *sah*, you must come,' like a kitchen Kaffir with a dozen words of English.

He led me to a patch of ground on the blind side of the mess stores, overlooked by the headgears of the Simmer and Jack mine. The air was thick with the acrid smoke of a dung fire. There must have been twenty of them there. I spotted Crathie with my corporals and a sergeant from the 47th, and was pleased to see Greig sitting apart from them. Before I could cross to his side and discover the cause of all the laughter and back-slapping, Robb hailed me with a sarcastic cheer. Somebody handed me a bottle of rum. I never felt less like drinking. 'Hae a guid swallae, man,' Sillars said. Then, switching to an over-aspirated attempt at the King's English, 'Take a proper swallow, Lieutenant.' They guffawed as if it were the grandest joke, Crathie along with the rest.

They were bragging of medals, sure it would be DCMs for Robb and Sillars and a DSO for the lieutenant. The enemy had paid us another visit. A daring plan: to blow up the mine. Even Crathie had not thought they would go so far. He feared a raid on our stores or a burning brand tossed into the forage barn, when he instituted the nightly search. They found three trenches primed with dynamite waiting for a Boer to light the fuses. Crathie dealt with one, Robb and Sillars the others. I asked Crathie why he had kept me out of it. 'Oh, come now,' he said. Sillars butted in, 'We had to keep it tight. We didnae want a Boer spy getting wind o' it.' I asked what he meant by that. Crathie tried to smooth it

159

over: we were all good fellows here. I said I wanted a straight answer, and Robb spoke up, 'We didnae want your hoor or her bastirts passin the word along.' *My what?* I said. Sillars laughed, 'Your Dutch bag o' bones, sir. But she still has some honey in her fud, eh?' Crathie sniggered. He was drunk. I should have reported him, but I knew it would never stick. He is too popular. Everyone likes Bill Crathie.

I know what you're thinking, Arthur. Why did I not assert my authority? I'm sure they're all jolly civilised wallahs in Bombay, but it's not like that here. It terrifies me: the thought of these men sailing home when the war is over, walking the streets in civilian clothes. You might as well dress leopards and cheetahs in starched collars. They will turn on anyone who thwarts them – turn on him and tear him to pieces. If you ever come face to face with them, you will understand what it means to be outnumbered by the pack.

I told them my dealings with the woman had been prompted by Christian charity. Sillars choked at this, spitting out a mouthful of rum. 'Are ye tellin us ye didnae get a horkin?' I said he should hold his tongue, but he laughed in my face. 'The besom owes ye that – she owes us all.' There was more of this lewd and drunken talk. I was itching to box their ears, but I could see they had the devil in them. Sillars jumped to his feet, a couple of sappers at his side. I guessed what they had in mind and ordered them to sit down, but they ran off into the dark, laughing. Johanna was safely under lock and key, and the charge-room guards knew it was more than their jobs were worth to give her up to a drunken second corporal, so I stayed put. The wind got up, driving a twisting column of sparks into the starry sky. Sergeant Greig started a sing-song. When they came to 'Auld Lang Syne' Crathie put an arm around my shoulder. He is a charming fellow when he wants to be. We must have passed an hour like this before Sillars and the others returned.

To cut a long story short, they got her. They must have

pulled her from sleep. She was in her shift, pinioned between them. She did not notice me at first. Terror made her blind. Sillars seized her by the hair. 'Gentlemen,' he boomed, 'I give you... the Boer hoor. She thieves and lies and feeds Brother Boer in the dead o' night, and what else, eh, what else do ye do for him?' He pressed his nose into her neck, drew back and spat. 'She stinks.'

Robb stepped forward: 'Brother Boer likes a bit o' filth.' 'And she's lousy,' Sillars said, 'they're lowping aff her.' Robb took out his knife. 'We'll need to clean her up for decent company.' It must have been then that Crathie slipped away. I wish to God I'd done the same.

Robb cut off her hair. He tossed the rat's tails on the fire. Their greasy smoke caught in my throat, worse than the dung. The men closed in. I saw the glint of the knife as Robb sliced through her shift. The fabric was half-rotten; in a moment she was naked. A bag of bones, as Sillars had said, yet her breasts were plump. He threw the ruined shift on the flames, which flared up, showing her more clearly. Her skull was boyish without hair, but she still had her hips and those white breasts.

I saw her look from face to face, seeking a glimmer of pity, or shame. Despite her terror, she still had hope. This is hard for me to write, Arthur, and hard to remember, and yet it never leaves me. I lie down to sleep and it is painted on the insides of my eyelids. The firelight, their avid faces, the moment her eyes found mine, just before they pushed her to the ground.

She cried out my name.

You must be able to guess what they did. Imagine the most base, and force your thoughts lower. I will not pollute you with the details. I am not sure I could furnish them if I tried. It comes back to me all at once, and in that same instant my brain and body convulse. The next day I was confined to my tent with a pain like a white blade in my skull. I rose from my cot only to vomit. If I avoid beer, rum and coffee, I can keep it down to a dull ache, but any thought of that night and it returns.

I am too queasy to continue. Write to me as soon as you get this letter, but remember your words will be read by others.

Herbert

1904

I ask, 'Do you remember a man with hair like blue smoke who used to sit at the lakefront café in Bellagio...?'

You are correcting my sketches. I have graduated from loaves of bread to wooden chairs.

'...I saw him in the square yesterday. He's touring with his mother, they're staying in Settignano.'

You have reached the drawing I did of a crow. Quite a good drawing, I think. You tear it out of the sketchbook and crumple it into a ball.

'I met him again just now. He invited us to lunch but I said it would interrupt your work. I suspect they're rather starved of company. I thought I might ask them to supper.'

I wait for you to accuse me of taking him as a lover.

'Why not?' you say.

Richard's mother is very old, with a high colour that reminds me of the shopkeepers in Como. Theirs is natural. Perhaps hers was once. Not now. She has taken her paintbox and given herself a set of features pleasing to her poor old myopic eyes. Two pencilled arcs halfway up her forehead; a light caramel glaze across her wrinkled cheeks; around her mouth, a waxy ring whose colour is unknown in nature. The effect is at once ridiculous and indomitable.

She crosses the threshold, tinkling in jet-beaded chiffon. Richard is in black tie. I should have told him we do not dress in the evenings. I thought the word 'supper' would be enough.

He shakes your hand. 'Ah, the talented husband I've heard so much about.'

In any introduction there is one who grants and one who solicits. Surprisingly, Richard takes the latter role. Through his eyes, I see you afresh. Your narrow, muscular frame; your dark, mistrustful glance. It piques his interest. He presents his mother, whose nod in my direction is unimpeachably courteous and unmistakably cool.

I assume she is Italian, until I hear that nasal drawl.

'Tell me, Mrs Jackson, do you find the air improved up all these stairs?'

You laugh. A dimple appears in her cheek.

'Less the air than the light,' you say, 'especially in the mornings.'

'You see, Ricardo: Mr Jackson is an early riser.' Her mouth twists into a smile that seems to say, *I'm old enough to be your grandmother, but in my prime I'd have led you a dance.* 'I'm always telling Ricardo, dawn is the best part of the day here.'

'It reminds me of Africa.'

'Ah yes,' she breathes, though I would bet my best dress she has never been south of Naples.

An almighty thumping echoes up the stairs. Mrs Moretti's charcoal eyebrows move towards her hairline. Magdalena, Tommaso's flat-footed niece, arrives with the vermouth.

We talk about Italy. The splendour of the best hotels, and the curious fact of their primitive plumbing. How every waiter pockets his tip as if doing one a tremendous favour. I wonder if Richard feels more American or Italian? Both equally, he says, but never in the same moment. Here his thoughts couch themselves in Italian. Back in New York, he will revert to thinking in English, although he will see his foreignness reflected in the eyes of everyone he meets – just as, here in Italy, they treat him as *Americano*.

His mother tells him he should not care what they think. None of them is fit to polish his boots.

He smiles at us, amused by this maternal bias, while accepting it as his due. The more intriguing matter, he says, is the way his temperament alters from place to place.

'Surely that follows from thinking in and speaking another language,' I say. 'How else are we to know ourselves, if not through words? Change those, and all sorts of changes follow.'

It occurs to me that you and I can spend hours, even whole days, quite mute. And without conscious thought. It is safer. You read my face so easily.

'For me,' Richard says, 'knowledge comes through the senses. New York's icy winters make me a businessman, but when the Tuscan sun warms my skin and I breathe the resiny air, I feel the awakening of a southern self that lives by scent and taste and touch. If I lived here, and nowhere else, I should be an artist.' He glances at you. 'Or try to be.'

The ensuing silence confirms my suspicions. While happy to talk to Mrs Moretti, you mean to ignore her son.

'Herbert is teaching me to draw, but I make little progress. All my ideas are wrong. The very *having of ideas* is wrong.' I hate the sound of my breathy laugh, but one of us must say something. 'Yesterday he did a sketch of me. It gave me the queerest feeling. I can see it is a likeness, and yet the woman it depicts seems a stranger.'

'"O wad some Power the giftie gie us, to see oursels as ithers see us",' Richard quotes, in a valiant but execrable attempt at the Scotch. 'I admire your enterprise – I should find it impossibly inhibiting learning to draw in the shadow of Leonardo.'

This you cannot let pass without comment.

'Three months ago, I would have agreed, until it occurred to me there's nothing to be gained by following in the foot-steps of the unimprovable. A new century demands a new kind of painting.'

'Like that fellow who paints everything blue?' Mrs Moretti suggests.

'The day I start painting blue ladies you may take me out and have me shot, Madam. I'm afraid I have no ready explanation. Unlike Catherine, I have no facility with words...'

It is odd to see Richard's flatteringly attentive look sideways on, rather than as its object.

'...If I were to paint this country, it wouldn't be the Colosseum, or Pompeii, or some magnificent *duomo*, but a railway station in an out-of-the way sort of town, with that notice about not crossing the rails...'

'*Vietato attraversare i binari,*' Richard supplies.

'...and dozens of travellers wandering across the tracks.'

Richard releases an explosive guffaw.

'That was my observation!' I say.

'What's mine is yours. And vice versa, I hope.'

Magdalena returns to ask if we are ready to eat.

Her aunt is an excellent cook. Mrs Moretti compliments me on the *bistecca alla Fiorentina*. The *zabaione*, too, is delicious. The evening is on its way to being a success. Richard is a skilful guest, steering between the rocks of formality and presumption to draw you out. If he is less attentive to me, I remind myself that we share a prior connection. Having been warned of your jealousy, he is doing his utmost not to provoke it. Still, it would be nice if he aimed the occasional remark in my direction.

The great revelation of the night is how you blossom in company. The two of you are getting on famously. Richard will think I was exaggerating. It falls to me to amuse his mother.

Even at her great age, she is impeccably soignée, false hair arranged in an elaborate pompadour, her widow's black dress glitteringly *à la mode*. I am fascinated by her hands, their loose, liver-splashed backs beautifully soft, fingers flashing with rings. Beside her, I feel like an untidy schoolgirl.

'It's good of you to entertain us at a day's notice, Mrs Jackson.'

'A week would have made no difference. We live very simply here.'

'Nonetheless, I'm in your debt. I don't often get to see Ricardo in company of his choosing.' She gives me a sly look, like a card player trying to guess my hand. 'He is such a dark horse about his friends.'

The talk moves on to continental fashions. She too has had clothes made by Italian seamstresses. She found the fit excellent but the stitching rather slapdash. I tell a half-amusing story about the Perugian dressmaker who made sheep's eyes at you and insisted on showing you every swatch of silk, ignoring all my attempts to state a preference.

You break off from your conversation with Richard. 'Why must you tell these lies, everything twisted out of true? It wasn't like that at all.'

'It's just a story.'

'A *lie*. You know it as well as I do.'

I drain my glass to mask my embarrassment.

Magdalena comes to clear the table. As the ladies can hardly withdraw to the bedroom, the gentlemen go down to the courtyard to smoke.

I send up a prayer that you will not stay out there too long.

'What brought you to Florence, Mrs Jackson?'

Why not tell the truth?

'We're avoiding Mr Pierpont Morgan, an American Croesus who turned up in Perugia.'

She looks startled.

'You've heard of him?'

'I have,' she says, 'but I didn't know he was in Italy.'

'On a shopping spree, apparently. He'll buy as many Renaissance masterpieces as he can get his hands on and ship them back to America. He's an old enemy of Herbert's, or Herbert is an enemy of his, I can never remember which. Well, probably not an enemy as you or I would understand it, but Herbert would rather our paths didn't cross.' I take a sip of wine, and, for want of anything more to say, another. 'Have you bought any antiques while you've been in Italy?'

We are both relieved to hear manly laughter echoing up the stairs.

'Cold out there,' you say.

Richard asks how long we intend to stay in Florence. For the rest of the winter, you tell him. In the spring we move on to Switzerland. Perhaps he and his mother will visit us there? I give you a surprised look. Richard says there is nothing he would like more. Unfortunately, he must be back at his desk in a fortnight. 'Left to themselves for too long, banks have a habit of going to hell.'

'Ricardo!' his mother exclaims. 'You're not in the smoking room now.'

'Sorry, Mama.' He catches your eye with a rueful grin.

The evening is drawing to a close. Richard and I have hardly spoken to each other. He asks if he might come back in daylight to see some of your work. You say you have nothing to show him at present, but if he asks again in six months, you hope to be able to give him a different answer.

'What I saw in the Transvaal banished any interest in the professors and society wives whose portraits had been my living. I began to think the muse had left me. But at last I'm planning a new painting. A big canvas, more ambitious than anything I've attempted before. It may even make my fortune.'

'A battle scene?' Richard asks.

'Like Prior or Fripp, you mean: a thousand men charging the enemy? No. This will be behind the lines, an intimate composition, and yet epic in its way.'

'I'm sure it will be most attractive,' Mrs Moretti says. 'All those redcoats under the glorious African sky.'

'I'm afraid we wore khaki on active service.'

'The Boers were sharp-shooters, Mama. The British needed to blend into the landscape.'

Mrs Moretti gives you a teasing smile. 'No one wants to hang a dirt-brown canvas on their wall.'

'It's a nocturnal scene,' I say.

'How do you know that?' Your voice bites like a whip.

'I happened to glance over your shoulder.'

'I told you I would show you when it was ready.'

'It was quite inadvertent.'

'Which is another *lie*.'

I send Richard a quick glance. *You see.*

'I'm sorry,' I murmur.

'Sorry to have defied me, or just sorry to have been caught? You creep around behind my back, going against my express wishes. You have no idea how delicate the early stages of a painting are. I told you I didn't want you meddling before the conception was settled, contaminating my ideas with your pretentious verbiage, but no, you had to have your own way.'

'I have apologised.'

'And you think "sorry" is a magic word to make everything all right.' Your voice rises into a whining falsetto. '"*Forgive me, Herbert. I'm sorry. I'm so sorry.*" I'm sick of apologies. I would rather you behaved decently in the first place.'

Our guests study the tablecloth.

'Can we not talk about this later?' I say.

'I would rather not have had to talk about it at all.'

'We have guests.'

'And you weren't the centre of attention, so you threw a hand grenade into the conversation.'

I know I should keep quiet, since everything I say provokes you, but I cannot bear Richard seeing me so downtrodden.

'I will not spend my life trying to appease you.'

You squint at me. '*What?*'

'You heard. And I won't be made into a scapegoat for your disappointments, either. No woman could give you what you want in a wife...'

Mrs Moretti takes the napkin from her lap and lays it alongside her plate.

'...someone as submissive as she is fearless, as invisible to other men as she is radiantly beautiful – even that wouldn't be enough. As it happens, I think I meet your needs admirably: what you want is to be endlessly dissatisfied with me!'

'When we get back to England I shall divorce you.'

I stare at you. Such an odd sensation in my chest, as if my ribs were too frail to contain my pounding heart.

Hurt. How absolute it is, and how hard to remember, after. The wound closes, a scab forms, and in the end a scar, a pucker of unsightly flesh to remind us of our resilience. One day we laugh again, although every one of us has curled up in our beds and sobbed like a child. Who does not long to live in love? Like moving from air to water, buoyed up, caressed all over, refreshed inside and out. Until we wake in the desert with our childish incomprehension. The heart splits, its secret shame exposed. *I thought you loved me.* Childish self-pity, and a childish faith in the power of my own hurting. How can you see me like this and remain unmoved?

Magdalena comes to take away the coffee cups. Unnerved by the silence, she is anxious to make her escape. A dropped spoon clatters to the floor.

We will never see either of the Morettis again. It is almost as if they have already left. Their faces are closed to us. Richard's pleasure in my company was such a source of strength to me, I almost loved him for it. Now I feel nothing for him or his mother, beyond a fervent wish to have them gone.

'Well...' he says.

Mrs Moretti nods.

Magdalena goes to fetch the coats.

Abruptly you ask, 'Which bank?'

Richard looks affronted.

'J. P. Morgan and Company,' he says.

Dear Arthur,

I have just received your telegram. I know you mean well, but what you urge me to do is impossible. You cannot imagine what it is like here. I am sending this through the normal channels, but I'm sure you will understand when I write that the Royal Engineers are not going to recognise such distinguished conduct. I was the only officer present. What happened was my responsibility. Did I mention that a lieutenant in the 47th suffered an accident last year? A lecture to his men on pistol safety, a telegram informing his mother that he died in pursuance of his duty, and the matter was forgotten.

I realise you are a civil servant, not a soldier. The world looks very different from India. Here, life is cheap.

Do not write to me of this again.

Herbert

1905

February finds us in Stresa, waiting to board a steamer. Lake Maggiore is vast and flat and cold. Fan palms shiver in the wind. The purser hands me aboard, his '*Buon viaggio*' the first kind words I have heard today. The boat is only a quarter full, with a couple of policemen among the tourists stranded past the end of the season. I have been able to bear these months because they were temporary. Now we are going home, to the rest of our lives.

And to a new life we have made between us. This time I am sure. My breasts are so tender.

I go below deck. The lavatories are occupied. No matter. It was just an excuse to leave your side. Further down the corridor are the sleeping quarters. So many doors. Trying one at random, finding it opens into darkness, I step inside and turn the key, locking myself in.

'You have the wrong cabin, Mademoiselle.'

I yelp. An electric lamp floods the little room with light. A sallow-faced Frenchman is lying fully clothed on the lower bunk.

'Or are you a thief?' On his feet, he is not quite my height. 'Should I restrain you?'

His unblinking stare says this is a joke. He has a used-up look: his thinning grey hair, his whittled bones, the yellow skin that only just covers his aquiline nose. Forty-five? Fifty? An old man, but he does not seem to know it.

'I'm sorry, I didn't mean to disturb you.'

'I thought I was dreaming.' He is standing very close to me. 'Are you a dream, Mademoiselle?'

I could lie down with him now, on his narrow bunk, and justify all your suspicions. I do not find him handsome, but I am stirred by his shameless glance. And if it were to happen, why not call it love, for the hour we lay entwined? A pure exchange untainted by the dailiness that breeds hate. Pleasure given and taken, delight in each other's mystery, simple gratitude: would that be so very wrong? I could swear he is having these same thoughts. He steps back. I unlock the door.

'My apologies, Monsieur.'

He returns a mocking, courtly nod.

When I get back on deck a muscle is twitching in your cheek.

'Don't bother to lie to me,' you say. 'I saw him come out.'

I follow your gaze to a young man in a grey overcoat, the least likely person to kindle my lust. I imagine telling you the truth: I am unfaithful, in my thoughts. When you cover me in the dark I conjure other men, but even then, such desire as I can muster is nothing beside the elemental compulsion to defend myself against you. I could refuse your touch or submit without pretence of pleasure, but how you would make me pay. Did I not promise at the altar to love you until death?

'I suppose you told him not to acknowledge you, but he can't keep away.'

'I hadn't even noticed him until you pointed him out.'

'You must think I'm a fool.'

I close my eyes.

You hiss in my ear, 'You're making a spectacle of yourself.'

Sure enough, one of the policemen approaches to ask if I need assistance.

'She is perfectly well, thank you, Officer, only rather ashamed at being caught *in flagrante*. I saw that gentleman come out of her cabin, which was locked against me. I'm taking her back to London to divorce her.'

This again. I cannot let you divorce me. How would I work with a child to care for? And who would employ an adulteress?

The officer frowns as if doubting his understanding of English.

'I have to keep a close watch on her. I think it very likely she will try to kill herself.'

You cannot mean this – but why say it, if you do not? Impossible to tell whether the policeman believes you. He withdraws without further enquiry. Later I see him laughing with his colleague on the other side of the deck.

We go below to unpack. Our cabin is at the other end of the corridor from the Frenchman's. Were I travelling alone, I would take such pleasure in the miniature appointments: the fluted-glass shades of the lamps above each curtained bunk, the wash-hand basin on its mahogany stand, and linen towels embroidered with the initials of the steamship company.

You claim the lower bunk. I hand you your nightshirt to stow under the pillow.

In the dining saloon, the young man you believe to be my lover is giggling with his sweetheart. Their mutual infatuation is obvious, even to you. We talk about our plan to walk across the Alps. You will carry our toothbrushes and a change of underclothes in a knapsack. The rest of our luggage can be sent on by post. I hope the exercise will ease your headaches. They have been growing more frequent, along with your nightmares. You accused Tommaso of putting something in your food.

After dinner I talk you out of a stroll around the deck. We would be sure to meet the Frenchman. Although it is much too early for bed, we return to our cabin.

I have not spent twenty-four hours out of your sight in

174

four months, but sometimes I feel as awkward as if we had just been introduced. 'Herbert, I have some news.' I do my best to smile. 'I didn't want to say anything before I was certain...'

I am brushing my hair, watching our reflections in the washstand glass.

'It's good news. I know you've been worried about... about yourself, but there was absolutely no need...'

You hate it when I do not come straight to the point. My tone is all wrong. I should not have begun this, not here, not now. My mouth dries, but something in my expression delivers the information.

I feel a rush of air across my skin as your fist shatters the mirror. My face crazes before my eyes.

'Whose is it – the Prince of Wales's?'

I am too amazed to reply.

'I knew you let him fuck you, but I never thought even you would try to foist his spawn on me.'

'You think I... with the *Prince of Wales?*'

'I will not be lied to!' You grab me by the hair, pulling me around to face you.

'You're hurting me!'

Your grip tightens. 'It's his, isn't it?'

'Prince George's?'

Your other hand smashes into the glass. 'You know who I mean! I've called him the Prince of Wales my whole life, I'm not going to stop now, even if he is crowned king. *My God*, I don't know how you can look me in the eye. You think I don't see you slavering like a bitch on heat over every man we pass? He took his pleasure and went back to Mrs Keppel, but you have a taste for it now. You don't care who it is, as long as they have a root. Then you come crawling back to me. You think I can't smell them on you?'

Always when you talk like this, a door closes in my mind. I hear your voice, but the words are just sounds. There is no possibility of understanding, much less making myself understood.

'You're not even going to deny it, are you?'

I look at you, perplexed.

You grab me by the throat.

Such a small cabin. The bunks, the washstand, a shallow press for hanging our clothes. Nothing to help me. Your hands squeeze. *Scream, someone may hear.* But how do I scream, when I can't breathe? I claw at your grip. Blood on my fingers. Is it mine? No – yours: cut by the mirror. My bulging eyes in the fractured glass. My head pounding, the world throbbing, the cabin walls receding. Your face before me, known and strange, flushed violent red.

Dear Arthur,

It is a long time since I heard from you, or Mater, or Lucie. No doubt your letters have been intercepted. I was surprised your telegram got through. Write to me soon, care of Warwick Road. They are sending me home, with a complement of informers. If I am not 'lost at sea', I will post this from Britain.

I am watched day and night, my every word reported. They have marked me down as an enemy of the crown. My crime? Keeping my eyes open, and drawing what I see. The Boers have wangled a pretty good deal out of their surrender. They will be running these colonies before long, under the fig leaf of British sovereignty. It makes me wonder why we fought this war: we could have waved a white flag three years ago and saved thousands of our lads the trouble of dying. As for the natives who fought alongside us, I would not bet on them gaining the vote (those that are left, after the Boers have finished their score-settling). And yet we claim our moral victory: the forces of civilisation have triumphed. I can hardly write this for shaking with laughter. Any British Tommy awaiting his passage home would laugh just as heartily, after making sure his commanding officer was out of earshot. The Great Lie must be upheld.

You remember I wrote to you of the Dutchwoman who was assaulted so grievously, although 'assaulted' is hardly the word. They set on her like a pack of wild dogs, and yet with a discipline in their turn-taking that made what they did a sort of drill. A few days later I was summoned before Captain Hunter. Crathie was there, his brow furrowed in a show of decent concern, along with a God-botherer, Simmons, chaplain to the concentration camp. The captain asked how I had spent that particular Friday evening? I said I could not remember offhand. Crathie piped up that he had seen me with my NCOs celebrating the foiling of the plot to destroy the gold mine. Clearly Hunter already knew this. He told me the chaplain had passed on very grave allegations about that night. Making a show of recovering my memory, I replied that I had retired to my quarters at the same time as Lieutenant Crathie. The captain nodded and told Simmons he would continue to investigate but he had yet to find any shred of corroboration for the woman's story. Crathie and the chaplain left. I was ordered to remain. The captain said he saw no reason to doubt Corporal Robb's assertion that I had been present all evening, supported as it was by Sergeant Greig. They claimed to know nothing of the woman and she seemed to him an unreliable witness, of proven bad character. She could not identify the men who had supposedly molested her, which made any sort of investigation next to impossible. The only name she had been able to furnish was mine.

He paused to let me speak, but I knew the wisest course was to keep mum. What he said next is burned into my memory. 'Look, man, we're all flesh and blood. It's a lonely business, war. A man needs a little comfort. The Boer women have caused us trouble enough, God knows. What right do they have to be treated as ladies? So I don't condone, but I understand. Now it may be she spreads her favours a little more widely than you were led to believe. It may be Greig and Robb and the rest were regular customers. When you find out, you take your pleasure without payment. Afterwards she's upset, of course. No money. So she makes an allegation. I'm not saying this is how it happened, but I would not be overly surprised. Now, this ludicrous tale is not going to go any further. The slanders of a woman of easy virtue – and a Boer, at that – against the word of His Majesty's loyal soldiers? She must be out of her mind, if she thinks that's going to wash. But we have to keep the record straight. The chaplain has helped her lodge a formal complaint. I want you to write the report. It may be that when she talks to you, she

178

will realise she was mistaken and withdraw these very serious allegations. If she does, there will be no repercussions. If she persists, she should understand that your enquiries will find her complaint frivolous. His Majesty's forces take a dim view of unfounded accusations. There has to be a deterrent, but it's a nasty business, flogging a woman. No one wants that, eh?'

I knew better than to visit her in the hospital. I got the use of a room in the mess, a place of bricks and mortar where the door could be closed and what passed within not easily overheard. She was carried there, being unable to walk without pain. I suppose it was a shock to see me again. She looked at me with the blank face of a child. I said her name. She began to scream.

Next day I told Hunter what she said was true. I could supply him with most of the names, and would pick out the remaining faces at the next parade. After a moment, he said, 'Have you gone mad, Lieutenant?'

That afternoon Solomon sought me out. His hands were shaking and he stank – not his usual strong smell, so abhorrent to Sillars, but the stench of desperation. 'You are a man of honour, *sah*. You give yourself up, and your men: you will all be shamed. For me, it is not the same.' He had no rank to be stripped of, no pension to forfeit. They would hang him. He was a black man accused of taking a white woman by force. That alone was enough to condemn him, but there was more. He had been a farm labourer employed by the old Dutchman I killed. For years they had beaten him, making him work like a dog on the land of his fathers. It was not by chance that he led me there. He had known her husband and brothers were on commando, and that if we did not find them hiding on the premises, we would find their cache of food and ammunition. His words ran on while I tried to make sense of the three he had uttered at the start, until I had to ask: what did he mean, 'give myself up'? He had the gall to look me in the eye as he told his monstrous falsehood.

I said he could not blackmail me, his lies would be disproved in court. 'No, *sah*,' he said, 'they will all say they saw you. They will swear it.' Well, then I saw how cleverly they had arranged it between them. I told him to get out. If he crossed my path again, I would not be answerable for the consequences.

My headaches returned. I reported myself unfit and was relieved of my duties. A week went by. The only living souls I saw were the mess servants bringing my meals. I had to make a choice: to finish what I had begun, or to retract the statement I had made. When I considered either course, the pain bent me double and I gave up my breakfast. I took my sketchbook and let my pencil draw what it would, with a faint hope that the sketches might shed new light on my dilemma. One morning I woke from fitful sleep to find the book gone. That afternoon I was summoned to the captain's quarters. He told me I need not worry about the Dutchwoman's accusations. She had been caught in Second Corporal Sillars's tent, where she had crawled from her hospital bed, armed with a knife. She was tried the next morning. She wanted to call me as a witness, but they told her I was too unwell to give evidence.

They hanged her, Arthur.

This was not all the captain had to say. My sketchbook sat on his table. He had shown the drawings to a doctor, who had pronounced them the work of a diseased imagination. When I insisted they were no more than truth, he warned me to be careful. If I was not suffering from nervous exhaustion, he would have to seek another explanation. Did I want to be shot as an enemy agent? He was not denying there were irregularities in the refugee camps, as a result of our wish to save the Boer womenfolk from starvation. Did I think we should be condemned for our humanitarian impulses? It would be quite understandable if I held myself responsible for the Dutchwoman's death and felt the need to atone, but I had to put my country first. The war was bleeding money. The

Germans were spreading slanders about our conduct which had been picked up by treasonous elements among our own countrymen. Pierpont Morgan and his fellow bankers took a dim view of dying children and violated women. What if he should withdraw his support at the very moment when victory was within our grasp? Was that what I wanted?

What could I say but no, of course not. His manner softened. Terrible things happened in war, he said, done by men who would never have committed such acts in peacetime. What good could come of bringing them to the notice of civilians who would never understand? I must put the whole sorry business behind me and forgive myself along with the rest.

There it was again: the hateful insinuation that I had taken part. Infuriated, I replied with words a cooler head would have suppressed. The captain burned my sketches, ordering me to draw no more of their ilk. From that day onward I received no letters. Officially I was 'unfit', but when I tried to leave my tent the lie was exposed. I was confined to quarters. My headaches worsened. I hardly slept, and when I did, I dreamed of little Mariam calling, 'Mammie! Mammie!' as Johanna danced on the rope. Other dreams too, from which I woke disgusted at myself. I have not entertained such visions since boyhood, when my root was ever ready for action, and yet if you were to lead me into a seraglio, offering me my pick of all the houris, I could not take my pleasure with them.

Weeks passed. I heard the cheers when the treaty was signed, but little seemed to change. It takes months to get 200,000 men home. At last, I recovered my resourcefulness. Not every guard posted outside was properly conscientious. One regularly kept me awake with his snores. I waited until his turn on duty and crept out to the internment camp. Johanna's tent had been struck. The moon cast just enough light for me to make out the patch of beaten earth.

I told myself Christiaan was a cunning boy. He would see to it that Pieter came to no harm. But how would Mariam live without a mother? I stole into the nearest tent, waiting for my eyes to adjust to the dark. They slept like animals, all huddled together, the children pressed into their mother's warmth. There was a scrap of flesh and bone small enough to be Mariam, but her face was hidden.

'*Wie is daar?*' the woman said, low and fierce. I told her I was a friend of Johanna's. '*Wys jouself!*' I struck a match. I must have walked past her dozens of times, but her features meant nothing to me. The flame burned out. I struck another. She gestured for me to bring it nearer my own face, and made a guttural sound of recognition. I said I was looking for Mariam, did she know where I might find her? The Afrikaans word came to me: '*Waar?*' 'Gone,' she said. Gone where, when? She made a hissing sound. I asked if someone was taking care of her, the chaplain perhaps? Or had her uncles come back to get her? No answer. I listened to the breathing of her sleeping children. Then I understood: one more sack tossed into the burial pit. How, I asked? She turned away. For pity's sake, I said. She growled at me, '*Sy het nie geëet nie.*' She had just enough English to translate, 'Not eat.' I asked about Christiaan and Pieter. She shrugged. The child beside her woke, and I left.

I spent the rest of the night waiting outside Major Burn Murdoch's tent. He knew me by sight. His brother and Walter had shared a dorm at Edinburgh Academy. He listened while I told my tale and, assuring me the matter would be looked into, sent an aide to summon Captain Hunter, but it was all a sham. The captain arrived with two military police, who took me to the charge office and locked me up.

A day or so later I noticed bluestone vitriol in my food. I have swallowed nothing but apples and figs and pawpaw for weeks, but still they find ways of drugging me. Every morning I awake to the proof. They think to discredit me with these nocturnal emissions, and to infect me with self-doubt, but I am stronger than they know.

This morning, out of the blue, Crathie appeared in my tent to bid me farewell. His father is ill. The captain had offered him my berth on the invalids' ship, I was now on the manifest to sail with Robb and Sillars on the SS *German*. When I asked if they were releasing me, he played dumb. They were sending me home, he said, to be cared for by my family. The sea air would do me good. With any luck I would be three-quarters well by the time I reached Southampton. I snarled at him that he need not keep up this pretence as there was nobody here but myself, and I was certainly not taken in. Still he did not drop his act, but held out his hand for me to shake. Fool that I am, I took it, and he gripped me like a vice, twisting my arm so hard behind my back I thought he meant to break it. He spoke in my ear. 'You cost us our medals with your damned talk, Jackson. It's just as well you're as mad as a hatter, or the fellows would have to pay you back.'

So now I know what they say of me. What I don't know is how high it goes. Robb and Sillars, Hunter and Burn Murdoch, of course. But would even the major have the authority to imprison me for so long without charge? Nothing happens in the British Army without being recorded on paper and passed up the chain of command. Up to a certain point, this is a safeguard. Beyond that point, the very opposite. There are so many implicated in this war, from the lowest NCO to the highest in the land. Each has cause for shame, and reason to discredit anyone who draws attention to the fact. I will not be the only one in their sights. We must all be silenced, one way or another.

I will finish here, lest they come for me and find me writing this.

Remember me in your prayers, Arthur. I have never been more in need of them.

Herbert

1905

We are in a larch wood on the side of a deep ravine. It is
snowing. Not the large, wet flakes that fall in Glasgow, but
a fine powder that veils the view. Your tweed suit is white
all over. My skirt is twice the weight it was when I dressed.
White lumps the size of tennis balls have formed in the loops
of my bootlaces. I scoop up a handful of snow to quench
my thirst. It makes me cough. The fingers I used are seared
with cold, yet my head is sweating. I take off my hat. Within
minutes, my hair is a crown of ice.

'Are you sure we're on the right path?'

You pretend not to hear me.

We set off at daybreak. The roadside fields were steeped
in mist. A pearly sky, the distant mountains a delicate pink.
Peasant houses huddled, higgledy-piggledy, below agricultural
terraces. Washing hung from balconies. Even the cemeteries
seemed untidily domestic. Our first glimpse of far-off white
came just after Varzo, then the crags closed in and all was
grey. Leafless birch and granite cliff, a fiercely cold wind with
the bite of mountain ice. Another hour, and the trees were
firs. Yesterday's snow trapped in their branches gave the hills
a speckled look. Wisps of chiffon cloud hung halfway up the
slopes.

At Iselle they were cutting a tunnel through the rock to
Brig. It is to be the longest in the world. They let tourists in
to view the hydraulic boring machines. I expected you to find

this of interest, but you barely turned to look as we walked past. We followed the riverbed to the border town of Gondo, a hellish place squeezed between sheer granite walls, the sky a crack of light impossibly far above us. I had hoped to see the famous waterfall frozen, but the river still flowed around boulders wearing mob caps of ice.

Leaving Gondo, our climb began in earnest.

Twenty miles as the crow flies from Domodossola to Brig, you say. Twice that at most, by the twisting road. We can easily walk fifteen to twenty miles a day. 'At this gradient,' I say, 'in a blizzard?' After an hour, the eye loses the ability to distinguish detail. All we see is white. Obstacles, a sudden drop, are equally invisible. One unlucky step, and our bodies will not be found till spring. You revert to silence, as always when you are at fault. You promised we would be in Simplon Dorf by lunchtime. 'My head aches like the very devil,' you snarl. 'I feel like blowing my brains out just to stop the pain.' I say you might feel better if you ate something. I have a veal sausage wrapped in a handkerchief in my pocket. You take a bite and spit it out, complaining that it reeks of the paper supplied in public lavatories. So now I must throw it away. To eat it would be taken as provocation. We trudge on. The wind gets up. The snow starts to drift. With each step I sink to the knee. Can that really be a chalet in the distance? Now that I can envisage the possibility of rest, I find myself exhausted. Getting there takes every last ounce of strength I possess.

It is shuttered and locked for the winter.

'Shall we stop at the next hamlet?'

'You can do as you please. I'm going on to Simplon Dorf.'

'You know we have to stay together.'

Your bitter, breathy laugh: 'It's a little late for that.'

So you are back to this old song.

'You need grounds to divorce.'

'Oh, I have grounds.'

'But no proof. A photograph. A witness. A hotel

chambermaid, it always seems to be when these things are reported in the newspapers.'

'I have proof.'

'How can you? There is none to be had!'

'Have you forgotten what you're carrying in your belly?'

'Your child? No, I haven't forgotten.'

A cunning glint in your narrowed eyes. 'When was it conceived?'

'Around the new year. I have a feeling it was the night after the gale.'

'You went out when I was asleep? No: you let him in, didn't you? You did it while I slept in the same room!'

Patiently I repeat, 'It is your child.'

You wheel around to grip me by the shoulders. '*You know I'm impotent!*'

And I thought nothing you said could surprise me.

'Do you mean infertile?'

'I mean what I say.'

'Whoever told you that, he was wrong.'

'I don't need anybody to *tell me* I cannot father a child.'

'I'm finding this rather confusing...'

'Will you make me spell it out? My member will not rise to it.'

I touch the place between your legs. Even in a blizzard, I feel the blood stir.

You knock my hand away. 'Have you no shame?'

'It's what married people do – what you and I have done at least a hundred times.'

Your mood turns. You study my face. 'Did he tell you to say that: the Prince of Wales?'

Sudden as a sneeze, a tree sheds the load from its branches.

Overcome by futility, I turn away.

We resume our trek. At least now I have a distraction from exhaustion, an enigma to unpick. What we do under cover of darkness is never acknowledged. I took your speechlessness, your rapt intensity, as proof of passion, but what if it was something else? When my brother Gordon was very young, he went through a sleepwalking phase. Mother would find him in the kitchen, or the parlour. He had thrown off the covers, reached up to turn the door handle, walked across the landing and all the way downstairs, yet when woken, was bewildered to find himself out of bed. Is that how lovemaking is for you?

At long last we reach a hamlet. I am sure, if we knocked at a door, the occupants would offer us refreshment. You say it is only another couple of miles to our destination. I lack the strength to argue, and perhaps a part of me longs for disaster, since it will be your fault.

The light has almost gone from the day before we glimpse rooftops on the far side of the ravine. Even on the outskirts of the village, catching the wonderful, homely scent of cattle warm in the shed, I am not sure I can walk another step. The white-moustached concierge of the Hotel de la Poste finds a seat for me in the inglenook and pours me a glass of pear brandy, colourless as water, breathtakingly strong. A clock chimes six. We have walked for eleven hours.

They bring us grated, fried potato served with shavings of burned cheese. You pull a face, leaving yours untouched. I eat every scrap. In the street outside, the diligence arrives from Domodossola. Porters hurry out with a ladder to fetch the luggage down. You will not let the concierge book us places in the morning coach. 'Gert!' He beckons a man drinking at the bar: a giant, broad and bearded, his red face scored by deep grooves at the outer corner of each eye. It is like shaking the paw of a faithful hound. He warns us the weather can change from minute to minute. The wind brings a risk of avalanche. If we are determined to proceed on foot, we will need alpenstocks and snowshoes, and coloured spectacles against snow blindness. At the very least, a piece of green crêpe to tie around our eyes. He is surprised to learn we have come so far today. He recommends breaking tomorrow's journey in the *Hospiz* run by the monks at the top of the pass.

You get up and walk out.

Later I tell you I have engaged him as a guide.

'Promising him what?'

'Twenty francs to get us to Brig.'

'And what else?'

'His bed and board when we stop for the night.'

You give a mirthless laugh. 'I saw.'

'Saw what?'

'You really think I'm stupid, don't you?'

'*Saw what?*'

'The way you looked at each other.'

I no longer waste my breath denying these accusations.

We are in bed by eight. Some time later I am roused from dreaming by your weight, your hoarse breath. I am so bone weary, I fall asleep again. Now I am wide awake. You are snoring. Downstairs, a brass band is playing. It is a novelty, lying beside you, free to think my own thoughts.

I will take no more drawing lessons. They are just another way for you to control me. You are enraged by my incompetence, as you would be by my skill. But still I crave some artistic expression. Why not writing? How you hate my *words*. I take heart from that. Perhaps by putting them down on paper I can recover myself – my true self, as distinct from the woman you insist I am. But I must go carefully. Imagine your fury if you found a jotter tucked under my side of the mattress, page after page filled with proof of my independent thoughts! I am not ready to take the risk just yet, but it is something to move towards, a reason to hope.

When I go down to breakfast next morning, you have already eaten. Gert is to meet us here at seven.

'He came,' you say. 'I told him he wasn't needed.'

The day dawns fine enough to see the larch-covered

mountains enclosing the village. The cold nips my skull. The sky is palest blue scored with faint, fine cloud like the blade marks a skater leaves on ice. The government pays peasants to sweep the road. Large banks of snow to either side of us testify to their efforts, but I am grateful for my *Schneeschuhe* all the same. Onwards and upwards. The sun has yet to clear the peaks. We are in a black-and-white world austere as an engraving in an old book. It is noon before we pass from shadow into light. The *Hospiz* basks in the sun, at once imposing and tiny against the Alps. *Food*, I think, *and rest*.

You leave the road, clambering over the snow bank to our left.

We are surrounded by frozen water, but the word in my head is 'desert': a high, white desert wind-sculpted into dunes. No knowing how deep the snow is underfoot. Here it is crisp on top, like walking on meringue; there, a freshly made-up feather bed, soft enough to sink in. Far below us, a ribbon of glacier like a misted mirror. Above us: sun, the blue-white Alps, the dazzle bounced from peak to peak, ice crystals sparkling in the air. The scale is barely conceivable, immense. Rousseau, Mendelssohn, Wordsworth, litter my thoughts. I wish they had not been here before me, but still, something untouchable in this landscape rings in my soul.

Lacking any green crêpe, I have veiled myself with a folded muslin scarf. Your face creases with irritation every time you catch sight of me.

How far from the road we have come. We are much, much higher than we were yesterday. An hour ago I felt a swoosh of air and speed as a flock of birds passed overhead. Since then, nothing living. A low screaming reaches us from down on the plain, like the singing of seals. The wind. Before long I feel its icy kiss. It sweeps away our footprints, raises lying snow into a blizzard, then drops again. The mist closes in. The air is soupy, the sun a pearl button in the cloud, now here, now gone. There is only white. Underfoot, overhead, all around us. I pull off the muslin, but see no more clearly.

'Shouldn't we turn back?'

My voice sounds strange after hours without speech.

'Herbert?'

'*Can't you just trust me for once?*'

So we are walking to some purpose. I recall a passsage in Baedeker about smugglers' paths over the Alps.

'I'm tired and hungry.'

'You're always hungry. Have a little patience. We'll be in Brig by dusk.'

You quicken your pace. I do my best to keep up, trying not to think about what might lie under the snow. Icy water, or a crevasse. My stomach turning as we fall through freezing air. My sternum vibrating with the rumble of an avalanche, the very last sound we would hear.

If I am ever going to write anything more substantial than letters home, what better time to start? The lack of notebook and pen is nothing, if I can make good the other lack. Time and again I have pulled back, telling myself there are words that must never be spoken, even in my head. Why have I followed you to this place – so beautiful in sunlight, with its otherworldly glamour, but so quick to change, and all the time inhuman, deathly? There is something in me that craves what is most inimical. Was I not drawn to you by your violence, your ruthless masculinity? But the better I knew you, the weaker you became. I do not understand how you can be so weak and still have power over me.

I am falling behind. I should have refused to go on without a day's rest. You would not have left me, lest I jump into the concierge's bed, or Gert's. I feel faint, and nauseous. Exhaustion? Mountain sickness? Or your child sapping my strength as its father has drained my will? I frighten myself with these thoughts. Surely I will love it, when the time comes (if only it does not have your mouth, your ready sneer). I was so tireless as a girl. I never understood why Mother fussed so over us, why our nurse used to say, 'The child's beyond herself.' That is how I feel now. Further than I have ever gone. Hollowed out. Quite broken. If I tripped and fell in the snow, would I get up again? The mountains don't care. God is busy in Mother's parlour, or in the incense-choked Italian churches. He is not here.

'Herbert, please, slow down.'

Surely you, too, will be glad to rest. I can hear your lungs heaving.

'*You think I don't know what you're doing?*'

I have no idea what you mean, and yet your tone is familiar. Your unshakable belief that you are the injured party, just as I cleave to my own blamelessness. It gives every exchange the drone of words said a thousand times.

'I'm sorry to have upset your plans.'

And taunting, that is another register of droning.

'What plans?' I say.

'Do you know, I think I resent your contempt for my intelligence more than your treachery. "*What plans?*" Your friends waiting to ambush me in the pass.'

Always this grain of justification amid the absurdity of your suspicions. I do have contempt for you.

'Well? Nothing to say?'

'You *know* what I have to say—'

Your hateful, wheezing laugh.

'I have no friends any more. You saw to that.'

'Richard Moretti? Believe me, he's no great loss. Such a perfect gentleman, he's still trailing after his mother. Is that what you want? A husband just for show? A cloak for your depravity? You'd drop me in an instant if you could do it without shame.'

So utterly familiar, I can predict every word, every frown and grimace, every silent flare of rage, and still you are not quite real to me. Like an actor on stage. I have a front-row seat, my sympathies are caught up in the play, but at the same time it has nothing to do with *me*. I feel like this for days on end, and then suddenly it strikes me: *I* am the chimera.

'Herbert, please...' I reach for your arm. You throw me off with such force that I fall headlong in the snow.

By the time I have retrieved my alpenstock, you are a dim figure dwindling into the murk. I set off after you.

We are walking in the clouds. I cannot see three yards ahead of me, or behind. My vision swarms with *mouches volantes*. My ears burn with cold. When I drape the muslin scarf around my head in a makeshift cowl, my breathing is loud within its folds. At long last, the grey shape ahead of me grows more distinct. Perhaps the mist is clearing, perhaps your pace has slowed.

Come here, Catherine.

Did you speak – or was it your thoughts I heard?

Stumbling, I look down.

Barely five feet to my right, the ground falls away. A sheer drop. You must be even closer to it.

Herbert! Be careful! Do I say it out loud?

You have stopped. Another seven or eight steps will close the gap between us. Tiredness makes me stagger. You are always complaining that I am clumsy. It could happen so quickly. A lost footing, a sudden lurch. Together one moment. The next, one of us gone. Why have you led me so far from the road? *Why did I follow?* That would be their first question. Why walk across the Alps at all? After everything that has happened. That hard push in the pine wood, and on the lake steamer, when you told the policeman you were afraid I would kill myself, and not six hours later, in our cabin... But we never speak of that. Something so terrible we can only pretend it never was, that we are not both waiting for it to recur.

You are standing on the edge. When you turn towards me, your face is eerily vivid: your eyes bloodshot, your cheeks mottled. I catch your bitter smell, deeper than breath or skin.

'If there was a word you could say to make me disappear, would you say it?'

Do all married couples have these conversations?

'Don't tell me you don't think about it.'

Oh God, what I would not give to own my own thoughts, free of your voice accusing me, casting every impulse in a sinister light, until I no longer know who or what I am. Would I say the word to erase you? Yes! *No*. Why must it come to this, why not admit our mistake and go our separate ways? Because that would be too rational, and you and I have made a world beyond reason, a world where love, hate, desire, revulsion, indifference, all coexist. How often have we said the irrevocable, the unforgiveable? Nothing changes.

Seconds pass. We are still here. You, me, the precipice. The distant screaming of the wind. An almost-silence, filled with our suspense.

I say, 'Do you remember what happened on the lake steamer?'

The carved look that overtakes your face when I say anything you do not wish to hear.

'After I told you I was carrying our child?'

'What are you talking about?'

'When you tried to kill me.'

Your face twists in theatrical disbelief.

'You kept asking, "Whose is it: the Prince of Wales's?" You cut off my windpipe.'

My throat burns at the memory. Even if I could have broken your grip, where was there to run to in the middle of the lake? I felt the fight going out of me, my hold on life weakening. A knock at the door. The cabin steward come to turn down the sheets. The handle moved, but you had engaged the bolt. My hands found the china washbasin. With the last of my strength, I pushed it to the floor.

'The steward heard us struggling and sent for the captain.

He locked me in an empty cabin for the rest of the journey.'
But handed me back to your keeping when we docked, under the approving eyes of the police.

I loosen my muffler. 'Here: you can still see the bruises.'

'I can't *see* anything!'

'Because you won't look.'

'Because I *cannot see*!'

I move my hand in front of your face.

You ignored Gert's warning about screening your eyes, and the dazzle has taken away your sight.

That bitter smell of yours is stronger now.

'Are you really blind?'

'I said so, didn't I?' You grind the palms of your gloved hands into your eye sockets.

I could leave you here. You would never make it back to the *Hospiz* alone. I could tell them we became separated in the mist. I would be free to start my life afresh. In time I might even square it with my conscience. Better for one to expire in the cold than for both to face this lingering death.

I step back from the edge.

You cry out, '*Mariam!*'

Tears run down your cheeks.

I have the strangest feeling. Pins and needles. Icy fingers brushing my face. I know now: you are not strained, or over-wrought, or letting things *get out of proportion*.

'Here, Herbert, take my hand.'

The *Hospiz* looked like a prison in the dark.

'What's happening?'

'Nothing.'

You hammered on the door again with the side of your fist, making contact with an iron stud. I could see it hurt, but you did not cry out.

We listened to the silence.

I decided to walk around the building, in the hope of spotting a chink of light. I warned you this would take some time. You gripped my arm, mortally afraid of me leaving your side. It had been hard enough getting you off the pass, watching your footing as well as my own, dreading the fall that would take me down with you. Would we have to go everywhere like Siamese twins from now on?

Somehow you knew I was smiling. 'What's so funny?'

A vision of me wrenching out of your grasp and running away very slowly on my snowshoes, with you in blind, lumbering pursuit. Wisely, I kept this to myself.

'What can you see?'

'Stone walls, shuttered windows.'

Hübschhorn gleamed blue-white under star glitter, lovely and ominous. Did the monks keep diurnal hours, rising at dawn and retiring at dusk? Had they closed for the winter? There were three or four other habitations in the distance. None showed the faintest glimmer of light.

'I can't walk any further,' you said.

'Then let's hope we don't have to.'

'We could sleep here, with the building between us and the wind.'

'No one could survive a night in these temperatures.'

Mentioning the cold made me feel it more keenly. I stamped to bring the blood back into my feet. If I blew into my gloves, would my moist breath turn to ice?

You lifted your head. 'I can smell smoke.'

The heavy pine door creaked.

On the threshold, framed in yellow light, stood a friar in the black habit of the Augustinians. Later, I would see that his rosy cheeks were the scars of repeated exposure to the elements. I would find the air not much warmer inside than out – unless I stood directly in front of the stove, depriving others of their meagre share of heat. The barley soup would be tasteless, the Glühwein lukewarm, the coarse linen bedsheets damp to the touch. Nevertheless, in that first moment, I almost swooned with pleasure.

He ushered us in, introducing himself as Father Maurice, explaining that the *Hospiz* was a travellers' refuge, not a hotel. There was no charge for bed and board, although most guests left a donation in the alms box. He would point it out to us when he showed us the chapel. But first, we must eat.

The room was large, with a vaulted ceiling, bare boards underfoot, close-fitting shutters over the windows. Five men sat at one end of a long table, having shed their overcoats but not their hats. They nodded at us, too intent on eating to make conversation. A brother brought plates of broth and glasses for the Glühwein.

A large brown-and-white dog nosed around our feet, hoping for scraps: a St Bernard, bred to dig men out of avalanches, though from his easy way with our fellow guests, he seemed more of a pet. His great head nudged my thigh, looking up at me with rheumy eyes. I scratched behind his ears, which he seemed to like. You were spooning barley soup down your chin.

'Do you want me to feed you?'

You nodded.

'*Vous avez la cécité des neiges, Monsieur?*' Father Maurice asked.

I answered, '*Oui, mon Père.*'

A bell clanged outside. The dog barked. You nearly jumped out of your skin. One of the travellers laughed.

There was a blast of cold air as a side door opened to admit a monk wrapped extravagantly against the weather, rabbit pelts around his feet, a bearskin over his robe, his head protected by hat and cowl. He was English: Brother Francis, a visitor from the Austin Friars in Shoreditch.

He shed his swaddling and joined us at the table. It was an effort not to stare. He was completely bald. No eyebrows or eyelashes, either. I could not decide whether it made him look very young or very old. One of the friars brought him a cup of aromatic tea sweetened with honey. 'That smells delicious,' I said, angling to be brought a cup myself. Brother Francis's face lit up. 'You are English, Madam?' Scotch, I said. 'Of course! From Edinburgh? No, wait, don't tell me. I have an ear for accents. Some way further to the west, I fancy. Definitely a lowlander... Could it be Glasgow? Ah! You see: I can always tell! What brings you to the Alps?'

It seemed a long time since I had last laughed with a stranger. Not that Brother Francis was particularly amusing, just talkative, with an amiable disposition. I had forgotten such people existed.

He was an admirer of Wordsworth and, instead of a Baedeker, had brought *The Prelude* as his guide. He was delighted to hear I was familiar with the lines on the Simplon Pass, when the poet lost his way and asked a peasant how far to the Alps, to be told, 'You have already crossed them.' He found this episode profoundly truthful. How often did we fix our hopes on a certain destination, only to find life's journey was more circuitous, and our Heavenly Father's purpose more mysterious, than we had anticipated?

You were tugging at my skirt. Brother Francis fell silent.

'Is something the matter, Herbert?'

You reminded me of a child mortified to find himself the object of adult attention.

'I am very tired,' you muttered. 'I should like to go to bed.'

When you were settled upstairs with a pewter hot water bottle, in what I was relieved to see was a single cot, Father Maurice bandaged your eyes. You seemed calmed by the blessing he murmured over your head. I took some money from your pocket to leave in the chapel. 'You won't be long?' How anxious you sounded. It wrung my heart, but I forgot nothing. When we were out of earshot, Father Maurice warned me not to expect his ministrations to speed your recovery. It would be two days before you were able to see again. In the meantime, the pressure of a blindfold eased the torment of the sightless mind. Two days? I queried. Three at most, he assured me. I said we must set off for home at first light.

The *Hospiz* had been built as a barracks, to guard Napoleon's road over the Alps. I found it hard to believe such an enormous structure, with beds for three hundred guests, was home to just seventeen monks. Father Maurice told me they arrived as young men and saw out fifteen winters (each winter, there, lasting between eight and nine months), after which their constitutions were broken and they had to be retired to a more clement post.

Hearing that, I was surprised there were as many as seventeen. He said the order turned away twice that number each year. The young were drawn to sacrifice. In some, it was a form of pride; in others, despair. I asked him what quality the postulants had to demonstrate to be accepted? Love, he said.

'Love of God?'

'*L'amour de Dieu, de l'humanité et de soi-même.*'

The chapel was almost as bare as a Scotch church, with a residual smell of incense and damp. Three thick candles cast their gilded fog over the altar. What a pastiche Walter would have made of this place, the St Bernard howling like a lost soul, and the terrified monks warning their friar that, by allowing a woman to cross the threshold, he had called down the ancient curse! But were the plain facts any less Gothick? A would-be murderess passing herself off as a solicitous wife. Would I really have pushed you over the precipice, or left you to stumble over of your own accord? The only answer I could find was that I had not. I wondered if you sensed how close you had come to death. Was it this, as much as your blindness, that made you docile now? If so, I could not regret it.

I dropped some coins in the box. Should I squirrel away a few francs before your sight returned? I could lead you into the middle of a busy railway station and slip quietly from your side. And then what? My name would be reviled by all who knew me. I could never go home.

'*Voulez-vous que j'entende votre confession?*'

'*Je suis protestante.*'

'God will understand,' he said, in English.

Our eyes met.

What would I confess: not loving my husband, dreading his touch, lacking the courage to abandon him, seeing the years ahead as a living death? Were murderous phantasies a worse sin than despair?

'*Mon mari est fou.*'

My husband is a madman. It seemed to me then I had always known it, and yet saying it aloud changed everything.

Father Maurice said snow blindness was a terrible affliction.

'*Je m'excuse, mon Père.* I'm so tired, I no longer know what I'm saying.'

Escorting me back to my room, he had an idea to make the journey to England less arduous. Brother Francis was due to return to London at the end of the week. If he was happy to advance his departure by a couple of days, we could travel together.

In the diligence you held my hand tightly, while Brother Francis prattled on. At Brig, he supervised the transfer of our luggage to the train. We had barely left the station when you fell asleep, your head lolling on my shoulder. At Martigny, Brother Francis interrupted his description of the Shoreditch slums to offer an apology: he had said little more than *good morning, please* and *thank you*, since leaving England eight weeks before. His French was halting, his German non-existent. What a pleasure it was to express his thoughts, but he would quite understand if I found his loquacity an imposition. On the contrary, I said, I was grateful for his company, and his conversation. (And even more grateful that he expected me to disclose so little in return.) He resumed his lament at the plight of the London poor. By Lake Geneva, you were awake and hungry, but reluctant to make a spectacle of yourself in the restaurant car. Brother Francis went to enquire if it would be possible to eat in our compartment.

'Is anybody here?' you said.

'Just us.'

Your face relaxed. 'Describe him to me.'

'About your age. Slightly built. No hair. His head is rather like a whiff-whaff ball.'

We laughed.

'How long before we're home?'

'This time tomorrow we'll be crossing the English Channel.'

You settled back against my shoulder.

Brother Francis returned with a waiter who served us with *omelettes aux fines herbes*. When I guided the fork to your lips, you opened your mouth like a baby bird.

PART III

I think you are the only woman I have met, who is so intrinsically detached, so essentially separate and isolated, as to be a real writer or artist or recorder.

Letter from D. H. LAWRENCE to Catherine Carswell,
16th April 1916

A friend of your late father rented us the lower floor of a terraced house in Barnes. An alley beside it led down to the Thames, where there were herons and sculling oarsmen. Your mother had been storing our wedding presents, a few pieces of furniture and three tin boxes of newspapers supposedly containing defamatory references to you. Even in the cartoons, you told me. When I got back with my shopping, the pages were strewn across the floor. The morning papers waited in a pile on the bamboo table. It would take you most of the day to get through them, reading every word. Your childlike sweetness had vanished the instant your sight returned, soon after we'd left Calais. You were as jealous and overbearing and mad as ever.

'Herbert, leave that.'

I picked a path across the floor and put the tray on top of the unread papers. A buttered muffin and a cup of coffee laced with brandy. You found the damp of England in March worse than Alpine cold.

'Where have you been?'

'To the shops.'

I waited for you to ask whether I had been served by a man, but your mind was still on the newspapers.

'I got some paint.'

'We can't redecorate. It's in the lease.'

'Not for the walls. I bought something else.' I dragged the

cradle in from the hall. 'With a lick of paint it'll be as good as new.'

You sprang out of the armchair. I stepped back, measuring my distance from the door. *Never again.*

'Are you *trying* to provoke me?'

'Six months from now we will have a baby. We need to be ready.'

You kicked the table, spilling coffee over the newspapers. 'You disgust me.'

'Herbert, this isn't rational.' I was less afraid in England, but still it took courage to say, '*You* are not rational.'

Something in your eyes.

'You know it, don't you?'

'Tell me, what's it like to care for nothing but your own debauched appetites? How can you go out there – to the shops, you say – and look decent people in the eye? No, don't turn away. I'd like to know.'

'I can look them in the eye, because—'

But you did not want to hear what I had to say.

'I realise you never loved me, but there is such a thing as loyalty. Of course, it means nothing to you. You won't even tell me why they're spying on me.'

'Herbert, listen to me. No one is spying on you.'

Your head jerked like a bridling horse.

'We will find you a doctor. You're going to get better and go back to teaching. You can paint in the evenings...'

Dear God, how would I bear it?

'We'll be a family – you, me and the baby.'

'I will strangle it at birth, if it's not already poisoned in there.'

'I will not put up with talk like that.'

'*Then get out!*'

I grabbed my coat.

A scouring wind flattened the daffodils on Barnes Green. I watched the wavelets scudding across the duckpond. By now you would be listening out for me. In another hour, you would be in a vindictive temper. Better not to go back at all than to return any later.

The mallards were in their breeding plumage. They blocked my path, begging for bread. The boldest quacked at me, his neck as iridescently green as a scarab beetle's wing. Yellow catkins dangled from the trees. The whole world was ready to bring forth new life. Perhaps you would feel more paternal when you held the baby. But what if you did not?

Fanny was surprised to see me. How long had I been in London? She looked past me, down the steps. 'Is Herbert not with you?'

'I made a mistake,' I said.

She looked at me with the astonishment of a woman counting the days until she could marry the man she loved.

Fanny's landlady did not allow overnight guests, but cousin Gussie and his wife Constance had a spare room in Hampstead. Heaven knows what Fanny told them. They were so reluctant to upset me that my marriage was never mentioned. Hop was less tactful. He would soon be my brother-in-law: duty compelled him to speak plainly. No one begrudged me a short holiday with relatives, but I would have to go back: I had surrendered any choice in the matter when I married you.

I wrote a letter to your mother, telling her you were determined to divorce me.

I spent hours walking on the heath, telling myself this was freedom, although my every thought was of you. I pictured you in the bright room that served as your studio. I told you what life had been like for me, since our wedding. I said, for you, love meant crushing every shred of individuality in the other, eliminating every trace of the person you had fallen in love with. I vented it all, every last grievance. You said nothing. Now I had control and you had none, your personality crushed. What had you done to me that I could wish for that, even in phantasie?

How cold it was in bed without you.

When not torturing you in daydreams, I tortured myself. For months I had longed to escape you. Before I met you, if not always happy, I had been hopeful and alive to the world. After, the world had shrunk to your dimensions. I had let you infect me with your suspicion and despair. You were death to me, but you were all I had.

I missed you.

You opened the door before I had time to use my key. In your shocked face I glimpsed my own power. A new thought. I stored it away. Four days since I had last seen you. The flat seemed much the same, except for the cradle stacked in splintery sticks beside the range and that sour smell pervading the unaired rooms. Your smell. Your cheek pressed hard and fervent against mine. And, yes, I was moved.

Henry Acland Munro, your best man, was resident surgeon at a private lunatic asylum in Catford. He was married to a short, bosomy Englishwoman some years older. They lived in a splendid tied house just around the corner from his patients. On the dining room walls were sketches by Dante Gabriel Rossetti and John Ruskin, both friends of his late father. I had forgotten he was a Scot. In fact, I had forgotten him altogether: his virile beard, his candid brow, his steady gaze. He complimented my umbrella, my dress. I gave you an anxious glance, although he meant nothing improper. These were the gallantries of a man so besotted, he loved all women for reminding him of his wife. How happy they were, their lips budding with the same smile, as if their life together were one long joke. She had the playfully bossy manner I had noticed before in women of diminutive stature. He gave way to her with charming helplessness, taking it for granted that you and I enjoyed a similar state of bliss. She was less misled. Her shrewd glance shuttled between us.

He told us Ellen had refused him at first, not wanting to tie herself to a man whose business was lunatics. Now she had come to know his patients, she would often call at Flower House to take tea with them.

'It's true,' she said, 'I am quite fond of one or two. Not the dangerous mad – they're locked away – but the poor unfortunates who wander freely in the house and grounds. Miss Collins, Mrs Tavistock. If you met them, you'd think they were as sane as any of us, just a little sad.'

In that case, I wondered how they came to be there.

Henry answered, 'Their sadness was inconvenient to their relatives.'

'*Ham*,' his wife growled.

'Mrs Munro thinks I will gossip myself out of a living.'

'Without meaning a word of it.'

It was pleasant to watch them teasing each other, to know that marriage was not always a bed of nails.

Henry asked how we liked living in Barnes.

'It's good enough as a stopgap until I leave England,' you said.

He smiled at me. 'Back to Italy?'

'Catherine will not be coming with me.'

I sensed Ellen's warning touch on his leg.

'I am divorcing her.'

I sighed.

'We were crossing Lake Maggiore. She went below deck. I followed and saw her enter a cabin. The door was locked. Some time later a *gentleman* came out. He wasn't the first. If she has any sense, she'll go back to Glasgow. She would be wise to keep out of Mrs Keppel's way.'

Glancing up from the table, I met Henry's steady look. Ellen rang the bell and told the maid the ladies would take coffee upstairs.

In her drawing room, I said you had been ill. It left you prey to odd fancies. I had thought seeing your childhood friend would do you good. I had had no idea you would say anything so embarrassing.

'Really, Ham is Arthur's friend. He attended your wedding as Arthur's proxy.'

'Oh,' I said.

She was a nice enough woman, but she did not want her husband bothered by lunatics in his leisure hours, and I could not really blame her.

The natives stand and stretch, easing their aching backs, wiping the sweat from their streaming brows. 'Tata!' the corporal barks. 'Get a move on!' Once more they bend to the task. A spade chimes, striking stone. The mounds of earth increase. The stink of sweat is overpowering, yet sweeter than the stench coming from the heaped sacks. A sapper arrives, salutes, bends double and heaves up his breakfast. Behind him a party of natives bring more sacks to be slung on the heap. The last of the corpses lands with a less percussive thud. Is that movement – or just the flies swarming over the sacking? The gravediggers drop their shovels, muttering a word the corporal does not understand. He quizzes the old darky who speaks English and Dutch along with a couple of local lingos. 'Bad spirit, sah.' The corporal knows these savages and their superstitions: if he does not stamp this out now, every Kaffir in the camp will get the vapours. He orders the sapper to untie the sack. The natives shriek. Inside is a two-year-old child, or maybe older, starvation makes it hard to tell. A girl, judging by those filthy rags. She blinks in the sudden glare.

'Ssshhh,' I said, touching my hand to your clammy brow. 'You're dreaming.'

'Help her!'

You were still inside the nightmare.

'Help who?'

Your eyes were desperate. My heart cleaved with pity. My head said *madman*.

You clutched my hand. 'Don't leave me!'

I lit the lamp. 'What were you dreaming about?'

Suddenly you were wary.

'Was it Africa?'

'You know it was.'

'Tell me.'

For once, you did.

'It's not real,' I said. But how could I be sure of that?

You muttered something. I leaned closer, into your sour smell. 'Marry *who*?'

You whispered, 'I hear her screaming.'

You wanted to know if I could skin a rabbit? You were off to the common to shoot one for dinner. No more butcher's meat for us. An omelette would do for lunch; the great advantage of eggs was their impregnable shells.

I went out to buy some.

On a bench by the duckpond, I opened Lucie's letter, redirected from cousin Gussie's. I was not to trouble your mother again: it was barely fifteen months since your father's death. I thought I might be accused of exaggerating, but she accepted my account of your condition. There was a Doctor Gemmell in Glasgow. If you were not well enough to make the journey, she was sure he would recommend a colleague in London. She could offer nothing more by way of help: her last three letters to you had been returned unopened.

Dear Lucie, thank you for your understanding reply...

It never crossed my mind to wonder why she believed me.

'Cathie.'

'Hello, Walter.'

How good it was to see him again.

'Jackson.'

You ignored his outstretched hand.

Your mother offered me her cheek to kiss.

'Please sit down, Herbert,' I said, 'you're making us uncomfortable.'

You took the empty chair. Your mother poured the tea. A sticky web of the unspoken tightened around us. So many criss-crossing loyalties – mine to Walter; his to your mother; mother's to son; despite everything, mine to you.

You pushed the cup away, slopping tea into the saucer. 'You drink it, I'll have yours.'

'Why?'

Your look said you were not such a fool as to answer me.

I exchanged the cups. You watched me take a sip.

Your mother offered me a slice of cake.

You asked why she had not cut your slice from the same side as mine. She looked at the plate in confusion.

'How was Italy?' Walter said, helping himself to the piece of cake you believed to be poisoned.

'Full of surprises,' I said.

For a moment his hooded gaze was mordantly amused. 'But you had been there before?'

'As a girl. It was very different seeing everything through a husband's eyes. An education, in all sorts of ways.' I had to stop this. It was too caustic, and at the same time too much like flirting. 'Herbert did a great deal of sketching. He is working up a new painting.'

'A portrait of Catherine?' your mother asked you.

'Why not? After Manet. Olympia on a bed embroidered with the coronet and three feathers.'

I was not sure she caught the reference, but Walter's throat-clearing made matters plain enough.

'It's to be a painting of the Transvaal,' I said.

'Oh yes?' There was a note of alarm in her voice.

Chimingly, you drove your teaspoon around the cup.

210

A silence settled on our little tea party.

Walter plied his cake fork. I remembered how deliciously self-conscious I used to feel under his scrutiny.

'You look well,' he said, 'less of a daisy, more of a rose.'

'Marriage will do that to a woman.'

'It suits you.'

'And to think, if I hadn't come down to Berkshire last September I might still be a spinster...'

You snorted. We all pretended not to notice.

'...I will never forget I have you to thank for introducing us.'

'Really, it was Lucie.'

'I draw no distinction between a man and his wife.'

'How very conventional of you.' He touched his lip with the napkin, dislodging a cake crumb. 'She'll be sorry to have missed you.'

'More tea?' your mother said.

Walter and Lucie had recently moved house. Your mother was eager to see their new home. Walter said it was an ugly redbrick villa with leaded windows and an open porch the builder had added so he could describe the place as 'Arts and Crafts'. Lucie was sure he was in league with Liberty's wallpaper department.

As if we were alone, you asked, 'What do you think of the portraits?'

I looked up.

Each of the paintings grouped around the mantel was dark as pitch, the subjects rendered in half-tones. Lucie as a girl, with her hair down. A lighter-skinned, less sensual-looking youth with your unruly hair. (Presumably your brother Arthur.) I guessed the bearded old man was your father. I recognised the other as William Makepeace Thackeray. Clearly Rembrandt had been an influence on you, although Rembrandt's faces leapt out of the frame, alive after two hundred and fifty years. Your subjects were uniformly costive.

'They're not very cheerful,' I said.

Your mother and Walter looked bemused at our laughter.

'Which do you prefer?'

'I like the way you did Thackeray's shirt front, but your father has more humanity.'

'He had none in life.'

'Then it's a bad likeness, but I prefer it.'

'Yes,' you said musingly, 'I knew you would. You have a weakness for old men. Royal lechers, pretentious windbags—'

'That's enough, old chap,' Walter said.

'Does he think he's the only one?' Your voice was husbandly, intimate. 'Or doesn't he care, as long as he gets his share of the fun?'

I stood up. 'I think I should go.'

'Am I embarrassing you?'

'You're upsetting your mother.'

'And we mustn't have that. Children can starve and women can hang, but we can't have Mater *upset*.'

My mother-in-law and Walter rose from the table.

'Thank you for coming, Catherine,' she said. 'You must come again soon, and tell us all about your travels.'

'You want to hear about Italy? My bride committed adultery with the Prince of Wales – the king, as you call him. She's such a devious slut, she'll open her legs to any man who flatters her.'

I crossed to the door. Your glance flickered. You did not want me to leave you there.

'She is trying to foist another man's whelp on me. I warn you: if you accept it as your grandchild, it won't be the last. She will supply us with a whole tribe of bastards—'

'*Bertie!*' your mother boomed, as she must have done when you were a boy.

'And of course you take her part. You'd believe anyone who spoke against me. Father, Lucie, that bitch of a land-lady, and of course, Major Burn Murdoch.' Your voice rose, parodically obsequious. 'Dear Major, may I express our heartfelt thanks to you for slandering our second son. You may be sure we will keep a close watch on him and spread the calumnies among all his friends so that they too account him a liar. Fortunately my husband is in a position to guarantee that his drawings will never be seen in the public prints.'

'Your father did a very great deal for you,' she said.

You laughed.

'His influence opened every door – he sent you to Paris!'

'To get me out of the way, when he got too old to thrash me and I got too big to be thrashed. He hated me, and I fully reciprocated.'

'Why do you say these things? You know they're not true.'

'What? That he thrashed me? And not just me. We all heard him. We all knew. If I'd been the only one, I might have put up with it. You wanted him dead as much as any of us.'

Your mother began to mewl. It was the most extraordinary sound. Walter's face was a mask of embarrassment.

'Oh, stow it, Mater.' Such a bleak look in your eyes. You got up from the table. I stepped back, out of your way.

The front door slammed behind you.

Your mother was still making that noise.

I reminded myself to let her take the lead in the following conversation. Once she and Walter had come to the inevitable conclusion, then I could say it: '*Henry Munro is a doctor...*'

In the middle of the night I woke to find you above me, lit by a blade of moonlight, your eyes open, unseeing. Was this sleepwalking, sleep-pawing? And if not, then what?

'Herbert, you're dreaming again.'

Your hands persisted.

'No!' I tried to push you off.

How strong you were. You parted my thighs as easily as a baker divides a lump of dough. I reached for the glass of water on the bedside table.

You shouted, rearing back, your face and hair dripping wet.

You knew me now.

I had never seen a grown man cry. Your mouth gurned as you folded onto the mattress.

Exchanging my damp nightdress for your dressing gown, I opened the curtains. Moonlight bled the colour from the bedspread.

'I'm cold,' you said, although your brow was burning hot, 'come back to bed.'

I sat on the edge of the mattress. 'What was it this time?'

You shook your head.

'Try to remember.'

'I *can't*.'

'About me?'

Evidently not.

'Some other woman?'

A sob.

I was so tired. Would I never sleep through till morning again?

'Was it someone in Liverpool – or Africa?'

Your smell was almost sulphurous, your eyes black. I thought of Mother's prayer circle casting out devils.

'*You have to help me.*'

'How?'

'*I don't know.*'

Our glances locked. You had made me suffer for so long, why should I care that you felt pain? And yet I did.

'If I found a doctor,' I said, 'someone with experience of—'

'*No one has experienced this! I'm in hell!*'

'But he would have some understanding. More than either of us. He might know of something to stop the headaches at least...'

You were listening. For the moment, desperation overrode your mistrust of me.

'Or a rest cure. A nursing home...'

I felt the change in you. 'Where I would not be your responsibility. You could wash your hands of me.'

'Herbert...'

'You must think I'm a fool.'

'I want you to get better.'

'You're like all the rest, calling me sick. Is this their idea? Did they put you up to it?'

I took a tramcar to Catford. The asylum was not used to casual callers. Dr Munro was on his rounds. I agreed to wait in his office. There was a photograph of Ellen in a silver frame.

'My dear Catherine, this is an unexpected pleasure.'

'Cathie, please.' I found it possible to correct him, as I never could you. 'Not a pleasure, I'm afraid, more of a consultation.'

It was his breadth that was so attractive. His barrel chest, that wide forehead, the flattish cheeks above his beard. Even his eyes were spacious, and full of light. I wondered why I had chosen your narrowness.

'I suppose you've come about Herbert,' he said.

A raw morning, the icy rain carried on a slicing wind. Early as I am, they are waiting by the duckpond. When Henry moves towards me, his companions tip their hats. The old man is tall, with skin that looks almost Indian against his snowy beard: Doctor Savage, an eminent alienist. He called at the flat two days ago. You were too worried about eavesdroppers to demonstrate your delusions in detail, but you mentioned the Prince of Wales. A magistrate has signed the necessary papers. I am to return home and expect them in five minutes. Do I have any questions?

What have I done?

When the doorbell rings you have no idea what is about to happen. I feel the urge to embrace you one last time, which I resist. I let them in. The look on your face will stay with me for ever.

'I've been expecting this for a long time.'

One of Henry's burly, bowler-hatted attendants closes the front door, fearing you will run into the street, but you go the other way, towards the bedroom. Guessing why, I move to intercept you. For a moment we are jammed together in the doorway before we burst into the room. My fingers close on the cold metal of the barrel. Your hand is on the grip. You jerk the pistol upwards, but I hold on. I can smell our sleep on the rumpled sheets, mixed with the oil you used to clean the

216

gun. The other attendant clamps his arms around your chest. You grunt in surprise. I wrest the pistol from your grasp and hurl it through the window.

You say, 'There was no need to break the glass.'

For a long time after they have taken you away, I cannot think what to do with myself. Your mother has offered to have me to stay. I foresee many breakfasts and suppers, each of us assuring the other that you are receiving the very best care. I should pack my clothes, go out and hire a glazier. In the back yard I retrieve the pistol. It never left your person in Africa, and all the months we spent in Italy. Should I keep it for you? There is no known cure for suspicious insanity. Henry was very sorry. I had to cover my face to hide my relief.

What have I done?

I remind myself you tried to kill me. You have enjoyed another two months of liberty since then, if 'enjoyed' is the word.

When I break open the gun, the chamber is empty.

I lock up the flat, although anyone could climb in through the broken window. Tomorrow I will have to visit you and show concern for your welfare, and you will call me a liar, and you will be quite right. I can hardly bear to contemplate the years ahead, but today, for now, I am free.

I walk down Barnes High Street with stinging cheeks and coat skirts flying, the March wind doing its best to tear the hat from my head. The greengrocer is hurrying to dismantle his pavement display of potatoes and onions. A collie tethered outside the butcher's barks at a piece of paper birling along the gutter. I look up into the racing sky and feel – oh, everything. Guilt, loneliness, wild exultation. I welcome every blast of air, the lashing rain, my soaking feet.

Around four the next morning, in your mother's guest bedroom, I wake and read a hundred pages of Middlemarch. I lie in warm sheets, the arm holding the book outside the covers almost numb with cold, and there is no one to tell me I will catch a chill, no one to treat reading a book as tantamount to infidelity. I watch the sun rise in a sky the exact hue of our first awakening in Como. Later, when I walk to the library, shopkeepers are sweeping the wind-wracked streets.

Dear Catherine,

I trust you are pleased with yesterday's work. I have often suspected you of devious and unworthy conduct, but I never imagined you capable of this. I know my mother and Walter had a hand in it, it may be you were not the prime instigator, nevertheless you have betrayed me. What a fool I am to have loved you so deeply, but I would rather own a fool's heart than a false one.

The bag you packed for me contained neither sketch-book nor pencils. I have need of both. Will you bring them tomorrow? I am sure you have no wish to see me, but you are still my wife.

Herbert

P.S. You will notice I have numbered this letter. Please do the same in your replies so we shall know if any of our correspondence 'goes astray'.

Rose House
21st March 1905
2

Dear Catherine,

Thank you for coming yesterday. I admit I expected a longer visit, if only for appearance's sake, although I cannot blame you for wanting to get out of here as quickly as possible. I feel the same. Without the same freedom, unfortunately.

I have been thinking about your remark that it did not seem 'too bad a place'. I suppose you meant that the chairs were upholstered and the floors swept. Did you not notice that you were in a room reserved for visitors, well away from the lunatics? I assure you, you would have gained a very different impression had we met in the gallery. I am surrounded by every sort of grotesque. I can hardly hear my own thoughts for their senseless jabber. There is no 'rest cure' to be had here, even if I were in need of one. I have been the victim of a gross fraud. I beg you, speak to my mother and Walter. I am prepared to believe you did not appreciate the full consequences when you plotted to have me abducted from our home. This is your chance to undo a great wrong.

Your husband

Rose House
25th March 1905
5

Dear Catherine,

It is now seven days since I came here. It seems like an eternity, and yet the shock is just as keen. I am watched day and night. Everything I say and do is written down in a ledger. To what purpose, God only knows. I am so afraid, Catherine. Eight days ago, I had no inkling that I was about to lose my liberty. How can I be sure there is not worse to come? But what could be worse than this? I have lost my home, the company of my wife, the freedom to come and go as I please. I am hemmed about by some who wish me ill, and others so bereaved of their wits there is no knowing what they might do. Yesterday I overheard two of the attendants discussing me. 'A crafty one,' they agreed. If I had had so much as an ounce of craft, I would not have let myself be kidnapped in broad daylight. I would have trusted no one, least of all the woman who held my heart. I am curious to know when they recruited you. Please tell me you were not working with them from the

very beginning. Leave me my tender memories, at least.
Your husband

My dearest Catherine,

I dreamed of you last night, such a happy dream. We were living in a wooden cabin in what I took to be America, a wild place with brightly coloured birds and meadow flowers and sweet, clean air. I was painting – imagine that! I am sorry you have never known me happy in my work. I am quite another fellow then. How different our lives would have been, if only they had left us alone. We would still be in Italy, you hunting through the flea market for treasures to adorn our home, me finishing a portrait to show at the Royal Academy. We might have had a little dog, a white terrier with a piratical patch of brown fur across one eye, to keep us amused with his antics.

In my dream the day turned stormy. You had gone out foraging for mushrooms and came back wet through. I built up the fire and boiled kettle after kettle to fill the tin bath. You sat shivering, hugging your knees, as I washed you. Then I wrapped you in a towel and carried you to bed, where I rubbed you dry until your skin was rosy pink again. How in love we were. How desperate I felt, on waking to reality. What a place this is. Who would have thought Henry Munro capable of inflicting such misery on his fellow men? As you know, I have been angry with you, but now I see we were both deceived by him. How bitterly you must regret it! Dear heart, let us look to the future. I am quite the model patient here, but my thoughts are my own (if you take my meaning).

221

Nil desperandum. We may yet live to laugh at our little white dog.

Your ever-loving husband

---

76 Longridge Road
Earl's Court
7th April 1905

Dear Herbert,

Thank you for your letters. I was not expecting quite so many, although I am always pleased to receive them. I hope you will understand that I cannot reply to every single one. I should use up all my news and have nothing to tell you when I next visit.

As you probably know by now, on Tuesday you will be transferred to the asylum in Oxford. Your mother thinks it best, and I am sure she is right. She can combine visits to two of her children, and Lucie and Walter will be able to see you whenever they wish. You can expect me before nine o'clock. Dr Mercier will drive us up to Oxford, I will help you settle in, and then spend the night at Lucie's, before taking the train back here on Wednesday.

There is one last matter I must mention. It makes me very unhappy that you will not share my excitement about the child I am expecting, or even acknowledge it. I have no wish to start another argument about its paternity, I have said all I have to say on that, but I must feel free to allude to a condition that is already beginning to affect me and will only become more obvious as the months pass.

Until Tuesday,

C

My dearest Catherine,

It did my heart good to see you yesterday, and to spend a decent amount of time with you. How is it that I still have so much to say? I suppose I should not be surprised. I chatter away to you all day in my head. It's the only thing that makes my life bearable.

I have been mulling over something you said which puzzled me at the time, but the conversation moved on and later I did not remember to ask what you meant by it. You seemed to imply that I was on the brink of severing my life from yours when I was kidnapped by Henry Munro and his ruffians – that if I were not incarcerated here, I should be instructing my solicitors to petition for divorce. In your heart of hearts, Catherine, you cannot believe this. I admit we exchanged rash words in the heat of a quarrel or two, but what husband and wife have not? I pledged myself to you until death. I am yours, body and soul, and you are mine. Whatever happens, that can never be in doubt.

You are always beautiful to me, as you know, but I noticed you were looking rather peaky yesterday. I remember you telling me how you once stole a piece of cake your neighbour had left out for the birds, and your childish conscience tormented you so much that you knocked at her door and confessed. I know that, inside, you are still that little girl, and I love you all the more for it, but it pains me to see you so guilty on my account. I forgive you, my dearest. Please try to forgive yourself. I worry that the extra strain of living with my mother will wreck your nerves. She seems such a harmless old body, but she can draw blood just when you least expect. I wish you would go back to Barnes. What is the point of me paying the rent for the flat to stand empty?

I hear my jailers approaching to lock me in for the night. I will seal this now and write again tomorrow.

Till a' the seas gang dry,

Your husband

P.S. Please remember to number your letters.

---

76 Longridge Road

24th April 1905

Dear Herbert,

I am sorry I could not get to Oxford yesterday. I telephoned as soon as I knew. I hope the message reached you.

I was going to wait to tell you in person, but you might as well know now. I have taken a job for three months collecting subscriptions for Gray's Hospital. They need me between nine and five on weekdays, and until half past twelve on Saturdays. It is reasonably well-paid (30s a week), but there is a great deal of walking involved. I start each day addressing envelopes and doing business at the office. At eleven, I put on my coat and head into the City, to call on banks and insurance offices where I ask the managers to display one of our cards. My first day was Tuesday, and so far I have met with very few refusals, but by Saturday lunchtime I was absolutely exhausted. I went for a 'nap' when I got back to your mother's, meaning to wake in good time to catch the six o'clock train. In fact, I fell into the sleep of the dead and did not open my eyes until eleven yesterday morning. Quite how I will manage a full five-and-a-half days this week I'm not sure. I am afraid I shall be poor company for your mother, dragging my weary bones up to bed by nine every night, but perhaps she will be grateful for the peace and quiet.

I promise to see you on Sunday, without fail, and will remember to bring the shirts with me.

C

My dear Catherine,

I will not have a wife of mine wearing herself out for thirty shillings a week. I thought I had made myself perfectly clear. Since you refuse to stay in Barnes, my mother is willing to feed you and keep a roof over your head. As for bus fares, stamps and other necessities, Mr Simons, manager of the Kensington branch of Barclays Bank, will happily advance whatever sums you need. I cannot imagine why you are being so contrary about this. Are you *trying* to cause me distress? I am imprisoned here, through no fault of my own. Visitors come, or they do not. Letters arrive, or they do not. I cannot recall when I last saw a newspaper. I have only the most piecemeal impression of what is happening in the world beyond these walls. It would be abominably frustrating for any man, but think how much worse it is for a husband, knowing that his wife is tramping the streets, prey to any passing scoundrel.

I insist that you tender your resignation with immediate effect. Let us say no more about this.

Your loving husband

P.S. I must remind you again to number your letters.

Dear Catherine,

I received a letter from my mother this morning. She tells me that not only have you not given up your job, but you have been staying with your sister for the past week. Do you have any intention of returning to Longridge Road? It is rather inconsiderate of you to keep Mater in the dark. Another surprise was the news that your friend Phyllis is in London. I wonder why you did not mention this to me in your own letter. Could it be because you were entertaining her at your sister's when you had promised to be in Oxford with me? Mater is under the impression that Phyllis will be helping you with the 'flitting' from Barnes. Frankly, Catherine, I am speechless. I told you that I wished to keep the flat. I cannot believe you misunderstood me. To put it in the plainest possible terms: St Ann's Terrace is our home and I mean to return there as soon as I secure my release from this place. In the meantime, I shall continue paying the rent. There will be no 'flitting', as you call it. I forbid it.

Write to me as soon as you get this.

Your husband

My dearest Catherine,

Are you all right? I have neither seen nor heard from you for two weeks. If your letters have not been intercepted, you must be ill. Mater tells me she expects you on Tuesday. I shall sleep easier once I know you are back at Longridge Road. Not that she is to be trusted, but I do not think any actual harm will come to you under her roof.

I am glad to report that spring is well underway here. It is such a relief to look out of the windows and see that sweet, sharp green. I suppose you hardly notice it in London. Will you do me a great favour and take a tramcar to one of the royal parks? I shall enjoy the thought of you marching across the grass, your hair ruffled by the wind, a healthy colour in your cheeks. You never look so well as when you're exerting yourself. I remember the day I came to Glasgow to ask for your hand. How nervous I was. I waited a good hour on the pavement, staring at your house, trying to pluck up the courage to climb the steps. At last I felt something – don't laugh, but it seemed to me the brush of an angel's wing – and turned to see you running towards me. I knew then that Fate had smiled on me.

Visit me as soon as you can. There are things I have to tell you that cannot be put in writing. Events here have taken an unforeseen turn – not good, but not altogether bad either.

I worry about you, my sweetheart, and I miss you unbearably.

Your loving husband

Warneford Asylum
21st May 1905
39

Dear Catherine,

It is now clear to me that your silence these past weeks, and your failure to declare yourself to me on your visits here, can only be a matter of choice. You have been hand-in-glove with them all along. Did you think I was so blinded by affection I would never see the truth?

There is one thing I do not understand. Why do you haunt

me here? I have heard you, and seen you too, at a distance. You went to such trouble to have me locked up, is that not enough for you?

I pity you, Catherine. One day, you will be held to account for your black soul.

Herbert

Warneford Asylum
4th July 1905
58

My dearest,

Do you know, it is ten months to the day since we first met. It sounds such a paltry stretch of time, does it not, but I believe we should trust our hearts over the calendar. I always knew we would meet one day. Even as a boy, I dreamed of loving a beautiful woman with your fierce heart and passionate nature. I searched for you in London, Paris, Liverpool. In my eagerness, I even thought I had found you once or twice. Despite these disappointments, I never lost my faith in us. I recognised you the very first time I clapped eyes on you, larking on Lucie's floor. You blushed so prettily as you got to your feet. Even then you must have sensed that I worshipped you. What sort of God would join us in marriage only to keep us apart? It is very hard, sweetheart, but we must not give up hope. Our love is stronger than all our enemies combined. We will come through this.

Forever your loving
Herbert

My dear heart,

Please send me word of how you are. I know you cannot mean to be cruel, but it is torture not knowing if you are alive or dead. Mater tells me nothing. You cannot imagine how miserable my days are here, how each minute drags. My friends were suborned long ago. Raleigh and Lucie pretend I no longer exist. Even Arthur barely writes. I am surrounded by lunatics and informers. Without you, my dearest girl, I believe I should give up all hope. It is a comfort sometimes to imagine dying by my own hand, all my troubles ended at a stroke. It could be managed with a little planning. But then I think of you receiving the news, and my heart breaks.

I beg you, send me a few lines. Even a postcard will do.

With all the love in the world,

Herbert

---

41 Kersland Terrace
Glasgow
17th August 1905

Dear Herbert,

As you see from the address above, I am back at Mother's. The Gray's Hospital job finished last month, and it is not long until my time. I am a little nervous, but the doctor says I am perfectly healthy, and I suppose other women give birth and live to tell the tale.

I am sorry I could not come to Oxford and break the news of my departure in person. Everything was such a rush. I am now quite a size, a ship in full sail, as my brothers say. Walking my great bulk up and down the pavements of London, I felt as if my coat pockets were crammed with a hundredweight of coal. Your mother kindly offered to let me stay on after the baby is born, but it would have been a dreadful imposition, and if anyone's mother is going to drive me to distraction, it might as well be my own.

In case you are wondering about your recent letters, your mother bundled them up in a brown-paper parcel which arrived this morning. I read the first few after breakfast and will work my way through the rest. I must be honest: some of your accusations leave me quite bewildered, and at other times your extravagant tone puts me in something of a false position. You must see that our circumstances hardly warrant the writing of love letters. I should have said this months ago, but somehow I was afraid to, and stopped writing instead. If you reflect on everything that has happened, you will see that I am right.

I am sorry to learn you are no happier at the Warneford Asylum, but as I do not pay the bills, I really don't see what I can do. Have you written to your mother? Perhaps she can bring some influence to bear.

With all good wishes,

C

Warneford Asylum
18th August 1905
79

My own dear sweetheart,

It brought me such pleasure to see your charming, untidy scrawl again. I should know it among a thousand different hands. Do you recall the shopping list I assumed you had written in Italian? I went to every grocer in Perugia looking for 'buller'!

I am glad you are back in Glasgow, away from my mother. She feels no compunction whatsoever about my confinement. Indeed, she is ready to pay good money to keep me here. If her bribes dried up, I should soon find myself out on the street. But I will not waste precious ink on her. I have been puzzling over the shawl you wore the first few days of our honeymoon, the one stolen with our trunks in Perugia. I can see it clearly in my mind's eye, and yet I cannot say whether it was green or blue. You will think it foolish of me to mourn the loss of such a thing, when so much else has been taken from us, but it seems to me that moment marked our exile from the garden, and afterwards our troubles began in earnest. Remember how happy we were in Milan? What a slugabed you were! Every morning I would lie for a good hour in your warmth, listening to the tigress purr of your snoring. Of course, I know you will deny that! You must not be embarrassed. When a woman is loved as I love you, even her snoring enchants. Ah my love, how sweet these memories are, and how unbearably sad. I must finish here, lest I blot these lines with my tears.

Keep well, my dearest,
Your husband

Glasgow greeted my return with an Indian summer. The Botanic Gardens were crammed with men and women tilting their faces to the sky. The compass needle in my belly swivelled, sending me back to Great Western Road. I was a slave to the whims of the creature forming inside me. It did not like crowds, or cooking smells, or loud noises, or sitting indoors, so I paced the streets as I had in London, only without payment. I had forgotten pregnant women were a scandal here, seen as shameless advertisements for copulation. We were supposed to stay at home, allowing our decent neighbours to pretend that children came straight from God.

Mother was touchingly pleased to have me back but, once the tearful reunion was behind us, I found her muddle-headedness as maddening as ever. Gordon and Grant made a great fuss of me the first night or two. Soon I only saw them at breakfast and dinner. I had the old panicky sense of Life passing me by, and yet I dreaded the turbid feelings stirred up by your letters. Phyl said I should burn them unread.

One morning on Buchanan Street I came across Don Carswell so lost in thought he did not notice me at first. He was still thin and pale and donnish – he even had a parcel of books under one arm – but he looked more at home in the modern world. It was twelve months since I had last seen him. Much could happen in the space of a year; he might even have fallen in love. I smiled rather woodenly in anticipation of this news.

'Cathie!'

Too many feelings flitted across his face for me to name them all, but astonishment and joy were among them. Dismay, too. My size must have been a shock. He mustered a smile not much less wooden than my own and asked after you. In hospital, I said, my stock reply, delivered with a pained look that inhibited the curiosity of neighbours and acquaintances. Don deserved better.

'Actually, it's a lunatic asylum. Delusional insanity.'

He put the books down.

It was not done to touch a pregnant woman in the street, and Don was the last man I would have expected to try. I caught his hand with a quick squeeze, which left us both embarrassed.

His face had a way of slackening when his thoughts were busy. Was he pitying me, or judging me?

'I don't know what to say,' he murmured.

He wanted to take me for a cup of tea, so I could tell him everything. I knew he meant only kindness, but I also knew that, afterwards, he would never look at me in the same way again.

'I have to get home – I'm late already.'

'This evening, then? Come to the *Herald*.'

The compass needle swivelled as if he were my North Pole.

The *Glasgow Herald* newsroom was more like a factory than an office. A wall's length of windows above me admitted light without the distraction of a view. Coolie lampshades hung low over tables. There were cast-iron columns, and a grid of water pipes across the ceiling to douse the room should the wastepaper baskets catch fire. The reporters were all smoking up a fug and clattering away on typewriters with their blackened index fingers. They typed on three sheets at once, interleaved with carbonic paper. As we watched, a man yanked the pages out of the roller, passing the first two to a running boy and impaling the third on a copper spike.

Don grinned. 'Not what you expected?'

I was a little jealous of him for loving it so much.

He took me down to watch the first edition being printed. The floor juddered under our feet. There was a smell of machine oil, and a noise like an express train with a cargo of loose knives and forks. The biggest press in the world, he said, capable of printing, cutting and folding fifty thousand copies an hour. I thought of you with your father in the basement of the *Illustrated London News*.

'Too noisy for you?' Don bawled above the racket.

I shook my head, mesmerised by the speed-blurred ribbon of paper above us, my eyes too slow to follow its zipping progress from off-white innocence to densely printed knowledge.

Upstairs, Don introduced me to the editor, who bore a passing resemblance to the king, being bald and bearded and avuncular-looking. He asked if I considered Shakespeare or Shaw the better playwright? I said Shakespeare for poetry, Shaw for ideas, but Marlowe for inspiration. He seemed to like this answer and wondered if I was available to attend the first night of *Man and Superman* at the Theatre Royal on Thursday.

'The curtain'll be down by ten, and it's – what, a ten-minute walk back here? That gives you an hour and a quarter till the deadline for the final edition. Does five hundred words sound all right?'

I returned a dazed smile. 'I think so – I mean, *thank you*.'

'We'll see you Thursday night, then.'

Don took me across the road to the Arcade Café. We ordered a pot of tea and two plates of macaroni cheese. Next time, he said, he would show me the canteen and introduce me to the sub-editors. I would find the job easier with them on my side.

'You told the editor about me this afternoon, didn't you?'

'He wants to increase our coverage of literature and the arts.'

'You asked him to give me a trial?'

'You impressed him.'

Another woman would have kissed his cheek for this. I punched his arm.

I passed my trial and joined the newspaper's permanent cadre of reviewers. Working to a deadline was surprisingly helpful. No time for dithering or second thoughts. If I trusted my first impressions, the review as good as wrote itself, proceeding by way of logical argument to a satisfying conclusion. I was not sure why I could do this when criticising a play or novel. If I thought about the sacred vows I had made; and your need to possess me utterly; and your rage when you could not; and what I had had to do to, or chosen to do, to save myself; and the affection in your letters; and your madness wound around your sanity as ivy strangles a tree, and what it meant to be husband and wife in these circumstances... all I managed was a deeper confusion. I told myself I had been impossibly lucky. Six months before I had been your hostage. Now I was surrounded by family and friends, earning my living as a writer. I should have been happier. Phyl said I was grieving for my phantasie of a perfect life. I was growing up, she said – and just in time. Soon I would have a baby.

In September Fanny married Hop. Gordon and Grant called them Tom and Mrs Thumb. I was a head taller than him, but neither of us doubted that he was the proper measure of things. It was impossible to imagine him undressed: surely he had sprung out of the womb in a morning coat and striped trousers. Fanny was quite transfigured by happiness. I was glad for her, but I found it very hard.

Diana Katherine Lewis Jackson arrived on Friday October twentieth. Labour was as terrible as all the auld wives said.

They gave me chloroform to dull the pain, which accounted for my clearest memory of the experience: your hand on my brow. I felt it quite distinctly, although you were four hundred miles away.

Mother was heartbroken that I had booked myself into a nursing home instead of giving birth in the mahogany bed where she had been delivered of me. Beforehand I felt selfish about this; afterwards, profoundly thankful. Baby was whisked away to the nursery. I lay numb and blanched, like a lightning-struck tree. Mother was admitted for five minutes, as a special favour, and told not to return. For the next fourteen days I was confined to bed. In the mornings they brought me bread and milk; then, at intervals, beef tea, toast, poached egg, milk pudding, cocoa, bread and butter, and a light beef broth. Every two hours a nurse reminded me to turn onto my side, or my stomach, or my back. I saw no one, other than Baby, who was carried in to be fed every two hours and taken away directly after. The rest of the time I drifted in and out of sleep, wondering if I had dreamed having a daughter.

On the sixth day, I was propped up on pillows for an hour with the window open. My room was just above street level. I could see the deserted pavement through the net curtains. I listened to the trams racketing along Bath Street. When Sister came to lie me flat again, she closed the window. I heard nothing more until a rustle of white apron when the red-haired nurse brought my barley water.

I wondered if your days passed with the same monotony.

One afternoon, Phyl appeared in my room: the first woman I had seen in ten days who was not wearing a starched cap. I had no idea how she had got past Matron.

'You look like the Queen of Sheba, lying there.'

I smiled.

'What's the matter?'

'I'm not meant to talk.'

'Seriously?'

I nodded.

'Whyever not?'

'"Mother needs her rest".'

'It looks like it,' she said sceptically.

I met her eye.

'As bad as all that?'

'Much, much worse.'

She winced. 'That's put me off. Not that I was particularly eager to begin with.'

Dear Phyl. It was just as she had predicted: now my marriage had gone wrong, she *was* the only one I could face.

We talked about her commission for McGeogh's warehouse. She could have it finished in three weeks, if only her mother would release the parlourmaids from their household duties. She was sorry she had not paid a couple of life models from the School of Art. Ethel complained that holding a pose for so long was giving her leg ulcers.

'I tell her, you can't make art without a little suffering.'

'Perhaps she thinks she suffers enough scrubbing your mother's floors.'

The Irish nurse came in with my daughter and was startled to find I had company. I insisted Phyl remain with me during the feeding. The nurse went off to tell Sister.

Baby strained in the crook of my arm, mouth puckering. She was a funny little creature, all dark-eyed hunger, no more human than a squirrel, but mysterious in her power over me.

I unfastened my nightdress.

Phyl had not had much to do with babies. Under her eye, I felt more expert, less like an accidental food supply.

'Well?' I said, fishing for praise.

'They all look the same to me: a baldy head and a bundle of broderie anglaise.'

Casting a precautionary glance at the door, I slipped the little pearl buttons and eased the nightgown over Baby's head. There she was, in the flesh: her mottled, mauveish skin so loose, it seemed another layer to be unbuttoned and shed; her arms and legs no fatter than a cigar. Her fingers still had the look of being steeped too long in water. Their fragility frightened me. I preferred her barrel belly, so nicely solid in its folded napkin.

Phyl had observed corpses in the anatomy room with this same dispassionate glance.

'She was green when she first came out.'

'*Green?*' Now I had her attention.

'Covered in slime. It took a skelp from the midwife and a wipe down with a muslin napkin to convince me she wasn't...' I bit my lip.

'Dead?' Phyl supplied.

I stroked the fine hair on my daughter's soft scalp. She opened her eyes wider, but carried on suckling.

'Would you like to wind her afterwards?'

'Kind of you, but no.'

'Have a sniff, then.'

She grasped my daughter's foot and brought it to her nose.

'The elixir of life,' I said.

'More like Vinolia and rose powder.'

There was a man on the pavement outside. Just the postman, I realised, but by then Phyl had seen my gaze flash towards the window.

'I thought it was someone else,' I said.

'A black-haired someone with a moustache?'

'For a moment.'

She fixed me with her sea-coloured eyes.

'There's a passing resemblance,' I protested.

'You had him put away in an asylum.'

'Strictly speaking, it was his mother did that.'

'He's not going to turn up in Glasgow.'

'No.'

'*No*,' she said pointedly.

We had this conversation, or one very like it, almost every

time we met. You were too much in my thoughts. It exasperated her, as if I had some choice in the matter.

Baby was guzzling. Cupping her crown with my hand, I hummed 'Ae Fond Kiss' to slow her down. Nursing hurt less after ten days of painting my nipples with glycerine and brandy.

'I can't just pretend he doesn't exist,' I said in my humming voice.

'I don't see why not.'

'Nor do I, really, but it seems to be beyond my control.'

Baby's mouth relaxed. I pushed myself higher up the mound of pillows and hoisted her over my shoulder to wind her.

Phyl's lifted eyebrow was waiting for a proper answer.

I sighed. 'Meeting him – marrying him – is the only really *fateful* thing that's ever happened to me, the one thing that can't be undone or forgotten. I'd give anything to go back to last year and tell Walter, "I'm sorry, I can't come to Berkshire".'

I glanced at the warm weight on my shoulder. Did I really wish she had never been born? A meaningless question. It was unimaginable. She was so marvellously alive. And as long as she lived, you and I would be her parents.

'But I can't change the past, and regretting it feels blasphemous.'

'Still your mother's daughter.'

'I mean blasphemous against *Life*.'

The Irish nurse put her head around the door to see if I had finished with Baby. We smiled at her, and she withdrew.

Phyl lowered her voice. 'Any other woman who'd got free of a lunatic wouldn't waste another thought on him – and not just any old lunatic: a lunatic who tried to kill you. Which you seem to see as a mark of distinction.'

'That's not fair.'

Yet I knew what she meant. For all the pain you had caused me, and the shame in others' eyes, I was not of the common run. I had lived an adventurous life.

'I wish to God he had divorced you.'

'Citing the king as co-respondent?'

'If necessary.' Something made her smile. She nodded at my daughter, still propped on my shoulder. 'You know all that milk you just fed her?'

'Oh no!'

I wiped away the sick, put her back in her flannel gown and gave her to Phyl while I changed into a clean nightdress.

'You could love somebody else, you know,' she said, making faces at Baby.

'Once was enough.'

'You'd be very unlucky to meet another man like Herbert.'

I was quiet for so long that at last she looked up. 'But?' she prompted.

Baby's hand curled around my index finger.

'But I'd be the same.'

WARNEFORD ASYLUM, OXFORD

1905

The way Joseph saw it, you had your cacklers, your thrashers, your screamers, your twitchers and your Bible-bashers. Aaron disagreed. He said God had made as many kinds of madmen as there were sorrows and it was his Christian duty to listen, which was why his wife had to wash drool and snot and greasy finger marks out of his uniform six nights a week, while Joseph's sister got away with giving his a damp press.

Eighteen years Joseph had been an attendant at the Warneford. It wasn't a bad job, if you kept the thrashers at arm's length. Being well in with Cook, most days he took home a leftover chop or a piece of apple pie. His fellow attendants were hard workers, in the main, and while he wouldn't go so far as to say he liked the inmates, they were manageable, as long as everyone remembered the golden rule. The mad were mad: there was no sense in 'em.

Eighteen years he'd believed that.

Mr Jackson was admitted in April. His wife brought him in. Not married six months, according to Aaron, who was always first to find out. The head surgeon at the Catford asylum had been best man at the wedding. It gave Joseph a funny feeling just thinking about it: that they could be back-slapping in the smoking room in autumn, and doctor and lunatic by spring. Aaron said the brother-in-law was a professor at the university. Handy for visiting. Not that they'd seen him, or the sister, or the mother who was paying the bills. The wife came every Sunday for a while, reluctance written all over her. Nothing new in that. What hadn't happened before – not to Joseph – was the suspicion he'd had for months now. That, for all his queer notions, Mr J wasn't so different from any other man.

Joseph kept this to himself. He was a senior attendant, one of the most trusted. If you started doubting the doctors, who knew where it'd end? The week Mr J arrived, Dr Neil had him in for a chat. 'I want you to keep an eye on this one. He could be a runner.' Dangerous? Joseph asked. 'Not that I've been told, but you wouldn't want to find out.' A former soldier, a solid hundred and fifty pounds, with that look in his eye: *Don't push me into doing something we'd both regret.*

The first few days, they were never happy. His relatives were plotting against him. He had witnesses to prove it, but he'd only produce them to the proper authorities. Joseph had heard it all before. Like a caged animal, pacing up and down the corridors. He was allowed into the superiors' courtyard for a blow of fresh air, but forbidden the gardens. When Dr Neil decided he was to work in the carpenter's shop, Joseph went with him to see he didn't pocket a chisel. He was handy for a gentleman. Turned out his father and his uncle had been wood engravers. Old Wheeler took a shine to him, told him some stories Joseph had never heard, about the years he spent apprenticed to a shipwright. It was an easy afternoon's work. On their way back to the ward, Mr J asked if he was a billiards man. Joseph said Dr Neil didn't pay his staff to fritter their time away in the games room, why not ask Mr Perks?

'I'm not going to play with a madman.'

There was something about the way he said it, as if Joseph was the cracked one for suggesting such a thing. They both saw the funny side of it, so there they were laughing in the corridor. Anyhow, Joseph gave him a quick game, both of them listening out so they wouldn't get caught. Mr J was the better player, but not by much. Afterwards, Joseph was expecting to be asked to smuggle in a bottle of beer, a French postcard, a copy of *The Confessions of*

Nemesis Hunt – the mad were quick to take advantage – but Mr Jackson went back to his room good as gold, so where was the harm in another game next day, and the day after? Before long, Joseph was winning as many as he lost.

He knew word would get out sooner or later. Still, it gave him a nasty turn when Aaron said Dr Neil wanted to see him in his office. It turned out he was all for it: 'You take a patient and put a tennis racket or cricket bat or billiard cue in his hand, and he'll gather his scattered wits. The pace of the game gives his brain no time for idle fancies, and leaves him too tired for unwholesome occupation in the privacy of his bed.' Well, Joseph knew it'd take more than a daily game of billiards to make Mr J leave off cleaning his rifle, but he didn't see anything to be gained by telling Dr Neil that. As a parlour patient, Mr J was entitled to fresh sheets as soon as they were sullied. Mrs Neil flat refused: a change of bed linen once a week was acceptable (once a fortnight being preferable), but not even the blessed King of England had clean sheets every night. Mr J could mend his dirty habits or stew in his own filth. Joseph agreed. He had enough to do without changing patients' bedding every morning. But Dr Neil said it wasn't right for a man to sleep in sheets stiff with seed when his family was paying a hundred pounds a year, so maybe there was a medical answer to the problem. After that, Joseph made sure he bathed only in cold water, and Cook was always most particular in pointing out Mr Jackson's cup of cocoa. Not that it made any difference that Joseph could see.

The weeks went by. Aaron got lazier. A new cook arrived. The menus didn't change, but the pies were heavier and she did something queer-tasting to her gravy. When the weather warmed up, Mr J was allowed to work in the gardens. First-class patients did the pruning, if they could be trusted with shears, or laced the canes in the fruit cages. Mr J called it 'sissy work'. His body was softening for lack of exercise. He wanted a spade to turn over the potato patch alongside patients who slept in the attics on straw pallets. It turned out exercise had nothing to do with it; Joseph

243

couldn't leave the other superiors unattended, and Zachary had enough to do keeping his eye on the third-classers, so there was no one to notice Mr J slipping away to the tool shed. Once Joseph got wise to him, he started ducking inside the rhododendron bushes. Every fine day was a game of hide-and-seek between them.

One Sunday, after Joseph had locked the parlour patients in for the night, Mr J started hammering on his door. Joseph had to let him out: he'd have woken the whole wing.

'Where is she?'

'Everyone's in bed, Mr Jackson.'

'But you heard her?'

Joseph would have told any other patient there was nothing to hear, but Mr J knew he was half-deaf. 'Heard what, Mr Jackson?'

'Ssshhh.' He raised his palm and cocked his head.

A shiver ran up Joseph's spine.

Their eyes met. Joseph knew it was a mistake, but he couldn't lie to a man he played billiards with every day.

'I might have heard something. I couldn't say what.'

'The first night or two, I wasn't sure.' Mr J lowered his hand. He looked sad. 'It's stopped now.'

The next time it happened, Joseph was ready for him. He told him his ears were playing tricks, the female patients were locked in another wing. The nearest he'd come to a woman in six months was in chapel, and that was the other side of a sandstone wall. Mr J looked at Joseph as if he'd thought better of him. It was queer how he could turn things so you almost felt guilty for not harbouring the same mad notions. Sharper than he should have, maybe, Joseph told him straight: there was no screaming lady. 'Then you won't mind if I go outside to check.' It was after dark, but Joseph couldn't get off home until all the patients were tucked up in bed, so out into the court they went. After that it got to be a habit. Joseph knew he was making a rod for his own back, but it was the quickest way of getting him settled for the night, and he was so worried about her. Every morning as soon as his room was unlocked, he shot up the stairs to try to catch the blackguard. Not that there was a blackguard, any more than there was a screaming lady, but she was so real to Mr J that Joseph could picture her, right down to her tear-streaked face and torn nightgown.

All through the spring they kept up their billiards. By then they were pretty much even-steven skillwise, which made the contests fiercely thrilling. Joseph used to dream about them, as if his brain was getting in some practice for the next day's match.

One afternoon he mucked up his first shot. His sister had been on at him all week: too hot, too cold, pains in her joints, what had she done with her life except skivvy for him? He wasn't one to snap at the patients as a rule, but Mr J moved his arrow on the scoreboard with a snigger. Said he wasn't laughing at Joseph, it was the number. 'The number? What – you mean one?' Mr J sniggered again. Then he clammed up. Any sort of gambling was strictly forbidden, but Joseph was nosy enough to propose a wager: if Mr J lost the match, he would explain what was so funny. 'And if I win?' Joseph knew what he wanted. 'I'll put you forward for an afternoon parole.' Well, Mr J played like a demon. They were walking back to the ward when he took Joseph by the elbow.

'Are you going to talk to Dr Neil?'

'I said I would, didn't I?'

'Now?'

'First thing tomorrow.'

Mr J looked at Joseph, weighing him up. Then he said the numbers were a code used by the soldiers in his camp in Africa when they took their pleasure with the enemy's women. Not professional tarts, but respectable women fallen on hard times, trying to feed their children. This wasn't something Mr J knew from personal experience, he said, but it was common talk around the mess. The men who made use of these women had to be careful when agreeing a price with them. Too crude, and there was a risk the lady would complain to the camp superintendent. But if a fellow requested a number one (the lady bringing him to his pleasure with her hands), or number two (with her mouth), or number three (to sodomise her), the lady could haggle without indelicacy. And the odd time she hadn't a clue what he was talking about, he could end the conversation leaving her none the wiser.

Joseph thought, *I've lived such a sheltered life.*

'So you see that my smiling had nothing to do with you missing the shot?'

Joseph said yes, he saw that.

'And you understand why I'm so concerned for the screaming lady?'

Joseph frowned. 'Not really.'

Mr J brought his mouth to Joseph's good ear. 'Number five.'

The next week, Mr J got his afternoon parole. By June he was allowed into town to draw the colleges. When it rained, he'd sit in the Oxford free library and read books about the Russian language. Joseph told himself it was a passing fad, but the weeks went by and neither of them picked up a cue.

The wife hadn't been seen for months, and all of a sudden there she was. Dr Neil said the visit might do some good, convince Mr J she wasn't running an elaborate scheme to deceive him. But Joseph had better be in the room, just in case. He showed her into the visitors' parlour. She was nervous, asking Joseph about himself, as she never had before. What part of Africa was he from? How long had he been in England? As a girl, she'd been friendly with a boy from the Congo. He died of sleepy sickness after he went back. Joseph said he was Oxford, born and bred, and she blushed. Served her right, selfish baggage.

When he brought Mr J in, Joseph just had time to think, *I should have had Aaron outside*, before Mr J crossed that room like a bolt of lightning. She went limp in his arms, like a cat held by the scruff. Next thing, they were kissing. He was pressing himself against her, and she was making these little sounds. Joseph didn't know where to look. The third time he coughed, her eyes moved but she didn't really see him. Mr J was the same. *All these months I've been your friend*, Joseph thought, *where was she?*

Still, they were awkward with each other when they pulled apart.

'How've you been?' she asked.

'Much the same as any prisoner.'

'But you're comfortable – the food's all right?'

'I miss my wife.'

That shut her up.

They took the chairs beside the fireplace. Joseph stood by the door. There was a wait for the tea tray to turn up. Mr J chafed her fingers between his palms. When Thomas came in with the tea, she looked round. Her eyes were wet.

She poured him a cup. No milk, two sugars, a good stir: the way he liked it.

He smiled, seeing that she remembered.

All in a rush, she said, 'There are things I can't seem to say in a letter, and the more you write to me the more impossible it is, so I end up feeling I'm not being honest when all I want is to behave decently...'

Mr J gave her the same look Joseph gave his sister when she got a bee in her bonnet about nothing.

'I can't bear it, Herbert. Anyone would think nothing had changed between us.'

'Nothing has changed, on my side.'

Joseph could see her sideways on. Her eyes closed for a second.

'How can I feel the same, after everything that's happened? I still care about you – love you, I suppose. When you write to me so tenderly, of course I'm touched. But if that tenderness is just a whim, in between accusing me of Heaven knows what, if facts mean nothing, then we mean nothing. Don't you see?'

'You mean everything to me,' he said.

She put down her cup.

Joseph had this funny feeling, like he wasn't there, not as himself, or maybe he was, but it was Mr J's heart beating in his chest.

The wife's hands were clenched in her lap. 'I've been working for the *Glasgow Herald*. It's wonderful, being paid to see a play or read a book and tell people what I think of it – a lot easier than trudging from door to door collecting subscriptions. Even so, it's been a struggle these past few weeks. I've not been getting much sleep...' Something furtive in her face. 'Still, I'm sure we'll settle into a routine.'

'When we're back in Barnes,' Mr J said.

She looked him in the eye. 'I gave up the flat.'

'I told you to keep paying the rent.'

'It was throwing good money away for nothing, and I need to be in Glasgow, so Mother can help with...' That shifty look again. 'With everything.'

'It doesn't matter,' he said. 'We'll be in Russia soon enough.'

'Russia?'

'We'll be safe there.' He took one of her fists, opening it up, smoothing out her fingers. 'I've been so worried here, knowing I can't protect you.' His voice cracked. 'I'm sorry, Catherine.'

'It's all right,' she said in a tight voice.

'No. No, it's not.' He pressed her hand to his cheek. 'I heard you screaming.'

She looked like someone had walked over her grave. 'You mean, when I had the baby?'

He dropped her hand. *That's done it*, Joseph thought.

'She's so lovely, Herbert.'

'So that's why you're here,' Mr J said in the quiet voice that always meant trouble.

'I've brought you a photograph. See, she has your colouring.'

'She has nothing of mine and I'll have none of her.'

'If you saw her, you'd love her, you couldn't help it. She's like the best of both of us. When she looks up at me with those blue eyes... it's like she forgives us.'

Mr J snatched the picture and ripped it into quarters. Then he was on his feet. Joseph moved without thinking, gripping his arms from behind, but he was as strong as an ox. His chair toppled over, the teacups went flying. The wife shrieked, scrambling out of the way. If she was hurt, Joseph'd get the blame, maybe even lose his job. He cursed himself for letting it happen, but it was something to see, all right: Mr J so wild.

The next minute, the fight went out of him. It happened so quick, Joseph pulled him off balance and had to break his fall.

'Take me back to the ward,' he said. 'Tell Dr Neil I don't want to see her again.'

Aaron arrived, too late to be any use, and escorted Mr J outside. Closing the door to the visitors' parlour, Joseph caught a last glimpse of the wife, white as a sheet, tearful, terrified, with this queer lost look on her face.

1906

Every day with a baby was a lifetime, but once in a while I looked up to find the weeks flying by. The monthly nurse left after New Year. We missed her at first, but Baby soon forgot. Such a pretty bairn, once the milk rash cleared up. She had your dark skin and my dish-shaped face and a gummy smile that was all her own. She laughed when I sang to her. I put her over my shoulder and patted the song's rhythm on her dear napkinned rump. I could have wept at the miracle of someone so sweet with such a bedevilled start.

At half-past six every evening I put her in the crib and resumed my other life. My reviews were published anonymously, which did not lessen the thrill of seeing my words in print. A Mrs Stephens, a friend of the editor, wrote to ask if I would give a talk to the Renfrew Ladies' Circle, and further surprised me by paying a fee. This led to bookings in Bishopbriggs and Rutherglen, and so I gained a second source of income, lecturing on the theatre, and modern literature, and art.

Mother was a terrific help, and I was not always sufficiently grateful, or even patient with her. At least once a day she turned the house upside down searching for a prayer book or handkerchief she had had in her hand two minutes before or a brooch already pinned to her chest. Determined to set her too-worldly daughter on the Heavenly path, she fretted over my clothes, my friends (those she knew about), my nights at the theatre. I reminded her that I was twenty-seven and a mother myself. She said, if I had listened to her eighteen months ago, I might have married a more suitable man and be mistress of my own household by now. It gave me no pleasure to reflect that she was right.

February brought a flurry of unwelcome excitement in the shape of a letter from your mother. You had written to her, making threats if she did not procure your immediate release and betray the names of her 'co-conspirators'. She begged me to travel down from Glasgow to reason with you. I replied that I could not possibly leave Baby for three days, and this was true, but I had another reason for refusing. Behind our cordial correspondence, your mother and Lucie and I were engaged in a game of Hot Potato. No one wanted to be left with responsibility for you when the music stopped.

After a lengthy silence, your letters resumed, still wooing me, and denouncing me, but showing a new preoccupation with your life in the asylum. You were permitted to go into Oxford. You complained that people spat in the gutter or scraped their shoes as you passed, but, mindful of the promises made to achieve your parole, you took no notice. Dr Neil often asked about your delusions. You were not so foolish as to answer truthfully. Instead you confided in me. You were being drugged by a fellow patient. You knew this by certain bodily changes you observed on waking.

In June you were confined to the ward for breaking the terms of your parole. You had approached the ladies' wing and spoken to a female patient through the window. I spent too many of my precious idle moments wondering about this woman, whether she was beautiful and almost rational, or merely susceptible and weak. Within a month, you had been moved to an asylum in York where you were fed a special diet and treated with sedatives and hydrotherapy. My mother-in-law wrote that this regimen had effected an impressive number of cures. I noted that York was two hundred miles north of Walter and Lucie: two hundred miles nearer to me.

Baby's first birthday in October coincided with a letter from our landlord giving notice that the lease would not be renewed the following year. Gordon found us a pretty house overlooking the River Kelvin, smaller than the flat in Kersland Terrace. Even Mother admitted we could not take all our belongings with us, but every object I suggested we do without, she wanted to keep: the cracked vase, the scorch-marked quilt, Father's meerschaum pipes. Next morning, everything I had sorted into piles, 'indispensables' and 'sentimentals', had been jumbled back into the press. I hatched a plot with Gordon and Grant. They would take her to Edinburgh while I went through the cupboards and kept an eye on Baby.

The Saturday in question was that rarity, a bright December day. As soon as the others left, I emptied the linen press. Baby entertained herself with the chess set. (Without the board. Although advanced for fourteen months, she was not a prodigy.) The low sun picked out the china figures on top of Grandpapa's cabinet: a Meissen gallant and coy shepherdess, a Staffordshire Bonnie Prince Charlie, a lion with the bibulous face of a Georgian squire. How dusty they were, being much too high to be reached by Lizzie, our maid. I fetched a pail of water and washed them. The doorbell rang.

Lizzie trudged down our long, L-shaped hall.

'A Mr Greiffenhagen.'

My heart turned over.

I put Baby down for a nap, with a chess piece to keep her quiet. When I walked into the drawing room, his profile robbed me of breath. The sensual, exacting line of his nose, that sybarite's beard, his warm ivory skin and silky white hair. Even the glint of his pince-nez gave me gooseflesh. Phyl said he was too old for me, but he was as strong as a blacksmith under his clothes.

He was examining Uncle Frank's unfinished canvas: another possession I would have been glad to leave behind.

'This is a surprise,' I said.

He looked up and I wondered yet again how a face so still could be so expressive.

'I thought it was time I saw you in your lair.'

I would have rushed into his arms, but Lizzie was there. I told her to bring us tea on the silver tray and she gave me one of her shrewd looks.

'My mother's lair, not mine,' I said, when we were alone. 'She's in Edinburgh today.'

'That's a pity,' he murmured in a tone that made me smile, although we could hardly retire to bed with Lizzie on the premises, not to mention Baby. (And I had no intention of mentioning Baby.)

I crossed the room, stopping just far enough away. Once in a while I liked to make him reach for me. But having to listen for Lizzie's footsteps, I could not lose myself in the kiss. I stepped back, putting a respectable distance between us.

'How are you getting on with the wall panels?'

'Much the same as the last time you asked.'

'You're sure I won't be recognisable? Mother would *die*.'

'Her life is quite safe.'

He liked to work with the morning light. I sat for him at least twice a week. Clad in a bedsheet toga, under the intensity of his gaze, I truly felt like a goddess.

'I wish I could be at the opening.'

'You could come in disguise. A veiled Salomé. Or a nun, if you prefer.'

'If you mean a Catholic nun, I might cause less scandal as Salomé.'

Greiffy did not really understand Scotch religion, so my joke fell a little flat. I picked up the silk shawl covering the worn patch on the sofa and improvised an eastern dance. His face told me this had the desired effect.

'You're a terrible woman,' he growled.

We met at a soirée at the School of Art. I remembered the person I had been moments before, climbing the steps from the street: I loved my child, my siblings, my mother, my friends, but that other sort of love was behind me. I walked into the party and a stranger turned his head to look: a man in evening dress, as most of the boys there were not. He stood with his weight on his back leg and his trunk slightly canted as if he were monarch of all he surveyed. No sooner had we been introduced than Phyl came to claim me, but for the rest of the evening I felt his eyes upon me and knew we would meet again.

He taught life drawing in Glasgow, as you had in Liverpool, but there the similarity ended. His work had been shown across Europe. He was a friend of Rider Haggard and the darling of fashionable London, though being less celebrated than Sargent and Lavery, he accounted himself a failure. A complicated man. When I was not working, all my thoughts were devoted to trying to puzzle him out: the proportions of romance and cynicism in his nature; his contempt for all tastemakers, and his ambition. Whether he could truly love any woman, if he did not love his wife.

I replaced the shawl on the sofa.

'You have a feather in your hair.'

My hand flew to my scalp.

'On the other side.'

I went to the mantel mirror and plucked out a curl of pillow down. Behind me, his glance dropped to the dress you had bought me in Perugia. Why on earth had I agreed to such an unflattering colour?

'If you'd told me you were coming, I would have made myself beautiful,' I said.

'I assumed you were always beautiful.'

I flashed him a look over my shoulder. 'As I am, to those broadminded enough to recognise it.'

'Yes, well, as you know, I am no Bohemian.'

Outside, the sun slipped behind a cloud.

Why did he mar our happiness with these sudden withdrawals? Did he not know what it cost me to love him, the tears of joy and terror I had shed at the thawing of my frozen heart?

Crisply I asked, 'Would you like me to change into my best dress?'

Lizzie brought in the tea tray. As she was setting it down, a jaunty *rat-a-tat-tat* sounded at the front door. There was only one caller who knocked like that.

'Maurice, this is Donald Carswell, a colleague on the paper. Don, Maurice Greiffenhagen, the painter.'

It was horribly apparent that each was as put out as the other.

Greiffy shook Don's hand and sat beside me on the settee, ignoring the empty chairs.

Regretting that cool word *colleague*, I said, 'Don has been my friend for ever and doesn't mind seeing me in old clothes.'

Lizzie came back with an extra cup and a plate of buttered bannock, which she left on the little table beside Don.

'Are you painting Cathie?' he asked.

A faint smile showed between my lover's Van Dyck beard and his salt-and-pepper moustache.

'I'm not really suitable,' I said quickly. 'He prefers models with athletic figures and strong jawlines, very powerful and inspiring. Only there is a pose they all seem to adopt, straining towards something – usually a man. It puts them rather off-balance.'

Greiffy's eyes glittered behind his pince-nez. 'The slanting line makes for a pleasing composition.'

'It does,' I allowed, 'but the men you paint always seem to be planted squarely on two feet.'

Don sipped his tea unhappily.

Changing the subject, I mentioned the newly hung gallery at the Palace of Arts. Don and I agreed that the selection of paintings was insufficiently Scotch. When Greiffy wondered whose work we would rather have seen, Don named Margaret Mackintosh and Frances MacNair, not knowing that the Spook School was one of Greiffy's pet aversions. The conversation lumbered on. Mutual acquaintances at the university. The Royal Scottish Academy's rather uneven collection. Inwardly I cursed the mischance that had brought them together. I knew what Greiffy saw: a tweed jacket patched with corduroy, an earnest cleverness that society would think rather bad form. I resented his judging Don, and resented Don for tainting me by association, but I found I was more concerned that my lover should make a good impression on my friend.

Forgetting he had already been told, Greiffy asked Don what he did for a living.

'I work with Cathie on the *Glasgow Herald*.'

'Don made me a writer,' I said.

'You were always going to be a writer. I just opened the door.'

Oddly enough, we had never talked about this.

'He's been marking up my copy since we were at university.'

'And you still can't spell "mediaeval".'

'I only misspell it to give you the pleasure of correcting me.'

He laughed, and I felt a twinge of shame at flirting with him to make another jealous. By way of amends, I said, 'Really, Don should be in London, working on the *Telegraph* or the *Times*.'

He reddened: a warning, which I failed to heed.

'I have sentimental ties that keep me here.'

'His parents,' I translated.

'And other ties,' he said, looking at me.

I blushed.

'Ye-es,' Greiffy said at last, 'you do rather entangle us in your web.'

This was the moment Baby chose to call out from the nursery, 'Mamma!'

Seconds passed. I could see Don wondering why I did not respond.

'*Mamma*!'

'I take it that's you?' Greiffy said.

My daughter tottered in, blue-lipped from sucking the black queen. Seeing Don, she held up her arms. He was a favourite of hers. He could bark like a dog, whinny like a horse, low like a bull: the proper sounds, so you would have thought there was a belted Galloway in the nursery. He scooped her up and, dipping his knees, pretended to drop her. She laughed in delight.

I recognised Greiffy's thin smile as a sign of unbreachable reserve. He stood up.

'Must you really go?' I said in relief.

At the door, showing him out, I could have explained that I had always meant to tell him, I was just waiting for the right moment, but you had taught me the futility of appeasement. I was finished with coaxing men out of their sulks.

Returning to the drawing room, I found Don staring at his boots while Baby delved in the coal scuttle. I cleaned her up with my handkerchief, and reunited her with the chess pieces.

'An interesting man,' I said, when I could bear the silence no longer. 'His work is really arresting, almost poster-like, and yet shaded with exquisite sadness – I find it terribly moving. Phyl says he's all surface, but after Herbert I find I've had quite enough of the depths.'

'He doesn't mind that you can't marry?'

'As far as marriage goes, we're both in the same boat.'

Don did not look any happier for hearing this.

I lifted Baby on to my hip. 'I must get on, or Mother will be back to find the contents of her cupboards strewn across the floor.'

Ignoring this hint to take his leave, he followed us down the hall. I knelt on the rug and began sorting through the piles of sheets and pillowcases. He sat cross-legged beside Baby. She giggled, thinking he meant to play with her.

'Cathie...'

I knew what he was going to say and, to forestall it, I told him what I had told Phyl: the hard-won lesson of my sentimental career. 'I am not the sort of woman who inspires a lasting passion.'

He looked a little stunned by this. 'So you throw yourself away on a heartless adulterer?'

'If his paintings are to sell, he needs to mix with London society. He can't afford to frighten them off by leaving his wife. And I would rather be desired by an adulterer than trapped by an ownership that is death to my soul.'

'Those being the only two possibilities...'

Don was not usually satiric, but I supposed no man liked to hear a woman defending her lover.

'So you've taken up with Greiffenhagen because he's nothing like Herbert?'

'That's certainly one of his attractions.'

'There must be other men who meet that standard. Unmarried men.'

'Will you stop harping on about marriage!'

Baby began to grizzle. She did not yet understand every word, but she was sensitive to the music of feeling. Don leaned towards her.

'*Look*,' he crooned, his voice full of wonder.

A circle of shimmering silver was in fractured motion on the wall. Baby watched, entranced. For a moment I too was spellbound. Then I understood: just sunlight deflected by the pail of water I had used to clean the china.

He lifted his gaze to mine. His eyes were the colour of the olives you loved in Italy.

'Am I like Herbert?'

I had never known Don so direct.

'You don't look like him, or behave like him, but...' I had to say it. 'If I let you love me, I'm not sure it would turn out so very differently. And I should miss your friendship dreadfully.'

He flinched. I felt at once afraid of his anger and obscurely pleased with myself.

'You think Herbert went mad because of you?'

What an innocent he was.

'When two people marry, they become unrecognisable to themselves, saying, *feeling* the most appalling things, behaving as they would never have done before.' I hesitated, wanting to make him understand, and yet if he truly understood, how could I keep his regard? 'It's as if you become someone else, a citizen of another land, with only one compatriot.'

'And Herbert is your compatriot, even now?'

I met his look.

'That's why you're so sad underneath – so hopeless?'

I closed my eyes. 'Please, Don, no more.'

When I looked again, he was taking something from his wallet. A newspaper clipping.

KENSINGTON MAN STRUCK NEIGHBOUR

An artist attacked his upstairs neighbour for 'making strange noises', West London Police Court heard yesterday. Herbert Parry Malpas Jackson, 36, struck fellow artist Joseph Brown several severe blows to the face, cutting him in two or three places. Elizabeth Smith, landlady of the artists' studios at 80 Redcliffe Square, Kensington, told the court her husband heard a commotion and rushed upstairs to find Mr Brown covered in blood. When remonstrated with, the defendant laughed and said, 'He won't do it again.' After summoning a constable, Mrs Smith informed Mr Jackson he was no longer welcome as a boarder. 'We'd had enough of him and his queer ways,' she said.

Jackson admitted assaulting Mr Brown, but claimed he had done so under provocation. Mr Brown had often made sobbing, sighing and crying sounds to annoy him, yet when challenged, denied it, or blamed his small boy. Jackson said the child was in the habit of running up and downstairs, making it impossible for him to work, and eventually he lost patience.

Fined 20 shillings.

The report had been cut from the top of a page. The date in the upper margin was 6th July 1904. Two months before I met you.

I read it twice, and then a third time while I thought about the trouble Don must have taken to get hold of it, perhaps bribing a compositor to run it off the press. The use of all four of your names; that staple of your nightmares, the sobbing child: surely these were suspiciously esoteric details, purposely added to convince me? At the same time, I knew it was all true. You had tried to strangle your wife; why should you not have thrashed a bothersome neighbour? The situations were alike enough, with one all-important difference. The second attack lived only in my memory. The first was recorded in cold print. *People knew.* Walter, Lucie, your mother, cousin William, so many of the smiling faces who had congratulated me at our wedding.

'Is this you handing me the key to unlock my cage?'

Don could hear this was a question better left unanswered.

'Setting me free to love you?'

His colour, which had settled down, flared up again. 'I thought you'd be interested.' He got to his feet. 'I wasn't looking for thanks.'

I had hurt him, my dear old friend who had always wanted what was best for me.

'Don, wait, I'm sorry. It's just a shock. All these months I've been telling myself no one else could possibly understand, hiding behind the idea of my marriage as a private tragedy, and now you show me proof that he was a public menace. Of course I would rather know, but it *is* shocking – and if I'm honest, not so completely surprising. I *do* feel Herbert and I are compatriots. I thought it was the very worst thing, but I wonder if it hasn't been shielding me from the worst...' I paused, what I was trying to say almost within my grasp. 'I suppose there had to be love between us, or else I threw my life away for nothing. But if I loved him, for love to be worth the name, it has to last. And now... I don't know what's true and what's just saving face. Perhaps I'm the sort of person who can bear anything, any amount of unhappiness, as long as I'm not just a silly goose.'

'Is being a goose really so dreadful?'

I knew he would say that.

Baby was grizzling again, not really upset, just wanting attention. When I picked her up she grabbed the clipping, crumpling it in her sticky fist. Gently, Don extricated the mangled evidence.

I was so eager for Phyl to see it, I ran all the way to her studio.

1907

The shepherd clasped his lass in sinewy brown arms. Voluptuous and ungainly, she averted her face from his ardent kiss. Poppies smouldered around their knees. Behind the coppice, the sun set.

The honourable Mary Dowdall turned to me. 'Captures the moment rather well, don't you think?'

'The shepherdess looks like an armful of wet sheets,' I said, and she did, although I was hardly an impartial judge. Mary looked at *The Idyll* and saw a courting couple. I saw the man who had painted it. I had been twelve then, and Greiffy twenty-nine. That pale, plump model had had the best of him.

I was ready to walk on, but Mary lingered, enthralled. '*Wet sheets*: that's very good. Isn't that just what it's like, the first time? You feel such a *lump*. Closing your eyes, waiting to be swept away, when that's not how it works at all.' She gave me an arch look. 'Or perhaps it was, for you?'

'There's something odd about his hat, too.'

'But the mood of the thing,' she persisted, so that I imagined saying it: *Mary, you're being a bore*. 'A rather inspired touch, to paint her big feet leaving the ground. All perfectly decent, and yet one can see exactly what's going to happen. Can't you feel those meadow flowers, springy and slightly damp under your back?'

In my experience he was strictly a chaise longue man.

'Greiffenhagen,' she mused. 'German, I suppose. It seems

wrong somehow. French or Italian, yes, but nothing northern European.'

'He's English,' I said, 'of Danish descent.'

Something in her face. There and gone.

'He teaches in Glasgow.'

'You know him! How simply thrilling! Do tell.'

That was when it struck me: 'He's a little like Walter Raleigh, only with artistic talent.'

'Oh, my dear,' she breathed, surely gleeful behind her shocked look, 'I hope you didn't let Walter break your heart?'

'My heart? Oh no, that's still intact: still beating faster for the wrong man.'

For once, the honourable Mary was lost for words.

We moved towards the next gallery, her yellow dress drawing admiring glances. I was in grey, a colour that flattered me when it was not so blatantly outshone. She slipped her arm through mine, causing me to startle and then to smile in embarrassment, which was all the encouragement she needed to start talking again.

'I always think there's a touch of the public house about this place. Built by our local brewer, bless his vulgar heart. One half expects the marble nymphs to wink and ask, "What're you having, dearie?"' She nodded at the wall to our left. 'That's where they hang me in the autumn exhibitions. I'm rather a fixture, always being asked to pose by someone or other. I suppose word has got round that Silky will stump up for the finished product. Trust Lucie Raleigh to keep count: "I can see you'd want to leave the little ones something to remember you by, but are you really going to have nine children?" I went home and checked and she was quite right. Robert Anning Bell, Francis Dodd, Charles Shannon, Augustus John... how many is that – four? Who on earth were the others...?'

'My husband?'

'Of course! Not the most accomplished likeness, I must say. If you come back for tea, you can see for yourself.'

The Dowdalls lived in a leafy suburb a half-hour tram ride from the centre of Liverpool. The house was ostentatiously large: doors, windows, ceilings all twice the usual height, as if built to accommodate a family of giants. Mary pulled a contrite face at the woodland garden ('our cat run') and said she spent half her life on the tram. 'All the interesting people live within a hundred yards of our old place in town. But then, the price of getting one's own way almost all the time is that, now and again, one simply has to put up with things. Don't you find?'

'Not any more.'

Her eyebrows shot up. 'My goodness, hasn't the grub turned into a butterfly!'

We laughed, and I felt suddenly hopeful. She was not a bad sort, only rather vain: she might relish standing in the witness box with all eyes upon her.

Petitioning the High Court for an annulment of marriage had turned out to be surprisingly straightforward. I was very glad Fanny had had the good sense to marry a solicitor. Hop had made me an appointment with a notary public in Glasgow who handed me three sheets of paper. The first two stated my address, your address, our address in Barnes, the date of our child's birth, the place and date of our wedding, and your unsoundness of mind on that day. The third sheet asserted that these statements were true. After signing them, I lifted my right hand above my head and repeated: 'I swear by Almighty God as I shall answer to God at the Great Day of Judgment that this is my name and handwriting and that the contents of this, my affidavit, are true.' That done, I was bade good afternoon.

Two carefree months had passed. Then I spent a week with Fanny in London. Hop drove me to his office in Finsbury

Square to discuss the case. While he would be acting for me free of charge, it had become necessary to incur the expense of counsel. The Official Solicitor had been appointed *guardian ad litem*.

'Please, Hop – in plain English.'

'Your husband is contesting your petition to annul.'

'But he's mad!'

'Mad, but very soundly advised. There was a hearing last week. A solicitor by the name of...' Hop glanced down at the papers on his desk. '*Alfred Bell* presented your husband's affidavit that he cannot avail himself of legal representation due to lack of means. Consequently, the Official Solicitor will be acting for him.'

Hop seemed nervous, which was quite out of character. What was I failing to understand?

'Are you saying...' *Surely not*, I thought. 'There will have to be a trial in open court?'

'It could become a leading case—'

I cut him off. 'With all the newspapers there?'

I had seen my colleagues in the *Glasgow Herald* newsroom, just back from the High Court, boasting about the shocking details, haggling with the editor for an extra two hundred words. What a story this would make. Our marriage held up for all the world to inspect, every sordid detail printed in the *public interest*.

'The Official Solicitor's costs will have to be found. They are recoverable, if the judge decides in our favour.'

I had no money. Every penny I earned went to support my child.

'Somebody must have been paying for Alfred Bell's time.'

As soon as I said it, I knew who: *Walter*.

'So *I* will be the one on trial – my fitness as a wife. Herbert can make any outlandish accusation he chooses.'

'We have a good case,' Hop said. 'No judge would want

to see a young lady like yourself tethered to such a person.'

'But we could lose?'

Since that day I had not enjoyed a night's unbroken sleep. Hop had urged me to leave everything to him, but the more passive I was, the more anxious I felt. I had written to Mary saying I had business in Liverpool and could we meet, half-expecting to be fobbed off with some excuse. But there I was, sitting in her enormous drawing room with a Wedgwood teacup in my hand.

Nurse arrived with baby Judith and was told to pass her to me.

'Another girl. I suppose Silky will keep at it until I present him with a son and heir.'

'She's very big for sixteen months.'

'Mmm, I'm afraid she takes after Silky's mother. How old is your little beast?'

'Diana?' Saying her name made me smile. 'She'll be two in October.'

This seemed to be as much baby talk as Mary could tolerate.

Nurse was sent back upstairs, *as Mrs Jackson is doing such a splendid job.*

When we were alone with the child, she said, 'I was so sorry when I heard.'

'Oh, I wouldn't be without her.'

Mary gave me a sidelong look. 'Actually, I meant when I heard about your marriage. I should have warned you. I knew they were looking for someone to take the burden, and we could all see he liked you, but I thought you were too gone on Walter to accept a substitute. And you were such a prickly little thing.'

I stared at her, transfixed by the obviousness of what she had just told me. Of course I had known Lucie was match-making, but I never guessed she had seen in me the makings of a lunatic's nurse. Walter must have approved, even as he slipped into my bed in the middle of the night.

I could not let Mary guess how obtuse I had been.

'I suppose I was jealous of you,' I said.

She looked quite delighted. 'No more than I was of you, I'm sure. So silly of us. Walter has much grander belles to ring, these days. He really is a dreadful man, with his little amanuenses, and his famously uxorious heart. I wouldn't change places with Lucie for a thousand pounds, and I don't believe you would, either—' she gave me a glance from under her brows '—now you've found yourself an artist who can really paint.'

Ah.

'You know about Greiffy?'

A roguish smile. 'I'm afraid I do. Oh, don't worry, I had a very discreet source, who only told me because I'm equally discreet. I must say I'm rather envious. A lover whose wife is four hundred miles away: couldn't be better.'

'I've been thinking I might move to London.'

'Oh *no*. You don't want to be bumping into her buying frillies at Harrods. Besides, it's always preferable to be the pursued in these affairs. The presents are so much nicer.'

Baby Judith smacked a fat hand against my neck.

'Greiffy says I chose him to indulge my taste for schoolgirl yearning.'

She looked appalled. 'I wouldn't let him get away with that. I suppose you're the sort to think love is a sacrament, or manna from Heaven, or some such?' She watched my face. 'Yes, I thought so. Whereas *I* know – well, most women know – being lovable is just a trick. Like dressing well, or being amusing at dinner. There's not much to it, once you grasp the basic principle. Men are babies, mostly, and those that aren't babies are dogs. You must have trained a dog: when they behave well, you give them a treat. When they don't behave, you punish them. But you mustn't be too predictable, then they get bored. Every once in a while, when they look for their treat, you withhold it. Torment them a little. It drives them mad.' She realised what she had said. 'Well, not *mad*, but quite unable to think about anything else.'

She assumed I was still the green girl she had met at Walter's, but being patronised was a small price to pay for what I had to ask, and so I played along.

'You have no respect for men at all?'

'Men? No! Of course, one would love to find a real man to make one swoon and submit without feeling one was casting one's pearls before swine, but I've never met one. Have you?'

'Not even Walter?'

'Oh, Walter! He says it himself: literary criticism is a spinster's trade. He'd have changed places with your husband in a second, if there'd been any hope of the army turning a blind eye to his shaky hands. No, as far as Walter's concerned, even stark raving mad, Herbert's twice the man he is.'

It was the first thing she had said that might just be true.

'But you don't think that?'

She pouted. 'I'm not altogether sure I don't. I mean, it makes no sense to *me*, challenging composers to duels and such, but it is rather magnificently *extreme*.'

'Duels?' I echoed.

'Didn't you know?'

I shook my head.

Her eyes softened.

I could stand anything but pity.

'So you think Herbert's a real man,' I said, 'but not a real artist?'

'Well, a really frightful artist.' The laugh died in her throat. 'My dear, I didn't mean to offend you.'

My belief in your talent gave what had happened between us a certain grandeur. But if you were just a hack painter, the tragedy became farce.

I said this.

'Mmm.' She was so visibly depressed that I wondered if

she was thinking of her own marriage. 'I can see how one would feel that.'

Baby Judith startled us with a noisy belch.

'Mrs Jackson, you *have* got the golden touch! Shall we take the little beast back to Nurse? We can have a look at your husband's painting while we're up there.'

Harold Dowdall's study smelled of stale tobacco and desiccating paper. There were glass-fronted shelves of legal casebooks and a table that could have seated twenty at dinner heaped with town council papers and ribbon-tied briefs. It took me a moment to notice the portrait: the witchy tendrils of hair across her brow; the bleak look in those sunken eyes; the tense line of her mouth. I remembered your words the day of the partridge shoot. *You have no idea of the evil there is in the world.*

'Oh dear.'

'Quite,' Mary said as if it were a great joke, but I noticed she kept the painting in her blind spot. 'Bad enough that it was shown in Liverpool – twice! Then I came across it at the Royal Academy in London. *The honourable Mrs Chaloner Dowdall.* He could have had the decency to call it something else. *Lady With a Nasty Cold* perhaps – or *The Barrister's Wife Contemplates Dinner With the Aldermen.* Silky wouldn't let me put it in the cellar, after he'd paid fifty pounds for it. I rather think he got his money's worth. All those weeks imagining shenanigans in the studio, and then to be presented with this!'

Gesturing for me to sit, she took her husband's chair at the head of the table. 'But I'm sure you didn't come all this way to see a bad painting?'

Now that the moment had come, I felt completely unprepared.

'If you had warned me about Herbert back then, what would you have said?'

'I'm sure you can imagine.'

'But I'd like to hear it from you.'

'Oh well, I'd probably have been rather vague about it.'

'And I would have pressed you.'

She gave me an assessing look. Whatever the test, I seemed to pass it. 'He was very different in those days. Rather louche and *French* somehow. I was carrying Ursula, my first. It felt more like nine years than nine months. I don't know if you've ever sat for a portrait? There's nothing quite like it. Day after day. You soon run out of ordinary conversation, and then all that's left is confessions and intimacies. It was rather fun for a while, but I had to tell him: I wasn't going to run away with him, three months gone with Silky's little beast.'

I glanced up at the portrait. It did not look like the work of a man in love.

'Then Violet came to stay, my sister. Naturally I wanted to show off my dashing admirer. I was rather slow to spot what was happening. One day I had to see Cook about some kitchen emergency and when I came back, well, it was all too obvious. I wondered whether I shouldn't throw a bucket of cold water over them. "Oh, it's all right," Vi said: they were engaged. I'm afraid it all got rather ugly. I said, after Mama heard what I had to tell, I had no doubt she would cut them off without a penny. Herbert took exception to being called a fortune hunter and Vi accused me of being jealous. I sent her home, and heard nothing from him for about a month. Eventually he asked Silky over to his studio to view the finished portrait and, well, as you see, he had his revenge. The next thing we hear, he's gone off to war. I must say Violet didn't seem too heartbroken. Within a couple of years she'd married Lewis, who was much more the thing. And Herbert seemed frightfully smitten with you.' Her voice, which had become less mannered in the course of this tale, resumed its habitual drawl. 'I imagine my being under the same roof added a certain spice to the experience.'

270

'Was he mad when he asked you to run away with him?'

After a frosty pause, she said, 'Not visibly.'

'So you must know when he lost his reason?'

Her head tilted. 'Why is it I have the feeling there's something you're not telling me, Mrs Jackson?'

The Official Solicitor had moved to dismiss the case because I could not give particulars of your insanity. Dr Savage would swear you were suffering from paranoia in March 1905, but what mattered was your state of mind the previous October, on the day we wed.

'I've petitioned the court to annul my marriage,' I said.

Surprise wiped her face clean of its languorous poise. 'And I suppose your daughter was a virgin birth?'

'There are other grounds—'

'I'm sorry, my dear, but I've never heard anything so ridiculous. "Whom God has joined let no man put asunder" – remember those words, after you *swore your vows*? Why can't you be satisfied with a lover, like any other wife? You've already had Herbert removed from your home, that's pretty good going. Now you want to expunge him from the record altogether? And what happens to your daughter, if her father never was?'

'As he won't acknowledge her, I can't see it will make any great difference.'

'She will be *illegitimate*.'

'In twenty years these things won't matter so much.'

'Oh, spare me. I suppose you think Mr Greiffenhagen would make a better father?'

I had to smile. 'Not on current form. He already has two sons. And, as you know, a wife.'

'In poor health, I hear.'

This had crossed my mind (how could it not?) but my conscience was clear. I did not want to become the second Mrs Greiffenhagen.

'I'm afraid marriage doesn't agree with me.'

'Do you think it agrees with any of us? The point is, there's nothing to be done. Unless Herbert is going to drag you through the courts as an adulteress.'

I could have explained that she was wrong about this, but why waste my breath? Mary would never give evidence for me. I dreaded telling Hop. I had heard nothing back from Kuno in Dublin, and I hardly thought Walter would oblige. Would she tell him about my visit? Of course she would: how could she resist? *I'm afraid I sent Mrs Jackson back to Glasgow with her tail between her legs.*

I said, 'It could have been your sister here today, telling you she'd married a madman.'

'Except that Vi had the sense to see she could do better. Anyway, there's no reason to think he would have been mad. He was perfectly normal before he went off to war.'

'It happened in Africa?'

She let her eyebrows rise and fall.

'The law does not allow madmen to marry.'

'Nevertheless, you were married.'

'Not lawfully.'

She shrugged. 'I'm not entirely sure I would call Herbert *mad*. Eccentric, certainly.'

'Challenging people to duels?'

'He never actually fought anyone. You know what men are like: it's all talk.'

I had Don's newspaper clipping in my reticule. Reluctantly, she took it from me.

'I didn't know about that.'

'He tried to kill me.' Phyl and Fanny were the only people I had told. 'We were locked in a steamer cabin. He had his hands around my neck. Luckily a steward heard the struggle and used his pass key.'

Two vivid red spots had appeared on Mary's cheeks. She cupped a hand around her throat. On the floor above, Baby Judith began to cry.

At last, she met my look. 'Walter and Lucie must never know I told you this.'

I nodded.

'Call at the University Club and ask for Robert Scott Macfie.'

1908

I went to London to meet Mr Barnard, the King's Counsel Hop had engaged. His crowded smile reminded me of my father. I could only hope he was more competent at lawyering than Father had been at trading with the Indies. He asked why you married me. Why does anyone marry anyone? I said. Hop frowned, but I was quite serious: why would we shackle our unknown selves to the hidden darkness in another?

I could see this was not a question that interested Mr Barnard.

'Herbert said he knew we would marry the first moment he saw me. Although it was his sister's house, he was rather an outsider there. As was I. He didn't like his brother-in-law much, and thought I had cause to dislike him too.'

'Did he dislike many people?'

'He seemed angry with almost everyone except me.'

Mr Barnard was pleased with this answer.

'He thought his old friends in Liverpool had turned against him.'

'In a conspiracy?'

'He thought they talked about him behind his back.'

Mr Barnard seemed disappointed.

'He did feel conspired against, but he didn't know by whom. He thought I might unmask them.'

Mr Barnard glanced at Hop. 'When did he say this?'

'I think it was on the packet steamer crossing the Channel.'

'On the day you married?'

'Yes.'

Mr Barnard leaned forward. 'Is it possible this was why he married you: so you could unmask his enemies, and protect him from their plots?'

Hop was smiling. I saw then why Mr Barnard was a King's Counsel. He understood it was not enough to prove that you had been mad when we married; you must have married me *because* of your madness. And what could be more insane than seeking protection from an imaginary plot?

'Think carefully, Cath,' Hop said.

Was there such a thing as love without ulterior motive? We all hoped to gain something. Was it any less deluded to marry for lifelong happiness, or to be completely understood, or to burn in passion's ever-renewing flame? I knew what Hop would say: the madness of humanity was not my concern. All that mattered here was us.

I had always wondered how people could lie on oath, and now I saw it was quite simple: they convinced themselves the most advantageous answer was the truth.

There was one more person to meet before I went back to Glasgow.

'Cath, this is Captain Hunter.'

Even without Hop's introduction, I would have known the captain for a military man. He had the papery-skinned, schoolboyish look old soldiers gained after a lifetime without women. Six years since the war had ended. What was it he smelled of? Ah yes. Peppermint humbugs.

'Captain Hunter was your husband's commanding officer in Africa.'

And just like that, I felt you in the room. The way your breathing shallowed when you sensed danger. The sideways flicker of your eyes. I almost turned to see if you were standing behind me.

'He witnessed the onset of your husband's madness.'

'Towards the end of the war,' the captain confirmed.

Hop's clerk was called in.

Captain Hunter said there had been a camp for Boer refugees at Elandsfontein. The African climate fostered epidemics. The camp authorities had done their best to impose hygienic practices, but the inmates were mostly women and children, undisciplined and poorly educated. You had been in charge of the burial parties. He glanced at me. I lowered the hand that had flown to my mouth.

'Did your husband ever speak of this?'

'No,' I said, because fragments of a dream recounted in the dark were hardly *speaking*.

The captain seemed reassured.

It was demanding work, he said: day after day spent on the shadeless veldt. And of course there had been the nature of the task. No one liked burying children, but you found it particularly distressing. Had you come to him, he would have reassigned you, but by the time the matter was brought to his attention, you were unfit for any sort of duty. The medical officer diagnosed a complete nervous collapse.

It was the explanation I had longed for, the final piece of evidence to clinch my case, so why did I not believe it?

Like the mills of God, the wheels of justice ground exceeding slow. The hearing was set down for March, thirteen months after Hop had filed my petition to annul. I arrived in London to learn that the judge had influenza. The case was adjourned for a further ten weeks. I went home.

In May, I was back, feeling quietly hopeful. Cousin William would say you were sane when we wed, but only out of family loyalty. I had Captain Hunter on my side, and three of your Liverpool friends – four, if I counted the composer you had challenged to a duel – and the man you had beaten bloody in Redcliffe Square, and the landlady who called the police, and, for some unfathomable reason, Walter. Plus my own testimony. It was disappointing that Henry Munro would be giving evidence for you, but I had three eminent alienists, all of whom agreed that delusional insanity was a disease of gradual and progressive growth. Surely they would carry more weight than your other medical witnesses: Turney, who had examined you for the life insurance policy, and Gemmell, Walter's Glaswegian general practitioner.

I liked London in late spring, its sense of possibility, azure mornings and gilded dusks and the taste of awakened earth on the wind. The cab driver took me past Regent's Park to see the trees all flagged with green. In my luggage were a pair of gloves for Fanny and a set of pearl shirt studs for Hop. I had no self-control with presents: so impatient to see the recipient's pleasure, I had to hand them over at once. My sister's face clouded.

'As soon as I saw them, I knew they were your colour,' I said.

She glanced at Hop, who had not opened his box.

'Cath,' he said, 'I have some bad news.'

My heart clenched, but I was determined to be cheerful. 'Not flu again?'

'Captain Hunter died on Monday.'

'*Why?*'

'A seizure.'

Why me? I meant. *Why now? Why could he not have keeled over next week, after the trial?* I was not proud of these thoughts.

'But it'll be all right,' I said. 'Won't it?'

The Royal Courts of Justice were a sort of legal cathedral, with trefoil arches, lancet windows and blind arcades. The ushers went about their business with solemn faces, the celebrants processed from court to court in their hallowed robes, but the public behaved like travellers in a railway station. Raising my voice to be heard over the hubbub, I breathed in a fetor of smoky overcoats and queasy stomachs.

A clerk consulted his register and directed me to court twelve, where the dark oak pews were packed with idlers seeking a free show. Beneath the lion and unicorn, an elaborately carved choir stall awaited the judge. I did not need to be told that the men lining the wall to my left were from the newspapers. The *Glasgow Herald* court reporters had that same combination of vigilance and slovenly ease.

When I slid in beside Hop, a ripple of prurient interest stirred the room.

The bench in front was occupied by counsel. Mr Barnard turned round to show me his crowded smile. His horsehair wig sat slightly askew as if he had just left off romping with a brood of unruly children. He introduced me to his junior, the rubbery-faced Mr Willock. The tall man who was all eyebrow and cheekbone and beaky nose was your Mr Rawlinson. He had the boiled-looking skin that so often goes with sandy hair. I thought he might be Scotch, until I overheard him speaking to his junior in the kind of English accent that delivered each word on the point of a sharp knife.

Directly behind sat the Official Solicitor, Mr Winterbotham.

The court clerk sang, 'All rise.'

Mr Justice Bargrave Deane was shortish, stocky, vigorous-looking for a man approaching sixty. I was heartened by the suggestion of appetite in his cushiony lips and those black eyebrows twisting into little devilish horns. Mr Rawlinson was the ascetic type.

All four counsel bowed to the judge. We sat down.

Still no sign of you.

Most of the day was taken up by Mr Barnard setting out the facts of *this unusually sad case*. His account was as carefully edited as any of my reviews, with certain details dwelt on at the expense of certain others. I realised this was what I was paying him for (or what Fanny was paying him for, until I could reimburse her), but it was disconcertingly like listening to a story that had happened to somebody else. On and on he droned in his mild tenor voice. Who would have thought such painful events could sound so monotonous? I had to hope this was part of his strategy.

We adjourned for lunch.

At two o'clock, Hop returned from the robing room with news. You would not be attending the trial. Your doctors believed the excitement would prove too much for you.

My relief felt strangely like disappointment.

'So I won't be accused of adultery.'

'No,' Hop said. 'And I was rather counting on that.'

Mr Barnard resumed his summary of the evidence to be led. The woman you thought was following us on the Channel crossing; the voice you heard coming from my dressing room; your behaviour at the circus; the spies blowing bugles and engine whistles; the intruders on the roof. *Dear God*, I thought, *can I bear to go through it all again, even to be free of you?* It was a relief when he moved on to what happened in Liverpool, the bizarre tale I had heard from Robert Scott Macfie.

At three o'clock the first witness was called: Dr Nisbet, your former friend. When Scotty Macfie introduced us, the doctor had been quite the blether, plying me with cups of tea and Dundee cake. In court, he gave the bare minimum of information. That you had always been rather reserved, but genial enough after a dram or two. You came back from Africa a changed man, morose and disappointed. He had once glanced out of a window to see you standing in the middle of the road, looking about as if you could not remember why you were there.

Your counsel declined to cross-examine the witness.

'All rise.'

In the car, Hop was quiet.

'I didn't think sitting still for six hours would be so tiring,' I said.

He drove hunched over the steering wheel so his feet could reach the pedals.

'It seemed to go fairly well,' I persisted.

He looked at me, and back at the road. 'There was nothing that could go wrong today. Tomorrow will be a different matter.'

Next morning, Fanny supervised my dress. The faintest trace of rouge on my cheeks. Not too much. His Lordship was partial to a pretty face, but on no account was I to flirt with him. Demure was best. No fidgeting or lip-licking. 'Don't worry,' she said. 'Just be yourself.'

I took my seat beside Hop in court, pretending not to notice every head turning to stare. Fanny had been careful to hide this morning's *Times*, but I passed a news-seller outside the court. *Madman's Marriage. Honeymoon With a Lunatic. Glasgow Lady's Demented Husband.* Mr Rawlinson surprised me with a courteous nod. It was just another day's work to him.

I was to be the first witness on the stand. Mr Barnard said the judge had heard enough from him yesterday: Mr Willock would take me through my testimony. Hop muttered some last-minute advice. 'Don't look at His Lordship unless he addresses you directly. When Mr Rawlinson cross-examines, answer the question, not the insinuation. Try not to—' *Not to do his job for him.* He had already told me this. Before he could repeat himself, the court clerk bade us rise for the judge.

'*Mrs Catherine Jackson.*'

Hop gave me a tight smile. I crossed the court, my shoes clomping horribly on the wooden floor.

I swore the Scotch oath, without the Bible, raising my hand above my head.

Mr Willock's gaze urged me to forget the echoing courtroom, opposing counsel, the judge, everything but the steadily escalating unhappiness of our honeymoon. Delicately he asked about our nocturnal relations. I had rehearsed this testimony so often, I found myself speaking by rote. The judge began taking notes at furious speed, as if I had just said something highly pertinent. I wondered what? He lifted his head suddenly and caught me staring. Mindful of Hop's advice, I looked away, to Mr Rawlinson, who was hanging on my every word. Once in a while he glanced at his junior, who scribbled something in his jotter.

'Thank you,' Mr Willock said, sitting down.

I tried to leave the stand.

Mr Rawlinson got up. 'If you would be so good as to remain where you are, Mrs Jackson.'

I stepped back, appalled at myself. I knew full well I would be cross-examined, yet had somehow managed to unknow it. I could almost hear Hop telling me not to get so flustered.

'You would have the court believe that Mr Jackson was mad on your wedding day, is that correct?'

He had the glassy eyes of a herring gull, a ring of palest blue around a pitiless black dot.

'It is,' I said.

'Forgive me, but you seemed to hesitate before answering.'

'I was giving it the same careful thought I give every question.'

'Most admirable, I'm sure.' His smile was perfectly balanced between courtesy and threat. 'Tell me, why did you marry a man who was bereaved of his wits?'

'I didn't know it at the time.'

'I would have thought madness was rather obvious.'

'Herbert was able to conceal it.'

'You're quite sure of that?'

'I am.'

A puzzled frown contracted his brows. 'How can you be?'

Of course, Mr Rawlinson felt nothing for me personally. It was his job to tear my evidence to shreds.

'Herbert was restless and unhappy.' My voice was not as steady as I would have wished. 'Later I discovered it was part of his madness.'

'Surely many people are restless and unhappy. You do not consider them *all* mad, I presume?'

'Once we were married, it became clear his enemies were purely imaginary. He thought ordinary gestures by strangers were signals about him. He heard voices on the roof when there was no one there – I said all this to Mr Willock.'

'Bear with me, Mrs Jackson. You said, did you not, that before the wedding Mr Jackson refused to explain his troubles, appearing very—' he took a sceptical breath '—*reserved*.'

'He told me a little. That he had been spied on, and his letters tampered with.'

'And you saw no cause to doubt this?'

'None. He spoke so rationally.'

'Did he, indeed?'

My face turned to flame.

'Not that I saw very much of him before we married.'

'But he wrote to you often?'

'Fairly often.'

In the public seats, a woman in a green dress was watching me – well, they were all watching me, but she was doing so with particular fascination. Beside her sat a stout man with scant yellow hair. His ruddy face seemed familiar. His hand rose discreetly, transferring something from his pocket to his mouth.

'And some of those letters Mr Willock read to the court?'

I did not like these questions that were not really questions.

'Letters in which Mr Jackson wrote that he was impatient to hold you and kiss you, addressing you as "sweetheart" and "dear heart", writing that the sight of you stirred his blood like a military band?'

'He did say that, yes.'

'And that if you continued to write to him in the way you had been, he would have to come and carry you off?'

I began to see where he was going with this.

'Mrs Jackson?'

'I remember something of that sort.'

'In short, he was violently in love with you?'

'He said he was.'

'Did you doubt it?'

'No.'

'Did you return that love?'

'I liked him very much.'

'You... *liked* him?'

'I was very fond of him.'

How coldly measured I sounded. Why not just say 'yes'? Because no love was *returned*. When was it ever an exchange, like for like?

Mr Rawlinson showed me his barbed smile. 'So Mr Jackson spoke rationally, and his letters were full of the sentiments one would expect of a man violently in love with his betrothed, a man so eager to marry he could not wait a month – and yet you describe him as "reserved"?'

'On the subject of his troubles.'

'And you paid those troubles little heed at the time?'

'I suppose.'

'Is it not possible, Mrs Jackson, that you paid them so little heed because they didn't matter greatly to Mr Jackson at the time: they were neither here nor there beside his great love for you?'

'But they *did* matter to him. I was to discover on our honeymoon that they mattered very much.'

He looked at me as if I were a child misbehaving at table.

'Did your friends approve of the match?'

'I think they did, broadly.'

'"Broadly"?'

'They thought it was rather rash, marrying after such a short engagement.'

'But you had good reason to do so?'

My blood froze.

'You must have offered them some explanation?'

'I forget what I said, probably something about Herbert being eager to see Italy in the autumn.'

'I see,' he said in his sceptical drawl.

'It wasn't as rash as all that. I didn't accept his proposal until my mother had met him.'

'So *she* approved, at least?'

The sun blazed through the courtroom window, a slanting beam of swarming motes.

'Mrs Jackson?'

'She wanted us to wait a little longer.'

Mr Barnard glanced at Mr Willock.

'If I might take you back to your wedding day. Would you be so good as to describe what happened?'

And now it came to me: where I had first seen the man sitting beside the woman in the green dress. He was one of the soldiers who burst in on our wedding.

'I arrived at the church a little late, expecting Herbert to meet me at the door—'

'Have you ever heard of a bridegroom meeting his bride at the door of the church? It would be a most unusual proceeding, would it not? His place would be with his best man, waiting inside.'

'It was Herbert's idea. He and his solicitor would take me to his studio across the road, to look over some papers. And yes, I did think it *most unusual*.'

Laughter in the public seats. Had I bested my adversary, or walked into his trap? Mr Rawlinson's glassy look gave nothing away.

'And on the journey to the Continent, did you think it unusual that a lady should stare at you both on the train?'

'No.'

'*No?*' He raised an eyebrow. 'Of course, I have no personal experience in such matters.'

More laughter.

'Many people like to see newly-weds spooning,' I said. 'It's very natural.'

'You were *spooning*? On a train?'

'In a modest way.'

'It strikes me, Mrs Jackson, that you take rather an original line on your own and others' behaviour.'

A pulse flickered under my left eye.

'If you mean do I worry overmuch about the done thing, I suppose I don't, but that doesn't mean I...' Hop sent me a warning look. *Try not to do his job for him.*

'That doesn't mean you *what*, Mrs Jackson?'

'There is a difference between not caring about minor social conventions and wittingly joining one's life to a madman.'

'When exactly did you decide your husband was mad?'

'In the February after we married.'

'The beginning of February, or the end?'

I glanced at Mr Barnard. Rawlinson's beaky nose smelled weakness.

'It must be rather memorable: the day a lady decides her husband is insane.'

'It wasn't a *decision*. He behaved so strangely for so long, insisting people were trying to poison him, Mr Pierpont Morgan was his enemy... In the end madness was the only possible explanation.'

'So there was no one particular factor?'

'No. Well, I suppose the matter of children. He'd always said he wanted them, and then suddenly they were an impossibility.'

'He refused to accept the child you were carrying was his?'

'As I have already said.'

'And he had no grounds?'

Was Mr Rawlinson suggesting I had been unfaithful?

In his silkiest tone, he said, 'Mrs Jackson, did your husband have any reason to doubt your child's paternity?'

'No sane reason.'

'Had you not formed a friendship with an American gentleman?'

I was not expecting this. Even you were not so mad as to imagine Richard my lover.

'My husband met him too. We entertained him and his mother to dinner in Florence.'

'But you had met him some weeks earlier without your husband, had you not? In Bellagio, and then in Perugia?'

'We met briefly in both places. It was more of an acquaintance than a friendship.'

'I see. Did you form any other acquaintances with gentlemen in Italy?'

'*I did not.*'

Hop made a discreet signal of restraint.

Mr Rawlinson regarded me with his air of languid surprise. 'When Mr Jackson denied he was the father of the child you were carrying, how did you respond?'

'I told him he was being absurd.'

'And what did he say to that?'

'He denied he was capable of conjugal relations. As that was patently false, and he was entirely serious, I realised he was insane.'

'And this realisation was distressing?'

I stared at him. 'It was the worst thing that has ever happened to me. All my hopes for the future were destroyed at a stroke. My child's father disowned her.'

'I take it Mr Jackson, too, was upset?'

'He was furiously angry.'

'Angry enough to be violent?'

The woman in the green dress was transfixed.

'No,' I said.

'Did Mr Jackson ever use violence towards you?'

Hop and I had been over this. I did not want Diana growing up to learn that her father had tried to kill her mother. I was ashamed, although *ashamed* was too mild a word. You had wanted me dead. That desire was something we created together, as surely as we made our daughter. And I had wanted you dead too.

Mr Rawlinson repeated the question. 'Mrs Jackson, did your husband ever—'

'He once pushed me rather hard.'

'Nothing more?'

'No.'

Mr Rawlinson's gown had slipped off his shoulders. He made a performance of hitching it back up. 'So all the time you were at Como, Bellagio, Milan, Perugia and Florence, you did not think your husband was mad?'

'I knew he had certain delusions.'

'But you didn't mention it to anyone, not even the doctor you asked to see him in Perugia?'

'I was determined not to. I thought he might get better. He was an artist, of a highly strung temperament. I thought it might only be a passing trouble.'

'I see.'

How I hated the way he said that.

'You said nothing at all until he repudiated the child you were carrying, at which point you, *ah*, knew beyond doubt?'

Had it been then, or before, when you first talked about me killing myself? When I began to feel it was a question of my death or yours?

'Mrs Jackson?'

I took a breath. 'That's correct.'

'And within a month he was taken to an asylum and certified insane?'

'He was.'

'And yet for two years after that you made no attempt to separate yourself from him legally.'

Put like that, it did sound odd.

'Were you dependent on him?'

'No, I earned my own money and went back to live with my mother.'

'So it wasn't a question of financial necessity?'

The whole court could see my twitching left eye.

'If I might press you, Mrs Jackson...'

'*I don't know what you want me to say.*'

Another mistake.

'I am trying to elicit the truth, Mrs Jackson. Only you know what that is. The rest of us must draw a reasonable inference from the known facts. For example, it strikes me as rather peculiar that you did not try to annul your marriage in March 1905. Unless you believed there was nothing to be done, since your husband had been perfectly competent when he made his vows. I have every sympathy. Insanity is a scourge. Some believe it should be grounds for divorce, regardless of when it arises, but that is not the law as it stands. You must see my difficulty: two years is a long time to remain in an invalid marriage to an absent party. On the other hand, it may have taken you two years to think up this ingenious way out of it.'

'That's not what happened.'

'Then why the delay?'

Such an obvious question. I wondered why it had not occurred to Hop.

'At first I did nothing for my daughter's sake, but the more time went by, the more I desired my freedom.'

'And there was no other reason?'

'None.'

My eye flickered madly, as if I had just lied on oath. As I supposed I had, by omission. But I could hardly explain that remaining married to you had been my penance for wanting you dead. That in my own mad way, I had continued to believe you loved me.

'I have to confess, Mrs Jackson, I find your story somewhat perplexing. You do not strike me as a shrinking violet. Rather the reverse. You give the impression of being a decisive person, admirably clear-headed about your own interests. The kind of person who, having had all your hopes destroyed at a stroke, might well think you are entitled to another chance at happiness, even if the letter of the law has to be... *bent* a little to achieve it. A fair assessment, wouldn't you say?'

'No, I would not.'

Hop moved his index finger. I understood why he would urge circumspection, but he was not the one being accused of bending the law.

'For those two years after he was committed to the asylum, Herbert was never out of my thoughts. I made sure he was supplied with clothes and drawing materials, I wrote to him, visited him – until he refused to see me. He had made my every waking moment a misery, but I hated to think of him deprived of his liberty. So don't you dare try to *explain me* – how could you, when I don't understand it myself?'

The judge looked startled.

289

'Thank you, Mrs Jackson.' Mr Rawlinson sat down.

The usher opened the door to let me out of the witness box.

When Scotty Macfie took the stand, I felt the same surge of hope I had felt when we met in Liverpool, followed by the same stab of anxiety. Thank goodness for an impartial witness to your madness! If only he had not had that florid face and bristling half-handlebar moustache. If only he had looked slightly less like a silly old buffer in a *Punch* cartoon.

Mr Barnard asked how long he had known you.

'Must be a good ten years now – no, tell a lie, it was ninety-seven he fetched up. Bunked across the landing from me. We had a fair few artist wallahs in the Varsity Club. Portraits were Jackson's bag. Did the chairman to a T, I thought. Some disagreed. Well, you know these painter chappies: jealous as cats in a sack.'

Mr Barnard wondered how you had seemed to him back then.

'Decent enough cove. Billiards secretary. Bit of a sportsman. Not one of those chaps who's always making clever remarks – awfully wearing, that. There was a dauber stood in for him at the art school when he went orf to Africa. Augustus John. Never stopped jawing, bit of a bounder all round. Jackson was more of a dark horse, kept his thoughts to himself. Though there was that business with the billiard room kitty: none of us was in any doubt that he had a bee in his bonnet about that! *Entre nous*, nobody bothers overmuch if a chap has the odd game when he ain't carrying any change, but Jackson pins up these stinky notes. *Gentlemen are politely requested to pay for their amusements*. Then he says money's gone missing from the honesty box. Well, forgetfulness is one thing, larceny quite another. Bit orf of him bringing it up, if you ask me, but the committee could hardly ignore it. They had a glass eye put in the door. Chalky Fry said, why not false teeth too? Ha! Rather good, that, I thought.'

Mr Barnard returned a perfunctory smile. 'Was there anything unusual about Mr Jackson at that point?'

'Ah well, that rather depends whom you ask. Bit of a bone of contention. Nisbet swears he was right as ninepence until he went to Africa, but if you ask me, what kicked it all orf was the billiard room ghost. Couple of the fellows said they'd heard knocking, but when they opened the door: nobody there. Ludo Phipps swore the cue ball had a mind of its own. There was a picaninny lived on Frederick Street, a tailoress. Earned a bit on the side as a medium. Baxter knew her somehow. Brought her over to the club one evening. Deuced pretty gel. She calls us all in there, gets us around the table, all the curtains closed, holding hands in the dark. There's a fair bit of sniggering. "Oh, Scotty, I never knew you cared," that sort of rot. Then she starts speaking – well, you can hardly call it speaking. Mumbling and moaning in this deep voice. More like a dock walloper than a chit of a gel. It's enough to give a fellow the willies. The balls start whizzing around the baize. Can't see a hand in front of m'face, but I can hear 'em all right.'

I remembered the creeping paralysis I had felt in the ladies' sitting room at the University Club, as it dawned on me that Scotty was quite capable of talking all through tea, and dinner too. Was it just my imagination, or were Mr Barnard's eyes beginning to glaze over?

'As it happens I'm holding Jackson's paw, until he pulls away and strikes a match. The filly screams and drops down in a dead faint. Baxter puts on the lights. Well, we look pretty silly: a roomful of chaps all holding hands. The gel has to be carried to the smoking room, which is strictly out of bounds to the fair sex, but the only place with a sofa long enough to lay her down flat. Judd finds a bottle of smelling salts, and when she comes round, she don't remember a thing. Jackson wants to know who put her up to it, reckons the whole show's been a ragging at his expense. Next day, Reverend O'Rorke's in there saying a lot of Latin mumbo jumbo to lay the ghost—'

'*Mr Barnard*,' the judge said.

Mr Barnard asked the witness if he would be so good as to confine himself to the question.

'Oh, ah...'

'Was Mr Jackson's behaviour in any way unusual?'

'Ah yes, well, a couple of weeks after this I'm having a bite of supper with Eddie Gordon Duff. In bursts Jackson. Turns out he's been creeping round the club, spotted GD in the billiard room, and got it into his head that he's the thief. Threatening to have him blackballed! Well, you can imagine. The chairman has a quiet word with GD, who agrees to steer clear of the premises for a month or two, entirely of his own volition, and Jackson struts about the place like St George after he's slain the dragon. When Jackson goes orf to the Transvaal, GD reappears. For a year or so everyone's happy as Larry. Then Jackson comes back. As soon as I saw him, I thought, *by Jove, what's happened to you?* Nisbet says to me, "Jackson's had a bad war". Well, that's as may be. War is war. You'd be a damn fool to enlist thinking it's going to be some sort of picnic. Whole show was an absolute shambles. Twenty thousand Afrikander mutton farmers running rings around the British Empire—'

Counsel cleared his throat. 'Was there anything *in particular* you noticed about Mr Jackson's behaviour?'

'I should say so. He tells one or two of the chaps he's been treated shamefully. No proper recognition of his service, while General Roberts gets a hero's welcome and a pot of gold. I mean to say, the general may have been less than inspiring as a C-in-C, but he did rather more for his country than fixing up a few horse troughs for the cavalry, eh, what?'

His Lordship gave the witness a pointed look.

'Anyhoo, for six months it's one thing after another. He don't like some bit of fun in the varsity magazine about returning soldiers. He won't let that chap MacNair do his kangaroo dance at a soirée the young ladies have organised at the art school. He tells Sampson some cock-and-bull story about Raleigh reading his post. There's this filly he popped the question to before he went orf, a married lady now. She comes back to visit her sister and crosses paths with Jackson at some charity shindig. Widows and orphans or some such. She tries to be pleasant, *have another macaroon* sort of thing, but when he spots her wedding ring he rather turns on her. Calling her a trollop and Lord knows what else. Titherley and Newell have to drag him away. *Then* I get this letter. He's still mithering over the billiard room business, only now he feels *he* was in the wrong, so will I arrange for Gordon Duff to turn up at his London studio so he can offer him a gentleman's satisfaction? Well, old GD wouldn't know one end of an eppy from the other, and if it's a question of who insulted whom, GD's an amusing fellow, but he's got a deucedly cruel tongue. Laughs himself silly, when I pass on the message. "No can do, Scotty old man".'

The judge propped an elbow on the bench and put his hand over his eyes.

'Of course, the story's all round the club. It gets to be rather a joke: *watch yourself! Jackson's about.* Turns out it's not the first time. He's sent a challenge to this composer chappie over some bit of doggerel he's supposed to have written in the club limericks book – only the poor chap's in bed with typhoid fever. Next we hear Jackson's *persona non grata* at the art school. They can't have a loose cannon teaching young gels. He chucks it as billiards secretary – frankly, rather a relief all round – but he's still hanging about like a bad smell, so Collins has the bright idea of making Sandy Mair's testimonial dinner a doubler. Sandy can be thanked for his years as club secretary and Jackson for his services to the baize and balls. Sampson draws the short straw of writing his encomium. Come the night, there we all are in best bib and tucker: *no Jackson.* Seems he's left Liverpool altogether. Last we hear of him is this extraordinary letter he writes to Harald Ehrenborg accusing us all of trying to wreck his nerves. At first he thought it might be some sort of ragging, or we'd hypnotised him, but now he believes we've committed some dastardly crime and we're trying to shift the blame onto him! I mean to say...'

The judge lowered his hand. Hop looked up.

The impossible had happened. Scotty had stopped talking. Mr Barnard blinked.

'No further questions, m'Lord.'

One by one, they stepped up to the stand. The composer recounted how you had challenged him to a duel, although you hardly knew each other. Your London landlady recalled you pacing the floor all night and lurking barefoot in the hall. Your upstairs neighbour told how you blacked his eyes and broke his nose. Through it all, Mr Rawlinson wore a look of utter indifference, but the next witness brought a glint to his seagull eye.

'Professor Walter Raleigh.'

There was a creaking along the public benches as people craned for a better view. He was so immensely tall. Imposing, too. Easily a match in gravitas for the judge. Three years since our last meeting. His hair was grey, and his moustache, but it was still a marvellous face. The irony in those hooded eyes, the subversive push of his lower lip.

Prompted by Mr Barnard, he said he had been introduced to you twenty years before, not long after meeting your sister.

'How did Mr Jackson strike you in those days?'

'He had rather a lonely life.'

'Unhappy?'

'In his shoes, I should have been, but he was always pretty much a closed book. Self-contained.' His eyes met mine across the court. 'Rather reserved and stiff.'

Again I wondered why Walter was my witness, not yours,

when it was thanks to him we were all here in open court, instead of disposing of the matter quietly in the judge's chambers.

He described a letter you had sent from Africa accusing him of tampering with your post. He had not held it against you, knowing you could only have written such things under great distress of mind. He sounded entirely reasonable and magnanimous. Mr Barnard thanked him and sat down.

To my surprise, it was not Mr Rawlinson who rose to cross-examine, but his junior, Mr Mills, a young man with the hectic cheeks of a mischievous choirboy.

'You said Mr Jackson came to stay with you on his return from South Africa. Did you think him insane then?'

'I did not think him insane at any time. I am not a medical man, and was not competent to form an opinion.'

'But you arranged for him to see a doctor the following year, did you not?'

'Yes, after Harald Ehrenborg showed me the rather extraordinary letter Jackson had sent him.'

'The letter claiming his former friends were conspiring against him?'

'The same. Ehrenborg wanted to know what he should do about it. As Jackson was coming to stay with us, I persuaded him to see my doctor, Gemmell.'

'By which time you were doubting his sanity?'

'As I said, I am not a medical man. He seemed normal enough to me in all things except these questions of "plots" and "opening of letters". I was always pleased to receive him as a guest.'

It was strange, seeing Walter so serious. I kept waiting for the old puckish twitch of his lips.

'And what was Doctor Gemmell's opinion?'

'I got the impression he didn't think Jackson was insane, merely brooding and in need of work and cheerful company.'

'So you felt he was sufficiently rational to introduce to the petitioner?'

'Cathie was visiting us. Jackson was staying in the same village. Naturally he spent a good deal of time with us. He seemed to have put these fancies behind him.'

Walter was a very convincing perjurer.

'And when they announced their engagement, did you warn the petitioner she was about to marry a man some regarded as of unsound mind?'

'If I had raised objections, it would probably have hurried on the marriage.'

Faces turned towards me. Hop grasped my elbow. I sat down again. The judge looked at Mr Barnard, who cringed in apology.

'Carry on, Mr Mills,' His Lordship said.

'So you did nothing to deter the match?'

'It seemed to me intolerable to pursue a man with stories of bygone things.'

'But consider the lady's position.'

Walter blinked.

The judge intervened. 'To have raised objections might have involved the witness in an action.'

Walter seized His Lordship's helpful suggestion. 'I would have regarded it as a slander. I believed him quite recovered.'

'And Mr Jackson's other friends, in Liverpool,' Mr Mills enquired, 'were they of the same opinion?'

'I had rather better hopes than they did – after all, a medical man was best man at the wedding.'

'Did you discuss Mr Jackson's state of mind with Dr Munro?'

'I considered it eloquent that he was there at all.'

'So you didn't discuss it?'

Walter's eyes turned to stone. 'I considered the question of Jackson's sanity most gravely.'

'You are very guarded in your answers, Professor.'

'I am very guarded in my thoughts, sir.'

'Mr Mills.' His Lordship did not care to watch an Oxford professor being harried by junior counsel.

Unwisely, Mr Mills persisted, 'Did the marriage go off all right?'

'Yes.'

'Mr Jackson answered the responses quite properly?'

The judge snapped, 'He was not a raving lunatic. The evidence is that outwardly he was nothing out of the common. The question is whether he was really insane. You are unduly pressing the witness.'

After a muttered exchange with Mr Rawlinson, Mr Mills said he had no further questions.

I had been dreading running the gamut of nudges and whispers and turned heads, but by the time Hop and I emerged from our conference with Mr Barnard the lobby was deserted. Hop went to get his motorcar, telling me to wait by the kerb.

Such a relief to stand and stretch. I should have liked to walk and walk until weariness bludgeoned the last thought from my head. And why not? At least, as far as Marylebone. Hop would try to dissuade me – the afternoon had been changeable, with sudden showers streaming down the court-room windows – but I was sure that, secretly, he would be relieved. We had been forced together since breakfast.

Something moved in my peripheral vision. I turned. The woman in the green dress came out of the courthouse. The soldier was behind her. I was the only other person on the pavement. I pretended not to recognise her, although our eyes had met across the public benches more than once. She was going to offer me a word of kindness, and at that moment kindness was as unwelcome to me as spite. I looked the other way, down the Strand, the nape of my neck prickling at her approach. The rain saved me. One moment we were dry; the next, it was like having a tub of bathwater tipped over us. She shrieked and dashed back to the shelter of the porch.

Her companion called out, 'Ye'll be droukit.'

I had forgotten he was Scotch.

The rain redoubled in ferocity, bouncing off the pavement. There was nothing else for it. I joined them in the cavelike space behind the Gothic arch.

The woman grinned at me, shaking the wet from her hair like a dog.

I returned the briefest of smiles.

'It's fair settin' in,' the soldier said.

I peered up at the louring sky. *Where was Hop?*

'Ah served under yir man.'

Reluctantly I turned towards him.

As if there were room for doubt, he added, 'Lieutenant Jackson.'

With my back to the daylight, I could see him quite clearly. He was barely thirty: young to have lost so much hair. Short legs; broad torso; big, blocklike head. The air was heavy with his animal reek of breath and feet and sweat-rotted cloth.

'You were hoping to see him in court?' I said.

He found this funny. 'Aye – naw. No for auld lang syne.' The humour drained from his voice. 'Nae sae many fond memories, ye ken.'

As chilly as Mr Rawlinson, I asked, 'And you are?'

'Davie Sillars – Second Corporal Sillars then.' There was an unmistakeable indecency in his slow grin. 'Ah thocht ye'd be rid-heidit like his Boer duntie. A rid-heidit radge. Till she turned cauld on him. He mowed her onieways, an all o' us watchin.'

'That's a lie,' I said, though how was I to know?

He laughed. 'Plenty lead in his peencil, yon nicht.'

Hop's Sunbeam drew up at the kerb.

'Tell the lieutenant ah wis askin' fur him,' he said.

In my dream I am swimming in a cold river under a dull white sky. The water is silky on my limbs, with a downward drag unlike the crude, salt buoyancy of the sea. My mind is very clear, at one with the push of my arms, the kick of my legs, my body's swoop and rise. Just before my head goes under, I breathe in the dank green smell of river.

And surface to hear shouting.

I break stroke and tread water, looking around. The breeze chills my wet face. Swallows dart past, chasing insects.

I swim again, easing back into the rhythm, slicing through the water. The river widens, its banks receding. The current grows stronger. All at once I see a rowing boat, a man pulling hard on the oars to stay in place. He glances over his shoulder. In the river light, your face is perfectly distinct: your tousled hair and broken nose. You let go of one oar and point at something bobbing in the water, some piece of jetsam, pale and luminous.

Our daughter.

I strike out towards her but it's no use, I am out of my depth, weak as a leaf against the racing current. In my panic I go under, swallowing water, flailing to the surface. A moment ago she was there, now she is gone. Drowned, I am sure of it. I roar my anguish to the sky.

In answer, a ragged sound across the water. Her squalling cry.

There!

The river has me at its mercy, sweeping me downstream. I can barely keep my head above water. A ghillie's cottage appears, and is gone, a reed bed, a fishing jetty, every moment taking me further from my last sight of her, on the bank, in your arms.

Friday's first post brought two letters, neither of them from Greiffy. Mother wrote to say she had been following the proceedings in the *Glasgow Herald* and was upset by references to her approving of the match. The second envelope contained a short note from Don wishing me luck, adding that the *Herald* had given the first day of the trial fewer column inches than the *Times*. The editor was looking forward to hearing what I thought of the Barrie play next week.

By which time I would be free of you. Or not.

That day it was Mr Rawlinson's turn to set out his stall. He would be calling four witnesses, to our ten. In the Sunbeam on the way to court, I said, surely this was an encouraging sign? Hop kept his eyes on the road.

'Is it not?'

'He doesn't need witnesses. The matter is already won, or lost, by us. All he has to do is remind His Lordship of the weaknesses in our case.'

It was a different Mr Rawlinson who rose to address the judge. Gone was the silky courtesy. Although he was not appearing for my daughter, he said, her welfare was much on his mind. Surely any court would hesitate before branding a child with the stigma of bastardy. Surely, where the evidence was evenly balanced, any court would decide in that child's best interests. And in this particular case, the evidence was not so balanced. Quite the opposite. Had the bridegroom suffered from delusions at the time of his marriage? Probably. But those delusions had had no bearing on the wedding itself. Your love letters showed the ardour to be expected of a man on the brink of marriage. Your sister and brother-in-law had approved of the match. There was nothing out of the ordinary about the ceremony. That very morning, you had dictated a new will to your solicitor. You had discussed the marriage settlement in a perfectly rational manner. The letters you had written to the insurance agent from Italy betrayed no fear of plots – nothing but newly-wedded happiness.

'And there is no evidence supporting Mrs Jackson's *recollection* of what happened on the honeymoon. If her husband had behaved as erratically as she maintains, would she not have insisted on returning home? Would she really have waited five months to call in a mad doctor? This case rests on the uncorroborated testimony of a lady whose evidence must of needs be... *tinged*.'

He was calling me a liar.

'Until this case came on, did the petitioner for one moment believe her marriage had been induced by delusions? Did she really believe Mr Jackson had married her not because he loved her, but because he thought she was a person who would protect him from imaginary enemies?

'If such a marriage can be annulled, one wonders, would a will be overturned on the same grounds?' His glassy eyes kindled in amusement at the thought. 'Naturally, there will be a desire to set aside this marriage, but to do so on the evidence here adduced would be straining the limits of public policy to the last extreme.'

Durham v. Durham was cited, and *Hunter v. Edney*, and *Dow v. Clark*, while the judge took copious notes. I scanned the public benches for your corporal and his friend. Absent, to my relief. An old woman had fallen asleep. Her rumbling snores were just low enough for the usher to leave her be. Mr

Barnard caught a sneeze in his handkerchief. Mr Willock's profile wore a troubled, interior look, as if his tongue were worrying at a shred of breakfast trapped between his back teeth.

Your witnesses were called. Cousin William said you had been given to melancholy silences since childhood, but were wholly rational on the morning of our wedding. Dr Gemmel claimed he had found you quite fit to marry. Dr Turney had passed you as a first-class life two days before the ceremony. Even Henry Munro said you had shown complete understanding of the responsibilities you were taking on.

Mr Rawlinson lifted an envelope from the shelf in front of Mr Mills, where it had sat all morning, unnoticed by me. 'Bearing in mind Your Lordship's regret that the respondent is not able to give evidence in person, with Your Lordship's permission I will read out a letter I received from him this morning.'

The judge nodded.

'Dear Sir,
I have just read a report of the first's day's hearing. Of course, I have no other means of hearing what transpired than through the newspapers, but if that report is correct, there are some statements which are absolutely untrue, and they must be contradicted and refuted. I was thirty-six years of age when I was married, not forty. I never told my wife that any woman was following me on the train.

It was my wife who informed me that Mr Joseph Chamberlain was on the same boat. I did not see him and certainly never said the Government had sent someone to watch me. My state of mind was that, whilst being conscious of being watched, I did not know by whom I was being watched.'

Such an odd sensation: hearing your words read aloud by another. I knew you so well. Your breathing. The timbre of

303

your voice. The sarcastic, residually tender inflection whenever you said 'my wife'. It was as if I could hear you speaking under him.

'As for my removal to the asylum in March 1905, I had no struggle. I had an interview with Dr Munro and consented to accompany him to Rose House. I threatened no one with a revolver, which was unloaded and under the bed. My wife seized it and threw it out of the window.

I paid no marked attention to any young lady at Liverpool in 1903. I only expressed a desire to again meet a young lady who had previously refused to marry me.

At Redcliffe Square Mr Brown (the artist) occupied the rooms above me. I was not friendly with him. His small boy ran up and downstairs making a noise. I have sometimes thought I heard cries like a child sobbing, and one night, hearing it more clearly than usual, I went upstairs to Mr Brown's rooms. He was very offensive and there was a row.

Please make what use you like of this statement, which I wish I could repeat on oath in court.

Yours faithfully,
Herbert Jackson'

It was just like you, I thought, to focus on irrelevant details when so much was at stake. Though I supposed you sounded rational enough, in your pedantic way.

The refreshment room was busy. Heads lifted as I passed. I sat at an empty table in the corner, half-hidden by a potted aspidistra.

A long shadow fell across the cloth.

'May I join you?'

'It seems you already have.'

A waitress followed with Walter's pot of tea. She insisted

on pouring us both a cup. That tremor of his had worsened. Sugar rained from the spoon.

'It's been a rough few days for you,' he said.

There had been more lurid headlines on the newsstand that morning.

'I was hoping it didn't show.'

'You forget, I know you very well.'

As well I knew him. Those long fingers, his smell of cloves.

'Lucie is rather displeased with me,' he said, anticipating my question.

'She feels you're running with the hare and the hounds?'

'"Sniffing after" were the exact words.'

'And you justified yourself how?'

'I hardly think that's any of your concern.' He used both hands to bring the teacup to his lips, and still it shook. 'Unless you're asking me to justify myself to you.'

'Why should I do that?'

'Don't be fatuous, Cathie. You always had a vigilant sense of your own deserts. It was the first thing I noticed about you, that and your peachy skin.'

I looked down at the spill of sugar across the tablecloth. *Not everything that brings us pleasure is good for us.* You taught me that.

He tipped my chin with his forefinger, making me look up. A chancy gesture, but very quick. 'You must see that I couldn't stand by and do nothing.'

'I suppose you're going to tell me you believe in the principle of marriage.'

'As I do.'

'And you're concerned for your niece's future?'

'Someone ought to be.'

I could have pointed out that he had never taken the trouble to meet her.

'I read her Byron after breakfast, and Lamb's *Tales from*

305

Shakespeare before bed. I am bringing her up to understand what matters, and to ignore the rest.'

'And when she finds herself a pariah?'

'You mean, she may not be asked to tea by titled ladies whose husbands accept other men's children as their own?'

He said nothing, knowing I meant the daughter his great friend Lady Elcho had conceived while her husband was two thousand miles away. The same Lady Elcho who had been Lord Balfour's confidante while he was prime minister. Walter's name was often in the society columns these days.

'Why *did* you give evidence for me?'

'You know why,' he said. 'I want you to be happy.'

I felt as if he had reached across the table to pull my heart out of my chest, and there it sat, beating in his hand.

'And I suppose you told Lucie the case will be decided on a point of law, so anything you say will make no difference?'

He laughed. 'My clever girl.'

'*Cath*.' Hop was standing over us. 'Mr Barnard would like a word.'

'I'll see him before we go back into court.'

'As soon as you can,' he said, departing. He did not trust Walter. Nor did I, of course, but I had almost forgotten until Hop broke the spell.

A stocking-coloured skin had formed over my untouched cup of tea.

'I was thinking yesterday,' I said, 'that the judge has no interest in uncovering what actually happened, only in satisfying himself that he can grant my petition without society descending into anarchy.'

'What a cynic you've become.'

'Then it occurred to me how many of Herbert's mad fancies have turned out to be justified. His Liverpool friends *were* gossiping about him. His letters *have* been read. He *is* watched day and night. We *did* act in concert against him. And still his suspicions are taken as proof of insanity.'

Walter was looking bored.

'I'm not denying he's mad, but you must admit there's a certain irony. So yes, I suppose I have been feeling cynical. But when I heard Mr Mills cross-examining you, I thought, *Perhaps truth will out after all.*'

He fumbled his teacup back into the saucer. 'And I forced you up the aisle at gunpoint, did I? What you tell the judge is entirely your own affair, and I do see that the blameless ingénue plays better than the Bohemian adulteress, but I'm an *Oxford professor.* I won't have it put about in the newspapers that my niece is a bastard and I married my pupil to a lunatic.'

'Although you did.'

'You're not on the witness stand now, Cathie. Have you forgotten? He knocked you for six. You should have seen yourself.'

'*You knew what he was.*'

'Yes, my wife's brother. You would have been my sister. We would have been free to meet—'

'As siblings!'

'As family.'

How horribly funny it was. I had to laugh.

'I married Herbert because I thought I was carrying your child.'

I had never seen Walter speechless before, even momentarily.

'But you weren't.'

'As I discovered, too late.'

'I had no idea,' he said in the voice he had used with Mr Mills.

An immense sadness settled on me. 'No. I had that comfort, at least.'

Was that a flicker of guilt in his eyes, guilt or pity, before it was overtaken by distaste?

'If you'll excuse me,' I said, 'I have to see my counsel.'

The morning of the judge's ruling, Fanny's cook makes my favourite breakfast, French toast soaked in egg, vanilla, cinnamon and cream, but I am too nervous to eat it. Hop sends me back upstairs to change out of my black dress. 'You're not going to the scaffold, Cath.'

'Am I not?'

Fanny turns away, as if distracted by something outside the window, and I see she fears the worst. As must Hop, behind his brave face, nodding his approval of my lilac silk as we climb into the Sunbeam.

The usher calls us into court. Hop, Fanny, Mr Barnard, Mr Willock, Mr Rawlinson, Mr Mills, the Official Solicitor, my sister-in-law, my mother-in-law, Walter, the press. Your mother meets my *hello* with a fluster of embarrassment. It is Lucie who has the sangfroid to cut me dead. Middle age has hollowed her cheeks, but she is very elegant.

The public benches are empty. The entertaining part of the trial is over. Anyone interested can read the judgment in the newspapers.

I should have listened to Mary Dowdall. I have gambled not just with my future, but with that of my child, and for what? *For freedom*, my thrawn self replies. At least I can say I attempted escape: I will have that comfort when your mother dies and Lucie drops the hot potato in my lap.

The door opens to admit a latecomer. What on earth is Don doing here? He smiles at me.

'All rise.'

The judge's colour is bad. A sleepless night? A quarrel with his wife? Our eyes meet. It can make no difference now.

He begins with a summary of case law and a reprise of the relevant facts. The grim specifics of our marriage have been retold so often they are utterly banal to me, but not to Don. He sits stiff-backed at the end of an empty bench; when the judge refers to you accusing me of adultery in front of a policeman, he turns to look at me.

'It is for the court to determine, not whether the respondent was aware he was going through a ceremony of marriage on 8th October 1904, but whether on that day he was capable of understanding the nature of the contract he was entering into, free from the influence of morbid delusions. The burden of proof rests upon the petitioner...'

I look down at my fingers in Hop's pudgy grip. Fanny is clutching his other hand.

'...and in my opinion she has clearly established that the respondent's disease was of gradual growth, had existed long before the parties had met, and had steadily progressed since then. There must, therefore, be a *decree nisi* of nullity with costs, and the petitioner will have the custody of her child.'

I squeeze Hop's hand. It is the least I owe him.

When the court rises, I return His Lordship's smile, thank Mr Barnard and Mr Willock, and slip away.

Finally: a deserted corridor. In the window, my reflection is pale, with bruised-looking shadows under each eye.

I am not your wife.

The judge has ruled that you married me out of madness. He did not ask why I married you. Because you were Walter's brother-in-law, and a good man beset by enemies, and I needed a husband at short notice. I too had my delusions.

There was no child in my belly. I was not the love of your life. You didn't even like me, once you got to know me. Yet until five minutes ago I feared love would thirl us for ever. Not love as others understand it, but a bond like iron chains, a death embrace.

Will I ever know what it means to be loved?

Having gained my freedom, I am no longer sure why it mattered. Even Fanny assumes I will marry again, but I have been as free as I need to be since Dr Savage took you away. What I wanted was absolution. And now that I have it, what in the world will I do with myself?

'*Cathie.*'

Don has come to find me.

'I got your letter,' I say. 'It was good of you to reassure me that I still have a job.'

'I knew you'd be worrying.'

'I suppose I'm the talk of the office.'

He meets my look. *Of course I am.*

We turn at the sound of laughter to see Mr Barnard and Mr Rawlinson passing the end of the corridor without their horsehair wigs, evidently on their way to an early lunch. *Thick as thieves*, I think, *you wouldn't like that.* But your likes and dislikes are no longer any of my business.

'I can't believe it,' I say.

'You won.'

'*Four years.*'

'But you found a way out.'

Perhaps I need time to get used to the fact. Perhaps tomorrow I will feel it is no small thing to look my daughter in the eye and tell her life is a gift, and mistakes can be mended, and every woman has the right to her own happiness.

But that is not what I feel now.

'I wish...'

'What?' he asks.

'Oh, I don't know. So many things.'

I wish I had paid more attention that fateful week in Berkshire, and made an ally of Mary Dowdall, and understood that Lucie never saw me as a rival, only as her dupe. I wish I had not kissed Walter. I wish that, having kissed him, I had kicked him out of my bed. I wish I had cared less, or been less vain, less eager to run into the arms of another man. And, *ah God*, I wish that man had not been you. That I had looked past your supple skin and heavy-lidded gaze to ask myself why everyone avoided you. I wish I had listened to Phyl, and to Mother, and told you it was too soon to marry. I wish I had gone to Liverpool and met your friends, or questioned the man I met on the stairs on the day of our wedding. But since I did none of these things while there was still time, I wish I had not been too proud to admit my mistake, and had bolted the morning I found the pistol, or when you smashed Walter's perfume bottle, before I let you put your hands around my neck.

I wish I knew for sure what sent you mad.

I will always wonder if knowing would have made a difference: if I might have helped you tell shadow from substance, each of us learning to trust the other, cherishing our daughter.

I wish I had loved you better. Or not at all.

But what good is wishing? It is the past; I must let it go. Waltzing in the midnight garden. Laughing on the roof of Milan cathedral. The afternoon I first caressed you into passion, the consummation that was our undoing. The judge has ruled: we were never truly married. I should be glad to forget, and yet even our worst times have their bittersweet nostalgia. How alive I was in my resistance. How relieved when your mad face became calm and handsome again. And so I wonder, would I do it all just the same, given the same combination of circumstances? I think of the couples I have watched at close quarters: Mother and Father, Walter and Lucie, even Fanny and Hop. None has the *magic*, the balance of freedom and loyalty that I crave, and yet I retain my stubborn faith in the impossible.

311

Why can I not see men as they truly are; why must I force them into the lineaments of romance?

No, not all of them: not Don.

'We should go and find your sister.' Underneath the gentleness, there is a grainy note of exhaustion in his voice.

He is so familiar to me, I rarely look at him – or rarely *see*. His face is pale as whey above his blue chin; his olive eyes red-rimmed. He is so thin. I worry that he will overtax his strength, that because his mind is tireless, he assumes his body will always keep pace. It is a long journey from Glasgow to London, and I know he will have been worrying about me.

'You shouldn't have come all this way,' I chide him.

He lifts an inky thumb and brushes the tears from my face.

Dear Mrs Jackson,
I humbly beg your pardon for writing this letter without introduction, and hope it finds you well. I had the honour of serving as secretary to your late brother-in-law, Mr Arthur Jackson. It was arranged that we would meet for supper on the very evening that his assassin fired the fatal shot. To spare his good lady wife any additional distress, I have assumed the task of sorting out his correspondence, among which I found the enclosed letters. I recall Mr Jackson mentioning that your husband is currently indisposed. As I would not wish to entrust such a delicate correspondence to those supervising his welfare in such a place, I am sending them to you, in the assurance that you will return them to him at your earliest convenience.

I am, madam, your respectful servant,
Bhupendranath Bose

1914

He was always 'Lawrence' or 'Lorenzo', except to his family, who called him 'Bert'.

By then Don and I were lovers, living in Hollybush House. I was forever whitewashing black mould off the scullery wall but, in summer, with the door open and the bees buzzing in the honeysuckle, there was nowhere lovelier.

It was my friend Ivy Low who sought out Lawrence in Tuscany. A few months later, he and Frieda came to London, and Ivy announced she was bringing them round to tea. They could only manage the Sunday, when Don would be at work. *Oh, any old cake* would do to feed them, but I was not to wear the blue tailor-made I had lent her to impress them in Italy.

I saw Frieda first. Her generous figure blocked the doorway. Later I was to appreciate her beauty, but that day she seemed a German *Frau* of the blonde, gushing type. I welcomed her inside and Lawrence stepped forward.

Ivy had warned me he looked like a workman in a third-class compartment and, yes, he was wearing a corduroy jacket.

'You're a writer, Mrs Jackson?'

'For the newspapers.'

I wondered if he had seen my review of *Sons and Lovers*, which I admired more than any recent novel I had read. Ivy winked at me. She herself had two books in print.

'And I'm writing a novel,' I said.

'About what?'

I laughed. 'Just about everything that has ever happened to me.'

'Except?'

I stared at him.

'Write about that,' he said.

'They'd never publish it.'

'All the more reason to write it.'

Ivy's friend Viola asked if he had read Arnold Bennett's latest. I got up to make more tea.

Frieda followed me through to the scullery. I feared for her horse-check skirt as it brushed against the whitewash.

'You mustn't mind Lorenzo,' she said. 'He's guessed right often enough for it to go to his head.'

Her smile had its helping of jealousy. I wanted to tell her not to worry, that of course her instincts were sound, I was powerfully drawn to the genius type, he was exactly the sort of man I had thrown myself at time and again, but I had not lived through the past decade without learning something. The only way of avoiding disaster with men like Lawrence was by keeping my hands off them.

'What a pretty dress,' she said.

It was a tea party, with all the limitations implied. There was a certain amount of persiflage for which I, as hostess, felt dreadfully responsible. Only Lawrence refused to waste his breath. After an hour or so, Ivy chivvied my guests to their feet. The Lawrences could not afford to return to Italy just yet. How splendid if we found a house for them to rent in Hampstead. We would all be neighbours.

I went to fetch my hat.

When I came down, everyone but Lawrence was waiting outside.

'I have a favour to ask,' he said.

'Of course. Anything.'

I guessed he wanted me to put a word in for him at the Manchester *Guardian*: would they take the odd column on the state of the novel? I knew he lived hand-to-mouth.

'Will you let me read your book?'

I could not bear the shame of wanting it so badly. I had to demur. 'It's not finished.'

'I'll bear that in mind.'

I remembered the way Frieda had smiled in the scullery. There would be many young women who had put their manuscripts into his hands.

'I think it's only fair to tell you,' I said, 'I'm the sort of person who is much more impressive at first meeting than subsequently.'

He found this funny, and I found I didn't mind.

'Luckily for you, I'm the sort of person who has no interest in being impressed.'

I enjoyed taking him up and down the banks and steps of our little hilltop, then back past the house to the end of Holly Mount. His eyes widened at the kestrel's view of London spread below us. I had no inkling that his insights would transform my rambling prose into a competent – indeed, a prizewinning – first novel, or that I would return the favour in a small way with *Women in Love*, but even then I sensed we would be friends.

They had to catch an omnibus back to Kensington. We walked them down to the Finchley Road, Lawrence and I forging ahead. His restless energy found sauntering a torment, and this suited my long stride. Both Frieda and Ivy were dawdlers. By the time we reached Church Row they were far behind. We stopped to wait where the road narrowed between the parish church and the little overflow graveyard. I thought of taking him to see Constable's stone. Instead, I gestured through the railings to our right.

'My daughter's buried in there.'

He looked startled.

The mock orange I had left the previous Wednesday was drooping but still put out its evening scent. He read the inscription on the low stone around the double plot. *Eight happy years.*

'Peritonitis. Last September,' I said, before my face crumpled.

'And the father?'

I did not tell him everything, but enough. With him, it seemed a waste of time to talk about anything but my real concerns.

We took a turn around the little graveyard, a pretty spot guarded by cedars, on gently rising ground, the grey stones and green turf splashed by evening sun. The place worked its magic on us and we were quiet for a while, until a blackbird swooped shrieking across our path.

'You should write about it,' he said.

Ivy called to us from the gate. We retraced our steps.

The talk moved on to the book he was planning about Thomas Hardy, but I knew he was turning the other matter over in his thoughts.

When the omnibus came, he said again, '*Write it.*'

'And if I do, will you read it?'

Frieda boarded the bus. He grasped the rail.

'Write it for him,' he said.

ACKNOWLEDGEMENTS

This is a work of fiction about real people, using imagination to patch the gaps in the factual record.

I urge anyone wanting to know more about Catherine Carswell to read her books, especially her piecemeal auto-biography, *Lying Awake*, her memoir of D. H. Lawrence, *The Savage Pilgrimage*, and her first novel, *Open the Door*. I have borrowed freely from all three. Jan Pilditch's *Catherine Carswell: A Biography* and the two volume-length selections of Catherine Carswell's letters she edited were enormously helpful, as was Jan herself. I also drew on: Thomas Pakenham's *The Boer War*; David Smurthwaite's *The Boer War: 1899-1902*; Anthony Sampson's *The Scholar Gypsy*; Michael Holroyd's *Lytton Strachey*; Virginia Woolf's essay on Walter Raleigh in *The Captain's Death Bed*; and *Letters of Sir Walter Raleigh*, edited by Lucie Raleigh. The poem 'The Artist' was published in a collection of Walter Raleigh's humorous writing, *Laughter From a Cloud*.

I would like to thank: Catherine Carswell's granddaughters, Deborah Kaplinsky and Harriet Wilson; my editor Moira Forsyth and agent Judy Moir; Jim Carruthers; John Coughlan; Geraldine Doherty; Katrina Macleod; Siobhan O'Tierney; Alex Patterson of National Museums Liverpool; Anne Pia; Heather Reid; Lindsay Reid; Elizabeth Sedgwick; Ivan Sedgwick; Alice Walsh; Archive and Local History,

AK Bell Library, Perth; Borthwick Institute for Archives, University of York; the archives of the Crichton Royal Hospital; Glasgow University Library; Liverpool City Libraries; the National Archives; the National Art Library; National Library of Scotland; Oxfordshire Health Archives; Royal Engineers archive, Gordon Barracks, Aberdeen; St Luke's Church, Redcliffe Gardens, Kensington; University of Liverpool: Special Collections and Archives; Wirral Archives Service; and Westminster School Archive.

Creative Scotland generously provided funds allowing me to retrace Cathie's and Herbert's journey across Italy into Switzerland and to spend a year writing. Love and thanks to Jim Melvin for keeping me company along the way.

I still don't know whether the love story pieced together in these pages is mine, or hers.

Donella Ferguson Watson's husband Hugh will offer no explanation for their sexless marriage. A prison doctor, Hugh seems haunted by a hunger-striking suffragette who was force fed and held in solitary confinement. What really happened between Hugh and his prisoner patient?

LONGLISTED FOR THE WALTER SCOTT PRIZE
FOR HISTORICAL FICTION

'Cunningly constructed and well written.'   *The Sunday Times*

ISBN Paperback: 9781910124611
RRP: £8.99

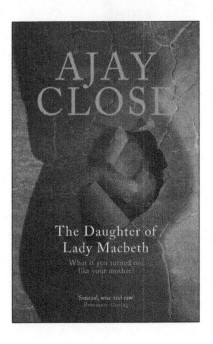

Freya and Frankie's longing for a baby has put their marriage under strain. IVF is their last hope – but how do you bring a child into the world if you don't know who you are? Freya's mother Lilias will tell her nothing about her father, not even his name. As lies and secrets unravel, it seems mother and daughter have more in common than either of them suspects.

'Close's handling of her themes is exceptional... a sensual novel which delves deep into the complex and dangerous relationship between mothers and daughters, in which tenderness and toxicity are laced together in an eternal braid.'

The Herald

ISBN Paperback: 9781910985427
RRP: £8.99

www.sandstonepress.com

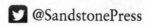 facebook.com/SandstonePress/

@SandstonePress